THE BRIGHTEST NIGHT

Jennifer L. Armentrout

THE
BRIGHTEST
NIGHT

THE BRIGHTEST NIGHT

Jennifer L. Armentrout

TOR TEEN

THE BRIGHTEST NIGHT

Copyright © 2020 by Jennifer L. Armentrout

A Tor Teen Book
Published by Tom Doherty Associates
120 Broadway
New York, NY 10271

www.tor-forge.com

Tor® is a registered trademark of Macmillan Publishing Group, LLC.

The Library of Congress Cataloging-in-Publication Data is available upon request.

ISBN 978-1-250-17577-9 (hardcover)
ISBN 978-1-250-78451-3 (international, sold outside the U.S., subject to rights availability)
ISBN 978-1-250-20831-6 (ebook)

Our books may be purchased in bulk for promotional, educational, or business use. Please contact your local bookseller or the Macmillan Corporate and Premium Sales Department at 1-800-221-7945, extension 5442, or by email at MacmillanSpecialMarkets@macmillan.com.

First U.S. Edition: October 2020
First International Edition: October 2020

Printed in the United States of America

10   9   8   7   6   5   4   3   2   1

To you, the reader. Always.

I

J ason Dasher."

The name thundered through the room as I stared at the broken shards of glass from the bottle General Eaton had thrown.

I stood there, stuck in absolute disbelief, watching the amber liquid seep over papers littering the floor. Some looked like junk mail from when Houston was a bustling city. A brightly colored advertisement for a new furniture store opening downtown. A blue pack of coupons never opened. White envelopes with the word *urgent* in red written on them. All were evidence of a life left behind by whoever had once called this building home before the electromagnetic pulse bombs were dropped, rendering the city habitable only by those desperate enough to remain hidden in a dead zone.

Had the owners evacuated, or were they lost in the chaos that followed the EMPs like so many hundreds of thousands?

Why was I even thinking about any of that? Someone's mail wasn't the most pressing concern. It was like my brain shorted out at the mention of *his* name.

Sergeant Jason Dasher.

The masses knew him as the fallen war hero, a patriotic icon lost in the war protecting mankind against the invading Luxen. I'd once been a part of those masses, but I'd since learned the truth. Dasher was an evil man responsible for horrific experiments on both humans and aliens, all in the name of the "greater good."

But he was an evil, dead man.

Nothing more than a ghost I couldn't remember, because his wife had shot him. The same woman I'd believed to be my mother up until I'd learned I wasn't really Evelyn Dasher but a girl named

Nadia Holliday. Which was roughly around the same time I'd gotten smacked upside the head with the knowledge mother dearest was also a Luxen.

Sylvia had married a man responsible for forced pregnancies between Luxen and humans, nonconsensual mutations, kidnappings, murders, and the subjugation of her own people. Not only that, she had worked for the institution responsible.

The Daedalus.

A secret organization that existed within the Department of Defense, one that had started out with the task of assimilating the Luxen into the human populace long before the public knew the aliens even existed. They'd studied the Luxen's unique biological attributes that not only made them resistant to every human illness but also enabled them to heal any number of physical injuries a human could suffer. The Daedalus sought to use the knowledge gained to better the life of millions, but all of that had gone sideways fast.

I still had no idea how to come to terms with any of that. I didn't think I'd ever truly be able to, but the fact it had been her who'd ended his life had helped.

A little.

She'd shot Dasher when he'd attempted to renege on the deal— the bargain that saved my life and robbed me of it in the same breath. The Andromeda serum had cured the cancer that had been killing me, but it had stolen my memories of who I used to be.

And it had turned me into . . . well, a thing I had learned was called a Trojan. Something that couldn't exactly be classified as just human.

Right now, that little factoid was taking a back seat to the latest *are you freaking kidding me* breaking news.

Jason Dasher was alive.

A dull ache flared in the pit of my stomach as I shook my head. I tried to take the next logical step that said Eaton wasn't the type of person to have misspoken, but my brain was so overloaded with all that had happened. And holy drama llama, *a lot* had happened in the last couple of months.

Jason Dasher was alive, and that wasn't even the most messed-up part of it all. I was coded to answer to him like I were nothing more than a computer responding to commands. A dead man who was now alive. A man who was a monster and could seize control of me at any moment.

"Impossible," a low voice growled.

Heart turning over heavily, I looked to my right. He stood beside me, not just any Origin—a child of a Luxen and a hybrid—but one who was more powerful than even the strongest Luxen.

Luc.

He had a last name now, one that he'd picked after I'd argued that just because the Daedalus never gave him a last name didn't mean he couldn't have one. He'd chosen the surname King, because of course he would, but *Luc King* sounded good—sounded right. And I'd just been happy that he'd given himself one, because the lack of a last name had been one of the many ways the Daedalus made sure their creations remembered they were *things* and not living, breathing entities that thought, felt, and wanted like anyone else.

The last name made him more human, but at the moment, Luc didn't look remotely human.

Not when the irises of his eyes were the color of jeweled amethyst and his pupils burned like bright diamonds. A white glow surrounded the taut shape of his body. The angles of his cheekbones appeared sharper, and faint, tense lines bracketed his full lips.

What surrounded him was the Source, a pure energy that was at the very core of the Luxen, making them so dangerous, so fascinating. The breathtaking power could give life, and it could end it in a nanosecond.

More times than I cared to admit, I'd found myself staring at him in a sort of astonished fixation, attempting to figure out what it was about the lines and angles of his face or how his features were pieced together that made him so beautiful. Everyone got a little lost staring at him when they first saw them, so I didn't feel too shallow. Male. Female. Young. Old. Those interested. Those not. All were affected to some degree, and right now, when he no longer hid what he was, there was a wildness to his beauty, primitive and raw.

Luc was as lethal as he was awe-inspiring, and I loved him—I was *in* love with him, and I knew deep down that I'd felt the same when I'd been Nadia. Everything about him fit everything about me, and what I felt for him now had nothing to do with his appearance or because there were residual emotions left behind from a different life. It was because of *him.* Love took root with his cheesy, horrible pickup lines and silly gifts that really weren't gifts at all. Love grew each time he looked at me like I was the most precious and cherished being in the entire universe. Love spread with his enduring patience that came with no ties or stimulations. He was there for me, always had been, with no expectation that I would feel anything for him. And I fell in love with him all over again when I realized that when he sincerely believed I'd never return to him, he still hadn't stopped loving me.

Until Luc, I didn't even know it was possible to love this deeply, this endlessly, and it was equal parts exhilarating and terrifying. The mere idea of losing him . . .

A shudder took me even as I reminded myself that very few things could gain an upper hand on Luc. I'd seen what Luc was capable of firsthand. Turning human and Luxen alike to nothing more than scattered ashes with just a touch. Tossing people like Frisbees with just a wave of his hand. Human or not, people didn't just fear Luc's strength. They respected it. He wasn't the alpha. He was the omega, and I didn't doubt for a second that one of the only reasons the world wasn't already under the control of the Daedalus was because Luc had turned on his creators.

But now one of them was somehow alive—the one who had made sure my life as Nadia, my life with Luc, had ended.

"I saw it." Luc's voice was thick and ragged with absolute power churning inside him. "I saw it with my own two, fully functioning eyes. Sylvia shot Jason Dasher."

"Just like you believed the Daedalus was truly gone?" the general countered, facing us. He was an older man, maybe in his sixties, with silver hair cropped close to his skull and a face lined with experience. A man who'd spent his life serving his country and should be enjoying his days in blissful retirement in someplace like Arizona or Florida. Instead, he was here, in what was now referred to as Zone 3, hidden among humans the government had decided weren't worth the stress of evacuating, unregistered Luxen, humans that Luxen had mutated—known as hybrids—and other Origins who'd escape the Daedalus.

"That with the destruction of the Origin Project, the Daedalus was simply no more?" Eaton said, referencing the program responsible for the creation of the Origins.

Luc went utterly still, and my skin pebbled in response. "Do you think I'm foolish?"

General Eaton's jaw flexed.

"Or naïve?" Luc's voice was soft now, scarily so, and when he spoke again, I really hoped that Eaton answered and did so wisely. "Well, do you?"

"No," Eaton clipped out. "I don't think that."

"Good to hear that. I'd hate to have to change your mind." Luc had moved forward a foot or two or three, and I hadn't even seen him move. "I never believed they were completely eradicated, nor did I think their goals would end with them. Humans will always want to be on the top of the food chain, and they will never stop seeking power."

The way Luc said *humans* made it clear that even though the mother he'd never met was human, he didn't view himself as one, and a last name hadn't changed that.

The gnawing ache in my stomach pulsed as he said, "But every facility I could find is nothing but ash now, along with a vast number of those who ran the Daedalus. I knew the Daedalus was still alive and well the moment that girl that Evie went to school with did the impossible and we found those serums at her house."

He was talking about April Collins, a frenemy who'd hated on the Luxen so much she'd rallied together like-minded classmates and held daily protests. The irony of it all was that April wasn't even human.

She was like me.

A Trojan.

Her hatefulness was engineered by the Daedalus and had the sole purpose of sowing fear and distrust of the Luxen into the human populace.

When Heidi and I had somewhat accidentally exposed her as something other, April nearly killed Heidi by putting her *entire* hand through my friend's body.

Luc and I had found a stash of serums at her place, but we'd had no idea what they were for and we'd lost them when Luc's club was raided. The serums weren't the only thing we'd discovered at her place. We'd also found her handler, who I'd . . . shot . . . in the head like it was something I'd done before.

For all I knew, it could be something I'd done countless times before, and I just had no memory of it.

"And the Daedalus survived only to grow stronger, to grow smarter," Eaton said.

"That doesn't explain how a dead man is supposedly alive," Luc shot back.

That was a damn good point, one I couldn't wait to hear explained, but I suddenly felt . . . *weird*. Wired, almost. Like I'd downed three of those espresso shots Zoe liked to drink. Had to be the fact that I was hungry and unused to not having at least several tablespoons' worth of sugary snacks by this point in the day. I pushed the odd jittery feeling aside and focused.

"Did you see Dasher die, Luc?" Eaton asked, shoulders sunken and weathered face tired. "No. All you saw was that he was shot and that he bled."

"He was shot in the damn chest, man." Luc's hands curled into fists. "He went down and didn't get back up. It was a mortal wound."

"Did you hang around afterward?" The worn leather couch shuddered when Eaton sat, his long legs stretched and boneless as he met Luc's stare fearlessly.

Luc didn't answer for a long moment, and a ripple of power flared around him, causing the air to thicken.

"I wanted to destroy everything that he was, erase him from this earth, but I couldn't." His chin dipped, head tilting to the side. "Jason had contacted members of the damn alien task force when I arrived. Officers were on their way. I feared my presence would . . ." He trailed off as the veins under his skin began to glow as white as his pupils.

"You feared if you lingered, your presence would jeopardize *her.*" Eaton jerked his head in my direction.

We were made for each other.

That was what Eaton had told us. That the Daedalus had a hand in us meeting the first time, when I'd been Nadia. That they were counting on him to form some kind of bond with her—with *me*—and through that bond, they thought to control him.

Like they'd tried with Dawson and Beth, Daemon and Kat, and most likely, countless others.

If that were true, it made sense they'd anticipate Luc doing anything to make sure I was safe. Even if that meant taking the risk to leave before being a hundred percent sure Jason Dasher was truly dead.

He wouldn't do anything that would ever hurt me. That was the one thing in this world I knew for certain. He would rip himself apart cell by cell before he harmed a single hair on my head.

But I . . .

Oh God.

Sudden clarity sliced through me like an icy wind. My next breath threatened to choke me. I could hurt Luc. Badly. In fact, I already had. If he hadn't gotten through to me, *reached* through to me, when I went all psycho Trojan, taking out the Sons of Liberty, a group that had been activated to take out the Trojans before it was too late, I would've killed Daemon.

I would've killed Luc, who I loved with every fiber of my being.

But in those woods, he was not the boy I loved before and the man I loved now. In those moments, Luc had become nothing more than a challenge to me—a threat this alien part of me saw and had been trained to take out. I . . .

I had peeled his flesh from his bones with just a *thought.*

Sickened, I squeezed my eyes shut, but that did nothing to stop the images of Luc going down on his knees as his skin tore, as he begged me to remember who he was.

I had believed in my heart of hearts that if I became what I had in those woods outside the safe house, Luc would be able to stop me. He'd find a way to get to *me* before I hurt anyone. But we'd been missing an important piece of information.

That I was *coded* to answer to Jason Dasher.

I had an idea of what that meant thanks to April's reaction to me after she'd used the Cassio Wave, a device that had awoken whatever training I'd had. She'd expected me to go with her without question, to return to *him,* a man nameless at the time but I now knew to be Jason Dasher.

My heart pounded against my ribs as panic seeded like a noxious weed. What if he or another Trojan used the Cassio Wave again? Or what if what happened in those woods occurred again?

What if Luc couldn't reach me the next time?

Then I'd turn into a mindless minion, and not even one of the cute yellow ones.

A laugh bubbled up, but it got stuck in my throat, where I felt like I was being choked, and it was probably a good thing, because it was the scary kind of laughter that ended in tears or blood.

Jason Dasher could take it all away from me again. Memories. Sense of self. Free will. Autonomy. My friends. Luc.

The mere idea of losing myself all over again burst open a door deep inside me, and out came a mess of emotions. A cyclone of fear and anger rose up, drenching every fiber of my being.

I would destroy myself before I allowed everything to be taken from me again.

"*Never.*"

My gaze jerked to Luc. Energy spit into the air, hissing and crackling as Luc picked up on my thoughts, something that annoyed the living crap out of me even though he couldn't always control it. According to him, my thoughts were often . . . loud.

"Never will you have to make that choice," he vowed, the surge of power emanating from him pulsing brightly and then easing off until there was no glow around him. The air in the room lightened, becoming easier to breathe. "He will never have control of you. No one will."

But I hadn't had control of myself in those woods, not when I'd attacked him and Daemon. That hadn't even been me—

"It doesn't matter." Luc was suddenly directly in front of me, his warm palms cupping my cheeks. Skin against skin. Like always, the contact sent a muted charge of electricity dancing over my skin and coursing through my veins. The brightness of his pupils receded until they were normal. Well, normal by Luc's standards. The fuzzy black lines around his irises and pupils were now visible. "That was you in the woods. Just another part of you that I haven't quite made friends with yet, but I will."

"I don't know about that." That power that was in me, the Source that had been twisted by all the serums and the alien DNA, wouldn't make friends with anything other than maybe a honey badger.

"Honey badgers are extremely intelligent creatures, did you know?"

"*Luc.*"

He gave me a lopsided grin. "To be honest, I think the honey badger part of you thought I was the bee's knees."

A strangled laugh broke free. "Bee's knees?"

"Yeah. Isn't that what all the cool kids are saying?"

"Maybe in the nineteen-twenties."

"I could swear I heard someone say it recently." He lowered his head, stopping when the bridge of his nose brushed mine. "I'm not worried, Peaches."

Peaches.

In the beginning, I thought that was such a weird nickname, but now? Hearing him say that made my heart feel as if it were being squeezed in the best possible way.

Genuinely curious and disbelieving, I asked, "How can you not be?"

"Because I have faith."

I stared at him.

"In me." His head tilted, and I felt his cheek against mine, curving up in a bigger grin. The next breath I took was full of pine and fresh air and so very full of *Luc*. "I have faith in you. In us. You're not going to turn into some mindless minion." A pause. "Unless it's Halloween."

He was referencing my last costume. "I thought you said I looked like Big Bird."

"My sexy little Big Bird," Luc corrected, and I wrinkled my nose. He slid a hand back, curling his fingers through my hair as he gently guided my head until our eyes connected and held. "You're Evie. You will not lose control. I won't allow that. You won't allow that. Do you know why?"

"Why?" I whispered.

"Because we didn't come all this way, survive all we have, only to lose each other again," he said. "You won't allow that. I know you won't, but if you can't believe in that yet, then believe in me until you can. How about that?"

Emotion swelled so acutely that when I blinked, my lashes were damp. His words broke my heart and also soothed the sting. I nodded as some of the panic died.

For a heartbeat, Luc rested his forehead against mine. The simple comfort released the rest of the panic. "Together," he murmured. "We're in this together."

The shaky breath I took felt clean. "Together."

Lifting his head, he stopped to press a kiss against my temple before pulling away. His hand dropped from my hair but stayed against my lower back.

"I thought you two forgot I was even here," Eaton remarked dryly, but when I looked over at him, his lined features had softened. "The Daedalus still haven't taken it into consideration."

"Taken what into consideration?" Luc asked.

"Love." A brief chuckle followed that one word as Eaton leaned back against the couch. "No matter what they do, they never take love into consideration. It's like none of them have ever experienced its power."

"You have?" I asked, not knowing much about the man.

"He has." Luc's hand moved in a slow slide, traveling up the length of my spine. "He was married once. Had a son."

I had a bad feeling none of that had ended with a happily ever after.

Eaton's smile was more of a grimace. "Why am I not surprised you know that even though I haven't spoken about Amy and Brent to Daemon or Archer?"

Luc didn't respond as his palm made another pass down my back. He didn't need to.

General Eaton didn't appear to need the answer either as his rheumy gaze met mine. I was sure that when he'd been younger, those blue eyes were as brilliant as the summer sky. "Sylvia healed him."

Luc cursed.

I'd already suspected as much, but hearing it confirmed knotted up my insides. Sylvia . . . would, God, she would always be Mother, no matter what she'd done. I couldn't change the way I saw her or how I thought about her, but she had lied so much, and those lies hid terrible things and ugly truths.

She had been so convincing when she told me about what my "father" and the Daedalus had been involved in—so convincing, so seemingly horrified by how the Daedalus had begun to exploit the Luxen in the pursuit of using the alien DNA to create weapons of destruction and by what Dasher had attempted to do to Luc.

How could she be that skilled of a liar? Convincing me wasn't an Olympic-level feat, as I hadn't known any better at the time, but to lie to my face like that?

"I listened in on their thoughts but didn't pick up on any of this." Anger vibrated in Luc's voice. "I knew they were using deflection, thinking about inane crap, but to be able to block all of this?" Bronze waves toppled over his forehead as he shook his head. "I should've known something else had to be going on there."

"It's not often you've had to go up against those who knew exactly how to be prepared when it came to an Origin's ability to read minds," Eaton reasoned. "They knew how to deflect your ability, because they had a hand in creating the Origins. It wasn't a failure on your part."

My heart pounded against my ribs as I opened my mouth, about to tell Luc that this truly wasn't his fault. I thought about when April had attacked Heidi. It took nothing for me to see Emery cradling Heidi against her as the Luxen had slipped from her human skin to her true form, a beautiful human-shaped light so intense that it had hurt my eyes to look upon her. Even though Emery hadn't been as skilled as other Luxen when it came to healing humans, she'd saved Heidi's life by placing her hands on her and summoning the Source.

You do not get between a Luxen and who they love, no matter what.

That's what Luc had said when Emery had taken Heidi, and within hours, there'd been nothing but a faint scar where April had put her hand *through* Heidi, destroying tissue, muscles, and organs.

So either my mom was skilled at healing, or she still loved that man.

The world seemed to shift under my feet. Feeling sick, like I might actually projectile vomit all over the floor, I took a step back. I needed distance from Eaton's words—from further evidence of the fact I never really knew my mother and I would never know what about her, if anything, was ever real.

Because she, too, was now gone, taking with her all her lies and whatever, if any, truths.

Luc's hand was a warm presence along the center of my back, stopping my retreat. His hand was just there, not holding me in place, but even if it weren't there, I wouldn't have bounced out of the room like a rubber ball.

Denial was a luxury I could no longer afford.

I needed to deal with this, and it didn't matter how much it hurt to realize that everything about her had been a lie. Yes, my mother could've had a change of heart at some point after I'd been returned to her with no memory of being Nadia or any of the training I'd obviously received. That much could be true—could be *real*. She had died making sure I escaped before the Daedalus could capture me, but none of that changed what she'd done, and I had to face that.

I had to deal with that.

Swallowing hard, I lifted my chin and squared my shoulders. I could do this. I'd already dealt with so much—the kind of stuff that would send most to the nearest corner where they'd do nothing but stare at empty space. I'd accepted that there had been a real Evie Dasher who'd died in a car accident. I'd processed that my actual name was Nadia Holliday and then realized that I was neither Nadia nor Evie but a mixture of both and someone completely different. I'd handled the truth that Sylvia and Jason Dasher weren't my parents. I'd survived an attack by an Origin who had one hell of a grudge/obsession with Luc. I'd stumbled across dead classmates, and it had been me—as a stealth assassin and sort of unaware of what I was doing, but whatever—that had taken out April. I was working on the knowledge that I was capable of doing some real harm and that there was someone out there that could seize control of me.

Sure, I had some messy baggage, a whole lot of missing memories, and I was possibly a psychotic alien hybrid that may or may not one day go completely banana pants on everyone, but I was still here. I was still standing on my own two feet.

Luc dipped his head and murmured into my ear, "That's because you're a badass."

"Stop reading my mind," I said, and he tilted his head up, winking. I sighed. "But thank you," I tacked on, because I needed to be reminded of that fact.

A half grin appeared a second later when my stomach grumbled, empty. The energy bars Luc and I had grabbed before meeting obviously hadn't been enough.

Cheeks flushing, I dragged my gaze from Luc's. Only *I'd* be hungry after learning such traumatic news. "Did she . . . Do you think she still loved Dasher?"

"I can't answer that." Eaton dragged a thumb along his chin.

"A Luxen doesn't always have to love the person they're healing." Luc's hand curled into the back of my shirt. "Remember, some are just extraordinarily good at it. Sylvia could've been, or she could've been properly motivated, something the Daedalus became very skilled at doing. Loving someone means they have a higher chance of being successful, especially for those who aren't adept or don't have the experience."

"And it also means it's more likely that the mutation would take hold without the human dying in the process," Eaton added. "That's the part the Daedalus could never figure out. There are degrees of science to the process, but there's a mysticism to it that hasn't been fully explained or understood."

Pressing my lips together, I briefly squeezed my eyes shut. What if she had loved him?

"She could've, Evie." Luc's voice was quiet. "Maybe she was feeling a lot more hate than love. Emotions are complicated." His eyes searched mine. "But it—"

"It doesn't matter." Eaton tipped his head back against the bare wall that once had been the color of butter.

Luc's gaze sharpened on Eaton.

"You're right. It really doesn't." And that was the truth, and it hit me with the speed of a racing freight train. There were more important things—stuff that mattered in the here and now. Placing a hand over my still-grumbling stomach, I considered the one thing that could make this situation so much worse. "Do you think she . . ." Throat dry, I tried again. "Do you think Dasher was mutated?"

2

Out of all those who could access the Source, a hybrid was the weakest. They became exhausted when using the Source, unlike Luxen or Origins, and they couldn't heal. However, they weren't something to take lightly. Doing so was like saying a ton of dynamite wasn't dangerous. Yeah, compared to a nuclear bomb, it wasn't as bad, but it could still take out a city block.

A hybrid, a trained one, wouldn't be easy to kill.

As soon as that thought finished, my eyes widened. Here I was thinking about how hard it would be to kill someone and not about the actual act of killing them. I wasn't even fazed, which probably meant I was a good candidate for some extensive therapy.

"What do you think, Eaton?" Luc asked. "Has Dasher gone and gotten an all-new upgraded, sporty version of himself?"

"I can't answer that, either." Eaton dropped his hand to his knee. "I haven't seen Dasher since the war ended, when I learned about the Poseidon Project. Obviously, we had a falling-out after that."

"But if he is, he's going to be harder to deal with." I folded my arms over my chest, chilled despite the lack of airflow.

"Hybrid, human, or chupacabra, he won't stand a chance against me," Luc stated. Surprisingly, that wasn't coming from a place of extreme cockiness. It was just the simple truth. "Or you."

It took me a moment to realize he was speaking to me. Surprised, I blinked. Not like I didn't remember what I'd done in those woods. I'd touched the ground and the soil had moved like a hundred vipers. My words and thoughts had turned to action without me even touching the men. I'd uprooted trees and broken entire bodies with a curl of my hand.

But it was still hard to think of myself as dangerous.

"He wouldn't stand a chance against me *if* I somehow learn how to . . . access those abilities and . . . you know, not try to kill you or any other friendly in the process," I told him.

"Technicalities," he murmured.

My eyes narrowed. "That's a pretty big technicality."

"Like I said, Peaches, I'm not worried."

"You should be," Eaton commented. "I am."

Man, this guy should give anti-motivational speeches.

"The Trojans are the Daedalus' crowning achievement. They succeeded where they failed with the hybrids and Origins, eradicating the whole idea of free will and sense of self. They have a true hive mentality, responding to who they view as their m—"

"If you say *master,* I may actually break something," I warned him, 100 percent serious.

"Maker," Eaton answered. "The Trojans see Dasher as their maker. Their god."

What in the screwed-up-ness in all screwed-up-nesses? I raised a brow at Luc and repeated, "Their god?"

A ripple of heat warmed the air when Luc growled, "He is no god."

"To the Trojans, he is. If he commands them to eat, they do. If he orders them to obey another, they will do so without question. He tells them to kill, they will slaughter without hesitation. He demands that they end themselves, they'd slit their own throats in a heartbeat if provided the blade."

Well, I wasn't sure how it could get any worse than that.

"I learned of the Poseidon Project shortly after the war ended. Dasher introduced it as the answer to any future hostile invasion and a way to keep existing Luxen in check so that those weaker would have protectors." Eaton's eyes went unfocused. "I think in the beginning, that was their purpose."

I frowned. "I thought the Poseidon Project's goal was to run the entire universe, like all cliché villains."

"Dasher—like most in the Daedalus—is complicated like Sylvia," he said, and I flinched. "There are threads of goodness in them, an initial goal of attempting to do the right thing. Dasher believes that the Poseidon Project is the way mankind survives."

"Because mankind won't survive another invasion," Luc mused, and then he nodded as if he were agreeing on what movie to watch and not the annihilation of the human race. "Not another sizable one. The invading Luxen were barely beat back last time, and that was only with the help of the Arum, which took a huge hit in the battle. There are still more Luxen who haven't come." He paused. "Yet."

That little factoid was something that had dominated the news in the wake of the war. Experts had estimated that there were still *millions* of Luxen who hadn't arrived during the invasion, but when the days turned to weeks, to months, and then finally to years, those statistics were chalked up to nothing more than fearmongering.

"But there are Luxen here who would fight back." I thought of Daemon and Dawson, Emery and maybe even Grayson—well, depending on what kind of mood Grayson was in. "Those who'd want to protect their homes and the humans they've befriended. Not to mention all the hybrids and Origins."

"The moment the Daedalus learned all they could from the Luxen, they stopped trusting them, especially when they discovered that many were aware that more were coming with plans to take over." Eaton shifted on the flat cushion, seeking comfort that couch had long since given up on. "It's why they are seeking to neutralize the Luxen through technology and fear. They don't want any aliens here, and if you ask me, I think they only want certain humans here, ones they deem worthy or necessary. Their thread of goodness has long since rotted."

My brows knitted. "You know, after what we've been doing to the innocent Luxen who just want to live their best lives, I wouldn't blame them if they didn't help fight back and just let us all go to hell in a handbasket."

"And there's that," Eaton agreed softly.

"Do you think other Luxen will eventually invade?" I asked.

Luc shrugged. "Possible, but let's not borrow trouble."

I wouldn't classify millions of human-hating Luxen as mere trouble, but that wasn't happening. *Yet*. The Poseidon Project was.

"My brain is starting to hurt." I sighed, and truthfully it was. There was a faint throbbing behind my eyes. Knowing my luck, I was probably coming down with a cold.

Wait.

Could I even get a cold now? I wasn't even sure. All I knew was what I could remember as Evie, and other than minor sniffles, I hadn't been sick. According to Luc, the Luxen DNA in the Andromeda serum would prevent any future severe illnesses.

Too bad it couldn't prevent a headache.

Luc's features softened. "I've got a cure for that."

Warmth invaded my cheeks when my gaze connected with his heated one. I had a feeling I knew what kind of cure he was talking about. Him. Me. Kissing. Lots of skin-on-skin activities.

Biting down on his full lower lip, he nodded.

The heat increased, spreading down my throat. "You're the worst," I muttered.

"I'm the best," Luc replied, sitting down on the computer chair. It didn't make a sound under his weight, whereas it had sounded close to dying when I'd plopped down on it earlier. "Tell me what you saw when you learned of this project."

"At first, I thought they were Origins, but I saw the way they moved, what they could do." One side of Eaton's lips quirked in a humorless grin. "He was so *proud* of them, like they were his children and he was showing them off. They moved like . . . God, like there was no humanity to them. Even you . . . there's a touch of humanity in the way you move." Eaton stared at Luc. "More so when she's involved, but whatever part of them that had started off human had been erased."

Unnerved, I swallowed hard. "They were like robots?"

"No." His eyes half closed. "They were primitive, like a pack of wolves, and Dasher was their alpha."

I think I preferred the robot comparison.

"As proud as he was of them, he didn't see them as people—not how you and I see each other," Eaton continued. "I learned that pretty quickly when one of them lagged behind the others. I think it was someone who had just been mutated. He wasn't failing at the tasks. He was just behind, and he was only a boy. Couldn't have been more than sixteen, but Dasher was disappointed." The older man's face paled as his eyes closed. "Dasher leaned in, whispered in the boy's ear, and that kid just turned around and ran into the cement wall opposite of us, slamming his head into it until—God, until there was nothing but a mess left behind."

My lips parted as nausea rose swiftly. "Jesus."

"Where was this facility?" Luc asked as he reached over, curling his hand around my bent elbow. He tugged, pulling me over, and I went. He settled me so I sat on his right thigh.

Eaton opened his eyes. They seemed even duller. "Dalton, Ohio. At Wright-Patterson Air Force Base—"

"Hangar 18? I know of the place." Luc folded his arm around my waist, his hand splaying out over my hip. "They were keeping Origins there."

"The Trojans were moved out before you razed the hangar to the ground," Eaton said, and I looked back at Luc, but he was staring at the general. "To where, I have no idea."

Luc's thumb moved over the curve of my stomach. "How many Trojans did you see that day?"

"Thirty." A pause while my foot began to tap. "And then twenty-nine."

Then twenty-nine. Sorrow swelled for a boy whose name I didn't even know but with whom I felt an odd kinship nonetheless. I remembered hearing *his* voice in the woods, right before what existed inside me took hold. *Prove to me you're worth this gift of life. Show them!* That voice had been full of unrelenting demand, and I now knew that voice belonged to Dasher.

All that guilt over being unable to recall how his voice sounded when I'd believed him to be my father had been wasted energy. The reason why was because I'd never heard his voice as Evie. I'd only heard Dasher's voice as Nadia.

Luc's arm tightened around me, pulling me back until my

entire side pressed against his chest. "Is it possible there are more Trojans?"

"Not counting her?" Eaton jerked his chin at me.

A shudder rolled through me. "Don't count me. I'm different from them."

The general's stare made me wonder for how long. "And not counting those activating now? There were at least a hundred fully trained that I knew of, but that was several years ago. Could be more now, but even if there aren't, that's a significant number. May not sound like a lot to you, but to put it into perspective, that's a hundred of you, Luc."

"There is only one me." There was no teasing quality to his tone or arrogance. It was the truth. There was no one like him.

A faint smile appeared on Eaton's face. "But there are at least a hundred capable of doing what she did and countless more who will be able to. Dasher will amass a small army, and what they're doing out in the Yard isn't going to make a difference. They'll be nothing more than cannon fodder."

"Ye of little faith," Luc murmured, his thumb moving once more along my hip.

"None of this has anything to do with faith." Eaton snorted as he scanned the room, his eyes narrowing on a carton. "Why don't you be useful, Luc, and summon me one of those beers?"

"I think you've had enough for the entire day."

He made another dismissive sound. "At this point, there is no such thing as enough."

I lifted a brow, deciding to ignore that. "You said that Luc was the Darkest Star and I was the Burning Shadow. They were code names for us." When he nodded, I continued, "What is the Brightest Night?"

"Dasher never explained what that stood for, and I did a hell of a lot of digging but never could get any clarification. All I can assume is that it's the end goal."

"World domination?" Luc huffed out a dry laugh. "He's got big aspirations with his itty-bitty army of self-destructive super-soldiers."

I blinked.

Frowning at Luc, Eaton shifted again on the cushion. "Hasn't the Daedalus always had lofty goals? You'd know. After all, other than the Trojans, you are their most coveted creation."

That reminded me of another thing I couldn't quite understand. "You said they used me to get to Luc, as some way to possibly gain the upper hand and reel him back in, but I don't get it. If they want to eradicate Luxen, hybrids, and Origins because they can fight back, why would they want Luc alive? Or . . ." My heart turned over heavily. "Or they want him dead and I totally misinterpreted all of that."

"I don't think you did, Peaches. They want me." Luc dropped his chin to my shoulder. "Can you blame them?"

"Yes."

That got a cackle from the otherwise stoic general.

"Ouch," Luc murmured, but a moment later, I felt the brush of his lips against the side of my neck. A quick kiss that sent a wave of shivers racing to all the interesting bits. I wiggled a little in return, and Luc's arm tightened, stilling me. Over my shoulder, I caught his narrowed glare, and I grinned. "Behave," he mouthed silently.

"With the Trojans," Eaton went on. "I don't know why they'd want Luc alive." A pause. "No offense."

"Offense taken."

Eaton looked like he couldn't care less. "If I were Dasher, I'd have a bounty so high on your head that the risk of certain death could be overlooked. You're a threat, a real one, but they want you." He looked between us. "So, that should be moderately concerning."

"Moderately?" I repeated. "I'd say that would be highly concerning."

"What it means is they have plans for me." Luc couldn't sound more bored than if he were watching a documentary about being placed on hold. "The Daedalus always has plans for me, and look how all their previous ones panned out."

Leaning back, I stared at him. "You are one of the few things that can stop them. Keeping you alive means they have even bigger plans than before. You're not at all concerned?"

Thick lashes lifted, revealing glimmering amethyst eyes. "I'm not remotely concerned. Their plans are always bigger than the ones before, and every single one of them involves controlling me. They've never been able to do that, and there's not a single thing they can do that would accomplish that."

"There's not?" Eaton asked quietly as he looked pointedly at me.

Tracking along the same line of thinking, my stomach sank to my toes. "They already have in a way. They got you to walk away and stay out of my life. They used me to do that."

"That's different." Luc held my stare. "And they will never get their hands on you again to be able to use you as a tool to control me. Never again." He repeated those two words as if they'd be etched in stone. "So, I'm not concerned."

"Concerned or not, at the end of the day, they want both of you," Eaton pointed out.

I dragged my gaze from Luc. "They can't have us."

The general shrugged. "You know, we've done everything to keep Zone 3 as safe from the Daedalus as possible. The wall is constantly patrolled; so are the city limits. We shut down the walking tunnels under the city and blew the entry points. That's enough for now, but if anyone were smart, everyone here, including both of you, would scatter to the four corners of the earth. Find a nice hole to hide in as long as they can, and scratch out some sort of life until no one can hide anymore."

I couldn't believe he had said that. Anger had been a slow burn from the moment he started talking, but now it rose to the surface, prickly over my skin like a heat rash.

"That's what I should've done, but I didn't. Look where I am now."

A pink flush crept across his weathered cheeks. "I tried to stop Dasher. I went to everyone above me, and I was warned to mind my own business each time, but I didn't listen." He shuffled to his feet. "I kept pushing, and you know what I got in return? I lost everything. I'm not talking about my career or my house. I lost"—he swiped his hand through the air—"*everything*."

My foot stilled, stomach sinking.

Luc leaned in, his lips brushing the curve of my ear. "His wife. His son."

"What?" I whispered, chest squeezing.

Eaton's shoulders moved with heavy, rapid breath. "They warned me to let it go, and when I didn't, they came for me, but they got them instead."

A knot lodged in my throat as I stared at him, having no idea what to say.

He sat on the edge of the couch. "I want to see Dasher and all of them punished in ways that would most likely disturb you. I'm helping the people the best I can, but I know what we're up against."

My right foot started tapping again. "I'm sorry about your family. I really am."

Eaton stared at me several moments and then nodded curtly. A long moment passed. "I know battle strategies. I know simple numbers, and I know what it means to be outgunned even if you're not outmanned." He dropped his elbow onto the arm of the couch. "I care about the people here. I even care about that one holding you now. I don't want to see anything bad happen to any of them."

"That warms my heart." Luc straightened behind me. "It really does."

The general shook his head. "And that's why I need to say what I'm about to."

"I'm all ears and a whole lot of warm fuzzies. I'm listening," Luc replied.

"We have a more pressing matter than when the Daedalus discover we're here and what we're doing." Eaton drew his right knee up, rubbing it with the palm of his hand.

"And what could that possibly . . . ?" Luc trailed off, and when I looked over my shoulder at him once more, I saw that his brows were knitted, head cocked to the side. His eyes flared an intense, brilliant purple, and then his expression locked down. His face nothing more than striking lines and hard angles. "No."

"Luc—" Eaton started, and my gaze snapped back to his.

"You've already thought it, and that's bad enough," Luc cut the older man off. "You can't take it back. It's already out there, but if you speak it, give it life to fester and spread, I will not forget that."

Really wanting to know what in the hell Eaton had been thinking, I opened my mouth, but the look on Eaton's face silenced me.

Sorrow etched into the lines of his face as he shifted forward, both hands on his knees. "I'm sorry," he said, sounding genuine. "I don't want to think or say it, and I sure as hell don't want it to be, but you know, Luc. You know it's the only way."

Luc was silent as we walked out of Eaton's home, his features still hard and gaze distant but blazing, his gentle hold on my hand completely at odds with the barely leashed anger thrumming through his body.

The sun had burned off the cool morning air. I imagined locals found the temps to be on the chilly side, but to me, used to much colder temps in November, it was the kind of weather perfect for grabbing the camera and getting outside.

A pang of wanting lit up my chest. I missed the rush of being behind a camera. It was such a silencer. I didn't stress or think about what the next hour would bring, let alone the next day or week. Every part of me, from my eyes to the fingers curling around the camera, would be focused on the moment in time I'd be trying to capture. The entire process was a contradiction, intimate and yet remote, sheltered and also like falling without a safety net. Even if my photos never made it beyond Instagram, I always felt like I was leaving behind something bigger than I was, whether it was proof that sometimes death truly was a renewal—like when leaves shifted from green to red and then finally gold before falling—or a candid smile or laugh.

And right now, my fingers itched to capture the looming city of Houston, its buildings stretching high into the sky like hollow skeletons and the freeways congested with cars but empty of people.

A dead city that should be remembered.

But I had no camera to grab. The old one had been destroyed

by April, and the one Luc had gotten me afterward had been left behind in the rush to escape the Daedalus.

I pushed away the heavy sadness. I had more important things to deal with.

The narrow street outside of Eaton's house was empty and the nearby houses silent with the exception of curtains and canopies snapping softly in the windows. I had no idea if people were living in the ranch-style homes or not, but there seemed to be no one around, which was perfect.

I stopped without warning, and Luc halted, looking over his shoulder. Warm sunlight glanced over his high cheekbones. "We need to talk."

An eyebrow rose, and a moment passed. "About?"

"You aren't reading my thoughts right now?"

"You're not being loud." Facing me, he held on to my hand as he stepped closer, his tall frame blocking the sun. "I try not to listen when you're not projecting."

"I appreciate that." And I really did, because I often thought about really random, stupid stuff like why blueberries weren't actually blue. "What was Eaton thinking?"

"When he decided to drink half a case of beer before noon?" Lifting his other hand, he caught a strand of my hair. "I imagine it's stress. Maybe even boredom. Hell, he could've always been a—"

"That's not what I'm talking about, and you know that. He was going to say something, but you picked up on it and wouldn't let him say it."

Luc tugged on the strand, wrapping it around his forefinger. "Did you know that in the sunlight your hair is like melted gold? It's beautiful."

"Uh, thanks." I snagged my hair free from his finger. Luc pouted, managing to look equally adorable and ridiculous. "Complimenting my hair isn't going to distract me."

"What about complimenting *you*? Will that distract you?"

I sighed. "Luc—"

"Do you truly know how incredibly resilient you are? How

strong?" he asked, placing the tips of his fingers to my cheek. A buzz of electricity skated through my veins. "You've dealt with so much, Evie. Your entire life has been flipped upside down and shaken. What you were thinking inside was right. You're still standing. Most wouldn't be. Some of the most physically strong people I know wouldn't be. I don't think you give yourself enough credit."

Even knowing what he was up to, he still managed to lead me right off the topic at hand. "All of that won't matter if Dasher has a way to take control or if I lose it again and don't come back."

"You're right," he agreed. "When April used the Cassio Wave on you, it awakened your abilities, but it didn't give control to her or Dasher. And in the woods, you may have been triggered and didn't know who you were, but you weren't attempting to get back to Dasher like a child called home, right?"

I thought about that. In the woods, I hadn't been me, but I also hadn't been a Trojan programmed to return to Dasher. I had been something . . . *other*. But who knows what I would've done had I succeeded in taking out Daemon and Luc? Would I have then gone on to attack the rest of the group, eventually returning to Dasher? I didn't know.

We needed to figure out if that was the case, because if I were triggered again, we all needed to know what we were dealing with. Not only was I a danger in the physical sense once I went full super-villain, Zone 3 was chock-full of unregistered Luxen and more. That knowledge in the wrong hands would be deadly.

"You're not going to betray the people here," Luc said softly, cupping the back of my head with his hand.

He was reading my mind again.

"Sorry." He grinned. "You were being loud then."

"Look, we need to talk about all of that, too, but to get back on point, I know Eaton was thinking something you didn't want me to hear. And I get you're probably protecting me, but whatever it is, I need to know."

Luc lifted our still-joined hands, pressing them to his chest, above his heart. My stomach took that moment to remind me and the entire world that I was still hungry, grumbling loudly. "Peaches," he murmured, lips twitching. "What you need right now is food."

"What I need right now is for you to stop being evasive." And maybe a hamburger, but considering where we were, I doubted that would be on the menu anytime soon.

"You'd be surprised. There's a lot of cattle here, and they have ice cellars and iceboxes," Luc explained. "If you behave, I'm sure I can grill you up a juicy hamburger."

My stomach was all about that idea. "If you don't answer my question, I'm sure I'm going to punch you somewhere it will hurt you."

"You're so aggressive," he murmured, dipping his head as he tilted me farther back. His breath danced over my lips when he spoke, sending a shiver through me. "I like it."

My pulse kicked up, flushing my skin. "You will not like it. Trust me."

He sighed even as he brushed his lips along the corner of mine. The breath I took caught as razor-sharp anticipation swelled, but he didn't kiss me. "Eaton is just worried that you're going to lose control."

Although I wasn't surprised to hear that, my shoulders still sank. "That's not breaking news, so why did you react the way you did?"

Luc was quiet for a long moment. "Eaton has a way of thinking things." He lifted his head. "He's a paranoid old man. Not that he doesn't have justifiable reasons for being just that, but his paranoia doesn't need to infect you."

Studying him, I wished the damn serum had given me the ability to read thoughts. Then again, not all Origins could do it. As far as I knew, only Luc and Archer could.

"As I told Eaton, there is no one like me."

I glared at him. "I'm going to punch you."

"I might like it."

"There's something wrong with you."

"Maybe." He started to lower his head, but I managed to evade him. Barely. If he kissed me, there'd be nothing but muddied thoughts and liquid bones.

"Eaton has a right to be paranoid," I told him. "I may not return to Dasher like a programmed toy, but that doesn't make me any less dangerous if I snap again."

"Then we just have to make sure you're not in a situation that can lead to you snapping."

"We don't even know what kind of situation will cause that."

"I'm thinking someone trying to kill you is the kind of situation we need to avoid," he reasoned.

"Uh, that would be great and all, but I have a sinking feeling with the Sons of Liberty out there and the Daedalus searching for me, that's going to be a hard situation to avoid."

Luc's jaw tensed. "I will keep you safe."

"I know you will." I squeezed his hand. "But I also need to keep myself safe. And we need to keep others safe."

He didn't respond to that, so I pressed on. "And we really don't know if that's the only thing that will trigger it. You told Eaton you would help me get it under control."

"I did."

"So, let's get started. Now." Excitement filled me, and yeah, considering what I was getting excited over, it was a little weird, but trying to get this thing in me under control was better than sitting around, doing nothing but stressing over it while everyone else also worried about whether or not I'd go all Thanos on them.

It was doing *something*.

Eaton had basically insinuated that a war was brewing, and it didn't matter if I wanted to be a part of it or not. I was already knee deep in the whole thing, and if I was something they thought they could use to take over the world, then why couldn't I be used to fight back? To help those here, who weren't just trying to scrape by but also building a resistance?

I wasn't Evelyn Dasher anymore.

Shock rippled through me as I stood on an unknown street, in a neighborhood that shouldn't exist.

I wasn't the same girl who'd walked into Foretoken with Heidi, who would rather run than face an uncomfortable truth. I wasn't even the same version of Evie who'd faced down an Origin, or even the girl who had been slowly coming to terms with who she was and who she was falling in love with.

Ever since I'd met Luc, I had been in a constant state of evolution, and it hadn't ended when I realized I was very capable of snuffing out life to protect someone I loved, nor had it ceased when I watched the life and light seep out of the only mother I knew.

I was now someone who didn't tuck tail and run even if I initially wanted to, who wanted to fight back instead of push back.

Luc's features tightened for a brief moment before smoothing out. "What we need to do right now is get some food in you before you start eating people." He dropped a kiss to the tip of my nose. "Those who live here wouldn't appreciate that, either."

I arched a brow at that, but when he tugged on my hand, I started walking, because he had a point. I did need to eat. We made it to the intersection before I said, "Luc?"

"Yes?"

"You're going to help me, right?" I asked as we crossed the street.

Luc had rather amusingly guided us to the crosswalk. "I will even if I don't want to."

"Why wouldn't you want to?"

Luc stopped, facing me. "Because I have a feeling to get what's in you to show up and play, I'm going to have to do what I know will kill a part of me."

Trepidation tiptoed its way down my spine. "What would that be?"

His eyes were like brilliant shards of broken purple sapphires. "I'll have to make you see me as a threat."

3

Luc's words sank like a stone in my stomach, quieting me as we walked toward the house. What he'd said made sense. Luc was one of the most dangerous and powerful beings to walk Earth. Whatever was inside me had sensed that and gone after him, but while Luc was a threat to everyone else, he wasn't to me. Never me. I had no idea how he'd make me view him as such.

And I had no idea how he could deal with doing that.

"Maybe we should have someone else work with me," I suggested after a few moments. "Like Grayson?" The surliest Luxen known to man would be beside himself with glee at the opportunity. "He'd be thrilled to scare me or tick me off. He'd think of it as a reward."

"Do you really think I'd allow anyone else to do what's going to need to be done?" he asked.

My lips pursed.

"I'm fully aware of the fact I have a vicious protective streak when it comes to you." Luc squeezed my hand. "The moment he goes at you, I'd have to kill him."

Sliding him a long look, I tightened my grip on his hand. "Or you could, maybe, understand that he wouldn't really be trying to hurt me and therefore not kill him?"

"I'd try and fail, Peaches. The same would go for Zoe or anyone else who meant you harm, even if I knew they truly didn't want to hurt you." He shrugged like what he'd said was no big deal. "Like I said, it's a flaw of mine. At least I'm aware of that."

"Yeah." I drew the word out. "At least you're aware."

One side of his lips kicked. "Awareness saves lives."

Having no idea what to say to that, I tried to come up with

some other way. Grayson only seemed to have barely begun to tolerate me after learning I was Nadia, and by *tolerate,* I meant he was only about 20 percent less of a jerk to me. But I didn't want to see him die.

I also didn't want Luc to do something that would hurt *him.*

We continued on in silence, and after only a handful of steps, a prickly shiver coursed its way down my spine, pulling me from my thoughts. Scoping out the quiet street, I couldn't shake the sudden awareness of being watched.

I felt *eyes* on me, on us. Dozens of them, and it wasn't paranoia induced by the nearly identical single-story homes with quiet porches and empty driveways. Even the trees lining the streets appeared to be free of birds, and the silence, the emptiness was creepy.

I knew beyond a doubt that even though the decades-old cars I'd seen that morning were now gone—cars made before electric ignitions and internal computer systems—some of those homes were occupied.

People were watching us.

As we made our way onto the street of the house we were staying in, the feeling heightened. I zeroed in on the faded brick home with a canopied carport. The breeze caught the fabric, lifting to briefly reveal outdoor wicker couches and chairs. A water bottle sat on a low table, next to an impressive, towering stack of books. The whole setup looked so normal, like something I'd see at home back in Columbia, Maryland.

The normalcy of it all sent another pang through my chest, and I could almost picture Zoe, Heidi, and James sitting on those brilliant, bright blue cushions, munching on junk food while pretending to study.

The image was part memory, part fantasy, because we didn't have a carport and Columbia wasn't home anymore. I didn't know if the four of us would ever be together again.

Steps slowing, my gaze flicked to the porch. Curtains blocked the sun, so I couldn't see anything beyond that, but I stopped.

I stopped the same moment Luc had, feeling a weird sensation along the back of my neck, as if fingers had grazed the skin there.

Lifting my hand, I slipped my fingers under my hair and rubbed at the skin.

The heavy curtains parted, and either Daemon or Dawson appeared on the porch. The dark-haired, emerald-green-eyed Luxen were identical, but as he descended the short set of steps, I knew it was Daemon. His hair was a little shorter than his brother's, face and body a fraction broader. That wasn't enough to truly tell them apart, but I'd always been able to after a few moments.

Which was weird.

My stomach grumbled again, and I dropped my hand from my neck to my stomach, rubbing it as if that would somehow help.

"You have been waiting all morning for me to walk by." Luc gave a slow grin. "Haven't you?"

Daemon strode down the flagstone sidewalk. "I've just missed you that much."

"Not surprised."

The Luxen nodded in my direction, and I gave him an awkward half wave, knowing full well that he wasn't currently a fan of mine. "How was your meeting with Eaton?" Daemon asked of Luc.

"Enlightening," was the response, and I almost laughed. Only Luc could sum up what we learned this morning in one word. "He dropped some pretty big news on us. Wondering if you've known all along."

My chest squeezed. I hadn't thought of that until now. What if Daemon knew about Dasher and hadn't given us a heads-up?

Oh, things were about to get ugly if that was the case.

"I'm going to need a little more detail before I can answer that." Daemon folded his arms.

Luc glanced at me, and I could read the question in his eyes. I even fancied that I could hear him saying, *It's up to her.* If Daemon didn't know about Dasher, Luc was giving me the choice of letting the rabid cat out of the bag.

There really wasn't a choice to be made. Daemon needed to know who we were dealing with.

"Eaton told us who's running the Poseidon Project, and guess who's pretty much in control of the Daedalus now." Tucking the hair the wind had tossed across my face back with my free hand, I braced myself for whatever reaction Daemon might have. "It's Jason Dasher."

Daemon went so still he could've been mistaken for a statue, but then he blinked and looked to Luc.

"Yeah, I thought he was dead, too," Luc answered, his hand a warm weight around mine. "Sylvia healed him after I left."

"How could you not know he was alive?" Daemon rang with disbelief as the pupils of his eyes turned white. "You seem to know everything else, even the stupid crap, but somehow, something as big as this, you had no idea?"

Irritation pricked at my skin like a swarm of fire ants, and I responded before Luc had a chance. "He had no idea, because they had their thoughts shielded while he was with them and my mo—" I started to correct myself, but the woman was my mother. "My mom had to have buried the truth so deep that Luc couldn't get to it. From what Eaton told us, she and Jason would've been extremely skilled at blocking their thoughts since they'd helped create the Origins, but you probably already know that little factoid, and I sincerely doubt you think Luc would keep something like that from everyone."

Dragging his teeth over his lower lip, Luc dipped his chin. He looked like he was trying not to smile or laugh, and I didn't know what he'd found so funny.

"What?" I demanded, staring at him.

"Nothing." His lips twitched as he glanced at Daemon. "She told you, didn't she?"

"Yeah." Amusement flickered across Daemon's striking features. "She did."

"Sorry," I lied. "I didn't like your tone."

"I apologize for said tone." Daemon bowed his head ever so slightly. "I'm just a little shocked. If I'd known he was alive, I would've hunted that bastard down."

Knowing what I did about Daemon's and Kat's time within the Daedalus, I didn't for one second think that was an empty threat.

"Why did Eaton keep that to himself?" The light behind Daemon's pupils began to fade. "Why wouldn't he tell us?"

That was something neither of us could answer.

A breeze carrying the scent of apples caught my hair again, whipping it around my face as Daemon looked over his shoulder, back to the house. "I don't want Kat to know," he said, focusing on us once more. "Not until after she has the baby. She doesn't need any extra stress right now."

"Agreed." Luc's gaze landed on the house. "She looks like she's about to give birth any second now."

"She's past due. Vivien said that's normal, but . . ." Daemon's shoulders tightened, and I assumed Vivien might've been one of the few doctors that were here. Concern bled into the air. "But if she goes too long, we're going to have to induce, and we don't have the best setup for that."

My stomach sank. "Do you have that medication that will do that?"

Daemon's stunning emerald gaze moved to mine. "We do bi-weekly runs for goods and supplies. We've scavenged all that can be from Houston, but luckily for us, lots of meds were left behind. The problem is many of them require certain administrative mechanisms that require a pretty steady flow of electricity, and we have to be careful on how often we power things up here."

That made sense. They wouldn't want to end up drawing attention.

"We need an easy-as-possible birth," Daemon added, unfolding his arms and thrusting a hand through his hair. "Viv is prepared for complications, just in case, but . . ."

What he wouldn't say lingered around us.

Women died in functional hospitals giving birth. Technology and medical advancement could only get you so far.

"Kat is a hybrid, and she has you." Luc's hand slipped from mine as he stepped toward Daemon, placing a hand on Daemon's shoulder. They were the same height, and it was hard to imagine a time when Daemon would've towered over Luc. "She has her family. She has me. We won't let things go south. Kat will be fine, and so will your baby."

Daemon clasped Luc on the shoulder. "You're her family, Luc. Don't separate yourself from that statement."

Hearing Daemon say that made me feel even worse for almost straight up killing him in the woods, because Luc needed to know that he was a part of a family, one that included Zoe, Emery, and probably even Luc. He needed to remember that even though he kept a wall up between him and almost everyone, there were those willing to chip away at that barrier.

"Then I'm thinking you and Kat have a little Luc or Lucy on the way?" Luc's reply would've been oh-so smooth if it weren't for the slight thickening in his voice.

The lines of Daemon's features softened as he let out a raspy chuckle. "We have two names picked out, and I hate to break it to you, but Luc isn't one of them. Neither is Lucy."

Grinning, Luc stepped back. "I don't know if I can forgive that."

A faint smile appeared, hinting at those deep dimples that must be breathtaking when he really let go and smiled. Daemon was beautiful. No doubt about that, but he didn't send my pulse skittering the way Luc did.

But within a heartbeat, the small grin Daemon had been rocking was gone. "You got time for that much-needed talk?"

Warning bells went *ring-a-ding-ding* as I clearly recalled Daemon referencing this "much-needed" conversation more than a time or three hundred since he learned what I was.

Since I was surely going to be the topic, I thought I should take part in said conversation, but before I could say anything, my stomach rumbled loudly.

I really hoped Daemon hadn't heard that.

"Don't really have time right now." Luc's gaze flipped from the cloudless sky to Daemon. "Evie's hungry. Sounds like her stomach is eating itself. I have a feeling if it doesn't get something that is considered red meat in her, she may start eating small animals and children."

Slowly, I turned my head and looked at him, lifting my brows.

Luc shrugged. "Just being honest."

"Pretty sure you could've described my hunger any other way than that," I told him.

"I don't know. It was impressively descriptive." Daemon grinned. "Look, feed your girl, and then come see me. This conversation can't be delayed forever."

"There's no point in hiding from it," Luc replied. "It's as inevitable as you getting on my nerves."

"If I had feelings, you might've hurt them."

"If I cared, that would concern me, but since I don't, you fill in the blanks."

Daemon chuckled even though I was watching both of them with wide eyes. Sometimes I wondered how these two hadn't seriously maimed each other yet. They had the weirdest friendship.

As Daemon and Luc went another round attempting to outsnark each other, I turned slightly, toward the city. We were on higher ground, which afforded a better view of what remained of Houston. I was struck again by how the city deserved to be captured before decay brought the buildings down. Swallowing a sigh, I started to turn back to Luc and Daemon.

Something snagged my attention. Unsure of what I saw at first, I squinted. I didn't know what it was, but as I scanned the landscape, sweeping over the skyscrapers on the outskirts of the city, I saw it.

A flash of light, easily mistaken for the glare of the sun off one of the windows high up in the sky, but it flashed three times in short bursts before a longer pause and then two more.

The sun didn't do that.

What the—

Out of the corner of my vision, I saw another burst of light coming from across the street, kitty-corner to the other building. Light flashed in a steady rhythm from a window lower down.

"Luc, look!"

He turned from Daemon as soon as I called his name, but he was focused on me. "Not at me," I told him, glancing back. "Those two buildings."

Luc did as I asked. "What?"

Doing the same, Daemon stepped forward. "What are we looking at?"

"You guys don't see the . . ." I trailed off, gaze darting from one building to the next. The flashing lights were gone.

"What am I supposed to be seeing?" Luc asked.

"I saw . . ." I waited to see if the lights would appear, but they didn't. "I saw lights flashing in the windows of those two buildings." I pointed them out to them.

"I don't see anything like that." Luc's brows furrowed. "Just the glare of the sun off the windows."

"That wasn't a glare. It was a steady flash in both windows at different times, almost like—" I cut myself off before I said, *Almost like the lights were communicating with each other,* because that sounded weird.

"Maybe the sunlight was catching something on the ground and it was bouncing off the windows. There's a lot of debris left in the city, along with abandoned cars," Daemon suggested. "And it's windy, so God only knows what's blowing around down there, but no one's there. Not even scavenger teams. There's nothing left of any value."

Luc nodded. "That or aliens. It's always that or aliens."

Daemon snorted as I rolled my eyes, but no matter how long I stared at the buildings, no flashing light appeared, and neither did a weird reflective glare. Daemon and Luc had to be right. It was the glare of the sun or a trick of the eye.

Because what else could be responsible in a city abandoned and dead?

Luc did end up "feeding his girl" with the most amazing charbroiled hamburger from ground meat provided, interestingly enough, from Daemon. He cooked it out on the little firepit that sat in the backyard someone had put a lot of effort into. Pansies that almost matched Luc's eyes flowed in abundance along the wooden privacy fence. Orangey-red marigolds bloomed in raised flower beds. Pale pink snapdragons blossomed along the flagstone pathway. There were other flowers, some red and some yellow that I didn't recognize, but it was beautiful, and I wished I knew how to tend to flowers.

Once, I managed to kill one of those tiny cactus gardens.

The firepit and an outdoor couch with deep red cushions sat in a small patio situated along the back of the secluded property. Faded metal signs designed as weathervanes tacked to the fence. As I wandered through the garden while Luc fiddled with the pit, I wondered who was taking care of this. The flower beds were free of weeds, and heads of the dead plants had been plucked away. Even the grass here had been relatively trimmed, and I figured the old-school reel mower propped against the fence was responsible for that.

There had been a few fresh slices of homemade bread sealed in the kitchen pantry, and Luc and I ended up turning our burgers into bread tacos. They hit the spot.

So did half of the second burger I ended up sharing with Luc.

I kept expecting Zoe to show up, but she didn't, and when I asked where she might be, all Luc said was, "I believe she is with Grayson."

Despite the fact I wasn't entirely sure Grayson was at all familiar with emotions like empathy or compassion, I knew Kent's loss had hit him hard, and I hoped Zoe was able to comfort him . . .

Without causing him physical harm.

Luc didn't head over to Daemon's when we finished cleaning up after our late lunch like I'd thought he might. Not that I was complaining. The idea of being alone in this stranger's house with only my own head for company wasn't exactly something I was looking forward to. He ended up coaxing me into the bedroom and into the bed, his arms settling around me and holding me close to his side, my cheek resting on his chest. Thoughts of the strange light I'd seen in the city fell into the background as we talked about what we'd learned from Eaton.

It was while we were lying there and there was a lull as I stared at Diesel, the pet rock Luc had given me, that I asked something that had taken up residency in the back of my mind ever since we'd left Eaton's. "What do you think the Daedalus would've done if you hadn't accepted me when Paris brought me to you? Like, if it didn't work, would they have kept finding people to put in your path?"

"What?"

I wrinkled my nose against his chest. "I know it's random, but Eaton made it sound like you and I meeting was planned from the beginning."

He was quiet for a bit. "I don't know how that would be possible, and it's not that I doubt their ability to orchestrate some screwed-up things, but how would they have played a role in you running away?"

"And you not knowing about it," I added.

"Well, there was some stuff about you that I didn't know. You were still loud then, but you rarely thought about your father or what made you run, and I didn't push." His chest rose with a deep breath. "It doesn't matter what they would've done if I'd turned you away. I didn't. The rest is history."

"I know there's no point dwelling on it, but it's just—I don't know. It's a big what-if."

"What-ifs are the STDs of the mind," he said, squeezing me when I laughed. "Seriously. They're pointless, and they end with you wanting to take a wire brush to your brain. Don't waste your time there."

I sighed. "You're right."

"I always am."

"I wouldn't go that far, but it's annoying when you are." I smiled when he huffed, and then he changed the subject.

Somewhere after discussing if Luc could take out an army of Trojans and me suggesting he could take the threat a bit more seriously, I must've fallen asleep.

Because I was suddenly back in the woods outside of Atlanta, surrounded by masked men with guns, but it wasn't raining this time, and there was no sound.

Nothing.

Heart racing, I looked around the small clearing at the men who did not move and did not breathe. They were frozen, arms outstretched and fingers on triggers of guns aimed at me.

"This is a dream," I said into the eerie silence. "I just need to wake up. I need—"

"Only me."

My heart stuttered at the voice echoing above me and in me, coming from nowhere and everywhere. A voice that wasn't mine. A voice I now recognized.

Jason Dasher.

Spinning around, I searched the trees and the shadows they cast, only seeing more men with guns—men I knew I'd already killed.

"Only me," he repeated.

I whirled, crying out as a flare of pain lanced the back of my skull before easing off.

"My opinions." His voice echoed through the forest, through me and my own thoughts. Every muscle tensed in my body as my hands curled into fists at my sides.

"My needs. My demands." His tone steady, oddly pleasant. "My opinions. My needs. My demands. Only I matter, your maker. Do not ever disappoint me."

"*Never*," many voices whispered back, a legion of them, and mine was one of them.

Pressure clamped down on my chest, squeezing and twisting. I started to speak, but my mouth was so dry it was dust as the masked men shattered into glimmering, golden ash.

A man appeared between two heavy trees, nothing more than a shadow, but I knew it was Jason. He was pulling himself out from the recesses of my subconscious, where years of memories had been buried.

My *maker*.

"No," I bit out, hands spasming as my skin flashed hot and then cold. "You're not my maker."

"I pulled you from the grasp of death and gave you life." His voice was fingers crawling inside my mind. I could feel them slipping over me, searching for a way in. "What would that make me if not your maker?"

"Nothing." Each breath was too heavy. "It makes you nothing."

"Do not disappoint me," he said as if I hadn't spoken. "Not when I have such beautiful plans for you, Nadia."

The sound of my name, my real name, was a bomb exploding deep within my mind, shattering open the locks and bursting open sealed doors.

Energy poured out of me, crackling through the forest and filling the air with static. Power filled the damp, musty space, licking over my skin and raising the hairs at the nape of my neck. The air warped—no, it was the trees doing the warping.

Groaning under the weight of the energy, the seams of the sky above stretched. Fine cracks formed, and a dusting of snow drifted to my bare feet. In the back of my mind, I knew this wasn't right. The sky couldn't crack. The dream and the reality flashed back and forth. I was standing in a forest, and then I was on my back, in a bed, and then the hard ground was rattling under my feet. My gaze flicked up to where he stood. Fury funneled into me, a whipping, whirling storm. I wanted to kill this man, to take back everything he'd stolen and to stop him from taking any more. Every cell in my body focused on him. I *needed* to kill him, because all those still tightly shrouded memories were expanding and shuddering, and they filled my mouth with the taste of blood and terror, of humiliation and the throat-clogging dirtiness of defeat and hopelessness. Those repressed memories screamed in rage and pulsed with uncontrollable hatred for every dark and soul-destroying deed the most hidden parts of my subconscious remembered even if I couldn't. They choked and smothered me, squeezing so tight until they crowded out every good feeling or thought I'd ever had and only they remained.

I hated him.

I hated myself.

I hated all of it.

The air heated, and at any moment I expected the trunks of old trees and the coiled shrubs to combust. The forest would ignite like a matchbox if that happened, taking everything in it in a fury of flames. Or the trees would simply cave in, burying us under the rubble of bark, dirt, and rock. Wind whipped through the trees, lifting my hair off my shoulders.

"That's it," he said, that voice of his still in my head, still digging in, and then I was no longer in the forest, but in a room. White walls. White light. A man standing before me. Fitted, plain white shirt. Dark, olive-green trousers. Brown hair dotted with gray.

A churning mass of shadow and light, a kaleidoscope of dark and light surrounded my arms and then my entire body. My feet were no longer on the floor.

"You're confused. Uncertain. Afraid. Most of all, you're so very angry."

"Yes," I seethed, my voice an echo of a long-hidden memory. The shadows continued to swirl around me, a white luminous glow streaking through the darkness like bursts of lightning.

"Good. Use it." He smiled, showing no teeth. "Take that fear and that anger and use it."

"Evie," a different voice intruded, softer and warmer. "Wake up. Wake up now."

"Use it, or it will swallow you whole," he said, staring at me with no fear. "And if it doesn't, I will take back the life I gave you. I will take *his* life. You know I will. You know I can."

Opening my mouth, I screamed the rage and the terror—

"Evie!" A hand clamped down on mine, and a jolt of electricity pimpled my skin as it shorted out my senses. The touch shattered the white room and the devil who stood before me, yanking me out of the nightmare and into reality.

My eyes flew open, and I saw I was in the bedroom. Lit only by slivers of moonlight, I was face-to-face with the blades of a ceiling fan spinning far faster than I thought it could, given there was no electricity to power it.

The hand on my arm was real, and it tightened, fingers imprinting on my skin. "You're safe, Evie. You're here. You're awake, and you're safe."

Was I?

The choking, smothering feeling lingered as I stared at the fan, wondering how I was so close to it. "I saw him. He was in the woods with me, telling me only he mattered. That he was my maker." I sucked in several ragged breaths. "Then I was in this room, and I saw him."

"You're not there anymore, and he's not here." Luc's voice remained soft and sure. "He's nothing to you."

The fan spun even faster. In the darkness, the bedroom door creaked, swinging open and then closed. "He made me," I whispered, squeezing my eyes shut.

"He did *not* make you."

"You don't understand." My thoughts were running at a rapid clip, making sense of the nightmare that had combined multiple realties together. "He made me do things."

"Evie, look at me." Luc's voice hardened into a tone that brokered no room for argument. "Look at me."

Opening my eyes, I forced my head to turn in the direction of his voice. Moonlight glanced over his cheekbone, and in the low light, his hair was a mass of dark, messy waves. White lights were where his pupils should've been, and he was several feet below me.

And the man in the white shirt and olive-green pants flickered in and out between us.

"It's Jason Dasher." I shuddered. "I saw him, and he told me not to disappoint him. He told me to use what is inside me."

"It doesn't matter. None of that matters." Luc was standing on the bed. Only then did I realize that wasn't moonlight on his face.

It was me.

My skin *hummed*. I could feel it now inside me, this rushing, roaring *power*. Pushing at my insides, at my skin and bones, stretching me. Shadow and light pulsed around me.

It wanted out.

And I wanted to lash out, to spin out of control. To free the vortex of fear and fury. I wanted to rage, wreak destruction. Tear down the walls until nothing stood but me, because I could still taste those sticky, blood-soaked realities.

"You're looking at me, Peaches, but you don't see me," he said. "*See* me."

I jerked as my gaze connected with his. "He said he would kill you. That he could and he would—"

"That was before, in the past, and Peaches, he couldn't kill me then." He pulled on my arm, his features straining and the diamond white of his eyes flaring. My feet touched the floor, and now it was Luc who towered over me. "And he sure as hell can't touch me now."

Another shudder racked me. "He was in my head. He's in my head. He has to be for me to dream that."

"You dreamed that because of everything you learned, but he's not in there. I can hear your thoughts now, and it's only you in there, and it's only us out here. We're all that matter." Luc touched his fingers to my cheeks. I flinched at the contact, at the way the power around me thickened, reaching out toward him like it was drawn to him. "And that man will never matter."

I trembled as he flattened his palms against my cheeks. Movement near the door had me turning—

"Look at me, Peaches. Just look at me," Luc coaxed, dragging his thumbs over the lines of my jaw. "It's just Gray. He was nearby. Heard you scream."

Grayson was in here, in the bedroom? I tried to look again, but Luc held on. "Don't pay him any mind. He knows everything is okay. That you just had a bad nightmare."

"That's one hell of a bad nightmare," came the bored, familiar tone of the Luxen.

"Yeah, it is, but we all have bad nightmares," Luc went on. "Don't we, Gray?"

The Luxen didn't respond.

"Now that he knows everything is okay, he's on his way out. Right, Gray?"

A heartbeat of silence and then a droll, "Right. Everything seems completely under control in here. Should I alert the locals to let them know you have everything handled?"

"That won't be necessary." Luc's lips curved up on one side, giving me that lopsided grin that was both endearing and daring. The same grin he'd worn the first time I'd met him as Evie, when his club was being raided. It was the same grin he'd had after being riddled with bullets. "Have a good night, Gray."

"Yeah, you, too," he said, and I felt him withdrawing without actually seeing.

The instinct to give chase, to stop his escape, cut through me like a swift wind. I didn't want to do that, wasn't even sure why I felt it, but the predatory impulse dug in deep. "I want to go after him."

"Who hasn't wanted to go after him?"

"You don't understand. It's like . . . there's this thing inside me. It wants to go after Grayson." I fought it as I lifted my hands, gripping Luc's wrists. The door still swung. "But I don't want to hurt him."

"I want to hurt him, but only a little. That's why you're better than I am." That smile of his wrapped its way around my heart. "You've always been better than I've been."

"How?" A strangled laugh made its way free. "I'm about to blow. I can feel it, Luc. I thought . . . I don't know. I thought we had time to fix this, but—"

"You haven't blown yet, so we still have time. Nothing has happened other than maybe a painting or a book falling." His features were now cast in shadows, but I could see his brilliant pupils searching mine. "I know we can, Evie. Together. Just keep focused on me. Not the memories. Not the nightmares. Just on me."

Heart hammering, I struggled to do just that when I felt like a balloon seconds from popping. I willed my fingers to relax. They tightened instead, until my knuckles ached and I could feel his bones. I could feel my body tipping toward him, and I managed to stop myself. "It's not like when I was in the woods. It feels different now."

"What's in you is a part of you, Evie. It's not a *thing* or an *it*. It's the Source, and it's you. Even when you don't remember me, it's still you," he said, dragging his thumbs over my cheeks. "You're just not familiar with how it feels or how to control it, just like

when Luxen or Origins are young. They have some hellish tan-
trums. Dawson and Beth's baby girl? Ash? She once blew out all
the windows in a room because Beth wouldn't let her climb the
railings on a spiral staircase. This other time, she threw a plate of
peas at the wall, and the plate *and* peas went *through* the wall."

"You think I'm having a *tantrum*? Like Ashley, who is a *toddler*?"

"Ashley, who is a toddler, has more control than you do."

I blinked. The blunt statement had knocked some of the pressure out of me. "Wow."

"When I was young—a baby Origin—I had trouble controlling the Source, too. All of us did at some point."

"A baby Origin?" I whispered, finding it difficult to picture
him as a small, confused child, but what formed in my thoughts
was an adorable, full-cheeked little face with mischievous purple
eyes.

"Yes, I was that cute." He'd picked up on my thoughts. "What?
You know I wasn't hatched from an egg or a test tube."

All I could do was stare at him.

"You're not having a tantrum. I think the nightmare—the
memories that nightmare woke up in you—caused you to have
an emotional reaction, one strong enough to call the Source to the
surface."

I thought back to the dream, how it had felt like locks had been
broken and doors thrown open. "In my nightmare—or the memory; I don't know what it was—but he called me *Nadia,* and that's
when I really felt it."

A tremor coursed through the hands that held my cheeks so
gently. "I'm going to have you tell me all about the nightmare
and what you remember, but right now, I just want you to focus
on me."

How he could sound so calm when the house trembled, when
anytime a nightmare seized me, I could lose it?

"Look at me, Peaches, and feel this."

Not even realizing I'd closed my eyes, I opened them. I saw
where he'd placed one of my hands on his chest, above his heart.
"Feel each breath I'm taking? It's slow and deep, right?"

I focused through the haze of panic and lingering fear. He was breathing deep and even, nice and slow. "Yes."

"Good." He stepped into me, and what was inside me stretched at the closeness. Our chests brushed with his next breath. "I want you to focus on each breath I'm taking, and I want you to slow down your breathing to match mine."

I started to do just that, but I saw the thick tendrils of moonlight and darkness slithering from my hand, licking out over his chest as something heavy toppled over in the house. I started to draw my hand back. "Luc!"

"It's okay," he said, keeping my hand in place. The tendons of his neck begin to stand out. "Just focus on my breathing."

My gaze darted from my hand to his neck. Even in the low light, I could see the skin around the collar of his shirt turn pink. Understanding dawned. "I'm hurting you."

"I'll survive. Just don't let go. Focus on my breathing—"

"No!" Breaking his grip on my wrists, I tore my hands away from him, but I saw the pulsing, twisting mass of the Source wash over his chest in a wave.

Horror punched through me as I stared at him.

"Listen to me." Faint white lines started to appear under Luc's cheeks, forming a network of veins, but he reached out, grasping me once more by the shoulders. "The way the Source builds in a Luxen or a hybrid is different from how it does in an Origin. When we start to tap into it, summoning it but not using it, we have what is like a critical breaking point. It's like a pressure cooker—" He sucked in a sharp breath. "If you can get it under control, you're going to have to let it out."

Use it, or it will swallow you whole . . .

I zeroed in on the energy coming to the surface of his skin as wetness trickled out of my nose. The power in me? Luc said it was a part of me, but it felt like a separate entity, and it was waking up. It wasn't the Source, that much I could tell. It was tied to it, though, and it was stretching and stretching, curling itself around organs and invading my limbs. It . . .

It *wanted.*

Shaking, I shoved it—whatever part of me it was—back as white dotted Luc's skin. "Let go of me, Luc. I'm hurting you."

White lines bracketed Luc's mouth as he slid a hand around to the back of my head. His fingers curled into my hair. "You're hurting yourself." He trembled—his tall, strong body *trembled*. "You're bleeding."

Pain flared along the back of my skull. The energy inside me felt like a bomb. These frail walls and old floors weren't going to withstand it, and neither would Luc. It was possible that the houses nearby would be knocked down. That was how big the power felt, and if I let it out, it would destroy everything. I didn't want that to happen—

"Then don't let it take control of you." He leaned in then, past the aura surrounding my body, and tipped his forehead against mine. I shuddered at the contact, at the way this foreign, new part in me yearned, not just to be let out but for *him*. That didn't make sense, but that was how it felt.

If I couldn't let it out and I couldn't get it under control, what would happen if I let it swallow me? Instinct or perhaps hidden knowledge told me that all this power would go inward, and I had a feeling that wouldn't end well for me.

But others would be safe.

Luc would be safe.

"You can't do that."

He was wrong. How I knew that, I didn't know, but I could suck it back in, pull it into me until it had nowhere to go.

"I won't let you do that, Evie." His hips pressed into mine, and there was nothing separating us. "You're not going to turn this back on yourself."

"You have to let go of me." An icy burn pricked along my skin.

"Never," he swore, brushing his lips over the curve of my cheek.

Another shiver whipped through me. Two reactions happened simultaneously. One was familiar. That warm, tight buzz of attraction that threatened to turn my body to liquid, even right then, when things were falling apart. The other was . . . different.

The new part Luc claimed was me shivered with anticipation, too, but a different kind I had no experience with before.

It wanted . . .

And it hungered.

"Let go," I begged as this *thing* poured into my chest. "Please. I love you, and I can't hurt you like this. *Let go.*"

"Evie." Luc's voice barely rose above the thundering of my pulse. "I will never let you go. Not again."

Muscles coiled tight to the point of fiery pain, jerking my arms. The pressure kept building and building—

"You can do this." His nose slid along mine as he said, "You just need time to learn how."

Before I could respond, Luc kissed me.

The feel of his mouth on mine was a shock to the system. It was a brush of the lips. Once. Twice. A soft caress that sent a rush of hot, shivery sensation from the roots of my hair all the way to the tips of my toes. I tensed, and it was nothing like the bitter burning anger, the icy fear or the slippery otherness that had been spreading inside me. Everything—*everything*—stopped out of shock, and all I felt was the sweetest burst of agony and wanting, and all of me went soft. My lips parted on a breath, and he shuddered against me, his hand fisting in my hair as the kiss deepened. His kiss was a demand, and I sank into him, my hands returning to his chest. The kiss ended on a ragged groan.

The sound . . .

My eyes fluttered open, and I caught just a glimpse of the pained grimace twisting his beautiful face.

"It's okay," he whispered, recapturing the distance between us, catching my lower lip with his teeth. He soothed the sweet sting with another kiss, and a gasp left me just before his mouth moved over mine again, causing another shock to the system.

I'm sorry.

As impossible as it was, it was his voice I heard in my mind, and I didn't understand what he was apologizing for when it was me hurting him.

One of Luc's hands skimmed up my waist and over my stomach to settle on the center of my chest. His palm flattened, fingers spreading wide as his other hand left the back of my neck. He curved his arm over my shoulders, holding me—

Luc broke the kiss, snapping his head back as he tore his hand away from my chest. The overwhelming strength of power pulled taut and then snapped.

I saw *it*.

Strings of white and black pulsing, twisting light streamed from my chest, attached to Luc's fingers. Pressure peeled back from my skull and my insides. Sweet, cool relief washed over me, so potent and so sudden, I cried out.

The pulsing mass washed over Luc, covering him completely until I couldn't see him at all.

Oh God.

Luc did it so I wouldn't. He'd taken the catastrophic power into *him,* letting it swallow him before it swallowed me.

4

The house stopped trembling, and above, the ceiling fan slowed to a lazy churn driven by the outside breeze. On one last creak, the bedroom door halted half-open. The threat of critical mass was over for me, but for Luc?

All around him, the whirling mass of shadow and light was like a battle between dawn and dusk. It consumed Luc, until he was just an outline of a man.

"Luc!" Panic exploded deep inside me, triggering a surge of the Source. I felt the ends of my hair lift from my shoulders in warning, and I tried to stamp down the power before it grew too big, too strong.

The streaks of white light around Luc pulsed intensely. Out of reflex, I threw out my arm, shielding my eyes from the glare as the moonlight shade of energy flared outward, licking and flicking over the darker, more turbulent shades until it became a rolling wave, the only thing that surrounded him—all of him.

His entire body was encased in the white glow of the Source, just like Luxen appeared in their true form.

Luc was as bright as a hundred suns, turning night to day. Anyone who was awake and within a block of this house would've had to have seen the light pressing against the windows and leaking out into night. Static charged the air around us, crackling over my skin.

I'd never see anything like this from him before. Normally, when he was really tapping into the Source for more than a few moments, it was only a whitish aura that outlined his body, and that was typically a sign that things were about to get froggy. This? This was totally different.

But he was alive and not ash and dust, something I knew wouldn't have been the case for me if he hadn't stepped in. The knowledge that it would've been deadly if I'd let the Source erupt inside me was instinctual, something I couldn't explain.

Tiny hairs raised all over my body, and it had nothing to do with the bursts of the Source still firing deep inside me. He was standing, but he wasn't moving.

"Luc." I repeated his name, reaching for him only to realize I was sitting on the edge of the bed. My legs had given out at some point.

There was no response from within the intense light.

I leaned forward, and the glow of light around him reacted to my proximity, flickering rapidly. I halted, fingers inches from the arm encased in the Source. "Please," I said, heart thundering. "Please say something."

Silence greeted me—cold, eerie silence.

For a heart-stopping moment, I didn't think he was going to respond at all, and that moment was one of the scariest seconds of my life, because I had no idea what he'd done to himself, and if I lost him? God. My heart cracked. I didn't know what I would do without him, because I couldn't lose him. Not again.

"I'm okay."

Relief caused my breath to lodge in my throat, but there was something wrong about his voice. His tone was thicker, the timbre deeper, and even I could hear the hum of unbelievable, uncharted power in those two words. The kind of power I doubted even the Daedalus had seen before.

And the alien part of me didn't know how to react to Luc. I could feel it, reaching out and pressing against my skin in waves as if it were sensing that Luc was a threat, like it had done in the woods, but it didn't take over this time. It withdrew into my core, seeming to give off the signal that it knew it would not be wise to go toe to toe with Luc while he was this . . . whatever *this* was.

And it reminded me of the inexplicable bad vibes I sometimes picked up from a person or strange place even if I hadn't known them or had never been there before. It was primal instinct warning me that the place or person was bad news, and that kind of intuition was never wrong.

That primal instinct was telling me right now that there was something very, very off about Luc.

"I'm not going to hurt you," Luc stated.

"I know that." And I did. Well, at least I thought I did. My eyes started to water from the intensity of the light surrounding him, but I couldn't look away. I pulled my hand away, though, curling it against the space between my breasts, where he had pressed his palm.

He remained where he stood, a brilliant, utterly otherworldly being. "I had to stop you before you killed yourself. You would've died. There would've been nothing left of you to even mourn." He confirmed what instinct had been telling me, but there was something different about his voice that went beyond the threads of power in his tone—something off about how he chose his words and even in how he stood there. "You would've taken down this building and everything around it."

"Thank you," I whispered, still unsure of what to make of it since he was, well, alive and all, but definitely not right. "How did you do that?"

"I took it from you," he stated as if he'd simply taken a coat from me and not a deadly mass of chaotic power. "And then I took the surge of the Source inside me."

I blinked the watery haze from my eyes. "Did you know you could do that?"

His head tilted, and then he nodded.

"Is it common knowledge that you can?" A tremor coursed through me.

"No. I've only done it once before." A pause as his head straightened. "With Micah."

I shivered at the mention of the Origin that had nearly ended my life. Micah had belonged to the last batch of Origins, but those kids had turned sour. Given God only knows what to increase the speed in which they'd physically developed, they'd become aggressive and dangerously violent. They'd thrown Kat through a window over a cookie, and eventually they'd killed a human. Luc had tried to intervene, but nothing he did seemed to have any impact on them, and he did what he had to do, putting them down, all except Micah, who then returned to terrorize the city of Columbia later.

It was another stain on Daedalus, but also one that Luc carried with him. What he had to do with those Origins was something he'd carried with him until the end.

"You didn't tell me you could," I said finally.

"It wasn't something you needed to know," he replied without hesitation. "It's not something anyone needed to know."

My brows lifted, and I struggled not to be offended or a bit hurt by his cool statement since now was not the time for achy feelings. There was something *wrong* with Luc, like scarily wrong. "Are you really okay?"

"Yes. I feel . . . invincible."

I opened my mouth and then closed it. How did one respond to that?

"It's strange," he continued in a way that was almost clinical as he took a step toward me. I tensed. "I thought I knew what that felt like, but I was wrong."

"I wish I were recording that statement." I watched him warily as I pulled my legs off the bed, tucking them against my chest. "But no one is invincible, Luc."

"I was the closest thing to invincible. Before you, that is," he amended rather factually. "Now that I know the extent of your power, I have concluded that I was not, in fact, invincible."

I was really beginning to wish for something I'd never had before: that Grayson was still around.

Luc took another step closer, and the heat of his body reached me. "But right now?" He lifted his radiant arms, his head turning to the left and then the right arm. "Even if you could control your abilities, you'd be no match for me."

"Congrats?" While he was busy checking himself out, I scooted back about an inch or five, freezing when the glowing mass of light that was his head snapped in my direction. My heart rate tripled. "Do you think you can, you know, dim down the light show?" If I could see him—his face and especially his eyes—I'd feel a hell of a lot better. Actually, I would probably feel better only when he returned to a little scary but normal Luc, and not this completely terrifying, inhuman Luc.

I glanced to where the pet rock sat on the nightstand. Above the eyes drawn in black marker, there was a Harry Potter lightning scar. Diesel was a goofy, senseless, and vastly useless gift, something that Luc would find great humor in.

This version of him standing in front of me would not.

"It has to run its course."

I swallowed. "What does that mean, exactly?"

"Once I absorb the Source, it will fade and I will be . . ." A pause. "A little scary, but normal, and not this completely terrifying, inhuman version of myself."

"Get out of my head."

"I can't help it. You're in me." Two incandescent hands pressed into the bed, a mere foot from my feet.

"That sounds . . . slightly disturbing."

"It is . . . different," he said, his voice still tinged with unfamiliar undertones. "The Source has an imprint of what drove it. I can't see what you were dreaming, but I feel it. I can taste your emotions."

I locked up, eyes going wide. I wasn't sure how to feel about that. While I'd wanted him to understand why I'd lost so much control, I didn't want him to gain such intimate knowledge of that choking, suffocating heaviness.

"It tastes like blood and terror," he said, and my breath caught. "Humiliation and defeat."

I was so caught up in what he was saying, I hadn't realized he was closer, on his hands and knees, prowling up the length of my legs.

"I can taste the residue of hopelessness," he continued. "What caused those feelings are still hidden from you—from me. Whatever he made you do during the time you were with the Daedalus does not matter. Only this does. I won't kill him, Evie. There will be no simple, quick death for him." Luc's hands were at my hips, and my back was pressed to the mattress. His head and shoulders were level with mine, and when he spoke, his words dripped fire. "I will flay his skin from his body and then shred his muscles and tendons until he cannot even lift a finger. I will slowly tear him apart, at the most sensitive parts, limb by limb, and then, when he sees death looming, he will see you. You will be the last thing he sees before you deliver the killing blow."

I shivered, a little scared by his words.

And I was also sort of . . . turned on. That probably meant there was something wrong with me. Okay, not probably. Most definitely there was something twisted and disturbingly wrong with me.

"There's nothing wrong with you," Luc said. "It's not the idea of violence that makes you feel that way. There's no one who deserves it more than Jason Dasher."

He was correct, but I shouldn't wish that kind of death on anyone. I should be better than that or some crap, and besides that, I shouldn't want to kiss him after hearing him say that.

Luc's head gave that odd little tilt again. "It's also because you know I'd do exactly what I said, that I would do all of that for you, and you also know how badly I want to be the last thing Jason Dasher sees."

Breathing turning shallow, I knew he was right.

"Humans are messy, Evie. Complicated and layered beings who sometimes find themselves in that uncomfortable, moral gray area," he said in that strange, power-heavy voice. "Just because you aren't exactly human doesn't mean you're not just as messy."

I wet my lips as my pulse pounded. It hurt my eyes to stare into the light, but as close as he was, I could see he looked nothing like a Luxen, who in their true form reminded me of liquid glass. Beyond the intense glow, I saw the almost perfect lines and planes of the face I still itched to capture to film like I'd done one afternoon in his club. "And you?"

"I am the mess," he stated.

I didn't understand what that meant, but he spoke before I could ask. "I wish you did not fear me now."

"I don't fear you."

"Your mind is completely open to me. I know what you think."

My watering eyes narrowed. "For the millionth time, it's rude to read people's thoughts."

"It does not change what I know," he replied.

"Okay. Yes. I'm a little freaked out. Can you blame me? You're speaking weird, and you haven't called me Peaches once since you sucked all that power into you—"

"I took it so you didn't stupidly kill yourself."

"And I thank you for that, but you could've left off the *stupid* part," I told him, and he just stared down at me with eyes full of white flames. "You also told me that you could easily take me out now—"

"What I *can* do and what I *would* do are two separate entities."

"Yes, I know that, Mr. Cold Logic, but that doesn't make it any less creepy to hear." My hands were tense at my sides, fingers digging into the blanket. It was the only way I could stop myself from punching him. "And in case you don't know, you look like the Human Torch right now."

"But I am still Luc." He dipped his head just the slightest, and I had to lower my gaze to shield my eyes from the brightness. "I am still yours."

My heart gave a happy little flop as my fingers eased off their death grip. "Yes. You are."

One of his hands shifted to the space beside my shoulder, and the heat he threw off should've been unbearable but wasn't. "I wish you didn't fear me," he repeated. "Because I want to remove the taste of what your memories held with something beautiful."

What my heart did next put the silly flop to shame. Filled with the bitter sweetness of his words, it swelled so much I felt like I could float off the bed. He wanted to erase what I knew he felt, because it had been in me first, and honestly, I wanted nothing more than to wash that taint away. I was scared of what he was right now, but not of him.

Never of him.

I couldn't count how many times he'd intervened and saved my life, only because I was sure there were times I didn't even know about. I couldn't fathom how he'd walked away and stayed away from me, because I knew I wouldn't have been able to do that. I was entirely too selfish, and that was where Luc was wrong about him and me. He'd do anything to make sure I lived, and I would do anything to make sure he stayed by my side.

Luc started to pull back, and I stopped lying there and I stopped thinking, because Luc needed me. I lifted my hands, knowing that the Source surrounding him would not harm me.

Electricity traveled across my fingers and down my arms as my hands slipped through the heated glow. I pressed my palms against his cheeks, turning his head back to mine. Tears crowded my eyes, and I wasn't sure if it was from the light or something else, but I closed them as I raised my head to his.

The moment our mouths touched, a much stronger current of energy washed over me, leaving my lips and throat tingling. I didn't pull away from the strong sensation or from the heat that now flared around him. I parted my lips and deepened the kiss, proving to Luc that I didn't fear him and doing my best to erase what we both felt, what we both now shared.

But then he slipped a hand to the back of my head, seeking for control of the kiss, and I happily handed it over.

A low rumbling noise came from the back of his throat; it curled my toes and twisted my stomach into tiny delicious knots.

Evie.

I swore I heard him say my name even as his lips moved over mine, and it had been *his* voice, not the frigid, apathetic one that had worried me—but that wasn't possible, and then I wasn't thinking about that at all. A hand on my hip tugged my body under his, and I gasped at the riot of sensation. The heat and the hardness pressed into me, obliterating all thoughts except for how he felt—how I felt.

Wherever he touched, static followed, dancing after the hand that slid down my arm, over my waist, and then lower, stopping to clutch my hip in a way that left me breathless, and then he gripped my thigh. His hips settled into me, and when he lifted my leg, I hooked it around his.

He didn't taste like bad memories or haunting nightmares. He tasted of sunshine and summer midnights. I was falling and falling into his warmth and in him, and when he moved against me, I gasped, "*Luc.*"

"The way you say my name like that? It's going to kill me," he said, his tone still that strange, power-heavy, cold one, but his words? They were all Luc as he caught my lower lip between his teeth. "You have no idea."

I didn't think he knew what he was doing to me as his mouth blazed a path of kisses down my throat. He dragged his teeth along that incredibly sensitive place just above my shoulders, causing my back to arch.

Okay.

Maybe he did know exactly what he was doing.

Luc chuckled as one of his hands slipped under my shirt, his hand a brand against the bare skin of my stomach.

"You're in my head again." I barely recognized my own voice.

"I am." No shame. "And it's not the only thing I want to be inside of."

My entire body flushed at the boldness of his words. "Shocker," I managed to whisper as his hand skated up my ribs, over the thin cups of my bra. The material did nothing to shield my skin from the heat of his hand.

His mouth returned to mine. "You want the same thing."

It wasn't a question. It didn't need to be. I did. I wanted the same so badly it was almost painful, but this . . .

This was Luc, but it also wasn't.

He kissed me then like he was staking a claim, like he never had the luxury of doing so before, and I was thoroughly claimed.

Things spun a little out of control as the intense glow that consumed Luc pulsed and flared, creating flickering shadows along the bed and the wall. His shirt came off, and his hair felt like strands of flames between my fingers as he kissed his way down my body, over clothing and then against skin.

How my pants and shirt came off had to be due to some nifty ability of Luc's, because I was completely unaware of it happening until I felt inches of heated, bare skin tangling with mine. The bra I was completely present for, because his fingers and then his lips chased the straps down my arms, and when it fell to the bed and clothing no longer provided a barrier between me and his hands, his mouth, I felt like I couldn't breathe past the way my pulse pounded all over my body. Our hands were everywhere, and I knew where this was heading. The intent was heavy in the air, a tangible third entity, and when I pushed at the last clothing Luc wore, I did so without really thinking. I just wanted to feel—to feel *him,* to relish in these precious, stolen moments while everything beyond us felt like it was on the brink of falling apart. We had no idea what was going to happen from hour to hour, and I just wanted the beauty of this, of him, of us together, and there wasn't a single thing wrong with that.

For one thing.

Our first time together should be ours, and not Luc's, mine, and whatever it was he'd pulled out of me.

Luc drew his mouth from mine in a slow, savoring kiss. "Evie?"

Opening my eyes, I saw that the radiance of power around Luc had faded just enough that I could make out the diamond brightness of his pupils. He was staring down at me, unblinking, his gaze familiar and yet not.

I placed one trembling finger against his shining cheek. "I want you. I want this," I whispered, and Luc shook. The Source flared brightly. "But not like this."

He was still for only a moment. "Not like this," he agreed, touching my chin. The Source crackled softly, spreading across my cheek. "You know what, though?"

"What?"

He dropped his hand to my hip. "There's a whole lot of stuff we can do instead."

My stomach dipped in the most exquisite way. We'd done other things, and I really liked those things. So did Luc. "Yes." The corners of my lips started to tip up. "There is."

Luc kissed me, and then, with one unbelievably quick move, I was half on my belly, half on my side, and the long, almost burning length of Luc was pressed to my back a heartbeat later.

Surprised by the sudden move, I let out a stunned laugh. "That was impressive."

"I know." The wet warmth of his mouth touched my shoulder.

I bit back a moan. "And here I thought you couldn't get any more arrogant."

"Is it arrogance if it's the truth?"

"Yes."

"Disagree." Stretching over me, his hand splayed over mine where it rested on the bed, the glow of the Source turning my own flesh iridescent, and as his fingers slid up my arm, sparks drenched my skin. "And you already know."

"Know what?" I tipped my head back against his chest, biting down on my lip as his hand roamed more freely.

"I'm always right."

My laugh ended in a sound that scorched my cheeks, but I got payback when I tipped my hips back, and he let out a ragged groan that sounded part curse. All laughter died within the next couple of seconds, because I simply didn't have the air in my lungs to do so.

His heated fingers slid over my belly, past my navel, and then halted. He waited.

Luc, still in there, still in control, waited for me.

I nodded as I whispered, "Yes."

He shuddered against me, and then there was nothing but raw, stunning tension as his hand drifted lower with unerring accuracy.

In those moments, we drove both of us to the point where neither of us were capable of coherent words. When he finally, really touched me, I lost all sense of time. I moved against his palm. He moved against me, both of us seeking, chasing after the explosion, and when it came, his hoarse shout joined my own sharp cry.

And it was then, when fine tremors rolled through me in waves that were mirrored in Luc, I realized that what had started out being about Luc had ended being about both of us. I didn't think until our breathing and hearts slowed that either of us realized how badly we needed the reminder that memories and the past, even the parts not remembered, didn't define us.

We wouldn't let it.

Ever.

5

Sometime later, a few hours shy of dawn, Luc no longer looked like the Human Torch. It had to have happened while I'd dozed, because when I opened my eyes, there was no glow, only shadows.

Luc had gotten an arm underneath my head, and I was currently using his biceps as a pillow. He was still curled around me, his chest warm against my back, but nowhere near as hot as it had been hours earlier.

"Your arm must be dead," I murmured.

He was tracing idle shapes along my waist. "My arm has never been better."

At the sound of his voice, I let out a tiny breath of relief. "You sound normal."

"You mean when I'm only a little scary?"

I cringed. "You're never going to let me forget that, are you?"

"Nope." His finger moved, and I thought he was drawing a figure eight.

Tilting my head to the side, I tried to see his face in the darkness, but all I saw was his neck. "You know I'm not afraid of you, right? Not even when you were looking a lot like a Luxen on steroids."

"I know." He shifted slightly, and his lips touched the tip of my nose.

"I mean, I was a little freaked out. You kind of reminded me of a robot. A horny robot, which are two words I never thought I'd say in my entire life, but you were . . . different," I rambled on. "And I'd be shocked if I don't end up with sunburn in some very uncomfortable places."

"Horny robot?" Luc laughed, his lips briefly touching mine. He settled back, his finger moving again. "I don't think you have to worry about any uncomfortable burns in unmentionable places."

"Good to know." I rubbed my cheek against his arm. "I'm glad you're not glowing anymore."

He didn't respond, instead drawing on my hip what felt like a . . . pair of lips?

Finding his other hand, I curled my fingers through his and squeezed. "I know I said thank you already, but—"

"You didn't need to thank me the first time, and you sure as hell don't need to thank me again. I would do anything to keep you safe, Peaches. It's just the way it is."

"That doesn't mean I don't have to thank you," I told him. "If you hadn't, I would've, well, you know what would've happened. I just couldn't calm down. I tried. I really did." I stared at the shadows across the bed. "I just couldn't pull myself out of it."

"It's good news, though."

My brows lifted. "How do you figure that?"

"Because now we know that the Source doesn't just respond to you feeling threatened. Extreme emotion can bring it out."

"And again, how is that good news?"

"Well, for starters, I don't have to make you feel threatened by me," he replied, tone dry.

"Oh. Yeah. Good point there."

"And I think . . ." He exhaled heavily. "I think working with it being emotion based gives us a better chance of pulling it out and controlling it."

I did a real bang-up job at controlling it.

"The Source seems to be reacting like a defensive mechanism in you, triggered if you're threatened or under extreme duress, and that makes sense. Like I said before, young Luxen or Origins have the same lack of control, but the thing is, you should be able to tap into it at least, use it when you want to. That's the part I don't get."

Maybe I was defective.

"You're not defective," he said quietly. "And don't yell at me for reading your thoughts. You practically screamed that one at me."

I sighed, and it was a while before I spoke my current innermost fear. "It was just a nightmare, Luc. And maybe some repressed memories coming through." Definitely some repressed memories, but whatever. "Could this happen anytime I go to sleep? What if this is something I just can't control?"

"What if you can't? Does that mean you'd rather just not do anything?"

I frowned. "No. But you can't take the Source from me every time I lose it. I don't want you turning into Robotic Luc—"

"But what if it's Horny Robotic Luc?"

"Oh my God," I moaned.

He chuckled again, and God, I was happy to hear it even though he was doing his level best to embarrass me. "We do it someplace safer. There are a lot of fields and abandoned areas where if you have to let it out, it's not a big deal."

"Not a big deal? What about you getting hurt?"

"I won't get hurt."

I cocked my head to the side again. "I'm going to remind you what Robotic Luc said. That you were wrong about being invincible."

"Besides the fact I'd be prepared for you to blow and will be able to take precautions, it'll take more than a building or two coming down on me to do any damage."

A building or two?

I really had no words for that.

But I had other words. "And if I go super-villain? The way you talked about my power." I looked away. "You made it sound like you knew I could take you."

"Evie? I don't know if you realize this or not, but from the moment everything went down in those woods, I knew you could take me out if you really wanted to. I wouldn't make it easy, but that's a fight you'd win."

I already knew that, but hearing Luc confirm it was frightening.

Now, if I could control it, it would be pretty badass, but until then? It was terrifying to know I could lose control and kill the person I loved with every bit of me.

"And that doesn't bother you? At all?"

"Honestly?" He rolled me onto my back, and even after what we just shared, I folded an arm over my chest. "I actually find it really hot. Like, I was a little turned on when you were peeling my skin off my bones."

Um . . .

"Yeah, that might be TMI, but look, it would be nice if someone else could take care of the bad guys while I got caught up on *Jersey Shore*."

I stared at his shadowed face. "Are you being serious? Because I can't tell. I hope you're not, but all of that sounds like something idiotic that you'd really mean."

His palm came to rest on my stomach, just below my navel. "Half of that was true. Well, ninety percent of it was. I think *Jersey Shore* is highly underrated."

Every time I was struck speechless, honest to God, I didn't think he could shock me into silence again. Each time I was completely wrong.

"But I won't let it get to the point where my life or yours is in jeopardy," he went on. "I will stop it before it gets to that."

"How? You going to keep sucking the power out of me?"

Tracing his finger around my belly button, he was quiet for several long moments. "I don't think that would be wise."

Unnerved, I asked, "Why?"

"I'm the only Origin that can do that—well, I'm the only Origin alive that can. In a way, it's similar to how an Arum feeds off the Source and how it heightens existing strengths and abilities, but it's not the same." He was drawing an invisibly squiggly line now. "Now I know why you refer to it as 'it' or something other in you," he said. "The Source felt like a separate entity."

"It doesn't normally feel like that?"

"It feels like an intricate part of me. What came out of you felt different. Maybe it's because I was engineered from birth. I don't think it's like that with hybrids, either. Probably because they have a Luxen to anchor the mutation. Maybe it feels that way because it's in you, but you're not really a part of it, at least intentionally?

Each time you've used it, it was forced upon you, either by physical threat or emotional distress. Maybe that will change as you grow more accustomed to it. I don't know. Either way, I've never felt anything like that before." His voice grew quieter. "That kind of power? What I felt with it in me? That could be addictive. I'm a smart enough boy to acknowledge that, but it was more than that. Like it was . . . I don't know, attempting to meld to me at a cellular level."

"That sounds really bad."

"Yeah, and it doesn't sound possible, either. It's not, so I could be reading what I felt completely wrong," he said. "But instinct is telling me if I did it often, it would change me, and my instinct is never wrong."

Ice drenched my insides. "You mean, like, you'd become Robotic Luc and stay that way?"

"I think I would become far worse than that," he said, and in the darkness, his eyes found mine. "I would become something to truly fear. It should only be the option of last resort."

It shouldn't happen again. If Luc was concerned something like that would happen, it couldn't. "I don't think you should do it at all."

Luc was quiet for a long moment. "There are other ways I can lock you down, Evie, if it comes to that."

Sensing there was a reason why he didn't use one of the other ways in the first place, I placed a hand over his. "Those ways would hurt me, wouldn't they? That would be the only reason why you didn't do that instead of taking my power."

"You know me so well." He slipped his hand out from under me. "I can do things you've never seen me do."

I managed to suppress the shiver his words incited. I'd seen Luc do a lot of things that were impressively powerful, so what else could he do that I hadn't seen?

"If I wanted to, I could reach inside your mind and shut you down. It wouldn't be painless. I imagine it would be like what you felt when the Cassio Wave was used," he explained, and that had been the worst pain I'd ever experienced. "I could make you think and see things that weren't there, just like the batch of Origins Micah was a part of could. That's not all."

My heart was beating heavily. "There's more?"

He laughed, but it lacked his warmth and humor. "The serum used to create me is a part of the Andromeda serum. I know this, because there were things you did in the woods that only I can do. Things Micah and the others were only beginning to develop."

I was almost afraid to ask. "What things?"

"The way you broke bodies with your mind? How you did it with a curl of your fingers without touching them? Those are things I can do." He lifted a hand, brushing his hair back. "But I'm nearly as fast and as powerful as you, and I couldn't do what you did with the earth, turning it into a weapon."

He was talking about how I'd turned the soil into ropes of death, basically. I honestly had no idea how I'd even done that other than I'd thought it . . . and it had happened.

"What about Archer?" And little Ashley and Daemon and Kat's soon-to-be-arriving child. "What about Zoe?"

"Neither Archer nor Zoe can do any of those things. I was a surprising fluke of perfection before they created the last batch of Origins," he said, and it wasn't said with a hint of arrogance. "Each Origin has its own unique abilities. At least that's how it's been. Ashley has a way of knowing things."

Like how she'd known I was Nadia?

That was still kind of creepy.

But I was also now kind of creepy.

"In the woods, when it didn't seem like I was going to reach you?" He shifted away from me, onto his back. Cool air immediately invaded the space. "I tried it." He exhaled heavily. "I hated the idea of causing you pain even though I figured by that point it wouldn't do lasting harm like it would with humans. Their minds can't withstand it. Scrambles the brains quite literally. But I couldn't get in. It's like that ability was taken into consideration when the serum was perfected."

Could the Daedalus have been that proactive? The answer was a resounding yes. They'd taken all the successes and failures of the previous serums and worked with that knowledge, not against it.

"I will just have to catch you before you tip over that ledge. It's the only way."

His arm curled under my head, as if he wished to pull it away, and I knew why that bothered him. Catching me before he couldn't get to me meant he would literally seize control of my mind. Luc hadn't minced words. It would hurt badly, and that would be the last thing Luc would ever want to do.

I rolled toward him, plastering myself to the side of his body as I threw one arm over his bare chest and a leg over his.

"Um . . . ?" Luc trailed off.

"It's okay. I give you permission."

Luc locked up against me. I don't think he even breathed.

"If I start to tip over, you have my permission to give me a mental bitch slap. It'll hurt, but it won't be your fault. You can't feel guilt over it."

"I don't think that's really an option, Peaches."

"It has to be done, Luc, or we're screwed. No one else can do what you can do." I kept my voice level, because I knew he wasn't being domineering or overprotective. If the shoes were on my feet, I would be drowning in guilt. So, I got it, but it didn't change the fact that it was our only option. "Are you okay with us being screwed?"

"I'm okay with us being the ones doing the screwing."

Rolling my eyes, I started to sit up, but Luc curled his arm around my back, keeping me against him. "No. You're right," he said. "It won't be easy. I won't like it, and neither will you, but it's better than the alternatives."

There could be no other alternatives.

A disquieting idea suddenly occurred to me. "What if the reason why it's happening like this is because I'm not meant to control it?"

Luc went very still. "What are you thinking?"

"We know I was mutated four years ago and then trained. My memories were removed only then, when I was placed back with my mom like some sort of sleeper. There were no signs of my mutation until April used the Cassio Wave, and since then there hasn't been any other sign, other than when I'm threatened or freaking out. Maybe that *is* just a defense mechanism and not something the Daedalus or Dasher planned."

"I'm not really following."

I wasn't sure I was myself, because the memories I had of Dasher were too brief, disjointed, and seemed out of context, but then there was what Eaton said. "The Trojans were designed to answer only to Dasher. Maybe I can only either intentionally use the Source or control it under *his* control, and that's why it feels like an entity instead of a part of me the same way the Source is a part of you or a hybrid. It's only a part of me when the Daedalus allow it."

God, the moment those words left my mouth, I wanted to take them back, because they sounded crazy enough to be totally on point.

"I refuse to accept that," he bit out.

"Luc—"

"It also doesn't make sense, Evie. There is only so much tinkering around with DNA anyone is capable of, and I don't care how much coding is in a serum, you're not a computer only capable of running one program," he argued. "It also wouldn't explain how your emotions could control it. Physical harm? Yes. That makes sense, because it would be a way for them to ensure you're able to protect their asset. But emotions? That's not an immediate physical threat."

Luc had a point there.

"It just can't be possible," he stated as if he could simply make that the case because he didn't want it to be.

Neither did I, because if it was and I was on the right path, no amount of training would make a difference if Jason Dasher held the ultimate ace up his sleeve.

I was nothing more than a walking liability or a possible bomb ticking down in the heart of what I suspected was the only place capable of forming any sort of resistance against the Daedalus.

Just like a true Trojan.

6

So, that was my night," I said to Zoe as I finished chewing a handful of peanuts I'd shoved in my mouth—the *fourth* handful of peanuts. I was so freaking hungry it wasn't even funny.

Luc was currently having that "much-needed" conversation with Daemon. Zoe had shown up minutes afterward, almost like she'd been summoned for Evie babysitting duty, wearing jeans and a shirt that fit so well I knew the items weren't borrowed but from a stash of her own clothing that had been held here.

Sometimes it was still a shock to realize how much of Zoe's life I'd had no clue about.

When I first found out that Zoe was an Origin and that our friendship in the beginning had been engineered, it had been hard, because there'd been a part of me that had feared that our friendship was as fabricated as my life as Evie was, but I'd gotten past that. How Zoe and I became friends didn't matter. What did was the fact that we had each other's backs.

We were currently sitting on the floor of the house that had temporarily become Luc's and mine, the worn coffee table between us loaded with the kind of food I normally wouldn't eat with a gun pointed at my head. Well, except for the small chunks of what Zoe had called *farmer's cheese*. I'd eat cheese all day and night, but the rest of the stuff?

Celery. Sliced apples. Carrots. Cucumbers and sliced tomatoes.

Other than the cheese I'd splattered over crackers that might've been a wee bit past their expiration date, Mom would've been proud of what I was consuming.

Mom.

A sharp slice of bitter pain lit up my chest before I could shut down that train wreck of emotions. I drew in a shallow breath. "How was your night?"

Zoe stared at me somewhat blankly, which was the expression on her face the entire time I told her what had happened last night. Granted, I hadn't told her *everything*. She didn't need to know what Luc and I had done, and I think she appreciated me leaving out those details, but I did tell her what Luc had done. I trusted her with my life, and I knew Zoe loved me like I was her sister, but I also knew Luc was something else entirely to her. She answered to Luc as a soldier would to their general. It wasn't just because Luc had freed her from a Daedalus hellhole but more than that, a loyalty born out of respect, the same with Grayson and Emery, even Kent before he was murdered. My chest ached when I thought of him, and it made me think of Heidi and if she was okay, and if James was wondering what had happened to us.

It made my heart ache even more because I then thought of Mom, and I didn't know if grieving her was right. If all the terrible things she'd done meant she was no longer worthy of me or anyone mourning her.

"Not nearly as interesting as yours," Zoe said, pulling me from my thoughts. "I had no idea Luc could do something like that." She shook her head as she dipped her apple in a glob of honey. "Actually, I didn't know any Origin could do that, which just makes Luc all kinds of extra-special."

"I know," I agreed, eyeing the golden goo dripping down the slice, wondering if that actually tasted good.

"It kind of reminds me of how the Arum feed. It sort of looks like a kiss when they do it." The slice of apple halted inches from her mouth. "Well, I guess they could do it while kissing, but they basically inhale, sucking out the Source."

"Luc didn't do it like that. He just put his hand on my chest and yanked it out," I said, mimicking what he'd done. "But yeah, he was super-weird until he absorbed it."

"Weirder than you eating healthy food?"

I snorted. "I think the amount of salt I dumped on the tomatoes zeroes out the health benefits of what I'm eating."

"True story."

"But yeah, he was different. Like he was still Luc, but he was something . . . other," I said. "He was colder and almost like, I don't know, coldly logical, if that makes sense? There was emotion there." There'd obviously been a lot of emotion there considering where the kiss had led. "But I could see where that wouldn't be the case if he'd taken more."

"But he's not going to do it again. Right?"

Exhaling roughly, I nodded. "Right. Even he said he shouldn't."

"And that's the scary part." Zoe nibbled on her honey-glazed apple, her expression thoughtful. "Like, if Luc thinks it'll end badly if he does it again? That's big. In a way, he's admitting to a weakness there. He can't control how he responds to the Source that's in you, and other than you, I don't think Luc has a weakness."

I wasn't sure how to feel about being Luc's weakness. Mainly because I knew it to be true. That was why Jason Dasher and my mom had been able to pull off what they had. They'd exploited his weakness.

Leaning back against the faded cream-colored couch, I watched the ceiling fan churn lazily. The wind from the open windows was catching the blades, keeping them spinning and moving air. It was pleasant in the house, but if temps skyrocketed, no amount of shade or open windows would keep that heat at bay.

My gaze flickered across the living room. I hadn't really paid any attention to the house before. Part of me didn't want to see the remnants of the previous owner's life, but now I couldn't stop myself from seeing it. A medium-size television sat uselessly on a wooden console, in the center of a row of dark brown bookshelves. Books of all shapes and sizes lined those shelves, broken up by random knickknacks like those white angel statues that looked like little kids. For the life of me, I couldn't remember what they were called. Some were praying, petting little dogs or cats, and others were on swings or looking up, their little wings spread wide.

Those little figurines always creeped me out. Like, little kid angels were kind of wrong.

The angel theme continued in paintings that adorned the walls. Two chubby thinking angels that also looked like children. A much more serious one of the archangel Michael battling demons hung above the television. Several smaller paintings of guardian angels watching over children and happy couples dotted the walls.

My lips pursed as I eyed the framed photos of Labrador retrievers with furry angel wings sitting on the end tables.

There were a lot of angels but no photos of who'd lived here. My gaze crawled over the walls, finding the outline of where pictures must've hung at one time.

I wondered if Dee had done that to prepare the house for Luc and me or if a team of people had gone through the habitable homes, removing the traces of those who'd lived there before to make it easier for others to take their places.

Either way, I couldn't help but think that if I'd been a part of that team, I would've probably taken some of those angel paintings down and stored them where they wouldn't be staring at the person moving in.

I knew why I was staring at the apparent angel obsession on display. I was trying not to freak out over what Zoe had said. There was no reason to worry. Luc wasn't going to do it again.

"Are you going to tell me what Eaton had to tell you and Luc?" Zoe asked. "Actually, on second thought, I'm not sure my brain can handle much more."

"Well, get ready for your brain to implode," I said, and then I told her what Eaton had told us. She was just as shocked and disturbed to learn that Dasher was alive and all the rest that I shared.

"God." Dropping the carrot, she plopped her elbows on the table. "Just when you think the Daedalus can't get any worse, they show up just to prove you wrong."

"I know," I murmured, hating the heaviness that settled over me. "I wish Heidi was here right now. She'd probably string together insults from five different countries in her anger—"

"And it would make us laugh, because not only would she probably pronounce them wrong but she'd be so serious about it, too." Zoe smiled.

"Like when she called my ex a *shitboot* in Swedish?" I said, laughing. "God, I really do miss her. I hope she and Emery are okay."

"They'll be here soon," Zoe assured me. "Emery is smart. Both of them are. They'll be okay. It'll just take them a bit to get here."

I nodded, dropping my hands to my lap. "I know." I couldn't let myself think anything else.

The humor faded as Zoe's lips thinned, and I knew she had returned to thinking about what I'd shared. "Eaton might believe it all started somewhere good, but I don't believe that for one second. He wasn't on the inside like Luc and me."

I was more inclined to believe Zoe's perception.

"World domination." She balled her hands into tight fists before slowly unclenching them. "Sounds stupid and cliché, like a plot of an Avengers movie, but it's not when you really think about it."

I nodded. "You know I wouldn't have believed any of this stuff—that our government was capable of this. And I like to think, pre-Luc, I wasn't all that naïve, but I wouldn't have believed it."

"You weren't naïve," she agreed. "And you also weren't on the Luxen-hating bandwagon even though you'd believed your father had died in the war, killed by one of them."

Anger and disgust slithered like a viper through me. I hated that I'd wasted even a minute feeling guilty over not remembering what my father's voice sounded like.

"I think it's just hard to really accept that people you trust—people you *need* to trust, who are supposed to be looking out for the health and wealth of their community—can be so evil," I said finally. "Even when you see evidence of it and know that people are capable of anything."

"It's just different when you see it happening with your own eyes. I think there's a part of our psyche, the human part of us, that automatically wants to believe the best in people and in situations. Maybe because it's easier or less scary. Maybe it's even a survival tool. I don't know," Zoe said. "But the thing is, there are groups of people out there who believe the one percent control the world.

Like some sort of shadow government is behind the wheel, and in a way, they're right. The public doesn't know the Daedalus exist, and that that organization has their hands in everything, but they haven't been able to stretch their reach to seize absolute control on a global level, not to a point where the impact on ordinary people's lives is no longer hidden and easy to overlook. To do that, they'll need to get rid of anyone who can fight back and then move on to humans they find undesirable. They could reshape the law, the government, and society to what most benefits them."

Pressing her lips again, she shook her head. "But is that really their goal? There are a lot of people they'd need to take out if they didn't want to spend every waking moment fearing a rebellion. And do we really know what their endgame truly is? We don't, but I can't figure out how they plan to accomplish any of this with a hundred or so trained Trojans and an army of recently mutated humans."

I mulled that over, thinking about how the world viewed Jason Dasher as a hero. "But if they make themselves out to be the heroes' like Jason Dasher did, and they make those they want to get rid of the villains, it may be easy for them to take control."

Zoe fell quiet, and there was a part of me that couldn't even believe we were having this conversation, so maybe Zoe was on to something about how the human psyche seeks to protect via levels of denial.

But like I'd realized before, the luxury of denial was something none of us could afford.

"It's already begun." Unease coated my skin. "Look at how the Luxen are being blamed for people getting sick. Something that's biologically impossible, but not a lot of people seem to question what they're being fed by people like Senator Freeman." I tucked my hair behind my ears. "We didn't really get to talk about the whole flu thing that the Sons of Liberty guy told us about. What was his name? Steven? I didn't get a chance to ask Eaton about it, but what if that's true?"

Zoe sat back, eyes widening with surprise. "God, I can't believe I forgot about that."

"A lot has been happening," I reminded her.

Raising her brows in agreement, she nodded. "Steven said that the Daedalus had weaponized the flu and have been releasing it in batches, right?"

I nodded.

Her gaze drifted to the rippling curtains. "They manipulated a strain of the flu to carry the mutation. People who get their yearly flu shot may still get pretty sick, but they won't mutate. Those who didn't get the shot will . . ."

"Mutate or die." Like Ryan, one of our classmates, who had gotten the flu and died. Or Coop and Sarah. They'd mutated. But then there'd been the outbreaks in Boulder and Kansas City. People died there, too. Steven claimed those cases were test runs, and the mutated virus hadn't been released widely.

Yet.

Even right now, I could hear my mom lecturing about the importance of the flu vaccine. Had she known what the Daedalus were going to do with the flu virus? Closing my eyes, I cursed myself. She had to know. She worked in infectious diseases, and God, she could've been a part of making that weaponized strain at some point. Was that why she'd been so pro–flu shot? Because she knew what was coming, and if so, was that further evidence of a change of heart?

It didn't matter.

Because it didn't undo what she'd done, and her change of heart didn't change enough. She could've warned people. She could've done something.

"I don't even want to believe it," Zoe admitted. "See? That's the human part of me screaming it sounds too impossible, but I know better."

And I now also knew better.

"Damn. If they release that flu more widely and a whole crap ton of people fall ill or if some of them start acting like Coop did, raging out like rabies-infected zombies, people are going to panic, and the Daedalus can then swoop in, giving frightened people someone to blame. The Luxen." She sucked in a sharp breath. "It will be bad."

It would be catastrophic.

"How many people even get the flu shot?" she asked, and I knew she wasn't expecting an answer.

"A little over forty percent, sometimes higher if there's a bad seasonal flu." When she blinked at me, a weak smile formed. "Um, Mom used to rant about vaccines a lot. I only know that because of her."

Zoe studied me for a moment and then said, "Well, over fifty percent will either mutate or die. That's a hell of an army, or that's a whole lot of thinning the herd."

And the herd had already been thinned when the Luxen invaded four years prior—220 million people had died then.

Fewer people who could think and who could fight would be easier to control.

Pulling my legs up to my chest, I folded my arms around my knees. "We have to stop them before they release that virus, because it will be too late by then."

Zoe's pupils gleamed bright white for a handful of seconds before returning to black. She didn't respond, and I figured she was too caught up in imagining what it would be like if that virus were released.

Anger resurfaced once more, but this time it didn't slither; it roared through me like a raging river. "Even if the Daedalus didn't have this flu virus, something needs to be done to them."

"Preaching to the choir, babe."

"I know I am. I know you and Luc and probably a hell of a lot of people here want nothing more than to see them gone, and I may not remember my time with them. I know that is probably a blessing."

Zoe's gaze flickered away. "It is."

I swallowed hard. "But I keep thinking about that Trojan Eaton saw—the one who slammed his head into the wall until he died. All Dasher had done was tell him to do so, and he did it without hesitation."

"I don't even know what to say about that," she said, jaw working. "They could never get that kind of control over us or the hybrids—definitely not the Luxen. Not that they didn't try. I think the only reason why the Daedalus haven't taken over was because they couldn't replicate the hive mind the Luxen and Arum can have."

"But they have now. Eaton said that the Trojans view Dasher as if the man is their god. Luc thinks that the whole coded thing doesn't matter, that I won't end up under Dasher's control, but we really don't know that," I admitted, then took a deep, steady breath. "It doesn't matter if I can control myself or not. Those other Trojans? They were probably like me or like you and Luc. They might not have had a choice before this was done to them, but they sure as hell don't have a choice now. We need to stop the Daedalus before they have the ability to command hundreds of thousands of newly mutated people who don't live up to their expectations into killing themselves. I can't let that happen."

Determination reverberated through me. I had to do something, because those Trojans and the ones yet to be mutated were like a part of me. Sounded crazy, but that was how I felt. I couldn't explain the connection with the other Trojans, faces and names I couldn't remember and might not have even known. Maybe it was there, buried deep within me, because I'd been trained with them. Perhaps it was far simpler than that and had everything to do with the lurking, insidious fear that I could become the Trojan commanded to do something too horrible to conjure to others or to myself. I had no idea, but the Daedalus needed to be stopped. They needed to be wiped from the face of this planet and from history, for real this time.

7

Our appetites pretty much shriveled up and died at that point. Talking about power-hungry organizations that had the potential to wipe out or mutate over half the United States population would do that.

Muscles twitching in my thighs, I unfolded my body from the near-fetal position. Having my legs stretched out helped. A little. Tiny twitches danced along the back of my thighs and then my calves, causing my legs to jerk.

"You okay?" Zoe asked.

"Yeah. I'm just . . ." I wasn't just feeling twitchy. There was more, a restlessness that pushed to the edge of frustration, the kind that made you want to cry or stomp for no apparent reason. I was *antsy*.

Antsy to the point it itched at my skin. I couldn't sit in here and stare at angel paintings. Probably had a lot to do with what we'd been talking about. "I need to get moving around. I can't sit here."

"Same," Zoe shared. "Not when we have all this heavy, dark crap in our heads. I can show you around, if you want."

Interest more than just piqued, I pushed off the couch. "Are you sure I'm allowed to roam like a free-range Trojan?"

"Free-range Trojan?" Zoe snorted. "If Grayson is allowed to actually come into contact with others here, I don't see why you wouldn't be able to."

Hearing his name made me think of last night. God only knows what he must be thinking, but I wondered how he was . . . well, handling everything. As much as he appeared to hate humans, he had cared for Kent, and even I could see he was taking Kent's death hard.

Sorrow poured into my chest as I gathered up the lids, placing them onto the containers of food. In comparison to Zoe and everyone, I'd barely known Kent, and Clyde and Chas even less so, but their deaths still hurt.

Especially Kent's.

"How is Grayson doing?" I asked, brushing my hands off on a napkin when I was finished storing the food away.

"He's doing okay." Zoe straightened the hem of her shirt as she walked around the coffee table. "He's not really wanting to talk about Kent or Clyde, but I know he feels responsible."

"It's not his fault." What happened to Kent happened before anyone knew what was going on. It had been so fast—a sniper and a bullet had found him, ending his life before any of us realized the threat had been there.

"I think he knows that, but sometimes it's easier to blame yourself than to accept that nothing could've been done," she said, sounding wiser than any eighteen-year-old I knew. "Grayson is . . ."

"If you say *complicated,* I'm going to hit you."

Zoe laughed as the front door opened before she reached it. Honest to God, a huge part of wanting to get control of the Source was so that I could be incredibly lazy like every being I knew with alien DNA was. "I was actually going to say *complicated.*"

I sighed.

"He's just . . . well, he's just very layered," she said after a moment. "He's definitely prickly."

"That's an understatement."

"But he'll grow on you."

"Like an STD," I muttered under my breath.

"Before you know it, you two will be the best of friends," she said. That was about as likely as me befriending a monkey carrying the Ebola virus like that little girl in that old movie. "Don't lock the door. There's no need here, and I don't know if anyone has the key."

As I followed her outside, my imagination ran wild with what could happen with an unlocked door. At least three serial killers who had a thing for blondes with missing memories could sneak in while we were gone and then lie in wait for my return.

Then again, if that happened, I could probably take them all out.

Feeling a little badass, a small grin tugged my lips up until I realized that I'd also probably take out anyone else who'd unfortunately be in the near vicinity.

Boy, that took the wind right out of my sails and also made me think of what I had asked of Luc. Wondering what Zoe would think, I announced, "I want to work at getting my abilities under control. I mean, not right this very second," I added when she looked sharply at me. "But, like, tomorrow."

"Oh," she said, and that was all she said while we walked past Kat and Daemon's place. There were no weird feelings of expecting someone to step out, but I wondered how Luc's conversation was going with him.

"Is that all you have to say?" I asked. "Oh?"

"I was still thinking about it."

"Didn't realize there was a lot to think about."

"There is," she replied as we continued down the still-empty street.

"Who lives on this street?" I asked.

"Daemon and Kat. Dee and Archer are in the house on the other side of the one you're in." She pointed to a brick home painted the color of ivory. "That's where Dawson and Beth are. There are a few more that are here, but you haven't met them."

God. If Luc hadn't done what he did last night, I could've seriously hurt so many people.

I had to push that thought aside, because if I didn't, it would send me into a panic spiral, and that was the last thing any of us needed.

Refocusing on the apparently barren street, I wondered if it was truly possible that everyone was out and about. I didn't feel like we were being watched this time. Then again, now that I didn't feel that way, I couldn't be so sure what I'd felt the day before hadn't been paranoia.

Before we turned the corner, I glanced out over the city, thinking of the flashing light I'd seen. I considered telling Zoe, but I imagined she'd have the same reaction Luc and Daemon had.

So I asked, "Are you done thinking about what I said?"

Zoe grinned. "I think it's a good idea."

"You do?"

She laughed then. Clearly, I hadn't been able to hide my surprise. "You didn't think I'd say that, did you? I'm just surprised that Luc agreed to it."

"Because he's going to have to coldcock my brain, basically?" I joked, even though I was so not looking forward to what that was going to feel like.

Or what it was going to do to Luc.

"Yeah, that. Which is why I'm not surprised to hear he won't let anyone else work with you."

The wind picked up, stirring the limbs. A few of the golden leaves shuddered free. "You sounded like there may be another reason."

She shoved her hands into the pockets of her jeans. "Luc only ever tried to train the Origins he freed, the ones Micah belonged to, and you know how that ended."

Nearly tripping over the curb of the street we crossed, I sucked in a sharp breath. I did know exactly how that ended.

"He didn't tell me that, either." There seemed to be a lot Luc hadn't told me. But right now, that wasn't the biggest issue at hand.

A cloud slipped over the sun as we walked past the street that led to Eaton's and continued straight. I hated the idea of Luc thinking about those Origins for even a few seconds. "I need to get control of this, Zoe."

"Agreed." Zoe's lips pursed. "But I just thought of a third reason or a potential problem."

"Goodie."

"What if continuously pushing you to tap into the Source kicks in that hive-mind mentality that Eaton talked about?"

Ice encased my insides. "I've considered that. I know Luc has to have thought about it, too, but it's a risk we have to take. The only other option is to do nothing, and I can't do that."

"Agreed."

"We need something in case I do turn into—"

"A robot programmed to return to the Daedalus?"

Shooting her a look, I nodded. "Maybe we can get ahold of an elephant tranquilizer?"

A thoughtful look crossed her pretty face.

My eyes narrowed. "I wasn't being serious."

"But a tranq may be an option."

All I could do was stare at her. "How about you think of something positive?"

Her laugh was soft, and it quickly faded in the wind swirling down the wide sidewalk. "When I think of one, I'll let you know."

"But I'd better not hold my breath?"

"You said it, not me."

Nice.

Up ahead, the ranchers and overgrown lawns gave way to what might have been a city park at some point. Among the tall reeds, I could just make out the shapes of benches and what might have been picnic tables. Thick vines obscured the sign at the entrance we walked past, and it was about then when I smelled . . . roasted meat, and then the breeze carried the sweet and spicy scent of cinnamon.

Despite all that I had just eaten, my stomach lumbered awake. "Something smells amazing."

"Fire-roasted chicken, and I'm praying to God it's those cinnamon-crusted pecans Larry and his wife make. Those things are like candy crack."

Larry and his wife?

My steps slowed as I heard people for the first time since we'd arrived. The low hum of conversation, of laughter, was the first proof that everyone wasn't lying and this wasn't a ghost town.

Curious, I got my feet moving at a faster pace. At the end of the street, we came to what had to have been a busy intersection before the war. Across the grassy median, behind a row of palms, was a shopping center.

Stores stacked on top of one another, most of the signs having long since fallen away or eroded to the point where only letters instead of words were legible. There'd been a nail salon once, kitty-corner to a liquor store. All that remained of the urgent care was the blue cross above shuttered double doors. Larger stores still clearly branded. The red letters of a now very useless electronics store were visible next to one of the pet store chains, and in their parking lots were dozens of stalls and people milling about, all under rolling canopies colored red, blue, and yellow.

"This is the market," I stated, donning my Captain Obvious hat. Now I knew where all those cars had been the afternoon before.

"Yep." Zoe was grinning at my wide-eyed face. I couldn't help it. There were so many people.

Hundreds of them.

And as I stood there, too far away to see faces or eye colors, instinct was flaring alive in me, telling me what I couldn't see but I could *sense*. Humans, lots of humans, and among them but not many were brighter . . . life forces. Luxen.

Life forces?

What in the hell kind of thought was that?

"This is how Zone 3 stays alive," Zoe was saying, yanking me from my thoughts. "Well, one of the ways. Food is traded here, along with supplies and other stuff. Actually, lots of random stuff. Last time I was here, someone was trading stuffed animals—you know, not the real stuffed animals, but the kind kids play with."

Blinking, I refocused on Zoe. "How? With money?"

"There's no need for money." She tugged on my arm, pulling me into the empty street. "Come on."

Confused by the prospect of there being no need for money, I asked, "Then how do people buy the things here?"

"Labor can be traded for food. Like if someone needs repairs on the house or help working one of the crops. Some people trade goods, but there is no currency," Zoe explained as we crossed the street, entering the market where the cement had cracked and little white-and-purple flowers had begun to grow. She kept her arm looped with mine. "And they make sure no one goes hungry, even if they are too old to barter with labor or have nothing of value to trade. That's what today is. On Wednesdays, the food is free to those approved to enter, and they can take as much as they need."

"And there's enough food for that?"

Zoe nodded. "It's kind of amazing how much work can be done and the amount of food that can be grown when you're not sitting inside watching TV or messing around on social media."

"Or when your next meal actually depends on you getting out there and growing something," I added.

"That, too." Zoe squeezed my arm as she stopped. "In a way, Zone 3 was lucky. A lot of farmers refused to leave during the evacuations. Their farms were their entire livelihood, and they couldn't just uproot and start over. So, there were people who knew the land and how to ensure an abundance of all kinds of crops. And those who were moved here have all been willing to learn."

"And the food and the stuff here is really free for those who need it?"

"All the necessities are," Zoe answered as I spotted a short, scruffy white-haired dog burst out from under one of the stalls, rushing to greet a group of people who'd stopped a few feet from the table. The little puppy yipped happily as it went from person to person, collecting pats and scratches.

"It hasn't always been easy," she continued. "Crops took a pretty bad hit during a drought last year, and along with a very hot summer, it was . . . hard. Not enough cool places to hold those most at risk for heat-related illnesses." She took a ragged breath. "There used to be more who needed assistance."

"That's sad," I whispered.

"But they didn't lose anyone this summer—not from the heat, at least."

Scanning what seemed like an endless procession of brightly colored stalls, I soaked in the sights and smells, but I was a little dumbfounded by it all. Who could really blame me? Having always existed in a world where nothing was free and where people were shamed for needing assistance, no matter how badly they needed help, this was entirely unexpected.

The people here had found a system that worked for everyone. Obviously, it was a much smaller populace, but it wasn't like the same mentality couldn't be applied to larger communities.

And then it hit me. If Zone 3 was able to survive, become a place where those left behind could thrive among those who needed sanctuary, then what about the other zones? There were three other cities that had been walled off and left to decay: Alexandria, Chicago, and Los Angeles.

Luc hadn't exactly said they were empty. He'd just said that people were left behind.

"What about the other zones?" I asked. "Are they like this?"

Zoe watched the wind rolling through the canopies. "In some shape or fashion, yes. All but Alexandria. It's too close to the capital."

"What about the people in there? Were there still people left behind when they built the walls around Alexandria?"

Zoe started walking again. "We don't know. It's been too much of a risk to get close. The bridge into Arlington has always been blocked, as are all the other roads that feed into Alexandria."

Pressing my lips together, I trailed alongside Zoe. It was hard to think of the people who could've been trapped. Four years without aid? Zone 1 had to be truly dead by now.

The invading Luxen weren't responsible for that. It was we who'd dropped the EMP bombs, and it was our government that walled up those cities, knowing there were people either too sick or too poor to leave. It was our government that told extended family members that their loved ones had died in the war when they could've still been alive in those cities, waiting for help that was never going to arrive.

The number of people who had to be involved to hide what was done was astronomical, and I couldn't understand how any of them slept at night.

As we neared the stalls, it became apparent who was approved to enter. Most of those moving about were elderly, their backs hunched and their speckled fingers with swollen knuckles clutching shopping carts used more for support than for goods. There were younger people, a few I spotted in wheelchairs or those who had other mobility challenges, and others who were younger but were being aided by older people who I knew weren't all human. The silvery-haired woman with eyes as glacial blue as Grayson's was definitely Luxen. Her pale arm was curled around the shoulders of a young human man who held a straw basket full of leafy greens close to his chest as they stood in front of a table loaded with potatoes in wooden crates.

She appeared to be the first to become aware of us.

Glancing over her shoulder at Zoe and me, the smile on her lightly lined face faded. She quickly turned to answer whatever the young man said. Her smile returned as she ushered him farther into the market, to where several firepits cooked meat.

"Are we allowed to be here right now?" I asked.

Zoe's grin was teasing. "Yeah, we are. Don't worry."

Not worrying was easier said than done, but I was caught up in the market and how all of this was possible. "You said 'they' make sure no one goes hungry. Who are they?"

"It's a group of people, kind of like a city council, that's made up of humans, Luxen, Origins, hybrids, and Arum."

My gaze jerked to her. "How does that work out with Arum and Luxen here?"

The two alien species were natural-born enemies, having destroyed their own planets in a way. That was how they'd ended up here in the first place. Arums could feed on Luxen or any creature who had the Source in them, taking the power within them and then using it, which made them a totally different kind of dangerous.

"There aren't a lot of Arum, but the Arum and Luxen know to behave. Obviously, no feeding on the Arum's part and no bigotry on the Luxen side. Neither are tolerated."

"And what happens if they don't follow the rules?"

Zoe's eyes narrowed. "As far as I know, there have only been a few instances where rules were broken. All of them have been resolved in one way or another."

I studied her profile. "And what do you mean by 'one way or another'?"

She didn't respond as we walked along the outskirts of the crowded tables, not for several long moments. "The people here don't want to leave, Evie. For many, their lives are better, but it's too much of a risk to kick people out. Luckily, it's never come to that. No serious rules have been broken, and there is a place to hold those who need a time-out from fighting or being a general pain in the ass."

Sounded sort of like a jail, which made sense.

An older man who'd just placed a bundle of ears of corn in his cart eyed us—or me—with open suspicion as he hurried as fast as he could to the next stall, the wheels on his cart squeaking.

"And no one has wanted to leave?" I asked. "To be reunited with family or friends outside?"

"I don't think so," she said. "But I wouldn't know. I'm not a part of the council, and I imagine if someone wanted to leave, that would be who they'd go to."

Unease trickled through me. I had a really hard time believing that not a single person had wanted to leave.

"That's Javier." Zoe pointed out a dark-haired man with skin the color of sunbaked clay. "He was a tailor before the war, and his skills are now just as useful."

A man waved from behind a table where clothing was folded and stacked neatly when he spotted Zoe, but the smile froze when his gaze coasted over me.

Zoe didn't seem to notice as she led me along, but I did. I couldn't help it. Each time someone noticed us, they noticed me and immediately appeared as if they wanted to bolt.

I was a stranger in their midst, and these people had every right to be wary, so I didn't take it personally. Or, at least, I tried.

The scent of cinnamon grew. The last table was the source, but the crowd around it blocked any access to Larry and his apparently magical pecans.

"Dammit," Zoe grumbled. "I really wanted you to try them. The pecans are amazing, but we're getting nowhere near the front of that line anytime soon. I'll check back later to see if he has any left. Right now, there's still more to see."

Tugging me around the last stall, she pointed out the urgent care I'd noticed on the way in, explaining that it was as functional as could be, serving as the only medical facility. Then I saw what was behind the plaza. Clothing hung from tightly stretched lines attached to bolted-down wooden poles. Men and women, all I inherently knew were human, sat on stools or in chairs above large plastic containers. The area smelled like fresh detergent.

I glanced back at the market. "Are they cleaning the clothes for the people shopping at the market?"

Zoe nodded. "Yep, and some do it full-time for others who really don't want to mess around with it."

"Labor?" I surmised.

"You got it." Motioning me to cross the street, she said, "The market is pretty much in the center, so a lot of stuff is here. The council meets here, and if anyone needs anything, this is the place they come to." She pointed to a three-story, concrete building with a sign LITTLE FISHER LIBRARY. "The basement area is also used when the temps get high."

Zoe didn't take me into the library. Instead, she followed a stone path shaded by heavy oaks as it curled around the side of the building. We only took a handful of steps when I heard the shouts and laughter of children.

"The school?"

Eyes a deep violet in the shade of the trees, Zoe smiled. "Mostly little rug rats. I think there are only like two a year or so younger than we are. They moved the school to this house because it's close to everything and easier to manage without power."

Someone had painted Sesame Street characters as if they were peeking out from the windows of the one-story, redbrick building.

Children—*tiny* children—were everywhere. Racing over sand and grass, climbing onto jungle gyms and playing on a seesaw that featured Snoopy and Charlie Brown. Jump ropes snapped off the asphalt part of the yard. Little ones smacked their hands in the sand shaded by the trees.

There were two sets of swings and both were packed, of course, as swing sets were the coolest piece of equipment in a playground. One was designed for smaller children, and the other was occupied by kids who looked around ten or so years old, but I was always terrible at figuring out kids' ages. To me, they all looked like babies.

Sitting at the picnic table were the two teens Zoe had mentioned. Two boys sat close, their heads almost touching as they shared a book in their hands. They must've had amazing focus, because I had no idea how they could read when they virtually sat in the middle of an outdoor *Romper Room*.

"Is this all of them?" I asked, counting them as best as I could since some of those little suckers were fast. "There's only like fifteen, and they're all . . ."

"They're all what?"

I had no idea how weird it would sound if I said I knew they were human. The three adults—two women and one male—weren't rocking any alien DNA. It was bizarre, because I felt like there was something else here. Someone who did have alien DNA. I didn't know how to describe that it wasn't so much a feeling as a knowledge, so I went with, "There are no Luxen kids, are there?"

Zoe looked at me for a moment and then leaned against the base of an oak, her hands tucked behind her. "There are actually sixteen kids here, but there aren't any Luxen kids. I went to the Chicago zone once and I saw little Luxen there, but many of the Luxen who were old enough to have kids died in the war, on both sides, and most of the ones who had children ended up registering. Young Luxen can't always control their abilities. They slip in and out of the form all the time, and having three children who can't control their forms was too much of a risk. Registering was safer; at least that's how it appeared in the beginning. A lot of other Luxen don't seem to want to bring a Luxen or hybrid child into this world, the same with the Arum. Well, except Daemon and Kat, but they're crazy and apparently decided condoms were for people with common sense."

I swallowed my laugh.

"Or maybe the condom broke," she rambled on. "I don't know, and I'm not going to ask, but I would be scared to death. Their kid is going to be crazy powerful one day, but until then, it'll just be a baby, and when—"

"Wait. I don't understand." I twisted toward her, remembering the Luxen I had accidentally barged in on when I'd gone back to find my phone at Luc's club. The male had nearly choked me out, but he'd been protecting his family—a family that included a little girl with pigtails. I had no idea if the other two siblings had been there and I hadn't seen them—because Luxen always came in threes—or if something had happened to them. "Luc had a family at his club. A little girl who was a Luxen. I saw her—"

"They didn't make it here."

My heart squeezed and then stopped. "What?"

Somberness was a heavy weight in her voice. "I think it was Daemon and Archer who were moving them. Halfway here, something came up and they had to hand them off to another who was going to take them the rest of the way. They were spotted. We lost Jonathan, too—the Luxen who was escorting them. They were taken to wherever the ART teams take unregistered Luxen." She watched the children, shoulders tight. "Luc has tried to find out where they're being housed, and you know Luc. He can ferret out just about anything. Same with Daemon and Archer. Between the two of them, they've probably done recon on at least a hundred locations."

All I could see when I looked back at the children was that little girl.

"We know unregistered Luxen are initially processed at ART offices, but where they're taken after? No idea. Whenever we think we have leads, it's a dead end." Zoe paused. "Either they have them someplace we just haven't thought to look, or . . ."

Zoe didn't finish, but there was no need. Mouth and throat dry like they were coated with ash, I folded my arms over my stomach. The unregistered Luxen didn't simply vanish, and if there were no leads, no evidence of a holding facility, then that left one possibility.

There were no holding facilities.

And that would mean the little girl with pigtails held by her frightened mother and her father who had been willing to kill to protect her were dead.

8

How many Luxen had been taken into custody? There weren't statistics on that as far as I knew, and the worst part—and there were a lot of terrible parts competing for top spot—was this horrific possibility made sense. If the Daedalus planned on eradicating anyone who could fight back, why would they detain the Luxen? What would be the point?

I had to breathe around the building nausea. "And no one apprehended by ART has ever been seen again?"

Zoe opened her eyes. "A few escaped, but it always happened before they were processed. As far as I know, no one has ever escaped after that."

Shivering at the implication, I watched the wind stir the tall reedy plants bordering the playground. What Zoe had said earlier about the human psyche defaulting to denial seemed to be right on point yet again, because I *almost* couldn't believe it.

But it wouldn't be the first time the human race committed genocide. It wouldn't even be the tenth time. We had a striking inability to learn from history.

"There's the sixteenth rug rat." A small smile appeared, erasing a fraction of the sadness on Zoe's face.

Following her gaze, I saw a tiny girl coming out of the door of the school, her dark hair pulled back from a face shaped like the cutest little heart. Her jeans were rolled up, revealing bare feet.

"Ashley," I said. Bethany and Dawson's daughter. "Is she the youngest Origin there is right now?"

"I believe so." Zoe paused. "At least until Kat gives birth."

Clutching some sort of stuffed toy to her chest, Ashley hopped down the steps like a little kangaroo. One of the other kids all but power-dived off a seesaw, nearly sending the other tyke flying into the air.

"Oh my God." I laughed as that little girl rushed across the playground, meeting Ashley at the bottom of the steps. The girl gave her a quick hug and then scampered off.

"They all love her," Zoe said quietly. "Probably because she's made a couple of them"—Zoe lifted her fingers, forming quotation marks—"'fly.'"

"Uh, what?"

Zoe grinned. "Watch the little girl who hugged her."

Finding the little girl in pink tights over behind the swing set, I about fell over when the child swept up into the air as if a giant, invisible hand had reached down, swooping her up.

Thrusting her little arms straight above her head like a baby Wonder Woman, she flew as high as the school and then as high as the tree.

Ashley was just standing in the center of the walkway, her stuffed toy dangling at her side while her little face was scrunched up into a mask of rather adorably severe concentration. I quickly glanced over at the teachers and saw, much to my shock and awe, they were surrounded by several of the other, very distracting children.

And they had a little lookout!

A boy with dark brown skin kept glancing between the girl in the pink tights levitating above the tree and the adults. Peals of laughter from Baby Wonder Woman sent the other children clamoring to keep the teachers focused on them.

It was a good thing they did.

Because Baby Wonder Woman was rolling in *midair,* not once, not twice, but three times before the lookout waved his arms like one of those flailing inflatable tube men.

Ashley brought her down swiftly. Perhaps a bit too swiftly. Baby Wonder Woman made a rough landing, losing her balance when her feet hit the ground, plopping onto her butt. Like a true warrior goddess in training, she toppled onto her back, giggling.

My mouth was hanging open.

"Ashley really needs to work on the landings, though," Zoe murmured.

Grinning as if she were entirely pleased with herself, Ashley lifted the stuffed toy to her chest and resumed her barefoot skipping.

"I don't know what I just watched."

"How baby Origins make friends with humans?" Zoe suggested.

I couldn't disagree with that.

"I bet you won't guess who taught her to do that."

I didn't need to guess. "Luc."

"Yep." Laughing, she pulled her hands out from behind her back. "He taught her when she was barely two, apparently starting with making her toys fly, and then Daemon when he visited."

Now my jaw had to be on the ground. It took me a moment to find my voice. "I'm sure her parents appreciated that."

"Dawson found it hilarious, but Beth's a bit of a worrier." A dark look crept across her face. "Let's just say that was the closest thing to a scolding Luc has received in his entire life."

I grinned at that, but it sort of got stuck as I stared at Zoe, realizing for the hundredth time in a short period there was so much I didn't know about my best friend. "You have this entire other life," I blurted out.

Her gaze flickered back to me. "It was harder than you can ever know keeping it a secret."

Considering all that was at risk, I understood why she'd had to. Turning back to the playground, I almost jumped when I saw Ashley staring directly at us.

"Hi, Zoe!" she chirped, waving the stuffed toy at us, which turned out to be a stuffed llama. I bet I knew who'd given her that gift. "Hi, Nadia!"

Um.

Unsure of what to do and also not wanting to correct her, I waved back at her.

"Bye!" Pivoting around, she tossed the stuffed llama into the air, and then she skipped back toward the other kids.

The stuffed llama bounced alongside her.

I picked my jaw up off the ground. "She's, um, so cute."

"And she's also super-weird," Zoe tacked on, and when I looked over at her, she burst into laughter. "What? It's true. She never met you as Nadia."

Glancing back at the little Origin, I thought about what Luc had told me. "Luc said each Origin has unique abilities. That Ashley just knows things. What about you?"

"Nothing as cool as knowing things."

"I'm sure it's cool. What is it?"

She rolled her eyes. "I can use the Source to charge up the atmosphere. If there is any humidity in the air, I can create one hell of a storm."

My eyes widened. "You're like an X-Man."

"I don't know about all of that. I mean, Luxen can do something similar. Charging up the air and causing lightning."

"But can they create storms?" I asked.

Zoe shrugged. "Some can get one going, depending on the environmental circumstances, but I don't know any who've been able to create a tornado."

I blinked slowly, thinking I heard her wrong. "You can create a tornado?"

Zoe shrugged again like it was no big deal. "And I can control it."

"You can create a freaking tornado and control it!" I repeated, gaping at her. "Dude, that's really freaking cool." I paused. "And kind of scary, but I totally want to see one."

"Maybe one day." She grinned, and now I was wondering what Archer could do. I knew he could read minds. Was there more? Like, could he walk through walls?

A sudden, strange tickling sensation erupted along the back of my shoulders. Smacking around, I prayed my hands didn't come in contact with a crunchy insect.

I could only imagine the size of bugs in Texas.

Nothing was there, but the feeling remained, intensifying until—

"We are about to have company." Zoe pushed off the tree, her attention focused on whoever was behind me.

Lowering my hands, I turned and saw a tall, beautiful woman with deep brown skin and hair in thick, neat braids. Some of those braids were dyed blue, the effect stunning as the wind played with her hair. Her eyes were a shocking amber color, reminding me of a topaz, and they matched the casual maxi-style dress she'd paired with a cute black cardigan.

And she was a Luxen.

"Cekiah!" Happiness lightened Zoe's tone as she strode forward, embracing the older woman warmly.

When they parted, Cekiah clasped Zoe's cheeks. "Ms. Callahan," she said in a way that was full of fondness. "It's been far too long since I've seen you. You doing well?"

Zoe curled her fingers around the woman's arms. "I've seen better days, but I'm doing okay."

The woman's angular features softened. "I heard about Kent. I'm so sorry."

My heart squeezed while Zoe took a heavy, visible breath. "He was one of the good ones," she said, voice thick. "He didn't deserve that."

"No, he did not," came the soft, sad reply. "He died with people he cared about, people he loved. A family that is thicker than those he shared blood with. Find some peace in that, and remember him as Kent would've wanted you to."

Zoe nodded.

Pressing a kiss to Zoe's forehead, Cekiah then straightened, her ultrabright gaze finding mine as she lowered her hands. "So, this must be Evie."

I gave her a half wave like a dork.

"I spoke with Eaton this morning," she continued. "He told me that Luc brought you the day before yesterday."

Having really no idea if that was the only thing Eaton had shared with her, I stepped forward and extended a hand. "Pleased to meet you."

The Luxen took my hand in a cool, firm grip. "It's nice to meet you. Has Zoe been showing you around?"

"Just the basics," Zoe answered before I could. She went to stand beside her. "The market and here."

"And what did you think of the market?"

"I was kind of dumbfounded at first," I admitted. "It's amazing that people who need help can get it here."

"Unlike in the world outside of these walls," she said. "We make sure that no one here is ever in need, no matter if they're human or Luxen, Arum or hybrid."

"The world could use more of that."

She cocked her head slightly to the side. "The world could use a lot of things."

"Cekiah is one of the council members," Zoe jumped in. "And one of the first Luxen who came here."

She was a council member? Eaton would've shared what I was with a member of the council, wouldn't he? "How did you end up here?" I asked.

"Before the war, I lived in a community of Luxen in Colorado, one of the ones the Daedalus helped establish for those . . . assimilated." Cekiah's gaze never wavered from mine. "After the invasion, I met Daemon and his siblings there. Luc, too. He was a very young man at that time, but even at that age, you listened when he spoke. He didn't trust the registration program that was being created even though many were hopeful, foolishly so. I, like Luc, had a feeling that numbering and tracking us was the beginning of something that would not end well. And when he and Daemon found evidence that there were people trapped within the walled cities, I had to do something. The idea that people were just forgotten, shut away from a world that believed them to be dead? It gave me nightmares. Thankfully, I wasn't unique in that sense."

"But you and everyone who came here to help are unique," I told her, meaning it. "You didn't stick your head in the sand because it didn't involve you. A lot of people I know, a lot of humans, would've done that."

"Thank you, but I'd be remiss if I didn't admit that there was a self-serving angle to my altruism," she replied. "It afforded a perfect way to fly under the radar."

Zoe laughed. "Yeah, you could've flown under the radar by leaving the U.S. like many of the Luxen did."

I blinked. That was the first I'd heard of that. "They did?"

Cekiah laughed, the sound rich and throaty. "Many fled to Canada when they pulled out of the ARP agreement, along with several of the European countries. I considered it," she admitted, and the humor dancing in her eyes faded into shadows. "But the nightmares—they were real. I wouldn't have been able to live myself."

"And it won't matter how far anyone goes," Zoe said, "if the Daedalus succeeds."

"True." Cekiah stepped forward. If she was surprised to hear about the Daedalus, she didn't show it. "I saw you two outside and wanted to say hello, but I won't keep either of you much longer." Finally pulling her gaze from mine, she looked pointedly at Zoe. "You, however, had better carve out some time so we can properly catch up."

"Of course," Zoe murmured, and it was evident she was pleased to hear the request.

Those powerful tawny eyes flicked back to me. "I need to be blunt with you."

Zoe stiffened, but I held myself still, unbelievably so. I had a sinking feeling I knew what was coming.

"Luc spoke with me about who you are, who you really are," she said, and Zoe's attention snapped to the older Luxen. "He stopped by with Daemon earlier. He told me what I needed to know, and he did so while requesting that the knowledge of *what* you are stays with me. Luc asked that I not share it, not yet, with the remaining council."

My heart started to thump. I didn't want the people here to know. If they were to find out, their looks of suspicion and distrust would no longer come from a place of wariness but from fear. Hell, they could even demand that I leave, and I didn't even want to think of Luc's response to that. Nor did I want to face a reality where I'd be out there, trying to get my abilities under control when I could be found by either the SOL or the Daedalus.

"Cekiah," Zoe started.

"Let me finish." Cekiah silenced Zoe with those three words. "My instinct isn't to lie to those who feel a bone-deep responsibility to those here, and Luc knows that. I don't know you, and I don't say this to be unkind, but I have a feeling you don't know yourself, either."

I flinched at the all-too-true words.

"I only know what Luc has assured me, and all anyone has to do is look at Luc when he speaks of you to know he cares only about your safety," she continued. "His request didn't make me remotely happy. However, as Luc was quick to remind me, I owed him my silence."

How many people owed Luc favors? Seriously. Still, relief swept through me.

"As I told him, if I for one second believe that you will endanger anyone here, I don't care what I owe Luc, I will not hold my silence."

Heart pounding, I lifted my chin. "That is more than understandable. I wouldn't expect you to."

I thought I saw respect and maybe even a little bit of relief flicker across her face, but her words were still a blade when she spoke. "For your sake and the sake of all others, I do hope we don't end up regretting our hospitality and generosity."

9

Cradling the jar of peanut butter I'd discovered in the pantry, I paced the living room, spoon in hand.

The restless energy was back, making it nearly impossible for me to sit. I had tried that already, having rooted around in the bookcases until I found an ancient copy of *A Dance with Dragons*, but I couldn't focus. Maybe it was the quiet? That was a part of my inability to concentrate, but it was also the warning Cekiah had rightfully given me before we'd parted ways and that Luc still hadn't returned. Maybe Daemon was pushing back, not wanting to stay quiet like Cekiah, and Luc was having to convince him.

I hoped they weren't trying to kill each other.

All of that probably explained why I felt like the Energizer Bunny on crack, but I was starving like I hadn't indulged in gluttony only a few hours ago.

I glanced at the door for the fiftieth time as if I could will Luc forward, which was kind of sad, but I was bored and I couldn't sit still and I already ate half a jar of peanut butter and I was . . .

Lonely.

The only person I really knew here was Zoe—Grayson didn't count—and she had gone to catch up with Cekiah, and I missed Heidi and James. I had no idea how James was doing back at home with all of us gone. What would happen to him if the Daedalus did end up releasing the flu on a wide scale? Had he gotten vaccinated? I couldn't remember, and there was no way to reach out to warn him.

With that thought, I scooped out another spoonful of peanut butter smoothness and shoved it into my mouth.

Wait. How old was this peanut butter anyway?

It tasted fine, but if it belonged to the previous owners, I didn't think it had a four-year shelf life. Maybe it had been picked up on one of the supply runs. Frowning, I lifted the jar until I found the stamped "best by" date was over a year ago.

I glanced from the jar to the half-full spoon, shrugged, and then thrust that spoon right back in my mouth.

I ate only one more spoonful before I felt I should possibly leave some for Luc. Forcing myself to put the peanut butter down, I was about to investigate the closed-up spare bedrooms when I felt the weird tingle of awareness along the back of my neck. Frowning, I turned toward the front door. Not even two heartbeats later, someone knocked on it.

Zoe would've just walked right in, and Luc had no reason to knock, so I was full of curiosity as I all but bum-rushed the door, throwing it open.

Dee Black stood there, her long black hair tucked up in a bun that would rival Zoe's in terms of neatness.

Her blue jeans were splattered with something brown.

Dee's emerald-green eyes followed my gaze, and she laughed. "I look a mess. I know. I was trying to melt chocolate chips with my hands." She waved them. "Microwave hands courtesy of extra-terrestrial awesomeness."

I blinked slowly. "You can do that? Cook food with the Source?"

"Well, pretty much anyone except me can. Every time I try to do anything outside of boiling eggs, it goes south fast, evident in the fact I'm covered in dried chocolate. I heated it too fast, and it sort of exploded," she explained. "No matter what, do not let Luc or anyone else try to convince you that Source-cooked meat tastes good."

"It doesn't?" I heard myself ask as I tried not to gawk at her so openly . . . and failed.

"Oh no. No. It tastes like meat cooked with charged air, and while that doesn't sound all that bad, it is. There's no amount of seasonings that can cover that burned ozone taste."

"Okay." I felt myself nodding.

"Anyway." She smiled brightly. "I was sent over here to retrieve you. Kat wants to talk to you."

"She does?"

Dee nodded. "Yes. And she's super-pregnant, as you already know, and you don't tell a woman *that* pregnant no."

Completely dazzled by Dee, I found myself walking into Daemon and Kat's house a few minutes later, not even remembering the short walk or if I had even agreed. The fact I was so, well, starstruck by Dee had everything to do with what her easy smile and somewhat flippant attitude hid. Dee was incredibly intelligent and possessed a quick wit that enabled her to spend many evenings from a secured location outside of Zone 3, arguing with bigoted idiots like Senator Freeman on TV without losing her cool. Not only that, she was remarkably brave, becoming the public face for all the Luxen. There couldn't be one person in the United States who wouldn't recognize her. I was sure she had a lot of fans.

I was also sure she had a lot of enemies.

Zoe had been right. I had a total crush on Dee.

She led me through a living room that was free of creepy angel paintings but looked like a bookstore. Neat piles of books were everywhere—on the media console that must've housed a TV at some point, stacked in towers on either side. Books were piled on either side of the couch and the gray recliner, and the rest of the space was nothing but rows of mismatched bookshelves, some tall and some white, others short and deep brown, and all of them bursting with books. I'd never seen so many books in one room before.

"Kat is a big reader," Dee said, noticing what I was staring at. "No one touches her books without permission. If she lets you borrow any of them, that means she likes you, but you'd better return that book back to her in pristine condition."

Considering I dog-eared pages all the time, I kept my grubby fingers to myself as we walked down a similar narrow hall to the bedroom at the end. Curtains were lashed to the sides of open windows, allowing sunlight to pour into the room. The breeze kept the room cool, giving it an open and airy feeling.

The first thing I noticed was all the *stuff*. It was like wandering through the baby section in Target. An assembled high chair waited in the corner of the room, next to one of those bouncy chairs I always thought made kids look like human spiders. Beside a folded Pack 'n Play pen was a changing table that featured three different diaper bags. On a small end table was a basket full of bottles and nipples, and there were two strollers and one still in its box.

Then there were the diapers. I didn't even know there were that many different diaper brands.

A soft laugh came from the vicinity of the large bed. Kat was propped up by a mountain of pillows, deep brown hair swept back from her face in a messy topknot. Her pretty face was flushed as if she'd been out in the sun, but based on the size of her belly, which seemed to have increased from the last time I'd seen her, I doubted she'd been outside. Beside her was a hardcover minus the dust jacket, a bookmark jutting out of the middle of the book. Forgotten on the floor was a basket of bright blue yarn and what might have been a scarf? The beginning of a sweater? Something I really hoped no one would be wearing.

"Daemon has been a bit of an overachiever when it comes to baby prepping," she said. "Thank God he's not into doomsday prepping."

"Actually, that would've been helpful if that were the case." Dee plopped down on the bed beside Kat, crossing her long legs. "But then that would mean Daemon would actually do something really useful."

Kat snorted. "At least we won't have to worry about running out of diapers." Looking down, she patted her rounded stomach. "That is, if the little glow bug decides to show up."

"Well, he's definitely taking after Daemon," Dee commented, peering down at Kat's belly. "Aren't you, little guy?"

"How did you find out that it's a boy?" I lingered just inside the bedroom, fingers clasped in front of me, unsure of what to do.

"We don't know a hundred percent, but Ashley keeps referring to the baby as a 'he' and, well, you've met Ashley. Sometimes she knows more than we do," Kat explained.

"Yeah, she does." Glancing around the room again, my attention was snagged by a stack of gardening gloves on the oak-finished dresser. They were all new, with their tags still on them, but . . . My gaze swept back to Kat. "Did you do the garden next door?"

Her eyes lit up. "I can't take credit for starting it. The previous owners did. I just take care of it. Well, as long as I've been able to. Hopefully, I'll still have time to pop over and keep it maintained, if you don't mind."

"Oh my God, please feel free whenever you can. I have the opposite of a green thumb. I have a black thumb of death, actually. The garden will need your help."

"Maybe I can teach you a few tricks to turn your black thumb of death to a muddy-green color." Kat gave me a tired smile. "Come." She gestured at the space in front of Dee. "Sit. We figured since Luc was with the guys, we could have some one-on-one time."

Nervous and wanting to, well, wanting so badly to make a good impression, I got my butt where she wanted me. I sat at the foot of the bed, in front of Dee. "I didn't know Archer was with them."

"I don't think they knew that until Archer invited himself along," Dee replied dryly.

Kat laughed at that. "But to be honest, I totally had an ulterior motive for inviting you over. I have a ton of questions for you."

Suspecting what her questions had to do with, I decided not to beat around the bush. "Daemon told you what I did to him in the woods."

"He did." Heather-gray eyes met mine. Eyes I knew had seen things weaker people wouldn't have survived. "And I'm relieved that he's okay. If not, I'd have to do my best to take you out, pregnant or not."

Getting the warning loud and clear, I pushed past the embarrassment driven by the uncomfortable truth of what I'd done and nodded. "Understandable." My cheeks warmed. "I really am sorry about what I did. I don't expect either you or Daemon to accept that. I just hope you all know that I am genuinely sorry."

"But I do accept your apology," Kat said, surprising me. "From what I understand, you had no control over what happened, and Daemon knows that, too."

Daemon may know that, but I doubted he was as forgiving as Kat. "Part of me wishes you didn't accept my apology. I know that sounds weird, but . . ." I trailed off, uncertain of how to explain it.

"But you feel like you should be punished. I get it. Trust me. We've all done things that ended badly for others, whether it was unintentional or not." Kat glanced at Dee, who nodded. "My actions led to the death of one of Dee's good friends. It wasn't something I did on purpose. In fact, I thought I was doing the right thing. Dee has forgiven me, but there are still days when it feels like she shouldn't have."

"But I did." Dee leaned into Kat's shoulder. "Eventually," she added. "And look, Daemon needs knocking down a peg or five hundred every so often."

I blinked slowly.

Kat laughed softly. "That is true. Usually, it's Luc who reserves that special place."

"They seem to threaten each another a lot," I acknowledged.

"That's their version of male bonding." Dee rolled her eyes. "Throw Archer in the mix, and it's like who can out-threaten one another."

"What about Dawson?"

"Dawson is the only normal one out of all of them," Dee said, and Kat nodded. "So, if he threatens someone, it means some bad stuff is about to go down."

"Noted," I murmured, thinking that Dawson and Daemon may appear identical, but their personalities couldn't be any more different.

"I'm pretty sure this kid has a foot planted in a vital organ." Kat planted her hands in the mattress and shifted slightly. Once settled, she breathed deeply. "I don't know if Luc told you this or not, but when I was first mutated, I had no idea what was happening. I was a mess. If I thought about wanting a glass of tea, the jug would open up in the fridge and spill all over the place."

"No way."

Resting her hands on her belly, she nodded. "Doors would open before I touched them. Clothing fell off hangers. There were a couple of minutes where I thought maybe my house was possessed."

Dee laughed.

"It takes a lot for a Luxen to mutate a human, and it's not something that happens often, so it wasn't even a thing I considered at first, but when I finally did tell Daemon, he knew what was going on." She paused. "I think he was as shocked as I was at first."

"How did it happen?" I asked, hoping I wasn't being too nosy.

"Short version of a long story, but it can all be boiled down to Daemon healing me one too many times."

"Okay. That is not even the correct short version. Yes. Daemon healed her a couple of times, but what did it was that Kat was all badass and saved our lives," Dee jumped in. "Before the invasion and everything, the biggest threat were the Arum."

"My, how things have changed," muttered Kat.

"Daemon had taken out this one Arum's siblings, and the dude was gunning for Daemon and me. Kat and Daemon were like archenemies at this point, and he said some stupid typical Daemon crap to her, and she ended up volunteering to be a human distraction, much to Daemon's displeasure—"

"Daemon and I didn't get along in the beginning," Kat said, grinning. "Actually, I sort of hated him at that point. Okay. I thought he was hot even then, but his hotness did not override his douche-ness."

"Anyway, she ended up basically sacrificing herself to save Daemon and me. She almost died."

"I would've died if Daemon hadn't healed me, and it was such a massive healing, it started to change me on a cellular level." The topknot on Kat's head slipped to the side. "The rest of what happened is long and convoluted and, to be honest, will just make me mad and depressed."

"You don't need to tell me any more," I rushed to assure her.

Kat's gray gaze flickered over my face, and silence stretched out between us. "We met a couple of times."

The next breath got stuck in my throat. "Daemon said as much. He told me you saw me in the club when you first met Luc."

She nodded. "And I saw you later, during the invasion. Luc had brought you to Malmstrom, an airbase in Montana. All of us were there, including Eaton. Luc tried to keep you hidden from us."

I frowned. "Why?"

"Have you met Luc?" Dee asked with a short laugh.

"I'm sure you've noticed he's a little protective of you," Kat said, and then it was I who laughed.

"Just a little," I said, rubbing my hands over my knees. "Did we talk then?"

She shook her head. "You were . . . resting most of the time you were there."

I understood what that meant. It must've been while I'd been very sick.

"After the invasion and things settled down, Luc visited us while we were living in Colorado and you weren't with him. We thought that you'd . . ."

"Died?" I supplied. When Kat gave an awkward nod, I grinned. "I think in a way, I did. I mean, other than a few brief memories that don't tell me much, I don't remember anything about my time as Nadia."

Kat's eyes met mine. "That's probably a good thing."

My hands stilled on my legs. "Yeah, I'm kind of getting that feeling." I looked down at my hands. "I mean, I want to know who I was, but I'm thinking it's a curse and a—" Words left me as a splattering of shimmering black dots spread across the top of my right hand.

"You okay?" Dee asked.

Heart stopping, I blinked. My hand appeared normal a second later. What in the world? I glanced at the girls and then back to my hand. Still normal. Had I seen what I thought I saw? Or was it some sort of trick of the eye? I didn't know.

Throat dry, I nodded. "Yeah, just thinking about the whole lack-of-memories thing."

A look of sympathy traveled across Kat's face. "I can't imagine what that feels like, not remembering who I was, but I do know what it was like to be trained by the Daedalus and how far they will go to advance their cause."

That caught enough of my attention that I shoved the weird hand thing aside. "I have . . . feelings sometimes," I admitted tentatively, only because I was unsure of how to explain it. "Like emotions tied to those repressed memories. They're not good, so there's a part of me that is grateful. A huge part of me, because I think if I did know, I wouldn't be okay."

Kat's hands stilled on her belly. "Daemon told me about Jason Dasher," she announced. "He tried to keep it from me, but I knew he was hiding something. I can't believe he's alive, but in a way, I'm not surprised. Hardly anything surprises me anymore." She exhaled roughly. "I knew Jason Dasher. He had a way of almost getting you to believe what they were doing was for the greater good. So did Nancy."

I zeroed in on that name. "Eaton mentioned her when we first talked to him, and Luc didn't seem to be happy to hear that name."

"He wouldn't be." Kat raised her eyebrows. "Nancy Husher oversaw the Origins; they were her pet project. She basically raised Luc until he escaped, and she was obsessed with finding the most powerful Luxen, believing that would ensure better Origin off-spring. That woman was a—" She clamped her mouth shut, shaking her head while I sat there in stunned silence. "Let's just say I would've loved to have been there when Luc ended her life."

"Luc never told you about her, did he?" Dee read me like an open book. I shook my head. "Well, he probably would rather not think about her."

"I know I prefer that," Kat remarked. "And if Luc hasn't brought her up, then I should shut my mouth."

I started to disagree.

"It needs to be Luc who tells you about Nancy," she cut in before I could demand answers. "I might've already said too much."

"It's not your fault. You probably thought he'd brought her up." I didn't know how to feel about not knowing about all of this, but . . . "A lot has happened since Luc and I . . . since we reconnected, and he's been mostly focused on me and what I've been going through. There hasn't been a lot of time for much beyond that."

I wanted to pat myself on the back. Look at me being all logical instead of getting my feelings irrationally hurt.

I deserved more peanut butter.

"Which leads me to my super-nosy question." Kat exchanged a look with Dee. "We want to know more about your abilities."

I told them what I knew I could do, and I was up-front about the fact I had no control over the few times I was able to use the Source. I left out what had happened the night before, because I just didn't feel Kat needed to worry about how close I'd come to possibly leveling their house. At no point did either of them make me feel like I was an out-of-control freak, and that bolstered my courage to tell them what I did next.

"Luc is going to work with me to get it under control. I don't want to risk anyone here, and I want to be able to fight back. I want to take the Daedalus down. Permanently. And if I'm as badass as a Trojan is supposed to be, I can help. I can fight with you all," I said, and there was no missing the quick looks Dee and Kat sent each other. I rushed on before they could rain on my parade. "I know that people are training in the Yard. I haven't seen it with my own eyes, but I know that's what's happening. And I also know that none of you have a reason to trust me, but if I can control this, you all will need me."

Kat was silent.

It was Dee who spoke. "You're right. If you can get control of your abilities, we would need you. I've never heard of anyone being able to do what you did."

Nodding, I didn't let myself get too excited. I could feel a huge *but* coming along.

And it did. "But I'm not sure what it will take for us to take that risk." Dee's bright green eyes held mine. "It's not something personal. I like you. Plus, according to Zoe, you have a girl crush on me. You have my vote."

I was going to punch Zoe.

Seriously.

"But it's not just me, and to be honest, what you are may be too much of a risk," Dee continued, and the weight of words sank like stones. "If there is just a small chance that you may link up to the Daedalus, it's too much of a chance."

Her words were nothing more than the truth—the raw truth—but before I could really feel the burn of those words, I compartmentalized like a pro and nodded. "I understand, but aren't I already a risk?"

"You are," Kat admitted. "If you were to link up and report back what you already know, we'd be screwed. All the innocent people here would be screwed."

"I know—"

"Then you have to know what we'd be forced to do," Kat cut me off, her gaze steady. "We won't let you take any information back to the Daedalus."

My heart turned over heavily as I held her stare, and I was surprised by how calm my next words were. "You'd kill me?"

"There was a time I wouldn't even think for a second that ending someone's life was a decision or an act I could be a part of," she said, her hand slowly rubbing her swollen stomach. "That it was something I would hate to decide but would do nonetheless. But that was a long time ago. That was a different life. We would not allow you to take any information back to the Daedalus."

I knew she was only speaking another uncomfortable truth. I also knew it wasn't personal and that she didn't want to have to say any of this to me. And like with Cekiah, if the shoes were on the other feet, I'd say the same and do the same. The warning still burned like I had face-planted in asphalt and slid, and it hurt in that spot of my heart that wanted nothing more than to belong here, to be friends with Kat and Dee, and to be a part of their plans to take down the organization that had undoubtedly done terrible things to all of us. And it hurt because I knew it meant I would never have any of those things, not beyond the superficial.

But I swallowed the thick knot of emotion and said, "If you all managed to be successful, you'd have Luc to deal with."

"We know," Kat said with a sad smile. "We know that none of us would live longer than the second it takes Luc to realize what we've done, but protecting the people and what we're doing here is worth our lives. And he knows even now what we'd do, but he believes it won't happen. I hope it doesn't, so let's hope together that day never comes for any of us."

Shortly after Kat told me I was as good as dead if I ever linked up with the rest of the Trojans, I left her place. Strangely enough, it wasn't because of that comment. Dee had quickly and smoothly shifted the conversation to her next on-air interview with Senator Freeman, and by then, Kat was fading out. I was betting she was napping before I even made it to the front door.

Troubled by what the future possibly held here and somehow hungry, I all but dragged myself into the silent house. With that jar of peanut butter in mind, I walked into the kitchen, the room lit only by the wide window over the sink. I heard the sharp inhale of breath that wasn't mine.

My head jerked in the direction of the small pantry. A kid stood there, several cans of vegetables gathered to his chest and the small bag of baked bread dangling from between his teeth. The moment my eyes connected with his wide, brown ones, I knew the boy hadn't been at the school. I would've recognized that shocking red hair that stuck up in every direction, but it was more than that. The kid was scrawny. Deep hollows under his cheeks and too-sharp collarbones jutting out above the collar of his dirty green shirt. That wasn't the only thing soiled. The fingers gripping the cans of food were covered with dust and dirt. His torn jeans were filthy, and those kids at the school had been clean and well fed. Not this kid.

He'd been frozen, just like me, but he snapped out of it. The cans slipped from his arms and clattered to the floor, rolling in every which direction. The bag fell next.

The kid bolted.

10

S top!" I yelled.

The kid didn't listen, rushing around the small kitchen island. I darted toward the back door, blocking his path. He spun around, starting for the entrance I'd come through, but I moved so I was in between the two exits. He jerked to a halt, behind the island, his frail chest rising and falling rapidly.

Heart thumping, my gaze swept over him once more. I had no idea who this kid was, but it was obvious why he was in the kitchen with his arms full of food. The kid looked like he hadn't had a good meal in weeks, if not longer, and I knew that meant he couldn't be living in this community unless he was being kept somewhere by someone who didn't allow him access to food or water to bathe.

Man, my mind went to some really dark places, but the world and the people in it could be darker than anything my imagination could drum up.

More importantly, though, the thing inside me hadn't come alive, so I was guessing that meant it didn't recognize him as a threat. The kid was definitely human, that much I just knew, but I wasn't naïve enough to believe that didn't mean he couldn't become one, but at this moment, I was going to listen to instinct or whatever was inside me.

I kept my eyes on him, preparing for him to try to make a run for it. "Who are you?"

The kid didn't answer as his gaze darted between the entrance and the back door.

"It's okay." I raised my hands, thinking that would help.

It didn't.

The kid threw his arms up over his head and bent, shielding

himself as if he expected me to throw something or to use the Source against him.

Holy crap.

What had happened to this boy? I quickly lowered my hands. "It's okay," I repeated. "I'm not going to hurt you."

He didn't move, but his small body trembled. The kid was beyond afraid, and while I had no idea what had caused him to be in such a condition, I said the only thing I thought could help.

"I'm not an alien," I told him, and that wasn't exactly a lie.

The kid didn't move for a long moment, but slowly, he lowered his arms. He didn't look at me, though. "If you're here, then you're friends with one of them. You're with one of them."

"I am friends with them," I answered. "But that doesn't mean I'm going to hurt you."

"Why would I believe that?" He stared at the door as if it were a lifeline, and I had a feeling he would bolt again the moment he felt remotely threatened by me.

"Because I don't understand why being friends with them would make you think I would hurt you," I told him, even though I knew why humans feared the Luxen, whether that was right or wrong. "And because I don't want to hurt you." I paused. "Even though you were in my house."

"I didn't know anyone moved in." His gaze nervously shot toward me and then skittered back to the door. "It had been empty all this time."

"We just moved in a few days ago. I'm new here, but I know some of the people here." That also wasn't exactly a lie. "Do you live here?"

The kid didn't answer.

My mind raced, trying to figure out what I could say that would keep him talking and wouldn't make him even more nervous. I decided it might help if I told him my name. "My name is Evie, by the way, and like I said, I just got here a few days ago with my boyfriend."

Another quick glance in my direction. "Is your boyfriend one of them?"

"Is he a Luxen? No." That was also not exactly a lie, but the kid wouldn't know that Origins or hybrids existed.

"But you're here, so you're one of them that support them," he said.

"I do. The Luxen here are nothing like the ones who invaded," I said, really hoping this wasn't the time Luc decided to show up. "Unless you know something I don't? If so, I really hope you tell me."

He didn't say anything for so long that I thought he wasn't going to answer, but he did. "We don't go near them."

"We?"

The kid took a deep breath and then looked at me, and this time, he didn't look away. I thought that was a step in the right direction, but there was a heaviness in his stare. This kid had seen far too much in his young life. "I was trying to steal your stuff." He lifted his chin, and his shoulders squared. "You caught me, and I don't believe you're not mad, so don't even try to lie."

"You caught me off guard. Scared me a little, but I'm not mad. I wouldn't be standing here and trying to talk to you if I were. Besides, it's not like you're stealing my food. That stuff was here when we arrived." I forced a casual shrug. "And it's not like you took the peanut butter. If you had, then I wouldn't be remotely happy."

He blinked.

"I like peanut butter." I smiled. "A lot."

A long moment passed as he did nothing but stare at me. "You're weird."

I laughed. "Yeah, I think I am."

"Definitely are," he confirmed. His wary gaze never left me, but he seemed to relax a little, no longer glancing at the entrance to the kitchen every three seconds.

"So, are you going to tell me your name, at least?"

"Nate." He shifted uneasily, scratching his fingers through his hair. "Just Nate."

Relieved and a bit surprised that he'd shared his name, I said, "Well, it's nice to meet you, Nate."

He stared at me again, this time as if I had a third arm sticking out of the middle of my forehead.

I didn't dare move closer to him. "You don't live in this community, do you?"

Nate moved from one foot to the other. "I don't live here."

Thinking of the flashing lights I'd seen, I almost shoved it aside. The city was dead and everything of value scavenged. How could anyone live there, let alone more than one person, and not have been seen?

But if he didn't live here, and I seriously doubted he could get through the wall without being seen, there could only be one other place. Houston may be dead, but it was a big city, and if the community had taken all the goods from the city, it would make sense that he was doing virtually the same, scavenging the community.

"Do you live in the city?" I asked.

He stopped fidgeting.

"I mean, where else could you live?"

Nate gave me a half shrug.

Even though I already suspected as much, it still sent me reeling. "How do you live there? Are you—?" Alone? Without parents? I cut myself off before I asked those questions. I already knew there were more than just him. He'd said *we,* and I had a feeling I had to choose my questions wisely.

"I make do," he mumbled, glancing at one of the cans of green beans.

"I guess you'd have to. Can I ask you something else?" When he gave a quick nod, I said, "Why are you living there and not here?"

"We aren't from here, and we don't trust them," he said, his eyes flashing. "They killed people. We all saw them, right after the invasion, before they dropped those bombs. We saw them touching people and becoming them, killing them."

He was talking about how the invading Luxen had rapidly assimilated the human DNA, virtually assuming the humans' physical appearance. Total *Invasion of the Body Snatchers* style, but . . .

"The invading Luxen were dangerous. They were killers, but the Luxen here didn't do that."

His chin jerked up. "How can you know? You said you just got here."

"Because I know that there are a lot of Luxen who were living here, on Earth, long before the others came, and the vast majority of them never hurt anyone. Some of those Luxen are here, in this community, living with humans—helping them. Some of them are even my friends I met before I came here," I explained, the last part a wish that rolled off my tongue all too easily. "And hey, I'm not saying all Luxen are perfect examples of, well, an alien race, but I think the ones here are good."

Nate went quiet again as he seemed to digest the news that the Luxen have been here. There was no shock or denial. I had a feeling this kid had been exposed to enough in his short life that he knew anything and everything was possible.

"Or have you seen something different from the ones here?" I pressed.

"How would I know if I have? The way they look isn't the way they always do," he argued, and man, he had a point. Luxen chose their human form, the ones who'd been here for a while having done so by slowly taking a little human DNA here and there, but some Luxen could easily change their appearance by mirroring those around them. "Any of them could be killers, but they just look different now."

"You're right." I took a shallow breath. "But the ones here and the vast majority of others, out there in the world outside these walls, don't want to hurt anyone. They just want to live. That's all."

There wasn't a single thing about the look on his face that said he believed me, so I wasn't surprised when he said, "I've got to go."

Knowing the only way I could stop him was to get physical— and that wouldn't do anything to help build trust for me or the Luxen—I nodded. "Okay. You can have the food if you want. I think there were some old plastic bags in the pantry. Would probably make it easier for you to carry."

His eyes widened slightly. "For real?"

I nodded.

Nate started to bend down to grab one of the nearest cans, but jerked upright. "Why?" he demanded. "Why would you let me take the food?"

I glanced at one of the cans. "Creamed corn? Not my food of choice."

There was a twitch of the boy's lips, a hint of a grin. "It's gross, but my . . ."

"But what?" I asked when he trailed off.

His gaze fell to the can, where it lay just at the corner of the island. "What's the catch?" he asked instead. "There has to be a catch."

Heaviness settled in my chest. "There's no catch, Nate. You need the food, right?"

His cheeks pinkened under the dirt, and I realized I'd said the wrong thing, but before I could slap myself, he said, "I do."

Relieved he hadn't denied that to his own demise, I moved backward until I was against the sink. "Take what you want. No catch."

Nate stared at me for several moments. "What about the peanut butter?"

"You can't have that."

Those lips twitched again, and then he didn't waste time, snatching a bag from the pantry and gathering up the cans and small pack of bread. I would've helped, but I sensed he wouldn't be comfortable if I got close to him. So many questions rose to the surface as I watched him. Like how did he get out of the city and move about without being seen? How many others were in the city? How old was he? Were there more kids? Adults? Others too afraid of the Luxen to reach out for help? I kept quiet, though. Nate may be taking the food, but that didn't mean he trusted me.

I waited until his bag was in hand before I spoke. "If you need more food or anything, you can come here. Or if you, you know, just want to hang out?"

He didn't respond.

Maybe the last offer was a bit much, but I wanted him to know that it was okay if he came back.

Cradling his bag to his chest, he inched his way toward the back door. He opened it as he looked over his shoulder at me. "Please don't tell anyone you saw me. You might think they're different and they're safe, but if you tell them, they'll come looking for us. The others—they'll run." His lower lip trembled. "They can't make it out there alone if they do. Please."

"There are more kids?" I asked.

He looked down at the bag he carried and nodded.

"How many?"

"That doesn't matter. Just don't say anything. Please."

It didn't matter, because I couldn't fathom how one kid survived, let alone more. I couldn't promise my silence. Even if I wanted to, because Luc would likely overhear my thoughts, and Nate was right. I had a feeling if Cekiah or anyone else learned of these kids, they'd go for them, and if they were afraid enough to run, they had a large enough city to hide in. I wouldn't hide this from Luc, but that didn't mean the others needed to know.

Lying was a necessity here. At least that's what I told myself, because Nate didn't need to know any of that. "Promise me if you need more food or anything, you'll come back here, and I won't tell the others."

His eyes narrowed. "You blackmailing me?"

"I wouldn't call it that," I reasoned.

"What would you call it, then?"

"Graymailing you?"

A surprised giggle burst from him. "You *are* weird."

"True," I murmured. "Do we have a deal?"

Nate was slow to nod. "Deal."

"Good."

Nate left then, without another word, and it was hard not to follow him. I released a ragged breath, hoping that wouldn't be the first and only time I saw him.

Finishing off the peanut butter, I roamed the backyard, looking for any sign of which way Nate had gone. There was none. Thoughts jumping from my conversation with Cekiah, Kat, and Dee, and Nate's appearance, I sat under the large oak with leaves of burnt gold. Looking up as I screwed the lid back onto the jar, I saw a tiny blackbird staring down at me.

Huh. That was the first bird I'd seen here.

Lying back, I watched the little guy hop along the branch. I didn't let myself dwell on what Kat or Cekiah had said. I couldn't. I was already afraid of losing control, and stressing over what would happen wouldn't help keep my panic at bay or whatever was inside me calm. My mind made its way back to Nate and the questions I couldn't ask.

How I dozed off after everything, I had no idea, but I must've, because the next thing I felt was the touch of fingertips against my cheek, and the hum of electricity skittering over my skin. When I opened my eyes, I saw impossibly long, thick lashes and slivers of violet tanzanite.

"Hi there," Luc murmured, a small smile playing across lips that were decadently full.

"Hi."

"I'm wondering something." Luc was stretched out beside me, lying on his side with his cheek resting against his hand.

"What?" I murmured, wondering how long he'd been there.

"Why are you lying in the backyard, under a tree, cradling a jar of peanut butter to your chest?"

"Huh?" My brows snapped together as I looked down, and hell if I wasn't cradling the jar. "I fell asleep with it."

"I feel like I need to be a better boyfriend if you're turning to peanut butter for support."

I let my head fall back against the grass. "You could never compete with peanut butter."

"That sounds like a challenge." One side of his lips kicked up.

Beyond the leaves, the sky was orange over Luc's shoulder. Dusk. "I must've napped the afternoon away. I'm probably covered in ticks."

He dragged the tips of his fingers along my cheekbone as he nodded.

"Great," I sighed, cuddling the peanut butter.

"I can check you over. Actually, I would be more than happy

to do so. I'm just going to need you to undress. Completely. I can also help with that."

"I bet you can." I laughed even as I shivered at the possibility. I refused to believe the attraction that sparked and burned whenever we were around each other could be engineered by a secretive government agency, no matter how many mad scientists they had on their payroll.

Those fingers skated down my throat. "I'm just being helpful. Wouldn't want to miss a spot and you end up with Rocky Mountain spotted fever."

"Can I even get Rocky Mountain spotted fever?"

"Probably not. I also don't think there are ticks in this grass." He drew his finger along the collar of my shirt. "But we can pretend. I can assure you it would be a lot of fun."

"You don't need to convince me of what I already know." Muscles feeling incredibly loose, I yawned. Loudly. Right in Luc's face. I flushed, looking away. "Sorry."

Luc chuckled. "Sleepy, huh?"

"Yeah." And I really was. There was a good chance I could easily fall back to sleep now. "It's a peanut butter coma."

"A what?"

"I ate nearly an entire jar of peanut butter." I turned my head to him. "Actually, I ate all the peanut better. Sorry."

His gaze flickered over my face. "You know, I don't like peanut butter."

I had to be hallucinating. "Come again?"

"I mean, I'll eat it if I have to, but just not a fan of it."

"How? How is that possible?" I demanded. "Peanut butter is life."

He simply gave me a half shrug.

"I don't think we can be friends any longer," I said even as I gave into my urge and reached up to run my fingers through his hair. Soft like silk. He turned his head, kissing my palm before I lowered it.

"Good thing we're not friends, Peaches." His gaze dipped to

my mouth, the heaviness and intensity in his hooded stare sending a fire sweeping over my skin.

"On second thought, this is actually perfect. This means we won't ever fight over the peanut butter."

"See? You and I go together like cheese and bread." His grin was brief. "Sorry everything took so long today."

"No need to apologize."

Amusement danced across his features. "Doubtful. I bet you were beside yourself with loneliness and need."

I narrowed my eyes at him. No way would I admit how lonely I'd been.

The grin that appeared left me wondering if he knew what I was thinking. Probably.

"I spent some time with Zoe. She took me around the zone. Then Dee came over. Kat wanted to see me."

"She did?"

"Yeah."

"How'd that go?"

"Good." I purposely didn't think about what Kat had said. Luc may know what they'd do if I proved a threat, but knowing and realizing I knew were two very different things.

His head tilted slightly. "Just good?"

"Yep. They have a lot of baby stuff," I went on. "And books. So many books."

"Kat is a huge reader. Back when she was living outside of here, she used to have a book blog. *Katy's Krazy Obsession* or something. Daemon used to stalk the hell out of it."

I grinned, picturing the dark-haired Luxen scrolling endlessly through posts and pictures of book hauls. The grin faded when I thought about what else I needed to talk to him about.

Luc plucked a blade of grass from my hair. "I didn't think it would take so long."

"I heard you had company in the form of Archer and you made a pit stop to talk to Cekiah."

Whether Luc was surprised that I knew about that or not, his expression didn't give it away. "Yes. She's sort of the unofficial leader around here, and I knew Daemon wouldn't keep what happened from her. Cekiah's a good woman."

"Who owes you a favor?"

"There is that."

"What did you do for her?"

"A gentleman would never share."

I lifted my brows. "Good thing you're not a gentleman."

"True." Returning to trace the collar of my shirt, he leaned closer. With every pass, he worked the loose neckline farther down. "I helped her locate her missing siblings."

"That's all?"

He nodded.

I had a feeling there was a lot more to that story. "How did the talk go with Daemon?"

"I know you were irritated about being iced out of the conversation with him. I'm sorry for that," he said, and surprise flickered through me.

"Yeah, well, I was irritated."

"I can't blame you for that." He continued dragging his finger along my skin above the collar. "Daemon needed to get what he had to say out of him, but you didn't need to hear it." Luc's lashes swept up and his gaze pierced mine. "Because you already knew what he was going to say, Evie."

I thought that over. Luc was right. I did know.

"And I know you feel guilt for what you did to him in the woods. You don't need him compounding that by running his mouth, and I don't need to throw him through a wall because he's hurt your feelings."

Shifting my gaze to the tree above, I saw that the bird was gone. "He told Kat about what happened. She said he'd eventually forgive me."

"He will."

Another yawn climbed its way out of me. "Do you really think that?"

"I do. Right now, he's just worried about Kat and their child and their friends, but that will change once he sees that won't happen again."

How Luc could be so confident about that amazed me, but even if he was right, I would never be fully accepted.

Pushing aside the disappointment and lingering hurt, I said, "Being iced out did irritate me, but I also got it. That's why I didn't say anything yesterday."

"I know," he said. "But I still needed to say something. There was some other zone-related stuff Daemon wanted to talk about." He'd gotten the neckline low enough that when I glanced down, I saw the scallop edging of my bra. "He wouldn't want to have that conversation around anyone he didn't know."

"Or trust?"

"I trust you, Evie. So does Zoe. Anyone who knows you does—"

"Grayson?"

"Well . . ." He bit down on his lower lip. "Everyone who knows you except Grayson."

I snorted.

"But those who don't know you? Like Daemon? They don't." Luc was as blunt as he could be. "But once they get to know you, they will. We just need to respect that they need time."

I was only mildly annoyed with his logically sound answer. "Did you and Zoe take Logic 101 classes?"

Luc chuckled as his gaze traveled to where his finger was slipping just an inch under the collar of my shirt. "Yes. We took one in between Killing Our Enemies 101 and Being Sexy as Hell 401."

"Oh my God." Only Luc could make a joke like that.

Grinning in a wickedly devilish way, he dipped his head, kissing where his finger had just passed. A pulse of shivery heat traveled from where his lips touched my skin to every point in my body.

"And while we wait for them to get right with their lives, that doesn't mean I can't fill you in," he went on to say, pressing another kiss where my heartbeat was skyrocketing. "But first, I have an important question for you. One that I really need you to think long and hard about. Okay?"

Knowing Luc, I had no idea where this was heading. I also wasn't sure I could even repeat my name when I felt the wet heat of his tongue against my skin, but I murmured something that sounded like a word from the English language.

Luc lifted his head as he shifted so that he was above me, the bulk of his weight resting on his arm and the heady warmth of him settling over me. "Are you religious?"

His question caught me so off guard that my thoughts cleared. "Uh, no? I mean, not really?"

"Well, I am." A pause. "Because you're the answer to all my prayers."

I stared up at him.

"You know what else?"

Lips curving up at the corners, I resisted the urge to tackle-hug him. Barely. This was the Luc that had been missing after he'd taken the Source from me, this playful, irreverent side of him that simmered under the surface even in the direst of circumstances. This was what had been absent.

"What?" I whispered, voice a little thick with the unexpected burst of emotion.

"I was feeling a little off today, but now, with you, I'm definitely feeling turned on."

"Oh my God." I laughed.

"Tell me, Peaches, are you a parking ticket?"

"How are you going to turn that into a cheesy pickup line?"

"Because you have *fine* written all over you."

"That was the lamest thing I've heard."

"Are you sure?" His hand slid down my waist to my hip, leaving a riot of sensations in its wake. "What about this? Is your name Google? Because you have everything I've been searching for."

I was grinning like there was nothing wrong in the world, and I had him to thank for that. "Okay. I was wrong. That was the lamest thing I've heard."

"And you don't ever have to worry about me becoming what I was last night," he said, voice quiet as his gaze locked with mine.

"That won't happen again. Never. I'm not going to lose you. You're sure as hell not going to lose me."

My breath caught. "Good."

"Like, ever, Peaches."

"I'm okay with that."

"You're stuck with me," he went on. "You're paper and I'm glue. We go together—"

"Like cheese and bread?"

"That's my girl." He leaned his mouth to mine—

Another yawn escaped me, heating my entire face. "God! I'm so sorry. You go to kiss me, and I yawn right in your face."

Laughing under his breath, he smoothed his thumb along my chin. "It was hot."

"That was the exact opposite of hot. I can't believe I did that. I don't know why I'm so tired."

"You really don't?" he asked, dropping his hand from my chin. "A lot has happened, and only a little bit of that included sleep."

There he went, being all logical and stuff.

"Come on." Folding his hand around mine, he hopped to his feet, pulling me up with him. "Let's get you inside, and if you're good, I'll dazzle you with some more pickup lines."

"If I'm good?" I smacked his chest, not at all surprised when he caught my hand with his unbelievably fast reflexes.

Curling an arm around me, he hauled me against his chest and kissed me.

It wasn't quick, like the one he'd given me before he'd left to speak to Daemon. This one went on until my head swam with the taste and feel of him. He kissed me like it was the last thing he'd ever do, like he was starving just for me, and he was. I could feel it in the press of his lips and the sweep of his tongue. I was his everything, and he was mine.

His chest was hot and hard under his shirt, and his heart was thumping just as fast as mine. I slid my hands up, clutching his shoulders, the nape of his neck and then his hair.

When the kiss ended, his breathing was as ragged and raw as every one of my nerve endings. "I am yours."

Opening my eyes, I didn't yell at him for being in my mind. "And I am yours."

He dropped his forehead to mine. "Cheese and bread. That's who we are."

"Mmm," I murmured, letting my hands slide off him as I stepped back. "That makes me hungry."

Luc chuckled as he reached for my hand. "Speaking of hunger, that reminds me of what Daemon wanted to talk about."

Probably because of that kiss we'd just shared, I was thinking about a whole different kind of hunger, and my mind immediately jumped into the land of naughtiness. I tried to blink away the images of Daemon and Luc.

And failed.

A slow smile pulled at the corners of my lips.

His eyes narrowed, but a teasing glint showed through. "Such a dirty mind."

"Whatever." I laughed. "What else did Daemon want to talk about?"

"One of the unofficial but entirely official leaders here is having a meeting outside the zone, and that's got everyone antsy, especially since a group that went out to pick up a package hasn't checked in like they were supposed to."

I thought about the Luxen family that hadn't made it here and the Luxen Jonathan who hadn't come back. "Can I ask you something and you be a hundred percent honest?"

Luc didn't answer immediately. I could tell he was thinking about his response. "Depends."

"It can't depend on what the question is."

His brows snapped together as he stared down at me. He gave a little shake of his head. "Ask your question, Evie."

"Do you think the Luxen that have been captured by ART . . ." It was harder to say out loud than think. "Do you think they're dead?"

His gaze met mine, and there was no hesitation in his answer, no thinking twice. "Yes, I do."

I closed my eyes, heart and soul heavy. "Zoe told me the family I'd seen at the club hadn't made it here, and that's what I feared." Drawing in a deep breath, I opened my eyes and met his gaze. "They have to be stopped, Luc. The Daedalus. All of them."

"Agreed." Luc smoothed his thumb along the bottom of my lip, and we stood there for what felt like a small eternity, neither of us speaking while the air was weighted with what could be the loss of thousands of innocent lives.

I broke the silence. "How do you move on from that knowledge? Think about anything else?"

"You just do, because you have to. Nothing good comes from traveling down that kind of road. I would know."

He would, far more than I, and that saddened me even more.

"We move on, but we don't forget, Evie. You know what we do? We get revenge. We get justice. That is what we do."

Swallowing hard, I nodded. He was right. I couldn't dwell on all that happened, but I would remember the faces of those frightened Luxen. I wouldn't forget Kent.

Or even my mom.

I would be a part of that justice if it was the last thing I did.

"That's not the only thing Daemon needed to talk about," Luc added as he took my hand, walking us back to the house. "He said some supplies have been coming up missing. Food. Med stuff. Other random things. He didn't know how long it's been going on, but I'm under the impression that it's been a while."

An image of Nate formed in my mind.

"Why anyone would need to steal is beyond me. Needs are met here," he continued. "Unless canned goods and jars of green beans are growing legs and making a run for the wall, someone is taking stuff."

"Green beans." I wrinkled my nose. "Ugh."

He grinned down at me as we walked into the kitchen. "What if we only had green beans to eat?"

I thought about that. "I'd eat them and complain the entire time."

"I can respect your honesty."

"I should probably stop eating everything in sight, then," I said as Luc turned on one of the lanterns. "I don't want to add to any problems here."

"If we need more food, I'll get us food. It will be like caveman days. I'll hunt and gather while you . . ." Luc trailed off.

I arched a brow, waiting. "I am dying with anticipation to discover which extremely sexist example you're going to give. Tend the home? Cook the previous night's kill? Wait patiently for my man to return?"

"I was going to say while you'll be right there beside me."

"Good save."

A downright boyish grin appeared, and it was almost shocking how adorable it was, and then he laughed.

I liked his laugh; it made me want to grin and snuggle close, so I did just that. Well, I did a less graceful version of snuggling. My face plopped against his chest. Surprise flickered through me at how easy it was to be like this with him, to be affectionate and close. I didn't think I'd ever get used to how easy it had become in what was such a short, tumultuous period of time.

But was it really a short time?

Our history, remembered or not, spanned years.

Turning my head, I rubbed my cheek against his shirt, welcoming the heat beneath the thin cotton. It was time to tell him what else had happened. I lifted my head. "Something happened today."

"Tell me all about it." Placing his hands on my hips, he lifted me up so I was sitting on the kitchen island.

"And I think it might have to do with the missing food and supplies Daemon was telling you about, but you have to promise me that you're not going to say anything to him or Cekiah or anyone."

"Done."

My brows lifted. "You're just going to agree that easily?"

A slight frown appeared as he braced his hands on either side of my legs and leaned in. "I live life operating on a need-to-know basis. You know that, but besides that, we're cheese and bread, Peaches. I have your back. You have mine. You tell me not to say anything, I don't say anything, because I know you have a good reason for asking that."

My heart squeezed as I blurted out, "I love you. I hope you know that. I love you so much."

His features softened. "I know that. I've always known that," he whispered, dropping a kiss on my forehead. "Tell me what happened."

Pushing past the knot in my throat, I told him about finding Nate helping himself to some of the food we had in the pantry, and what little information I could glean from the kid.

"Damn." Luc had moved away from the island, running his hand through the messy, bronze waves. "How old do you think he was?"

"I don't know. I'm terrible at judging ages, but I would think he's probably around thirteen, give or take a year? He looked like he'd been wearing the same clothes for weeks if not months."

"And there's more?"

I nodded. "I don't know how many or where they are in the city, but if the rest are in the same condition, they have to be close to starving, Luc. And he was terrified of the Luxen. I can understand it. At least to some extent, but it's not like he's had access to the news to be fed more BS about the Luxen."

"God only knows what he saw during the invasion and afterward, and he's young. Hell, that kind of stuff traumatizes adults and creates the kind of fear that's not easy to get over." Crossing his arms, he turned to the dark sky beyond the kitchen window. "If I went to Cekiah with this, she'd launch a party immediately to find these kids and bring them in."

"To help them?" I asked hopefully.

He looked over his shoulder at me. "Yes, to help them. They have to be barely getting by in that city."

"I know, but if they are as scared as I think they are, they're going to hide, Luc, and considering that they've moved unseen in the community, they know how to hide."

"True." He returned to the window. "It's a bit concerning that they've snuck past the guards that patrol the walls and the city outskirts, but I'm not surprised. Getting past the wall is one thing, but the city limits is a big space. Anyway, we can't have them running off and hiding. I'm actually surprised."

"By what?"

"That you didn't try to follow him."

"I thought about it," I admitted. "But I knew it was too much of a risk. If he saw me, he'd never come back, and I want to be able to help him—help them. I can't even begin to understand how those kids have survived four years in that city."

"I can't, either." He turned to me. "But following him presents a whole different risk, Peaches. You don't know anything about this kid, and while I'm not inclined to think it's some sort of trap related to why we're here, that doesn't mean where that kid is heading is remotely safe."

"I know that, and it's not like I think I can really take care of myself out there. Being able to kick butt and protect myself isn't exactly cool if it means losing complete control." I crossed my ankles. "But that doesn't mean I'm not going to try to help him. I hope he comes back."

Luc was quiet, and I thought I knew where his mind was heading.

"I know you're suspicious. You have every reason to be, but this was just a hungry, scared kid, and I didn't get the impression that there were any adults. If there were, wouldn't they have been the ones looking for food?"

"You'd think." Luc sighed as he returned to the island. "I'm not going to say anything to anyone, but you've got to promise me you'll tell me the moment you see him again."

"That's graymail, by the way."

"What?" He leaned against the island.

"Nothing." I laughed quietly. "I will. I promise." I knocked my shoulder against his. "I'm kind of surprised you didn't already know about the kid."

"I told you, Peaches. I don't read your mind if I can help it. You weren't being loud."

"I feel proud."

Luc snorted.

I rested my cheek against his shoulder. "Do you think he will come back?"

"I think so."

"Why?"

"Because after meeting you, I don't see how anyone could stay away."

11

After the most organic dinner I'd ever consumed and the quickest, coldest shower in my entire life, I sat on the bed, wearing one of Luc's borrowed shirts as I tried to comb all the tangles out of my hair in the bedroom lit by several candles and lanterns. While Luc showered, I thought about something else Kat and Dee had told me, something that had taken a back seat after their warning and Nate's appearance.

Luc was like a fireproof safe, and I wanted to crack the lock on him. He was always about me, focused on what I was going through or how I was feeling. It was like a full-time job for him, and that wasn't fair. I wanted him to be able to lean on me like I—

Coherent thoughts took a mini vacay when Luc exited the bathroom, a pair of sweats hanging indecently low on his hips as he rubbed a towel over his hair.

"Peaches," Luc murmured as he lowered the towel. "You're going to make me blush."

I was definitely blushing as I got back to combing out my hair. "I don't know how you can last so long in the cold water."

"Skill." He tossed the towel to the hook on the bathroom door. He had to have used the Source to have made that work. "You know, if you'd like to take a warm bath next time, I could make that happen."

Lowering the comb, I looked over at him and all I saw was a steaming bath. "How?"

"We could run the water, and then I heat it up with the Source."

I stared at him. "Why are you just now suggesting that?"

"Didn't really think of it until now." Soft shadows danced over his face and shoulders as he prowled toward the bed. "The shower would be too tricky. I imagine once you start working with the Source, you'll be able to heat up your own baths."

My gaze shifted to the bathroom, and dreams of hot baths danced like sugarplums in my mind. If I asked Luc to heat a bath, he'd do it right now, so I knew he'd do it for me tomorrow. The request was already forming on the tip of my tongue.

You'll be able to heat up your own baths.

Asking Luc would be so easy, but doing it myself would be so much more fulfilling.

Luc sat in front of me. "What are you thinking?"

Returning to combing out the tangles, I said, "I want to do it myself."

"Okay."

"It could be a goal, you know? Like something to work toward," I continued. "And it works like a reward, too."

"It does."

"So, we start tomorrow, right?"

"We do," he replied after a few moments. "Daemon recommended a place I think would be good and safe."

Relief almost caused me to drop the comb. "I thought . . ."

"You thought I wasn't going to push back." Damp hair fell to the side as he leaned down onto his elbow.

I nodded, lowering the comb. "I know you're not looking forward to the idea of hurting me, and I know you tried to train Micah and the other kids."

"Someone's been talking."

"Someone other than you." I tapped the comb against his arm.

Tipping his head back, he caught the comb. "I did try to train them, and in the end, I think I just made things worse."

"You couldn't have known what they would do."

"I couldn't have known what they wouldn't do," he added, tugging the comb free from my fingers. "But you're not them. I won't be thinking of them while we work together."

"You promise?"

He tossed the comb aside. "Yes."

I wasn't sure if I believed him or not. I knew what had happened with the Origins had carved a deep wound in him. "If you did think of them, it would make sense. No one could fault you for that."

"I know, Peaches. I'm more worried about hurting you than any bad memories that may or may not surface."

"But I'm more worried—" I gasped as Luc moved with the kind of speed I just couldn't track.

He was suddenly in front of me, on his knees. Gripping my hips, he tugged me onto my back. In the span of a heartbeat, he had me under him. "Sorry," he said, keeping his weight braced on one arm. "But you looked like you needed a Luc-size blanket."

My pulse thrummed as I placed my hand on his chest. "You're trying to distract me."

"I would never." His voice was full of mock outrage, even as he eased some of his weight onto mine.

The next breath I took was shallow. Neither of us were wearing much, especially me with just his shirt and undies, so there weren't many barriers between our skin.

Dipping his head, he pressed a kiss to the corner of my lips. "I like this." His hips shifted, and a sharp swirl of sensation ricocheted through me. "Being your blanket. A lot."

Feeling a little breathless, I brought my hand to his cheek. "I can tell."

He lifted his head, and I could see the sudden diamond brightness of his pupils. "Evie . . ." His gaze roamed over my face. "The things you fill my head with."

There were things I wanted to talk about with him, important things, but knowing what I filled his head with seemed highly important at the moment. "Like what?"

He turned his head into my palm, placing a kiss against the center of my hand. "You. Me." Lowering his head, he coasted his lips over my cheek until he arrived at that sensitive spot below my ear. "And things I only ever fantasized about."

Heat swamped my senses as wanting burst through me in waves. He pressed a kiss to where my pulse beat wildly, and then he went lower. My eyes drifted shut as my head fell back and to the side, allowing him free rein.

"To do anything?" he murmured against my skin, hearing my innermost thoughts.

My toes curled. "I don't even know what anything could entail," I admitted.

Stroking his hand up over my waist, he lifted his head and lined up his mouth to mine. "We can discover what anything entails together."

That sounded like a plan I could really get behind, and boy did I ever want to, but . . .

Opening my eyes before I got completely swept away, I tugged his head up. "There's something I want from you."

His gaze was heavy with intent. "Anything."

"Tell me about Nancy Husher."

The change that swept over Luc was as startling as it was expected. Light receded from Luc's pupils, and the drowsy look vanished from his eyes. His shoulders tensed as his features lost the razor-sharp edge of desire, becoming hard and unforgiving.

"*Someones* have really been talking." His tone was as flat as paper.

"And that someone isn't you," I repeated quietly and then went on before I lost my nerve. "Her name has come up more than once."

"Which is too many times." Candlelight flickered across his jaw. "What could you possibly want to know about that woman?"

I kept my hand on his cheek. "Anything and everything."

His lashes swept down, shielding his gaze. A heartbeat passed and then another. He didn't look up when he spoke. "Nancy was a woman who, in place of a heart and a soul, had nothing but obsession and ambition. Kindness and empathy were tools she used to either gain the trust of others or to ensure that she was underestimated."

As Luc spoke, his voice didn't change inflection. Absent of emotion, he sounded as if he were reciting a speech, but against my palm, I felt the tiny spasm of the muscle along his jaw. "The only thing she cared about was the Origins, and don't mistake the word *cared* for any semblance of human emotion. The forced pro-creations and mutations? They were her idea when the Daedalus either failed to convince others of their pure intentions or when they started to run out of willing Luxen and hybrids. There was nothing that woman would not do. Kidnap people? Murder loved ones? Use innocent people to control those she needed? There was no line she would not cross, and she was just as obsessed with Dae-mon as she was with me, thinking that if she no longer had me to tote around as the shining example of a success, she needed the strongest Luxen to either breed future Origin or to mutate willing soldiers who bought into her cause—lock, stock, and barrel."

Although I already knew that, horror still rolled through me.

"She was consumed with creating the perfect species, and she came pretty damn close to it."

"With you?" I asked. "Or with the group Micah belonged to?"

"She believed I was perfect up until I escaped. It was then when she and the others began working on the Prometheus serum. If I had stayed, she would've never created Micah and—"

"If you'd stayed, you would've never freed Zoe and countless others. If you'd stayed, the world would probably be even worse off," I interrupted, needing him to know that there wasn't a sin-gle thing Nancy or the Daedalus did that was his fault. "If you'd stayed, we would've never met."

His jaw flexed against my palm once more, and then his lashes lifted. I couldn't make out his eyes. "She was the only mother I ever knew."

Swallowing words of sympathy I knew he wouldn't want to hear, I lifted my hand and kissed his stubborn jaw.

"Do you know there was a short period of time where I ac-tually thought she was my mother?" Sandpaper coated his voice as he looked away, causing my hand to slip. "Before I could hone my ability to read minds, I didn't know any better. I thought that woman was my mother."

"I'm sorry," I whispered, because if anyone knew how that felt, I did, and I knew there was little anyone could say in response to something like that. "How did you find out?"

"Archer." He worked his head side to side as if he were working out a kink. "A few years older than I was, he was the only Origin left from the previous batch. Back then, we only knew what we only knew. The Daedalus was our home, for better or for worse."

I couldn't even imagine that.

"Even as a small child, I knew I was treated differently from the others. Given far more privileges. Better dinners and snacks. Candies. I was allowed to watch TV, and Nancy would often allow me to stay with her while she worked late in the labs. Jealousy drove Archer to reveal the truth. It was a . . . shock."

"I'm sure it was." I ran my thumb over his chest, above his heart. "I know it was."

"You would," he said softly. "But it was also eye-opening, and the only thing that matters now, when it comes to that woman, is that she's dead. And not like Jason Dasher dead, but a hundred percent dead. It was a joint effort between Archer and me, but that woman is not coming back." His gaze shifted back to mine. "She's nothing but ash, fertilizing a patch of ground somewhere in Montana, and I cannot find a single ounce of regret in me for doing it. Does that disturb you?"

"No," I said without a second of hesitation. "The ground deserves better than to be covered with her ashes, and I'm glad she's no longer here. She sounds like a monster, worse than Dasher."

"She was, but she's gone and has absolutely no impact on my life today. That's why I don't talk about her. There's no reason to give her any space in my mind or anyone's, especially Kat's and Daemon's. She doesn't deserve that."

"I can agree with that, but—"

"No impact, Evie. I refused to allow that," he cut me off. "I hope that tells you enough about her."

"It does." For now. There was way more than what he was sharing, but even I knew when to stop pushing.

"Good." Luc shifted off me and onto his side of the bed, the one closest to the door. Always that side. "We should get to sleep. If we're going to start working with the Source, you're going to need all the rest you can get."

"Okay." Sitting up, I scooted over, tucking my legs under the covers as the flames from the candles flickered and then went out. The lanterns followed. I looked over at Luc. His back was to me.

His back was *never* to me.

Folding an arm over my waist, I stared at the outline of his body. I didn't think he was mad. Irritated I'd brought up Nancy Husher? Perhaps. But I knew that whatever had him turning away from me had nothing to do with me.

Despite what Luc claimed, he wasn't as apathetic to Nancy as he wanted to be. And who could blame him? No one. I wished there were something I could say other than what I already had. Then he could understand that it was okay to still be furious and sad over what this woman had done to him and others, just as it was okay that he was glad she was dead.

That he'd been the one to ensure it.

What disturbed me was that Luc wouldn't let himself feel any of that, and that wasn't something I could change in a few hours or one night. But what I could do was what I wanted to be able to do. I could just be there for him, even if he didn't know why or didn't want it.

Lying down beside him, I rolled onto my side and wiggled toward him until my chest was pressed against his back. I threw an arm around his waist. Luc didn't move or respond, but I held him tightly. "I love you," I whispered against the warm skin of his back. I fell asleep like that, with not an inch separating us.

Sometime later, I awoke long enough to feel Luc threading his fingers through mine.

A few hours after dawn, I found myself standing in an abandoned packing warehouse on the outskirts of Houston. Faint sunlight filtered through the dirt-caked window and inches of dust-covered workbenches.

I looked up at the high ceiling, guessing it was made of steel and plaster. In other words, things that would probably hurt if or when they came down on my head.

Standing several feet in front of me, Luc followed my gaze. He was back to normal this morning, as if we hadn't talked about Nancy Husher last night. Part of me was relieved, but I was also worried he'd just shoved all those messy feelings back into the vault that was Luc. If I knew anything, that wasn't healthy, not even for an all-powerful Origin.

"Are you sure it's a good idea that we're doing this inside?" I asked.

"I figured it would be better if we did this without prying eyes," Luc explained.

A laugh as dry as the high school cafeteria meat loaf came from the corner. "Good luck with no one noticing the building collapsing on our heads."

My jaw locked. "Does *he* have to be here?"

Luc slid a long look in the direction of said corner, to where Grayson lounged on some kind of large cable spool. "Why are you here?"

The icy-blond Luxen grinned. Like all Luxen, with his sapphire-colored eyes and chiseled features, he was blessed with great DNA, but he always seemed the most inhuman of all the Luxen I'd met.

Probably because those near symmetric features lacked any touch of humanity.

"I'm here for moral support," he advised.

I rolled my eyes. "More likely he's here to make sure I don't kill you."

Luc grinned. "You're not going to kill me, Peaches."

"What if I kill Grayson?" I paused. "Accidentally?"

Grayson arched a brow as he reached into his pocket, pulling out a sour apple Blow Pop.

"That would make me sad," Luc replied. "Gray is useful."

"About as useful as a wooden frying pan," I muttered as Grayson unwrapped his lollipop.

Luc chuckled. "All right. I figured it was best to start simple."

"Simple sounds good."

Grayson snorted.

I drew in a deep, long breath.

"Ignore him," Luc ordered.

"Easier said than done."

"Easy or hard, you need to learn how to also ignore external influences. When you get out there and use the Source, not everyone is going to be quiet and peaceful," Luc stated. "Most likely, a whole lot of crap will be going on. You will not have the luxury of concentration then, and you won't have it here."

"So that's why he's here? To be an annoying distraction? That makes sense." I smiled at Grayson. "Thank you."

Grayson's eyes narrowed.

Snark point one for me.

Luc shot another pointed look in Grayson's direction, one that went largely ignored. "We know that the Source is triggered in you if you're mortally threatened or experience a high level of emotions. How you use the Source during those times is something that only the most skilled of us would be able to do. To harness it, turn it into a weapon, or to use it to shape or mold other physical objects is something extremely difficult to do."

"Too bad she doesn't know how she does that."

Snark point one to Grayson.

"But what that tells me is that you're more than capable of doing the simplest thing with the Source," Luc continued as if Grayson hadn't spoken. "I've been thinking about what would be easiest for you to try first."

"Breathing?" Grayson suggested.

Snark point two to Grayson.

"With us, it would be summoning the Source. Like this." White crackling light danced over his knuckles. "All I did was summon it."

I stared at the Source. "What do you mean by summon it?"

"Man." Grayson sighed. "This is going to be a long day."

Snark point three to Grayson.

I was really falling behind on the snark points.

"What I mean is that I called it from here." Luc placed his hand on his sternum, the central part of his chest. "Do you feel it there?"

"I . . ." I trailed off, unsure. Did I feel something there? "I don't know. What does it feel like?"

"You don't know what it feels like?" Derision dripped like syrup from Grayson's tone.

"You're about to feel my knee in your junk," I snapped. "Let me know how that feels."

Grayson shoved the Blow Pop into his mouth. Snark point two to Evie.

Luc's lips twitched. "To me, it feels like . . . a coiled rope nestled in the chest."

A coiled rope? Well, nope. I did not feel that.

"Doesn't feel like that to me." Grayson drew one knee up, resting his arm on it.

"How does it feel to you?" Luc asked.

The Luxen lifted one shoulder in a lazy shrug. "It feels like restless energy. A buzz. Sometimes all over. Sometimes in the sternum."

Heart rate kicking up, I glanced at Grayson. Now that I had felt. Often.

Luc's gaze sharpened on me. "Is that how it feels to you, Evie?"

"I've felt more restless since the Cassio Wave, especially lately. Like I can't sit still." I placed my hand on my chest. "And I have felt it start here, like a weird antsy feeling. I figured it was just because of everything that was happening."

Luc shook his head as the Source disappeared from his hand. "It's the Source in you. You're going to feel more wired than you did before."

"Ha. Look at me." Grayson smiled around the stick. "Being actually helpful."

He had been.

Ugh.

Whatever.

"Okay. Do you feel it now?" Luc's gaze roamed over me. The small grin returned. "I'm thinking you are."

I stilled, realizing I'd been slowly swaying back and forth.

"Listen to your body." Luc's voice was closer, quieter.

I wasn't sure how to listen to my body, but I focused on why

I'd been swaying in the first place. The antsy energy was there. I hadn't noticed it, but it was like a buzz in my veins. Yes. A *buzz*. Like a low electrical current, but it wasn't just in my veins. I could feel it in the center of my chest. I pressed the heel of my palm in, and there was something there.

My gaze flew to Luc's. "I can feel it."

He smiled. "Good. Now I want you to call on it." He must've read my confusion, because he added, "I want you to picture this." The Source flared to life along his knuckles once more. "I want you to picture you doing this."

My gaze lifted from his hand to his face and then fell back to his hand. "It's that easy? I just picture it and bam! I have electric fingers?"

He laughed. "Calling on the Source is easy. Using the Source to do what you want is a whole different story, but like we already know, you're able to do amazing things with it already."

"Scary things," I amended.

"Powerful things." His eyes met and held mine when I lifted my gaze. "That's what you're able to use the Source for. Powerful things, Evie."

That was right.

What I'd done to April, what I'd done in those woods, and even what I'd done when I'd started to lose it a couple of nights ago, all had been powerful. The trick was to control it.

I glanced down at my hand still pressed to my chest. The hum of energy was still there. It was always there. Maybe even before the Cassio Wave had been used, and I hadn't recognized it, but I felt it now.

"All I had to do was picture it? And that was it?"

"Yes," Luc said. "That's it."

I opened my mouth and then closed it. "Really?"

Grayson sighed so heavily, I was surprised he didn't blow us away. "Yes. It's that easy." His head cocked to the side as he spoke around the stick. "It should be. Unless there's something else wrong with you."

I shot him a death glare. "There's nothing else wrong with me except for the fact you're here."

"Wait." The Source winked out once more as Luc frowned. "You've never tried to summon it before?"

"Well . . ." I shifted my weight from foot to foot as both guys stared at me. "I mean, not really."

Luc blinked.

"What?" The lollipop slid out as Grayson's mouth dropped open. He caught it before it could hit the floor. "You haven't even tried to use the Source? Not once?"

"No." Feeling about seven different kinds of defensive, I crossed my arms over my chest. "Why would I? Do I need to remind you two what happened the only times I've used the Source? Not only did I have no control, two out of those three times, I had no idea who I was. Why would I go around purposely summoning something that could potentially hurt the people I care about? You're not included in that statement." I glared at Grayson, and he frowned. "And let's not forget that everything just happened."

"No, you're right." Luc snapped out of the only stupor I'd ever seen him in. "This isn't second nature to you, and there'd be no reason for you to even try it, especially considering what has happened. I should've considered that."

"Damn straight," I muttered, but I was feeling kind of dumb now. Like *I* should've known to have at least tried.

God, I was worse than baby Luxen everywhere. I didn't even know what the Source felt like and—

"You're not dumb." Luc was suddenly in front of me, his hands clasping my cheeks. "You're not worse than a baby Luxen."

I wasn't so sure about that.

"If anything, I should've figured this out." His eyes searched mine. "All of this is new to you, and barely any time has passed. There is nothing wrong with you. Okay?"

I nodded.

Grayson was slowly shaking his head, but he wisely kept his mouth shut.

Dipping his head, Luc pressed his forehead against mine. "You've got this. I know you do." He touched his lips to mine, the kiss short but so incredibly sweet. Sliding his hands off my cheeks, he backed off. "This is actually good news."

I glanced at Grayson. He was staring at one of the dirty windows, the Blow Pop gone. "How is this good news?"

"Because this may mean you can use the Source and control it intentionally," Luc explained. "And if that's the case, that's a big hole in your 'only the Daedalus can control your abilities' theory."

"Her what?" Grayson was focused on us again.

As Luc explained to Grayson my theory about Dasher being the key to my control, or at least attempted to, I thought about how if Luc was right, this would be a huge hole, but . . .

Staring down at my plain old hand, I didn't think about the weird effect I'd seen while at Kat's or what the Source looked like when Luc summoned it. Could it really be that simple? I almost couldn't wrap my head around it, but what if it was? I just had to picture it and that was it?

A sense of rightness swept through me as I opened and closed my hand. From what I knew, that *was* what I'd done in the woods. The images of what I wanted had flickered through my head so fast, and the Source had responded even faster, replicating what I saw. With April, it hadn't been the Source I'd used. It had been physical training, and I'd been on autopilot, my sense of self taking a back seat.

The hum in the center of my chest increased, almost as if it knew what I were thinking. Could that be why I'd felt more restless? It wanted to be used? But what if I did and it triggered something in me that I couldn't control?

Fear was a shadow pressing on my back, and that restless buzz intensified. If I didn't try because of what *might* happen, then what would happen?

Nothing.

Nothing good was what would happen. I would be worse than useless, because I would be choosing to do nothing.

I was not going to be useless.

Determination and absolute refusal to sit back and do nothing became a fuel that burned away the fear. The hum in my chest pulsed like a faint heart palpitation. What I was feeling wasn't anxiety or restlessness. It was power—power building inside me. And if that were true, was me not using the Source possibly leading to situations like the night I'd had a nightmare, when I'd hit critical mass? I didn't know, but I closed my eyes. In my mind's eye, I saw Luc's hand, crackling with the Source, and then I replaced his hand with mine, and I *willed* it to happen.

12

A *spark.*

That's what it felt like, like striking a match. A tingling sensation swept outward in a rush, shooting down my right arm. All of it could've been my imagination or wild, wishful thinking, but if it was, it was some of the most realistic imagining I'd ever had.

"Peaches? Open your eyes and look."

I did just that, finding both Luc and Grayson staring at me.

"Not at me." Luc's smile was full of reassuring warmth, and when his gaze met mine, there was the kind of heat in his eyes that made me think of hard kisses and soft touches, and there was also everything he'd never spoken.

Why in that moment I realized Luc had never actually said those three simple yet powerful words was beyond me, but I did. I didn't need those words when I could see them in the way he looked at me, when I could feel them in every one of his actions.

Drawing a shallow breath, I looked down at my hand, and I wanted to shout hallelujah upon what I saw even if I couldn't help but notice how different it was from when Luc did this.

White light encased in shadows swirled around my palm, threading between my fingers. It sparked and pulsed tiny licks of power that resembled arcing electric lines.

"I did it." I almost couldn't believe it as I turned my hand over. The Source followed the movement. Glancing at Luc, I felt my lips curve up as excitement bloomed in my chest. "I did it."

Luc smiled, and it was a big one, the kind that transformed his features from beautiful to simply breathtaking.

Then I saw it—the strange mottling of the skin of my arm I'd seen at Kat's. Shimmering onyx-colored dots appeared under my skin.

"Do you see that? My arm?" I asked, glancing quickly at Luc.

He nodded as he looked me over. "It's not just your arm, Peaches."

"What?" My eyes widened.

"It's all over," Grayson said from his corner. If he weren't talking, I'd question if he were breathing, he was so still. "Splotches of it. On your neck. Your right cheek."

"It's all over?" I looked down but somehow resisted the urge to pull up my shirt to see if it was on my stomach. "I have an outbreak of glittering black dots."

"Could be a worse outbreak," Luc said, and I gaped at him. "You looked like this before, Peaches, while you were in the woods. And the night before last, I saw the marks on your cheeks."

"And you didn't think to tell me that?"

"I didn't want you to freak out." He paused. "Obviously."

"I'm not freaking out!"

He cocked his head. "You're not?"

I snapped my mouth shut. The spots seemed to move under my skin, crowding closer and then stretching farther apart. "I thought I saw this yesterday while I was with Kat and Dee. I didn't say anything because they didn't seem to see it. I thought I must've been imagining it."

"Interesting," murmured Luc. "It could've been a spike of the Source. What were you feeling or thinking when you saw it?"

My thoughts raced back to that moment. "We were talking about me not remembering my time with the Daedalus."

"Makes sense, then. I'm sure there was emotion attached to that conversation." Luc's gaze roamed across my face in a way that made me want to see what he saw. "It must've only been on your arm, then, because there's no way they wouldn't have noticed this."

"I want to see what I look like," I said, looking around, but there was no window clean enough to even attempt to see a reflection in. Did they have bathrooms here?

"When we get back to the house, you can look."

Impatient but knowing there were more important things than checking myself out, I let it go. "I bet I look weird."

"It's actually kind of beautiful," Grayson said, and I about fell over in shock. Did he just sort of compliment me? He must've surprised himself, too, because he also looked like he was about to topple over. He averted his eyes—wait. Was he . . . *blushing*? "But yeah, it's also really weird," he added. "I'd be uncomfortable if I were you."

My lips pursed.

"It is beautiful," Luc said, and when I looked back to him, he was smiling. "And it is different. You know what a Luxen or Origin looks like when they use the Source. Sometimes there are no other visible signs. Other times—"

"It's white light in the veins or the pupils turning white." I swallowed. "Do I have black veins?"

He shook his head. "Not right now, but when you were in the woods, there was a faint darkening in the veins, and you had the aura of the Source around you."

Like with the nightmare. "What does it mean when there's an aura?"

Luc studied me. "What does it feel like to you when it happens?"

I mulled that over. "I felt . . . I don't know, like the power—the Source—was building up in me. Like it was expanding outside of me." And then, just like that, I answered my own question. Anytime I'd seen a Luxen or Origin do that, it was when they were very angry or about to go toe to toe with someone.

"There you go," Luc said.

Realizing Luc wanted me to figure out what I already knew, I narrowed my eyes at him. "You're annoying."

"And sexy."

I shook my head, returning to watch the white and dark light swirl over my knuckles. "Do Arum get black dots on their skin?"

"Not that I've ever seen. They are a near mirror opposite of the Luxen. I imagine this is how the Arum DNA shows in you."

"This is just crazy."

My gaze shot to Grayson. I hadn't heard him move, but he was no longer perched on the cable spool. He stood only a few feet away.

Curiosity marked his face as he stared down at my hand, shaking his head. "It really is a mixture of Arum and Luxen."

He sounded so surprised that I asked, "You didn't see me in the woods, did you?"

Still staring at my hand—at *me*—he shook his head. "Dawson and I had gone after the other members of SOL. I saw the aftermath of what you did in the woods, and I know what Steven claimed, but . . ."

"Seeing is a whole different type of believing," Luc finished for him.

"I've never seen anything like that." Ultrabright blue eyes lifted to mine. "You would have the abilities of both, to use the Source to push outward and to draw it in."

"I guess." I closed my palm, and the Source flickered out of existence. Oh no. "I didn't mean for that to happen."

"That's common," Luc assured me. "If you're not using it for something, you'll have to make it stay there. How do you feel?"

I shrugged. "Normal, I guess."

"No urge to kill us?" Luc asked. "Well, no urge to kill me?"

Grayson arched a brow, appearing entirely unimpressed with that statement.

I, on the other hand, thought it kind of sucked that the question had to be asked. "Not at the moment."

Luc grinned. "Call on it again."

Nodding, I did, and I felt the spark—the taut pull from the center of my chest and then the rush of energy. The shadowy light erupted over my hand.

I lifted my hand, turning it slightly as I stared at the display of the Source. Completely awed by what I was able to do on command, I felt a little weak-kneed and silly, but this was . . .

God, a handful of months ago, I would've laughed in the face of anyone who suggested I was able to do such a thing.

"Now I want you to make it go away," Luc instructed. "You can do this several ways—"

I pictured it vanishing, and the Source did just that, flickered and then faded out.

"Okay." Luc laughed.

Smiling like a fool, I curled my fingers inward. "I just pictured it disappearing in my mind."

"That was one of the ways I was going to suggest." Leaning against the bench, he folded his arms. "Do it again. Summon it and then make it go away."

I did it again and again, so many times that I lost count, and each time I did, the glittering dots appeared. Grayson went through four Blow Pops, leaving me to wonder multiple times how many of those things he had in his pocket.

Luc didn't move on from that until there was no doubt I could control summoning the Source. Then he found an empty white carton, placing it on the center of the table. He faced me. "I want you to move this carton. You don't need to summon the Source for this, but it works the same. You want the carton to move. Picture it happening."

Ignoring my grumbling stomach, I turned to the table. Once more, I found myself wondering if it was really going to be that easy. *Picture it, and they will come.* I swallowed a giggle.

"Focus," Luc ordered softly. "You should try to focus."

"You know, I'm going to be really annoyed if I picture that box moving and it does. Because that means I've lost days of being incredibly lazy."

"Peaches . . ."

"I could've been willing doors to open and close, clothing to unfold, peanut butter jars to come to me," I explained. "I could just lie in bed all day and will food to enter my mouth."

"Such lofty goals you have." Grayson had returned to his cable spool and his high horse.

"I don't know of a goal any loftier than having food come to me while I'm in bed," I retorted.

"Let me guess, you haven't even tried to see if you could move anything?" Grayson snorted as he peeled a wrapper on another Blow Pop. "I thought every human tried that at least daily."

I rolled my eyes. "We try that every once in a while. Not every single day." Well, at least I didn't, because the disappointment of not being able to move things with my mind was real. "And no, I haven't since everything happened."

"Shocker."

Forget that stupid white carton. I pictured the cable spool sliding out from underneath Grayson.

Nothing happened.

"Evie," Luc warned, but he sounded like he was choking on laughter.

Grayson looked up from his Blow Pop. "What?" He lowered the sucker. "What are you doing?"

"Nothing," I lied.

"Are you trying to do something to me?" The Luxen laughed. "I'm not remotely worried." He popped the lollipop into his mouth. "At all. Want to know why? Moving objects is one of the hardest things even for the youngest and brightest of Luxen to learn and control. You might've been trained and all that, but obviously you have no recollection. So, go ahead. Give me something to laugh about, because this is getting incredibly boring."

Oh, I was so going to give him something, all right, because it struck me then that picturing anything moving wasn't the key. It was the intent behind it. The *will*. Most importantly, it was *knowing* that I could.

I didn't picture the spool shooting across the floor. This time, I *willed* it. The pulse in the center of my chest was faint, something I probably wouldn't have noticed if I hadn't been paying attention.

It happened so fast, a split second after the thought entered my mind. It was like an invisible string had been attached to the spool and it had been yanked *hard*. The thing spun across the floor, sending dust into the air as Grayson went down, hitting the floor with a satisfying thump. He sat there, the Blow Pop hanging limply from the side of his mouth, his eyes such a startling unnatural shade of blue.

"Are you bored now?" I asked sweetly.

Grayson popped to his feet and whirled toward me. Where the Blow Pop went, I had no idea. The pupils of his eyes went diamond bright, and the center of my chest pulsed. Tiny hairs all over my body rose as every part of me, including what was in me, hyper-focused on the Luxen.

His gaze darted over my shoulder, and I saw his jaw harden. He took a step back as the light receded from his eyes. "If you were anyone else . . ."

The warning hung in the air between us, and I knew it wasn't me who stopped him. It was who stood behind me.

That ticked me off.

The Source flared intently, pressing at my skin a lot like it had the night I'd had the nightmare. I didn't need to look down to know that I had an aura.

"It's not Luc you should be worried about," I said, and that was my voice, those were my words. I meant to say them.

"Should he be?" Luc asked quietly from behind me. "Should he be worried right now, Evie?"

I had to think really hard about how I wanted to answer that. A deep, hidden part of me wanted Grayson to come at me, and I wasn't sure if that had anything to do with the Source or not.

But as much as I wanted to knock Grayson off his pedestal, I didn't want to seriously hurt him, and I would. I would totally destroy him if I let loose.

"No," I said, exhaling roughly. The tension in my chest eased off, and the shadowy light faded like smoke in the wind. "He shouldn't."

Surprise flickered across Grayson's face, and then he looked behind me again. His brows rose.

"What? Do you want me to peel the skin off your bones?" I demanded, and I spun to Luc. He was *smiling.* I blinked. "Why are you smiling?"

"I'm smiling because you really wanted to take Grayson down," he said, eyes glittering.

"Why would you smile about that?" I was dumbfounded.

"Because you chose not to," Grayson answered. "Let that sink in."

Shooting him a look over my shoulder, I was about to tell him I was considering changing my mind, when it did hit me.

"I stopped it." My head cranked back to Luc. "Holy crap, I felt the Source. It was ready to go, but I stopped it!"

Luc's smile grew. "Yeah, you did. You have control, Peaches. Now move the damn carton."

Grayson hadn't been lying earlier. Moving objects wasn't exactly easy. While I'd been able to move the spool out from under him, the carton proved to be a different story.

I wasn't angry with the carton.

Which showed the correlation between emotion and accuracy. If I was angry, everyone had better run for the hills. If I was ambivalent, everyone could take a nap.

I was able to move the carton after several misfires. It wasn't until Luc had said, "Picture having multiple, invisible arms—arms that can stretch hundreds of feet. And yes, I know it sounds ridiculous, but take those dozens of arms and encase them in the Source. Not what it looks like with Grayson or me, but with your Source."

That did sound ridiculous, and it had led me to picturing all kinds of random invisible things that had nothing to do with the task at the hand, but when I finally focused and did what Luc had instructed, the carton winged right at my head.

And that was right about the time I learned that if I was going to move an object, I needed to also plan where I wanted to move it.

Some days, I felt dumber than others. This was one of those days.

When Luc finally called it a day and Grayson disappeared in, like, a nanosecond, I was only slightly relieved to be heading back to the house. I was tired and hungry, but I also wanted to practice more.

Emboldened by the success that we had and a wee bit confident, I actually felt truly hopeful, like for the first time I thought maybe I could take back some control in my life. I was *juiced* to do more. Okay, maybe I shouldn't use the word *juiced* since that just sounded weird, but I wanted to see exactly what I could do.

I thought again of how fast Grayson had disappeared.

"I wonder if I can run fast now," I said as we walked down a road empty except for abandoned cars that had more rust and sun damage than paint. I kept scanning, hoping to see Nate, but knowing it was probably too soon for him to come back.

"That's actually a good question. I don't know. Hybrids are physically stronger and faster, but not like a Luxen or Arum or Origin. So, technically speaking, you should be able to run pretty fast. As fast as I can or they can? I can't answer that."

I wasn't sure what I would do if I could actually run measurably fast, since the only time I had was when my life was under immediate threat. Even then, I ran like a turtle with a broken leg. "Can we practice more when we get back to the house?"

"I think you should take it easy the rest of the day."

I frowned.

"Before you can ask why, and I know you're getting ready to, it's because I don't want you to overdo it until we get a better handle on what comes naturally to you other than knocking Grayson on his ass."

My frown turned upside down. "Man, that was great. I will never forget that. Not as long as I live."

"What was better was the fact it proved you can control your Source, even when angry."

That it did, but . . .

What else did it prove? Yes, I'd been angry with Grayson, but that had been nothing like the fury I'd felt in the nightmare, nor the panic. What I had done today didn't mean I wouldn't lose control again or that I wouldn't go hive-mind Trojan on everyone.

And just like that, my earlier confidence belly flopped out of a window. "But what does that really prove?" I asked as a cool breeze rolled down the street.

"It proves a lot more than you were just thinking, Peaches." Luc took my hand. "You can use the Source, and you can control it, but it's almost like a muscle that has wasted due to lack of use. I think with a couple of sessions, you'll be shocked by what you can do."

A dozen or so different scenarios played out. Opening and closing doors with the power of my mind just because I could. Lighting and extinguishing candles. Summoning a jar of peanut butter and a spoon from the kitchen. Heating up my own—

"Peaches." Luc chuckled, lifting my hand to his mouth. He kissed the back. "Not even I can summon a jar of peanut butter from a totally different room and have it do anything other than smack into a wall."

"But I'm supposed to be awesomer than you, so maybe I can."

"You are already awesomer than I am." He tugged me along as we came to the overgrown field that bordered the street. Off in the distance, I heard the mournful call of cows. "We'll practice moving some more stuff, and then we'll move on to seeing if you can move harder things."

"Like?"

"Like people who are able to resist."

My eyes widened. "Like you?"

He nodded. "Grayson. I'm sure Zoe will volunteer."

"But what if I hurt you guys?"

Luc glanced down at me. "You didn't hurt Grayson today, even though you wanted to."

He was right.

I stared out over the field, wondering how much more my life would change. "Does that make me a bad person? That I did want to hurt him?"

"Who hasn't wanted to hurt Grayson?"

I choked out a laugh.

"Grayson was purposely trying to get a rise out of you," he added. "And he's exceptionally good at it."

"That he is," I murmured, thinking that over. "You're saying that he wasn't pushing my buttons because he just wanted to be a jerk to me, but to see what I'd do?"

"Yes." He paused. "And because he's a jerk. It's one of his strengths."

How that was considered a strength, I didn't know.

"Today was a good day. No one had to hurt anyone. No one got hurt," he said, eyeing the cloudy sky. "Well, except maybe

Grayson's pride and a Blow Pop or two, and we didn't have to make you panic or really upset. I'll count this as a win and proof that we're on the right path."

Squeezing his hand, I decided that I would also count today as a win.

"So." He drew the word out. "You want to see if you can run fast?"

I came to a sudden halt. "I thought you said I should take it easy."

"If you can run faster than before, it will be the mutation—the Source fueling it—but it's not the same as what you were doing today." A mischievous glint settled in his eyes. "Or are you feeling tired? If so, I'm sure I can carry you back. Here." He tugged on my hand. "You can hop on my back—"

"I don't need you to carry me." I pulled my hand free. "Let's do it. Where are we running to?"

That boyish grin of his surfaced, the one that made it feel like there was a nest of carnivorous butterflies in my chest. "Back to the house. You can find it from here?"

"If we cut through the field, yes."

"Then let's do it. On the count of three."

There was no time to second-guess this or ask questions. Luc fired off the countdown, and when he hit three, he was already a blur of motion, racing into the knee-high weeds.

"Dammit!" I shouted.

His wild laugh echoed around me, and I cursed again as I broke out into a run. At first, I noticed nothing different. Luc was so far ahead, he was just a blip, and that was so unfair. How could I not be able to run fast? That would seem to make me a very inefficient Trojan.

I had to be able to run like Luc. I *had* to.

The hum of energy cranked, and then I wasn't thumping through the field. I was *racing*.

I didn't know exactly what second my speed picked up, but it did, and holy crap on a cracker, I was running fast—so fast that the little pieces of the grass and dirt pelting my cheeks and bare arms stung. There was no burning in my legs or seizing of the stomach and lungs. My heart was racing, but it didn't feel like it was going to burst out of my chest. Up ahead, Luc came more into focus. I was *catching* up to him.

I moved so fast it was almost like flying.

And it was freeing. There was no room for thoughts as the wind whipped strands of hair from the knot I'd twisted the hair back into that morning. I wasn't thinking about what I'd done, what it could mean, and what it might not. No space to think about Jason Dasher or the Daedalus. There was no room for the throat-clogging mixture of grief and anger that accompanied any thoughts of my mom. I didn't worry about Heidi or Emery or James as I ran. I didn't wonder if Nate would come back and how many more kids were out there, barely getting by. There was just the song of my pounding heart and the crunch of grass under my sneakers.

When I overtook Luc and blew past him, I knew I was going to beat him, and I did, slowing down only when I reached the front door and all but threw it open.

I spun, breathing fast but not heavy. Luc appeared in the doorway a heartbeat or two after me, hair blown back from his face in wild waves.

Laughing even as my heart still pounded, I backed up into the living room. "I can't believe I beat you."

"Me, either." The door swung closed behind Luc as he stalked forward, his eyes shards of amethyst. My stomach fluttered at the intensity in his gaze.

"How does it feel to not be the best?" I asked, stopping when my calves hit the coffee table.

"I'm a sore loser." His hands landed on my hips, and before I knew it, I was up in the air and then I was lying on the couch. Luc was prowling over me. "You're going to need to make me feel better."

"You're going to have to suck it up."

Dipping his head as his hands slid up my shirt, he whispered something in my ear that scorched my cheeks and a whole lot of other areas. "I'm sweaty," I told him.

"So am I." He kissed me, and an exquisite pulse shot through me.

I gripped his shoulder and fisted my other hand in the hair along the back of his head. "I'm dirty."

"I don't care." His mouth came over mine again, and his body moved over and against mine. I felt it all in the sharpest, most delicious way. "Before everything, when you were feeling better, we'd run like that all the time. Used to drive Paris crazy, because we'd often be in the house, knocking everything over, and it always ended in an argument between us."

Now my heart thundered for a whole different reason. "Why?"

"Because you'd get mad when I let you win," he said, and I laughed at the absurdity of it. He kissed me again, an almost greedy clash. "I missed that."

"You didn't let me win this time."

"No." His lips curved into a smile against mine. "I didn't, and hell, you have no idea how relieved I am to know that."

I knew why he would be. My chest tightened. It was more proof I was no longer sick—no longer dying. Luc knew that, but I imagined it was a lot like me having a hard time believing that using the Source could be that easy. There was still a part of him that couldn't believe I wasn't sick.

Pressing my forehead to his, I hoped for once he was listening to my thoughts when I said, *I love you.*

Illogical as it was, I thought I heard him whisper, *I know,* but I knew he couldn't, because his lips were busy with mine once more.

My fingers tightened in his hair, and his hand was slowly tracking northward, reaching the satiny material—

I felt the strange buzz along the base of my neck at the same moment Luc froze above me. He rose, looking over his shoulder, toward the door. Before I could share what I felt, he spoke.

"It's Dee," he said, and a moment later, there was a knock—a *pounding.*

13

There was absolutely not a single thing about giving birth that remotely appealed to me.

Sure, babies were cute when they weren't competing with your insides for lodging, and the whole circle of life was a miracle in itself, but—

Another scream tore through the night sky, followed by a litany of the most impressive combinations of the F-bomb I'd ever heard in my life. Most were directed at Daemon.

I winced.

Actually, all the curses had been directed at Daemon.

Poor Kat.

There should be some sort of cosmic law that required men to feel everything women felt while giving birth.

I really had no idea what time it was. I had dozed off at some point, before the whole screaming thing jarred me awake. Someone had draped a colorful fuchsia-and-turquoise patchwork quilt over me. I didn't think it had been Luc, since I figured he would've woken me up.

According to the last update given by Dee, which had come hours after she'd showed up at the house, everything was going "typically."

How typical could it be when Daemon had called for Luc, and I hadn't seen either of them emerge from the inside of the house? And it was now well past midnight.

Luc would've definitely checked on me if he were able to, and while I hadn't seen Dr. Hemenway with my own two eyes, the old gas-powered vehicle that reminded me of a dune buggy was still parked just beyond the carport. Zoe had told me the all-terrain utility vehicle belonged to the doc and that there were several like that scattered about Zone 3, used by humans who didn't have the handy ability of running with supersonic speed.

Worry pecked on my shoulder. I didn't know a lot—okay, I didn't know *anything*—about giving birth, but I was thinking something not so typical was going down.

I didn't really know Kat, and Daemon would probably rather see me anywhere other than where I was, but I hoped with every fiber of my being that both the mother and child came out of this whole and healthy.

They had to.

Kat was a hybrid, nowhere near as weak or prone to death as a human. Plus, if medical intervention failed, she had Daemon, his siblings, and also had Luc, who could harness the Source into a healing energy.

Kat and the baby *had* to be okay.

That's what I kept telling myself as I sat on one of the brilliant blue cushions of the wicker couches seated under the twinkling warm white light of solar string lights hanging from the top of the carport. I watched the breeze toy with the canopy, alone at the moment. Zoe had left with a young man I'd pegged as a Luxen before he'd even parted the canopy. Cekiah had sent him for Zoe, and I apparently wasn't privy to why.

I glanced down at the quilt. If she had been the one to bring the blanket, where was she now? I guessed it could've been any-one. People had come and gone throughout the evening and into the night. Luxen and hybrids I'd never met and humans who some-times accompanied a Luxen. I kept feeling that weird cobweb-type sensation, but at the moment I was too tired for the brain energy required to truly consider it might be the Source inside me recog-nizing it in others . . . or the possibility that I was continuously walking through actual cobwebs or lying in a giant one.

If it turned out I was covered in cobwebs, I'd set myself on fire. For real.

Anyway, all of them quieted when they saw me. Not a single one approached me as they stopped by to see how Kat and Daemon were doing and if there were any news or anything they could do. Only a few brave people sent a tentative smile in my direction, which I returned, probably a little too eagerly.

There was such a sense of community here. I doubted Kat and Daemon were best friends forever with all who stopped by, but people cared enough about them to show up, and I thought that said something amazing about both Daemon and Kat and those who came by.

I knew that Nate and whoever else was in the city would be welcome here, cared for, and would have access to all the food they needed. They would be accepted, and I just hoped I was given a chance to convince the kid of that.

But me?

Would these same people become more comfortable with me once I'd been here awhile? Once I proved I didn't fall into the stranger-danger category?

I hoped so, because for the foreseeable future, this was my home. *Our home.* Luc and I actually had a home together. Sort of. Wasn't like we went out and picked out an apartment or something, but it was just us. Either way, the flutter in my chest had pterodactyl-size wings.

Zone 3 had to become my home, because not only did I need to be somewhere where I could continue to work on the Source, neither the Daedalus nor the Sons of Liberty could find me here.

Hopefully.

Right now, I was safe here. It took no leap of logic to know I wouldn't be if I were out there. I needed to make this work.

I had Zoe, and Heidi would be here soon, and they were more than enough, but I needed to make friends here, too. Connections. Something that led to something other than a half-scared smile. Hell, I'd be happy with a hello. Seemed silly in the big scheme of things, but I wanted to feel like I was a part of what they were doing here and not like an unwanted guest.

They just needed time. That's all.

I added that thought to the "Kat and baby would be a-okay" record and hit the mental Repeat button.

Shifting on the couch, I unfurled my legs. My stomach ached a little. The quick dinner Zoe and I had ended up eating while we'd waited for news had only tempered my appetite. Maybe I was having sympathy contractions.

Man, Kat was a boss. When Dee had given us an update, she'd briefly mentioned there were no pain meds. Kat had opted out of them in case someone else needed them more than she did. Like, who needed it more than someone pushing out a tiny person? Au naturel childbirth had *nope* written all over it. There was absolutely no way I could do that without being high as a kite.

The wind kicked up the heavy canopy, and outside the carport, the night was dark and silent with the exception of the occasional cricket . . . or pain-filled scream. Snuggling under the quilt, I glanced over my shoulder to the side door that hadn't opened in quite some time. I hadn't gone inside with Luc, because even though Kat and I had gotten to chat the day before, I didn't know her like that. I didn't want to intrude in moments meant to be shared with family and friends. I didn't want to be in the way, and well, I hadn't been invited.

Not to mention I really didn't want to see what was going on in there.

The strange tickling sensation danced its way over the nape of my neck, and this time, I didn't do the is-there-a-bug-on-me dance. I waited to see if a Luxen showed up or if a giant spider crawled across—

I jerked my head toward the side door as an exhausted scream shattered the calm, ending in a weary groan. I grimaced, lifting the quilt to my chin. I really, really needed to find out if Origins and non-Origins could make babies, because there was nothing about any of what was going on inside that house that I wanted a part of. Ever.

"You look officially traumatized."

Gasping, I spun my head around. Grayson stood just inside the canopy, the string lights casting a warm glow over his form, and yet, he still reminded me of one of those carvings done in ice. Wariness trickled through me. After today, I was confident he was fantasizing about turning me into an episode of *Forensic Files* in which I was murdered and my body fed to hogs.

He arched an eyebrow that was only a shade or two darker than the swept-back blond hair. "I scared you."

"No." I still held the quilt to my chin. "You didn't."

"Is that so?" Grayson smirked, and boy, he could deliver some of the most impressive smirks I'd ever seen. He glanced over my shoulder to the closed door, and then his glacial-blue eyes settled on me. "You do look traumatized."

Slowly lowering the quilt, I mulled over how to answer that question. Grayson and I had probably only had one *almost* noncombative conversation since I had known him, and while he might've said that the dotted effect my skin took on earlier was beautiful, he also could've been suffering from extreme brain trauma at that point. I had no idea what he'd been doing before he'd joined Luc and me. He could've been repeatedly banging his head against a wall for all I knew.

"Listening to someone in labor is a little traumatizing," I finally said.

Reaching into the pocket of his jeans, he pulled out a Blow Pop. One of his Luxen talents had to be conjuring an endless supply of those things. "Then I hope you and Luc are being careful."

My brows lifted.

"Or you'll find yourself screaming into the wee hours of the morning." He leaned against the side of the carport, meticulously unwrapping the sucker. "Because it's not entirely impossible for you two, so you and Luc had better be engaging in some Teflon-level protection."

For a long moment, all I could do was stare at him, and then finally I was able to formulate a coherent response. "I really do not want to talk you about what Luc and I do and how we do it—"

He held up a hand as he said, "I don't need details, but thanks."

"I wasn't offering details," I snapped, my fingers now digging into the edges of the quilt.

"All I'm saying is that it's not impossible. He's an Origin and you are . . . well, you're whatever you are, but I'm betting you have enough alien DNA in you to make it probable." Sliding the discarded wrapper into his pocket, he raised the Blow Pop as if he were making a toast. "So, congrats."

I shook my head, dumbfounded. Luc and I hadn't exactly discussed protection, even though we'd come close to actually doing it a time or two. And yes, we probably should've had that conversation long before it even got close to the actual act, but neither of us would go into having sex with just thoughts and prayers as our only protection. "Let me say it again: what Luc and I are doing or not doing isn't any of your business. So, I'm going to pretend this conversation didn't happen. Okay? Great."

Chuckling in a way I knew he was laughing at me, he popped the sucker into his mouth.

And stared at me.

Tiny hairs all over my body started to rise. The old me would've looked away and wondered how quickly I could get away from Grayson. I wasn't her anymore. I met his stare. If we were going to have an epic stare down, I was in it to win it.

"Do you need something?" I asked, my voice so sweet it dripped diabetes.

Smiling around the stick of the Blow Pop, he crossed his arms over his chest. "Just waiting for an update."

"And you can't wait somewhere else?" I asked.

He lifted a shoulder. "Here seems like as good as any other place. If that's okay with you?" He paused. "*Nadia?*"

I had no reaction to him using my real name, not even a flinch, and my brain didn't take a trip down missing memory lane. "There's plenty of seating." Easing my death grip on the quilt, I made a broad, sweeping gesture toward the other furniture. "Help yourself."

"I'm fine standing. Thanks." A muscle ticked along his jaw.

Knowing he was annoyed I didn't rise to his bait, I smiled. I might've even batted my eyelashes.

"The couch is so much more comfortable," I pressed, refusing to look away. "I imagine the chair is, too. Better than standing and holding up the carport."

"Better stay where I am," he replied. "Wouldn't want it to collapse on your head."

"Let's be honest here." I leaned back, kicking my legs up on the cushion next to me. "You'd love to see it fall on my head."

His head tilted slightly, the stick moving in a slow circle. "You have no idea what I'd love."

His vague comments almost always came off sounding either like a thinly veiled threat or something someone who was seeking attention would post on Facebook. They'd normally leave me sputtering, but I was too tired and worried about Kat to pay it any mind. "You're right. I wouldn't."

"There isn't much you *do* know, is there?" he challenged. "No memory of who you really are. No idea of what you've become. You hadn't even tried to use the Source until today, and you don't have a single clue on how to prevent yourself from going apeshit and—"

"Killing a bunch of innocent people? True story," I cut him off. "I'm sure there's a lot more I don't know. We can write them down if you have a piece of paper and pen? Make a list, and then when I figure things out, we can check them off."

The white stick stopped moving as his lips thinned.

"Together," I added.

Grayson broke eye contact then, his jaw clenching so hard I was surprised the stick didn't snap in two.

Snark point explosion to Evie!

I wanted to jump off the couch, run around the yard, and shout my triumph. Ha! I won. I actually won the stare down, and he could go kiss my—

"This has been going on too long," he stated, bringing my gloat fest to a sharp standstill.

"What has?" I was half-afraid to ask.

"The labor." His gaze flicked to the door behind me. "That's an Origin in there trying to be born. Usually, the labor is fast and hard." His eyes were more like midnight pools as his gaze returned to mine. "And before you ask, no, I'm not an expert, but I know enough and definitely more than you."

The last part didn't irritate me whatsoever, and it had nothing to do with me being tired and hungry. God, I was hungry again. "You think something bad is happening."

"I think there is a damn good reason why Luc has been in there this whole time." His attention drifted back to the closed door. "Many don't survive the birth of an Origin."

Anxiety flooded me. "But Kat's a hybrid, and Daemon can heal—"

"Sometimes those two things are simply not enough."

I started to argue that they had to be enough, but . . .

Oh God.

Just like sometimes all the medical advancement in the world wasn't enough.

Curling an arm across my stomach, I glanced back at the door. That's when it occurred to me. My head snapped back to Grayson. "If Kat dies . . ."

"So would Daemon," he confirmed what I didn't want to even think. "Their life forces are irrevocably tied. One dies, so does the other. If the child survives, it would be an orphan."

I opened my mouth, but I had no idea what to say, and then, as a knot of emotion swelled in my throat, I realized there was nothing I could say. There were no words for situations like these. I sank into the couch, my gaze dropping to my hands. "Is that what happened to Luc's parents?" I asked, thinking that perhaps Grayson knew. Luc had told me that he was pretty sure his parents were both dead, but that was before I knew I was Nadia, and at that point, he was only telling me half-truths.

"Possible," Grayson answered after several long heartbeats. "Either that or after the Daedalus got what they wanted, his parents were no longer of value."

"That's horrible," I whispered the obvious.

"His parents may not have even known each other. They could've been nothing like Kat and Daemon," he stated in such a matter-of-fact way my entire body jolted. "He could've been the product of a forced mutation and conception. Most Origins were."

"That doesn't make it any less horrible."

"No." He still stared at that door. "It makes it even more horrible."

Yes. Yes, it did.

Over the next couple of minutes, I thought about how Luc had threatened both Daemon and Dawson more than once. "They were empty threats."

"What are you talking about?"

"Luc threatening Daemon and Dawson," I explained. "He said once he didn't want to leave Beth a widow, but he knows how it works—"

"How empty his threats are depend on how angry Luc was when he made said threat, but if I were you, I wouldn't assume any of his threats are empty."

"He wouldn't take out—"

"Luc is capable of anything," Grayson interrupted as my gaze lifted to his. "Perhaps that's something else you've forgotten."

I didn't care what Grayson insinuated; Luc was not capable of killing Daemon, knowing it would've ended both Kat and the baby's life. Same for Dawson and Bethany.

Silence descended between us as we were both succumbed to our own thoughts. My earlier mantra—*Kat and the baby will be okay*—no longer was repeated with confidence. Humans died every second, and just because Luxen and all those who carried their DNA fought death and often won, that didn't make them immortal. As Grayson had said, sometimes it was simply not enough.

And Luc's parents? God, I didn't even want to think about it. Had they loved each other? Had they even known each other's names? Luc had to think about that, and if I was feeling it as hard as I was, I couldn't even imagine—

"I miss Kent." Grayson said those three words so quietly I wasn't even sure I actually heard them. "He would've said something so stupid right now. Something incredibly off the wall. It wouldn't even make sense, but . . ."

Sort of stunned by his soft admission, I watched his impressively stoic face, absent from the usual smirk or curl of distaste, crack just a little. It was a small fissure, barely noticeable, but I saw it. The break was in his eyes, in the brief moment when he closed them and his skin tightened. *There.* There was the touch of humanity I'd only witnessed twice before, when Kent had died and, bizarrely, when he'd discovered I was really Nadia.

If Grayson were James or Zoe or a rabid kangaroo, I would've gotten up and hugged him. But he was Grayson, and if I did that, I had a feeling he wouldn't appreciate it, and I'd regret it.

That didn't mean I couldn't sympathize from a safe distance.

"He would've made you laugh. He would've made me laugh," I finished, throat thick. "I know I didn't know him long, but I miss him, too."

Jaw working, Grayson gave a curt nod. "Kent was the first human I met."

"You've known him since you were a child?"

Luc had explained some of the Luxen who'd been here before the invasion lived in communities, kind of like neighborhoods, and rarely, if ever, associated with the outside, human world. The general public probably thought those "strange" communities were just run-of-the-mill cults or something.

We had an amazing ability to find logical answers for the illogical.

Wait.

I couldn't quite include myself in that whole *we* part of mankind now.

Grayson's gaze coasted back to mine, stare eerily intense. "I met Kent when I was sixteen."

Mentally repeating what he'd said, I put two and two together, adding in that look he was giving me, and ending up with *holy evil Luxen,* Grayson was one of the invading—

Ghost fingers danced over the nape of my neck, the sensation startling me enough that I reached back and smacked my hand down on my skin. Nothing but flesh greeted me. I looked over my shoulder.

The door opened, and all thoughts of what Grayson could've possibly admitted slipped aside. Daemon's brother came out, and even though half of his face was in shadows, there was no mistaking the tension lining Dawson's features.

Every muscle in my body tightened, my lips and tongue unable to form the words I wanted to ask.

Luckily—and God, I would never admit this—Grayson was there and had absolutely no filter whatsoever. "Are they still alive?"

I shot Grayson a wide-eyed look.

Okay, maybe I wasn't *that* grateful for his lack of tact.

Dawson must've been used to the other Luxen, because all he did was nod and say, "For now."

That wasn't exactly the best of responses, but it wasn't the worst.

"Daemon is watching out for Kat, and Luc is there for the baby. I need to check on Ash. Zouhour is watching her," he explained. I had no idea who that was. "She normally wakes up around this time wanting a glass of water and . . ."

Wanting her daddy.

He started past the carport and then stopped. "Beth's labor wasn't easy, either." His voice was full of gravel, the kind that could hurt. "She's in there with Kat. I think it's helping, you know, seeing Beth? It's a reminder that someone else went through the same as what she's doing now and came out on the other side."

I didn't know if that helped or not, but I nodded and then realized Dawson couldn't see it with his back to me. "I think so."

"Yeah." His voice was barely above a whisper, his hands clenched at his sides, and I knew he had to be beside himself with fear for his brother and for Kat. "I'll be back."

Leaning against the back of the couch, I watched him disappear into the night. All of them had been through so much. It would be too unfair, too cruel to take Kat and Daemon or the baby. "What do you think he meant by Luc is there for the baby?"

"Luc's probably keeping the baby from going into distress while Daemon does the same for Kat."

"He can do that with the Source—for a *baby*?" A baby that was still inside its mama?

"Luc can do almost anything with the Source," Grayson answered, and I was awed by that. "Evie."

Still staring at where Dawson disappeared to, I wondered why I hadn't heard another labor-induced scream. "What?"

"Why are you rubbing your neck?"

I was? I frowned. Yep. I still was even though the odd feeling had faded shortly after Dawson appeared. Surprised that he noticed that and unsure of how to answer, I faced him. "I don't know. Why?"

His eyes were narrowed as he watched me. "If you're anything remotely like an Origin or a hybrid, you didn't get a cramp in the neck."

"Uh . . ." I drew the word out. "No. I didn't."

The stick jutting out from his lips had stilled again. "Did you feel something there?"

Curling my hands inward, I shrugged.

"How do you not know?" He took a step toward me.

Wariness returned, seeping into me. "Why do you care?"

"You know Luxen can sense other Luxen, right?" he said. "Hybrids always know where the one who mutated them is. Origins sense both and feel when an Arum nears. The proximity of when they feel the other varies from Luxen to Luxen, Origin to Origin, hybrid to hybrid. But when an Origin or hybrid feels the presence of a Luxen, they say it's like the touch of invisible fingers along their neck or between their shoulders."

I was tracking what he was saying, but I suddenly felt weird. Not ghost-fingers or cobwebs-on-the-neck weird, but as if my body were moving even though I was sure I wasn't.

Was the couch moving?

"It would make sense," Grayson was saying as I placed my hands on the couch. Nope. It felt like it was steady. "You felt it right before I walked into the carport, didn't you? I saw you wiggle your shoulders like something was crawling on you, and just now, you looked right at that door the same time I felt Dawson drawing near."

"Wait." That caught my attention, and I asked the least important question possible. "You were watching me?"

"I'm always watching." He stated that WTF bomb like he'd only just admitted to liking tea in the afternoon.

"Okay. That is the creepiest—"

A sudden whoosh went through as the entire carport seemed to spin around me.

I stumbled to my feet, pressing my hand to the side of my head. For a second, it was as if I were tilting to the far right, but I was standing straight. I closed my eyes. Wrong move. Horrible, terrible, bad-idea level of wrong move. The entire world seemed to rock.

Grayson was suddenly next to me. "You okay?"

Was I? My heart pounded against my ribs. Swallowing, I took a shallow breath as I stared . . . at Grayson's jeans? I was bent at the waist. When did that happen?

"I'm fine." I blinked, the dizziness gone as quickly as it had hit. At least I thought it was. I straightened, my gaze falling to where Grayson's hand lay on my shoulder.

Grayson was touching me.

He never touched me.

Well, there was the one time when Luc was shot and my skull had done an up-close-and-personal meet and greet with the roof of an SUV. Grayson had healed me and Luc, which meant he probably had to touch me then to do it. But despite what Luc claimed, I was confident he'd threatened Grayson with grave bodily harm to get him to heal me.

Grayson saw what I was staring at and jerked his hand back as if it were on fire. This close, his eyes were like the sky before a storm. "Are you messing with me?"

I took a step back. I couldn't believe he even thought to ask that. "Oh yeah. You know, I thought there wasn't enough going on, so I thought maybe I should pretend to be sick."

His lip curled. "Wouldn't surprise me."

Ignoring the comment and wondering how I could've ever thought Grayson had a bit of humanity in him, I snatched the quilt off the cement.

"After all, you're not the center of attention right now." Grayson's voice was as poisonous as a viper. "Are you that needy that you have to fake—"

"You are so lucky that stupid Blow Pop is no longer sticking out of your mouth, because I would seriously shove it down your throat."

Grayson laughed as his lips curled in a mockery of a smile. "Should I be worried now?" he asked, calling back to what Luc had said when we were training. "Or was that a fluke earlier? If I recall correctly, it only took a hundred tries to get you to move the carton."

It had not taken a hundred tries. More like a couple of dozen.

"Whatever." His features hardened to stone. "Other than stand there and get other people killed, there's not much you can do when it really counts, is there?"

Sucking in a sharp breath, I took another step away from him, his words a knife to the chest. I stared at him.

"Shit," Grayson muttered, looking away. "I didn't mean—"

"Yeah, you did." I tossed the quilt on the couch. Turning from him, I started walking. I didn't know where I was going. Maybe to the house. Maybe I'd just keep walking. All that mattered was that I got away from Grayson, because there was a good chance that if I stayed there, he would need to be worried.

Because I felt even weirder.

Wrong.

Jittery, like my blood and skin were buzzing. Pins and needles erupted in my toes and traveled rapidly up my legs. This was more than before, and it was the Source. I could feel it throbbing in the center of my chest. A fine sheen of sweat dotted my brow.

Grayson was suddenly in front of me. "Evie . . ."

"Move," I muttered, or at least I thought I did.

The air shifted—no, the temperature of my body did. Fire flashed over me, and yet I was cold, freezing, and my eyes . . .

Something was wrong with them.

Grayson looked as if he were surrounded by a freaking *rainbow.* A prism of colors surrounded his entire body for a few seconds before he returned to normal, lit by the glow of solar lights.

And yeah, that was not right at all.

My steps were jerky, shaky as I blindly swept an arm to brush the canopy, and the material parted as if a hurricane-force wind had caught it.

I couldn't tell if I had even touched it, because my skin was . . . I couldn't feel my skin.

Heart thundering and pulse skyrocketing, I inhaled, but it was like breathing through a clogged straw. Pressing my hand to my chest, I felt my heart thumping too fast, way too fast. Maybe this wasn't the Source. Maybe this was a panic attack. I'd never had one before, but Heidi used to get them when she was younger, before I knew her. She described them once to me, and it sounded a lot like this—like all my internal wiring just shorted out and my entire body was out of control.

I made it to the middle of the dark driveway when it hit.

Stunning, sweeping dizziness exploded, and it rolled through my body in a powerful wave that pulled me down, pulled me under.

I didn't feel the hard impact with the ground. I didn't feel or see anything, but I heard Grayson calling out to me. I couldn't answer. Not when Luc's voice replaced his. Not even when I heard Luc beg for me to open my eyes.

I was gone.

14

E*vie.* I heard my name called in different voices and at different times. I thought I recognized some, and Luc's voice was the one I heard the most. Sometimes it was just him saying my name, and then other times he was speaking to me, having a one-sided conversation.

"Zoe is worried about you, Peaches. Everyone is, even Grayson."

Grayson? That sounded like a lie, but why would anyone be worried? My head was too thick with sleep to figure it out, and I was just tired and needed to sleep. There was nothing to be upset about.

"You've got to wake up, Evie." Luc's voice was a silky, warm whisper in the soothing darkness. "Open those beautiful eyes of yours for me. Please."

I wanted to do as he asked, because Luc wasn't one to beg for anything or anyone, but I wasn't ready, and dreams were beckoning me.

And I dreamed I was home.

I walked through the quiet living room that smelled of crisp apples and pumpkin spice, drawn to the kitchen.

With her back to me, she sat at the kitchen island, her blond hair smoothed back into a neat ponytail and her white blouse impossibly wrinkle-free.

She.

Sylvia Dasher.

Luxen.

Creator.

Betrayer.

Mom.

I'd come to a complete stop, unable to move as I stared at her, heart racing as a mix of emotions exploded within me. Anger was there, like a poison. So was confusion, because I knew I was dreaming, but this felt like a memory, and underneath those messy, explosive emotions was also happiness. Despite everything I knew and everything this woman had done and lied about, I was happy to see her. Relieved.

She sipped from a mug as she flipped the pages of a book I could not see, and I realized that I now smelled rich coffee and more.

Coffee. Apples. Pumpkin spice.

Home.

Willing my legs to move, I took another step and then stopped. Something about the dining room table caught my eye. A flower sat in the center, white lilies in a clear vase, flanked by two tapered candles in iron holders. There'd never been flowers there before. I'd remember that, because Mom wasn't a flower person. She'd once said she didn't like to watch something beautiful die.

My gaze flicked up to the wall. An unfamiliar painting hung there. A mountainous landscape in black and white. Slowly, I refocused on her. I was almost afraid if I spoke, she'd vanish, return to wherever the dead went.

I took a step forward and then stopped once more. There was a small, roughly round spot where something had stained the hardwood floor. It had been scrubbed clean, but not soon enough.

"Don't worry about the floor. It will be replaced soon, and it'll be like none of that ever happened."

Jerking my head up, I held my breath.

Mom inclined her chin slightly to the right. "I was waiting for you to join me."

I squeezed my eyes shut as tears rushed them. That was her voice. Warm. Calm. Each word spoken as if she'd put thought behind it. Nothing like she'd sounded the last time I'd heard her.

The woman was a liar, and God only knew if anything she ever said was the truth, but she was my mother.

"Come sit with me," she said. *"It's time."*

Drawing in a ragged breath, I asked, "Time for what?"

She patted the stool next to her with a pale hand. "I'm not going to hurt you. I promise."

Cool air stirred as a body brushed against mine, silencing me before I could respond. Startled, I turned and felt the floor drop out from under my feet.

A girl with blond hair slowly inched forward, as if each step required effort. Her hair fell to a waist so narrow I was confident two hands could span it. She was slim, too slim. The plain black shirt hung from shoulders and arms that were so frail and so thin, they looked like they could be broken with a snap of the wrist. Legs that were absent of fat or muscle appeared as if they were barely holding her up. This wasn't someone who was just naturally thin with a hyper metabolism. This was someone who was sick.

Someone who was dying.

And it was me—when I was younger, when I went by the name Nadia.

Eyes wide, I watched her sit on the stool, arms folded at the waist, shoulders bunched, but she met Mom's stare with no fear.

Confusion flooded me as I stared at Mom and the younger version of me. Was this a dream or a memory?

"He promised not to hurt Luc, but he tried anyway," she stated, *incredibly pale jaw hard.*

"Why would I trust you?"

"Because I kept my promise," Mom replied.

The dying version of me laughed—laughed right in her face, and I think I developed a girl crush on me, which was as weird as it sounded. *"None of you tell the truth."*

"And who do you think tells nothing but lies?"

"The Daedalus. You're not saving my life because you have a soft spot for sick girls. You want to control him, and I'm a way to do it."

"And Luc still brought you here. He still left you here."

"That's because he's an idiot."

I blinked.

Mom laughed, though, the sound painfully familiar. "No, it's because he loves you even if he doesn't yet know what that means. He's willing to do anything to give you a second chance at life."

"Like I said, he's an idiot." Her chin lifted. "And there's nothing you can say or do that will make me trust you."

That was me.

The boldness in her words and in her gaze drew a smile to my lips. She was fearless.

I had been fearless.

Empowered by who I used to be, I walked toward the end of the island, my gaze falling on Mom first. She was looking at Nadia, but that was her profile, her face, the faint lines marking the skin at the outer corners of her eyes the only sign of her age.

Sylvia Dasher was beautiful in a crisp sort of way. Straight, chin-length hair the color of champagne. High, angular features and pale skin devoid of makeup. I could count on one hand the amount of times I'd seen her wear mascara and lipstick. This was definitely Sylvia.

Then I looked at Nadia, really seeing myself for the first time. I saw my features in the shape of her face. She was so pale, though, the freckles standing out starkly, and the shadows under her eyes were like bruises. Her eyes were puffy as if she been crying recently, and I thought I knew why. Luc had just left her here. Left me here. My chest squeezed tight. Weariness clung to her mouth, and her lips held a slight, bluish tinge to them. Each breath she took was labored, as if it took everything in her to get her lungs to inflate.

How much longer would I have lived if Luc hadn't brought me here? Definitely not months or even weeks. Maybe only days. That was how close I'd come to dying.

"You will," Mom said after a long moment, and she almost sounded sad, resigned. She tapped her finger on the book. "Look at this."

Brows furrowing, I did as she asked, and so did Nadia, her expression doing the same as mine. It wasn't a book that rested on the island. It was a photo album, and Mom's finger lay on the picture of a small blond girl sitting behind a birthday cake. A candle proudly proclaimed the number eight. She beamed at the camera, her smile so happy and big.

It was the picture of Evelyn Dasher.

The real one.

"You look so much like her," Mom said. "You could've been sisters."

Nadia leaned in just a little, her eyes widening as she stared down at the photo. "That's . . . disturbing."

Yes. Yes, it was.

Slowly, Nadia lifted her gaze and drew back, putting as much space between herself and Mom as she could.

Good to know the old version of me was just as wigged out as I had been when I'd found the photo album.

"The first time I saw you, I couldn't look at you. It was too hard when all I saw was my Evie." Sylvia mashed her lips together and then slowly loosened her jaw. "She died in a car accident. Three years ago."

Nadia stared at the photo.

"She may not have been my daughter by blood, but I was her mother in every way that mattered." Her shoulders tightened, and then she turned the page. "Your resemblance is uncanny. I knew that was why he'd chosen you."

Why he'd chosen you . . .

Nadia lifted her gaze, watching her for several seconds before asking, "When was the first time you saw me?"

I held my breath.

"A very long time ago," she answered.

I exhaled harshly, wondering if it was possible to hyperventilate in a dream, if this was even a dream. If Mom had seen me long before I came to them with Luc, then that—

"This was a setup from the beginning," Nadia accused, tiny beads of sweat dotting her forehead. "How? How did you—"

"There is very little the Daedalus cannot do, Nadia. Luc knows that better than anyone else." Mom smoothed a hand over an imaginary strand of hair out of place, a habit that caused my heart to squeeze. *"Do you remember how you found Luc?"*

Nadia's pale lips pressed tight as she stared mutinously at Sylvia.

"You told Luc you ran away from your father when he was passed out one night," she said, staring at Nadia. "Why did you lie?"

Surprise gripped me as I saw the same emotion dance across Nadia's flushed cheeks.

"*Your father was very good at hiding who he was,*" Mom stated. "*Alan was once a soldier with the kind of medals only bravery could earn.*"

She knew my father—my real one? And he had a name. My real father had a name. Alan.

"*He went to war overseas with Jason, fought side by side with him. Jason considered him a friend, but he didn't know who Alan really was. I don't think many knew what kind of monster was under the mask he wore when your mother was still alive.*"

I felt like I needed to sit down.

"*Why didn't you tell Luc the truth?*" she asked. "*Once you learned what he was and what he is capable of, you knew he could at any time reach into your mind and take those secrets.*"

Nadia was quiet for so long. "*I didn't think about it around him.*" Her voice was barely above a whisper. "*I don't think about it.*"

"*Of course not.*" Sympathy softened Mom's tone, and, like a fool, I wanted to believe it was genuine. "*You were protecting yourself against a monster.*"

"*I know what he was,*" Nadia snapped, her slim chest rising and falling rapidly. "*I know what he wanted. He was going to sell me to—*"

"*If we had known what your father was doing, we would've stepped in sooner. We wouldn't have—*"

"*Tried to buy me from him like I was a piece of meat?*" Tears clouded Nadia's eyes. "*Because it was him that I saw talking to Dad outside? It was Jason Dasher who came to the house that night? I couldn't hear his voice or really see him, but it was him, wasn't it?*"

Sylvia nodded.

"*Dad . . . he told me that he was going to sell me to him. That I'd finally be worth—*" She sucked in a deep breath. "*He'd said that it was our last night and I knew he wouldn't stop this time.*"

Oh God.

A knot of nausea lodged in my throat.

"*I couldn't stand it. I just couldn't.*" Her little hands balled into trembling fists. "*When he grabbed me, I don't even know when I picked up the knife.*"

Nadia closed her eyes. "I don't remember even . . . putting it in him. There was just so much blood and I ran. That part wasn't a lie."

Holy crap.

Nadia killed her father.

I killed my father.

"He deserved far worse than that," Mom replied. "Soon enough, you won't have to worry about those thoughts ever intruding on you again."

Nadia looked at her then, her brown eyes slightly unfocused but still filled with so much steely will and sharp intelligence. She was no one's fool.

"The kid I ran into two days later, by the park with all the ducks?" Nadia's voice roughened. "He was the one who told me about Paris and the club Harbinger—said that Paris had a soft spot for street kids. That I could get something to eat there. That kid . . . that was no accident, was it?"

"No, it wasn't." Sylvia smiled briefly. "We needed you to meet Luc. Paris isn't the only one who has a soft heart when it comes to broken things."

A strangled laugh wheezed out of Nadia. "What is the Daedalus? A psychotic Match.com? What would you have done if Luc had kicked me out? He hated me at first. Told me I smelled and looked like a Garbage Pail Kid."

Sounded like something Luc would say.

"We would've found another, but that's irrelevant, because he didn't. He took you in and made you his."

They would've found another, confirming what I'd already suspected. They would've kept putting people in Luc's path, little time bombs waiting to be exploited.

The pink in her once pale cheeks deepened. "I guess you all just—" A rattling cough shook her entire body. "I guess you all just got lucky with the whole cancer thing."

Sylvia turned back to the photo album, her fingers trailing over the photo of Evie. "There is no such thing as luck, Nadia."

My lips parted. No. There was no way she could mean what I thought she did. The Daedalus couldn't give people cancer.

But they could take alien DNA and meld it with humans'. They could create entire species and use technology the public had no idea even existed. They were capable of anything.

"Evie, I need you to wake up."

The weird dream rippled without warning, the gray countertops and white cabinets fading until everything went black. It lasted seconds, maybe minutes. There was no concept of time, and then everything came back into focus.

"Why are you telling me this?" Nadia asked, wincing as she shifted on the stool. "Because the serum doesn't work and I'm going to die anyway? If that happens, Luc will find out. He will kill you."

"The serum worked, Nadia, and that's why. You're going to get very sick, very soon. You already are starting to feel the effects. I can see the fever in your skin. I bet your joints are beginning to ache."

Nadia shuddered.

"The fever will get worse, and it will feel like you're dying. I'm going to make sure that doesn't happen." Mom closed the photo album. "And then a new life begins."

A dawning sense of horror crept into Nadia's watery eyes. "You're going to mutate me."

Mom didn't respond.

Another tremor coursed through Nadia's body, and then she was scrambling back from the island, turning as if to run, but she only made it a foot before she doubled over, her knees giving out.

Out of reflex, I moved, but Mom reacted with Luxen speed, catching Nadia before she could hit the floor. Scooping Nadia's hair out of her face, she carefully placed her on her knees. And it was in the nick of time, too.

Nadia's entire body spasmed violently, and then she threw up blackish-blue bile that shimmered. I knew what that signified. She was mutating.

I was mutating.

"What have you—?" Nadia heaved again, tears streaming down her face. Black stained her lips. "What have you done to me?"

"Saved your life," Mom whispered, kneeling beside Nadia. She reached for her, but Nadia shrank away from the touch. "You will never get sick again, Nadia. You will be better, and then they will make you stronger."

Nadia stared down at her hands, her body trembling as the veins under her skin became inky.

"The reason why I told you all of this?" Mom asked. "Because eventually you won't remember any of this. You won't remember ever being here as Nadia. You won't even remember Luc."

Nadia lifted her head. "No."

Sylvia nodded. "I'm sorry."

"No!" she cried. "You can't do that. You can't take my memories. I won't forget him."

Sylvia said nothing as my heart cracked in my chest. She would forget him. I would forget all of him and all of this.

"I won't forget him." Nadia's head jerked as her back bowed, the angle unnatural. "I won't forget him. I won't—"

She screamed as her arms twisted, her body bending as if all the bones had turned to liquid. Her head snapped to the side, and I gasped.

Nadia looked straight at where I stood, black seeping across the whites of her eyes like an oil spill. "Don't forget."

The abyss came for me and held me tight in its grasp until a new voice, one I was unfamiliar with, tugged me from the recesses of sleep. Drawn into a semiconscious state, I wasn't sure if I was still dreaming or not.

The woman spoke softly, so I heard only bits of what she said, and it didn't make a lot of sense. "It's the same as it was last night. Her vitals are, well, they're perfect. Like an athlete in her prime." Her voice faded out only to return in the same quiet, calm tone. "All I can say is that she's sleeping."

"There is no way she's just sleeping."

Luc.

That was definitely Luc, and there was a heavy thread of concern along with a razor-sharp edge of anger. I wanted to tell him it was okay, because it was, but my bones felt like they were weighted with lead.

"I know, but there's no physical reason that I can determine that explains why she won't . . ." The woman's voice faded as I slipped back into a deeper sleep and stranger dreams.

Flashes of images that formed with crystal clarity before fading and disappearing from my memories. Others that lingered and became shadows in my mind.

And I found myself standing in a city of steel that held centuries of memories and millions of voices but was now quiet. Before me, a sea of yellow cabs and black cars sat unoccupied, doors closed and engines turned off. Storefronts and hotels were silent and empty of light. Tiny hairs all over my body were standing, electrified by the currents of power in the air—in the currents of power snapping over my knuckles, light outlined in shadows.

My gaze fell to the cracked and broken asphalt. Pools of ruby liquid seeped through the fissures, humming with rage and power. Above and all around me, the city trembled. Buildings that were as tall as mountains shattered into themselves. Cement and brick crumbled into ash that glimmered like fireflies. Buildings collapsed in screams that tasted of metal. Fire the color of night blanketed a sky that could no longer hold the sun.

Coldness seeped into world.

The power radiating from me was icy heat.

"Open your eyes and talk to me."

His voice punched through the dreams, tearing a pinprick-size hole in the rippling black flames, and brilliant diamond light appeared like a star in a far-off galaxy. Time passed, and then his voice spread that tiny hole. Light grew.

"If you were letters on a page, you'd be fine print." Luc's voice clashed with the dreams of cities falling, and the white light spread.

His voice was closer. "You're going to love this one. My doctor says I'm lacking vitamin U."

The hole widened, and I felt the warm touch of his fingers against my cheek, the strong curve of his arm around my waist as, farther in the city, billboards evaporated and giant screens cracked before turning to shimmering dust. Cathedrals decayed rapidly, caving into themselves. The world fell apart around me until nothing remained but the gaping hole of crackling, stunning light and the warm, hard feel of Luc's body pressed to mine.

We stayed that way for a while, caught between the nothing of sleep and the life that existed beyond it.

"It's time."

Turning toward the voice, I saw myself standing there, wearing a shirt that was too big. A black shirt that featured a UFO sucking up a *T. rex*. It had to be a shirt straight from Luc's closet. Wind lifted the strands of blond hair in the mirror image of me, but where I stood, the air was stagnant.

"Time for what?" I asked once more.

Ink bloomed under her eyes like shadows, and her eyes were the darkest night lit by lightning, and it was the same under her skin, the network of veins a kaleidoscope of darkness and moonlight.

She was power.

She bled death.

"It's time to end this." She lifted a hand and pointed to the ground—to a grassy knoll that had not been there before, to the boy who stood there, a bronze-haired god of enormous power.

"Luc?" I whispered.

Slowly, he turned to me—to us. All of his body, his veins were lit from within. The light poured into the air around him, crackling and spitting with the power of the Source. His pupils were the sharpest diamonds, brilliant and cold, and he didn't look at me but to the version of me who was not his equal—something deadlier and far more powerful.

"*Never,*" he vowed.

That one word was a punch to the chest, and I fell apart. Shattering and breaking into a million tiny pieces that scattered until I became a part of the dead city and the glimmering ashes falling to the ruined ground.

And then I was nothing.

No memories. No sight. No sound. No sense of being, and I slipped further away into the nothing, to where dreams that felt like memories and nightmares of destroyed cities couldn't reach me. I stayed for an eternity.

Then I heard Luc's voice again, and I heard him call to me with one word.

Nadia.

15

Slowly, I became conscious of the body beside me, noticing first the weight of an arm curled around my waist, then the tangle of legs and finally the thigh tucked between mine. Only a few seconds later, I became aware of the solid chest pressed to mine and the soft, steady breath against the top of my head.

Then I felt, against my lips, warm skin.

My heart skipped a beat and then sped up in recognition. My soul *knew* the feel and weight of him, the taste and scent of his skin, because it always knew even when I didn't.

Luc.

He was holding me like I was the most cherished treasure in the universe.

I focused on each breath he took until my body seemed to naturally meet his, falling into a rhythm. His were deep and steady, but he wasn't asleep. I knew this, because his hand moved along the center of my back, tracking up and down my spine. Each pass of his hand caused the skin along my back to hum in a pleasantly distracting way.

Drawing in a shallow breath, I took a deeper, longer one and willed my eyes to open.

Nothing happened.

I had no idea why, but I tried again with the same result. Thinking I could move another part of my body, I tested out my hands. Turned out my arms were folded against a hard stomach, so that was no go.

Should I be concerned that moving was proving to be so difficult? Probably. But other than my muscles not responding to the commands my brain was sending, I felt okay. Granted, that was a pretty big deal. Maybe I needed to start with something small.

My toes.

And holy hallelujah, I *could* wiggle them!

Approximately five seconds later, I *almost* regretted my achievement.

Pins and needles swept up my legs in a quick succession. I wanted to stop moving my toes, but I pushed through it. The rush of sensation cooled mere seconds later. Feeling confident about the progress, I flexed my foot.

Luc's hand stopped, bunching my shirt under his grip, and his breath stilled against the top of my head. "Evie?" The way he said my name—it was full of restrained hope but sounded like it came from the other side of the room.

Were my ears still asleep?

Okay, that sounded next-level idiotic.

I managed to move my lips, mouthing his name against the skin of his throat.

Luc shifted, drawing back until an opening formed between our chests and cool air glided into the space. "Evie?" A moment later, I felt his hand leave my back to come to rest against my cheek. "Have you come back to me?"

Come back from where? I'd been sleeping and dreaming some weird dreams—dreams that felt like memories—but now I was worried. It wasn't just the fact my eyes felt glued shut and my limbs useless, but now I remembered hearing his voice while I slept. He'd been concerned then, and now? He sounded *desperate*.

And Luc never sounded desperate.

I needed to wake up and figure out what the hell was going on. I hated how Luc sounded. I needed to do more than flex my stupid foot.

Luc was incredibly still for several moments, and then he shuddered. "It's okay." His thumb dragged over the line of my jaw, the caress a brand on my skin. "I'm here waiting for you, but, Peaches, please don't take too much longer. I miss you."

Pressure clamped down on my chest as I thought, *I miss you, too.*

His hand jerked against my cheek, and I felt him move again as if he were half sitting up. "Evie?"

Trying and failing again to respond, I was starting to drown in frustration. Why was everything so hard?

"God," he said in a rough exhale. "I want to hear your voice so badly that I'm imagining it in my head. I'm losing my mind."

I wanted him to know I was okay. Well, sort of okay. This whole not-waking-up thing probably spelled trouble, but I was fine. I'd just been sleeping—

Wait.

Memories were slow to form. I didn't just fall asleep. I'd been with Grayson while waiting to hear about Kat and her—oh my God, did Kat have her baby? Was she all right? Okay. I needed to be able to wake up to find out the answer to that, so baby steps. I'd felt dizzy, and I'd seen weird rainbows around Grayson, and then I didn't remember anything else. Obviously, I'd passed out. Since I wasn't exactly human, I didn't think I could get migraines or seizures.

Something happened.

So maybe I was a little comatose? Holy shit, did I have that locked-in disease I'd seen in a Netflix documentary? Oh my God, what if—

"What if you wake up and you've forgotten yourself all over again?" His words were just a murmur, but they knocked me out of my panicky downward spiral. "What if you've forgotten me again? That's all I keep thinking about. That all of this? All the crazy, all the unknown, and all the terrible things that have gone down? That it was still too damn good to be true, because we knew each other. We had each other," he continued in a whisper, breaking my heart in ways I didn't even know were possible. "We were *finally* together."

Emotion welled in my chest. The back of my eyes burned as he pulled my heart all over the place, twisting it into mushy knots.

"But even if you wake up and you don't know who you are and you don't know who I am, it'll be okay. I'll be here, and I'll help you remember." His lips brushed my forehead. "I've got enough love for you that I'm overflowing with it. It'll be more than enough if you wake up and see me as a stranger." Luc's next breath sounded as ragged as my heart felt. "No matter how you come back to me, as Evie or as Nadia or someone else, I'll still love you like I do now, like I did yesterday and the day before, and that'll be enough."

I'll still love you.

Even though there wasn't a single doubt in my mind that Luc loved me, the shock of hearing him say it was like touching a live wire. His actions from the first time I'd met him as Evie screamed those words even if he'd never spoken them, and actions carried so much more weight than pretty words.

Within a few heartbeats, his words were tattooed on my skin, flowed through my veins, and etched into my bones. They'd forever be there, no matter what, that I was sure of.

A tiny, nameless muscle twitched along my pointer finger. It was such a minuscule movement that it went unnoticed by Luc, but that frustration in me became a fire that forged steely determination. I pushed past the heavy fatigue.

"It's okay," he repeated, his voice weary and gruff with exhaustion as he settled back beside me. "It'll be okay."

But it wasn't.

Not when he sounded like this. I wanted to make him better. I wanted to remove the weariness and concern in his voice and his thoughts. I wanted him to stop hurting and for him to laugh and to feel the tension seep from his muscles. I wanted him to tell me more stupid pickup lines. And I wanted to see how his lips moved when he said he loved me.

A lot had been taken from us. Memories, people we cared about, and actual years' worth of time, and I'd be damned if we lost any more seconds or minutes. Luc would do anything for me—he'd done just about anything for me, and the least I could do was open my eyes and speak, dammit.

The burst of anger was fuel for my determination, and when I took my next breath, it was stronger, deeper.

I opened my eyes.

And found that I was face-to-face with Luc.

Everything in me seized as I stared at him, not seeing his features at first. Instead, I saw a strange display of colors, a swirling transparent whirl of white and deep violet light that seemed to dance around his face and shoulders before fading out.

Then it was as if I were seeing him for the first time, in vivid, striking clarity. The tumble of locks against his forehead was a mix of gold, red, and brown, as if each strand had been hand-painted. His brows were a strong slash, a slightly deeper brown against skin that held a warm, golden undertone. Those lashes truly were an enviable thick fringe, like I'd remembered, but under his closed eyes were shadows that hadn't been there before. My heart twisted once more, knowing that worry and fear had put those dark smudges there.

He had what Heidi called a beauty mark, a faint brown speck under the center of his bottom lip. How had I not noticed that before? Nor had I noticed how defined his Cupid's bow was until now.

I blinked slowly, and the strange array of lights didn't return, but his eyes remained closed. I knew he wasn't asleep. Not when he still cradled my cheek and his thumb traced idle circles along my cheek.

My heart started thumping heavily as I forced my lips to move again. "Luc."

His eyes flew open, and his thumb stilled at the hoarse, low sound of my voice. Deep, brilliant violet eyes locked with mine. "Evie?"

Taking a deep breath as I held his gaze, I told him what I knew he needed to hear even if I didn't fully understand it. "I'm still here."

He didn't move or speak.

Neither did I.

And then he did move. He jerked halfway up, and then his face was right in front of mine. I thought he might kiss me, but his mouth halted mere inches from mine. His hand trembled against my cheek, and several long moments passed before he said, "Peaches, I've been waiting for you."

Such simple words but so incredibly powerful. "I've . . ." I cleared my scratchy throat. "I've just been sleeping."

"Just been sleeping?" He let out a shaky laugh full of relief. "You've been *just* asleep for nearly four days."

I opened my mouth and then closed it. "Four days?"

"Yeah." His wide eyes searched mine. "Evie, you've been gone for four days."

I stared at him, unsure how to process that news. Only one thing came to mind. I hadn't brushed my teeth in four days? "Thank God you didn't just kiss me," I blurted out.

His brows climbed.

Wait. That meant I also hadn't showered in four days, and I did not have the kind of hair that looked or felt like anything other than a grease slick after that many days. His hands had been all up in that. "I must look like a mess. Smell like one, too."

Luc stared at me, and I had never seen him like that, as if he didn't know what to say.

"What?" I rasped.

"You've been unconscious for four days and you're worried about me kissing you?" He sounded utterly dumbfounded.

"But that means I haven't brushed my teeth or bathed in four days," I pointed out.

"God." He laughed again, and this time it was even realer and more relieved. "Evie. I don't know if I should yell at you or hug you."

"Hug me?" I suggested.

Luc leaned in, slipping his hand from my cheek to my back, and that hand still shook as he tightened his arm around me and pressed his forehead against mine. He was rattled, and that was big. "I don't care how you look or if you've brushed your teeth or showered. You're still the most beautiful being I've ever seen. I would kiss you right now, but as much as I want to prove that to you, I need to get the doc in here to see you."

"You always say the right things," I murmured, uncurling my fingers and pressing them against his chest.

He shook his head as he stared down at me. "No, I don't. There's a lot wrong in a lot of things I say."

I started to argue, but Luc pressed a quick kiss to my forehead. "I'm going to get the doctor."

"I feel okay," I told him, and that was the truth. "Just a little tired."

Luc blinked once and then twice. "Just in case you didn't hear me the first or second time, you've been unconscious for four days, Evie. I'm getting the doctor."

Realizing Luc wasn't going to be swayed, I quieted, and then I thought of Nate. My stomach dropped. That food wouldn't have lasted four days. "Has Nate come by?"

Luc's brow puckered. "The kid? I don't think so, but I imagined if he did and saw me or anyone else here, he probably headed in the other direction."

That would make sense. I sighed, hoping if that was the case, he'd come back.

Luc rose from the bed, and I'd never seen him so wrinkly. He'd changed since the last time I'd seen him, having switched out jeans for a pair of black cotton jogger pants and a plain shirt, but it was clear he'd spent the last four days in those clothes.

I looked down at myself, brows raising when I saw that I was in a shirt—a black shirt. Unease blossomed in the pit of my stomach as I lifted a tingling arm and pushed the thin, yellow blanket down with fingers that alternated between numb and prickly.

The shirt featured a UFO sucking up a *T. rex*.

My heart skipped a beat. "This is your shirt?"

"One of the ones I had here. Zoe changed you," he explained, reaching for a bottle of water on the nightstand. "She thought you'd be more comfortable, and it didn't feel right for me to do it."

My gaze lifted to his. How was I wearing the same shirt in a dream before I'd even seen it? Had I at some point woken long enough to have seen it and didn't remember? That was possible, I supposed. But it was still bizarre.

"Thirsty?" Luc asked, and boy, was I ever. I nodded. "Do you think you can sit up?"

I thought about that, and then I nodded once more. Sitting up wasn't nearly as hard as opening my eyes had been, so I figured that was progress in the right direction. Luc handed over the water, and with the first touch of liquid on my tongue, I started to guzzle it.

"I think it would be wise to slow down." Luc gently tugged the bottle away from my mouth. "Slow sips until we get the all clear. Okay?"

Although my throat and mouth still felt like a desert, I took a dainty sip.

"I'm going to get the doctor." He started for the door, but stopped, shoulders tensed. Watching him, I lowered the bottle to my lap. "I don't want to leave."

Pressure clamped down on my chest. "I'm here. I'm awake, and I'm okay—at least, I feel okay. I'm not going anywhere."

Slowly, he turned back to me, brows knitted. His gaze met mine, and he didn't speak. He just stared at me with those intense purple eyes until I started to squirm.

"What?"

"Nothing," he said, and a moment passed. "Are you sure you're okay?"

"Yes." I nodded for extra emphasis.

An emotion flickered across his face, widened his eyes for a fraction of a second, but it was gone before I could figure it out. "I'll be right back."

Luc made it to the door, and I'd just taken a *tiny* sip before I remembered. "Kat?" Water dripped down my chin. "Is she okay? The baby? Daemon?"

He turned back, the skin around his mouth tight. "She and the baby are fine, as is Daemon," he answered, and sweet relief swept through me. They were okay. "They're the happy parents of a healthy baby boy. They named him Adam."

16

Dr. Vivien Hemenway arrived about ten minutes after I'd convinced Luc I was okay enough to walk to the bathroom without him following me inside. The moment I saw and heard her, I knew hers was the voice I'd heard on and off while I'd slept and that she was also human.

Maybe Grayson had been right and I was beginning to sense things the way Luxen and Origins did, because I just knew she wasn't rocking any alien DNA. I felt nothing when I looked at her. No weird vibes, nor did I see any weird light shows. But if Grayson was right, why would that randomly start happening?

I didn't have an answer as I remained quiet and watched the doctor do her thing. With brown hair pulled back in a haphazard ponytail and a face that held the kind of earthy beauty that reminded me of the pictures I'd seen of women in the '60s and '70s, she had an air of calm authority surrounding her that only a doctor could muster.

Perched on the edge of the bed, she'd already taken my pulse and temperature, looked in my ears and mouth, and was currently listening to my breathing—or maybe it was my heart. I had no clue. I was just supposed to take deep breaths while Luc watched from where he stood by the bed like a silent guardian, arms crossed and hips aligned with his shoulders.

Luc looked like he was ready to go into battle.

Smiling at me while I stayed still and quiet for what felt like an eternity, she finally lowered the stethoscope and sat back. "How are you feeling?"

"Um, okay? Just a little tired, Doctor—"

"Call me Viv," she insisted. "All my friends call me that, and I think we'll be friends."

Yeah, it was weird calling a doctor by her first name. "I feel normal."

"But tired?"

"Not extremely tired, but it doesn't feel like I slept for almost four days."

She nodded. "Have you gotten up and walked around at all? And if so, were you dizzy, or did you feel weak?"

"I went to the bathroom—"

"And washed her face and brushed her teeth," Luc added.

I shot him a narrow-eyed look, wishing he'd return to being a silent guardian and not a tattletale guardian. "Yes, I did that, too."

"And she was shaking when she finally came out of the bathroom," he continued, ignoring my death glare even though what he claimed was 100 percent true. "So, I think she was feeling weak."

"I was feeling *a little* weak," I said. "And thanks, but I can answer for myself."

Luc didn't even have the decency to look properly chastised. The smile he gave me dripped charm. I needed to stop looking at him. I focused on the doctor, who was watching both of us with open amusement.

"I have never heard someone speak to Luc like that before," she said.

"I've been telling her that for a while." Luc let out a long-suffering sigh that had me rolling my eyes so far back in my head I was surprised they didn't fall out. "No one speaks to me like she does."

"As if you don't like it," I muttered.

"I do like your attitude. In fact, I love it."

Remembering what I had heard him say while I'd been waking up, I felt my dumb heart turn to mush.

"Interesting," the doc murmured. "And you really aren't experiencing any dizziness or nausea?"

I shook my head. "I feel like someone who hasn't moved in four days."

"Which would be common for anyone inactive for that long. You may still experience muscle weakness for the next couple of hours, and you'll probably still be tired, but I have good news for you both."

"You do?" My brows lifted as I leaned against the headboard.

"Your vitals are almost perfect," she said, folding up the stethoscope and slipping it into the front pocket of a black book bag. "I can see no overt signs of any type of illness."

"What do you mean by 'almost' perfect?" Luc questioned, latching onto that one word.

"Well, her temperature is a little high." She crossed one extraordinarily long, denim-clad leg over the other. "It's about 101.2, but from what I know, Luxen, hybrid, and Origin temps all run higher than human, so considering that you aren't quite human, that may not be abnormal at all."

I glanced at Luc in surprise.

"I had to tell her about the serums," Luc explained. "And what you are. I didn't want her to attempt to treat you without knowing everything."

"Doctor-client privilege is still a thing, even in Zone 3," Dr. Hemenway advised. "You can trust that what we discuss here goes no further."

"Okay."

She tucked back a stray piece of hair behind her ear. "Full disclosure. I'm no alien-human hybrid specialist. Before everything went to hell in a handbasket here, I worked in human genetics—focusing mostly on cancer and hereditary diseases, which means I've had to dust off my med school days to be of any real help around here."

"But we couldn't have gotten luckier to have someone with her background," Luc stated, and man, he couldn't be more right. "We were planning to send those serums we found at April's house to Viv."

"I'm still upset that I can't get my hands on them," she said with a sigh. "How they concocted those serums is truly fascinating."

I thought the how was a little horrifying, but whatever.

"I've been able to study the LH-11 and the Prometheus serum," she continued. "Well, to the best of my ability with the limited access to the necessary equipment and power to be able to use said equipment." Dr. Hemenway folded her hands on her bent knee. "I've been able to learn a lot from the Luxen and the others—the ones who've let me tinker around with them to satisfy my own curiosity. Y'all have some bizarre genetics going, so there is a whole hell of a lot I don't know. And on top of that, I've never seen a Luxen or Arum hybrid. Luc over here isn't the special snowflake anymore."

A slow grin tugged at my lips.

Luc pouted. "No matter what you say, I am still a snowflake, unique and pure."

Dr. Hemenway snorted. "Luc also gave me a background on your health before . . ."

When she trailed off into awkward uncertainty, I filled in the rest for her. "When I was Nadia?"

She nodded. "It's only been in the last four years that I've learned anything about how Luxen and human DNA could be blended or that these serums had the potential to cure certain cancers. To think of all the lives that could've been saved." Sadness pinched her features. "But these serums and cures didn't come without a price."

"No," Luc agreed quietly. "No, they did not."

"So." She drew the word out. "With all that being said, I may be of no help whatsoever beyond confirming that you're alive and breathing." She paused. "Which you are."

Unable to help it, I laughed. "At least you're honest."

"The only good doctor is an honest one," she said. "It may help to know exactly what you felt before you passed out. Luc filled me in on what Grayson told him, but I want to hear it from you."

Fiddling with the edge of the blanket, I told her exactly what I remembered, even the weird light I'd seen around Grayson.

Luc jumped on that tidbit immediately. "What do you mean you saw a weird light around him?"

"I saw what looked like a rainbow of lights around him. It was brief, and I know that sounds bizarre, because when I think of Grayson, I don't think of rainbows."

Dr. Hemenway leaned forward and said in a conspiratorial whisper, "Me, either. I think of dark storm clouds and frigid winters."

I smiled again, really liking this woman.

Luc, however, was not amused. "Was that the first time you'd seen anything like that?"

"Yes, but I saw something around you when I woke up." I peeked at him, and his expression was impressively blank. "It was probably my eyes just adjusting to the light."

"What did you see?" he asked.

"Like an aura of white and purple light?" I pulled the edges of the blanket tight. "I know it wasn't the Source, but it was very brief, so it might've been my eyes."

"I don't think it's your eyes," Dr. Hemenway interjected, looking at Luc. "Grayson also mentioned that you might have been able to feel him before he showed up? The same with Dawson when he came outside, right before became dizzy?"

"Yeah." I resisted the urge to reach around and rub my neck.

"Did you feel anything when I neared the house?" she asked, and when I shook my head, she scrunched her forehead. "And had you felt this before?"

"Well, the last couple of days, I'd been feeling weird stuff. Sort of like the sensation of cobwebs on my neck, or I'd feel like a nerve twinge between my shoulder blades," I said, also telling them how I'd felt like I'd been able to pick out those with alien DNA among the humans at the market and at school. "But I don't think I felt anything before that."

Luc unfolded his arms. "Why didn't you say anything to me?"

"Well, a lot of stuff has been going on, and I didn't know if I was feeling something or just imagining it. It wasn't constant, so I had no idea if I really was feeling them or not. I was planning to mention it." And that was the truth. "It just didn't seem all that important."

"Any new thing you feel or experience is important." Luc did not look happy. "It could be a sign."

"Of what?"

"Of you evolving," Dr. Hemenway answered.

My gaze shot to her. "Evolving?"

She nodded. "We have had a few humans go through the mutation process while living here, so I've been able to witness the process. It's quite fascinating."

"I'll have to take your word on that," I murmured, suddenly remembering the dream I'd had of Mom and me. As the details started to come back to me, I wasn't all that sure it *had* been a dream, and a good portion of me wished that was all it had been. I sank into the pillows propped against the headboard. If that was a memory resurfacing, some of it could've been false, but if any of it had been real? The Daedalus orchestrating Luc and me meeting? What really happened to my father?

"Each of them started to experience things before the mutation took hold. Able to move things without touching them, usually accidentally. They were able to start to feel the presence of the Luxen who'd mutated them, among other occurrences," she explained, drawing my attention back to her. I had to think about that possible memory later. "Luc mentioned that earlier that day, you'd begun training with the Source? It was the first time you used it. Purposely, that is?"

I nodded.

"You were mutated several years ago, so we know this isn't like what a hybrid goes through during the beginning of a mutation."

"Right," Luc agreed.

"Ever since you fell into this superlong nap, I've been thinking everything over, and I have a theory." She tapped her finger off her knee. "It's batty, and I could be way off. Everyone understand that?"

Luc and I nodded.

"Great. We're all on the same page." She smiled. "When I think of the genetic coding we were working on in humans and the similarities I've been able to find in the serums I have seen, I think the

DNA in the Andromeda serum is more like a computer code or a virus."

"A virus?" I repeated.

"Have either of you ever heard of virotherapy?"

I stared at her blankly, but of course Luc had a response. "Viruses bioengineered to fight cancer?"

"Yes." She snapped her fingers at him. "You get a gold star."

I rolled my eyes.

"Certain oncolytic viruses can bind themselves to the receptors in tumors but not to healthy cells. I imagine the Andromeda serum followed a similar path. Attacked the cancer cells without harming the good ones. And if that serum is anything like the two before it, it carried a dual purpose—not just to heal you but also to mutate you with the blending of Luxen and Arum DNA. However, this new one that I really, really would've loved to have seen could have unique coding features. It's those features that remind me of certain types of viruses and their ability to remain dormant."

This conversation was so above my pay grade.

"Like herpes?" Luc suggested.

"What?" I gaped at him.

Grinning, he picked up a fresh bottle of water. "Herpes is a virus that lies dormant in the host."

"He's right," confirmed Dr. Hemenway.

"You couldn't come up with a better virus than that?" I took the bottle.

"Malware is a virus that can be dormant in a computer," he went on, eyes glimmering with humor.

I glared at him as I took a rather large gulp of water.

"Chicken pox is also a form of the herpes virus. Billions of people have some form of it," Dr. Hemenway clarified. "But back to the subject at hand. What if the Andromeda serum mutated you and then was coded to push that mutation into a dormant stage, designed to be activated under certain scenarios, just like some viruses only became active under a perfect storm scenario?"

"Like how some astronauts can have herpes flare-ups while entering space?" Luc added.

I closed my eyes and then reopened them when I was sure I wouldn't throw the water at him. "How you even know that is beyond me."

Dr. Hemenway ignored Luc. "How they sent the mutation into latency is something I can't even begin to figure out. It could've been the Cassio Wave used to send it into a dormant stage and also to activate it. That's just a huge guess, but what's not a guess is that when some viruses wake up, it's not a *bam*"—she smacked her hands together, startling me; I almost choked on my water—"the virus is everywhere and symptomatic. Some are slow to get moving, to become active. Symptoms, or in your case, abilities, start to pop up here and there."

"So, you're saying that my mutation is slowly becoming active?"

"Yes." She paused. "And no."

I blinked.

"To tackle the yes part of that equation, you're starting to experience new abilities."

"Arums see the energy around other living species," Luc chimed in. "I've heard that Luxen looked like rainbows to them, which is how they're able to pick them out in a crowd. It's why Luxen used to live in communities near natural-forming deposits of beta quartz. The crystal distorts Luxen wavelengths until they cannot be distinguished from humans. The same with hybrids or Origins."

"Oh," I whispered, shaking my head. This was a lot. "But that doesn't explain how I was able to do what I did with April and in the woods." I stopped. "I'm assuming you know about that?"

"Luc told me enough to have a general understanding," she replied.

"I think I'm following," Luc said.

"Of course," I muttered around the mouth of the bottle.

He winked at me, and the flutter in the pit of my stomach irked me. "When the Cassio Wave was first used, it woke up the mutation, and there was a burst of abilities, of symptoms, before returning to something like a base level. Your mutation was activated at that point and started interacting with your cells again. And in the woods, it was more or less triggered into a flurry of activity again by a perfect storm scenario—a threat to your life, but it wasn't a full-blown infection at that point."

Dr. Hemenway clapped enthusiastically. "Yes! Pretty much that. In a way. Your mutation was activated out of dormancy. The two incidents were like flare-ups, and it makes sense given what you began to experience along with the manifestation of new abilities. Luc mentioned that you've been extremely hungry?"

Lowering the bottle, I nodded. "Yes, always."

"So, just to recap where we are at this point. The mutation was activated out of dormancy by the Cassio Wave. Like many latent viruses, this mutation slowly began to interact with your body. You had flare-ups triggered by extreme emotional or physical distress, but all along, ever since the Cassio Wave, the mutation has been slowly taking hold, explaining the ability to sniff out other alien DNA. Now, what I think happened, what sent this mutation into a flurry of activity, is the training—purposely using the Source. It was the straw that broke the horse's back." She paused, wrinkling her nose. "Wait. That doesn't sound right."

"Camel?" I offered.

"Ah. Yes. That's it! Anyway, working with the Source kicked the mutation into hyperdrive—it's the *bam*!" She smacked her hands together again, and this time I saw it coming. "The sleeping could've been because of what was going on in your body. I imagine the mutation was doing a lot of work, and I think you'll probably discover more abilities going forward."

"Oh." I tried to not freak out, but my heart was racing. I had to ask, even if she couldn't answer. "Did Luc tell you about what I'm supposed to be? How I'm coded to answer to one person?" When Dr. Hemenway nodded, the plastic crinkled under my fingers. "When I was in those woods, I had no idea who I was, and when I looked at Luc and Daemon, I didn't see them as anything more than a threat. If you're right and the mutation is just now fully waking up . . ." My stomach twisted with equal knots of dread and hope. "Is it possible that is why I didn't go with April like she thought I would? And why I'm still myself now? Because the mutation hadn't fully taken hold then?"

Dr. Hemenway opened her mouth as she sent Luc a sideways glance.

"He can't answer that," I said before Luc could say a word. The ripple of charged heat that rolled through the room told me he didn't like what I'd said, but it was the truth.

"Neither can I," she said after a few moments. "Even if I had that serum here, I don't have the expertise or the equipment to determine exactly what it is capable of. This group—the Daedalus? They are light-years ahead of anything I've seen in bioengineering. All I can do is make poorly educated theories based on what I do know and what I've seen."

"And what would be one of those poorly educated theories?" Luc asked. "I know you have one."

Dr. Hemenway leaned back, brows raised as she pulled her lips in, making a popping sound. "Based on what I have seen and on the flare-ups where the mutation seized hold? You may not have remembered who you were at first, and you may have gone after Luc and Daemon, but you snapped out of it one way or another, and during that time, you didn't feel an overwhelming compulsion to seek out someone else or leave. In a way, it reminds me of a new computer. You buy it and it works for a couple of days or weeks, and then you have all these software updates that need to run."

I really had no idea where she was going with this. She must've read the look on my face, because she said, "Think of it this way. The mutation just came out of its dormant state, and it either was or still is running updates. Your memories, thoughts, and feelings were all there, but the day in the woods just took a little bit of time for *you* to come back online. Perhaps if the mutation is fully active or once it's completely integrated, there will be no need to reboot. But I'm guessing that if you're triggered again, the best thing to do is remove all threats until you can reboot."

"So, you think I will remain myself?" I asked, half-afraid to allow myself to think that was even a possibility.

Luc's gaze shifted to me as Dr. Hemenway said, "I think there is no way of knowing for sure what the Andromeda serum has done, even if I had that serum here and all the tools and knowledge necessary to be able to break it down to its very core. I don't think the Daedalus would even know, unless there were someone just like you."

"What do you mean?" Luc's attention snapped to the doctor.

"You haven't considered this?" She looked surprised as she stared back at Luc, and then she nodded as if she'd answered her own question. "A lot of stuff has been going on, so I can see how this was overlooked." Her gaze flicked to mine. "You weren't just given the Andromeda serum. You were given LH-11 and Prometheus before, correct? And while Andromeda healed and mutated you, LH-11 and Prometheus are still in there. How do those serums interact with Andromeda? It would be safe to assume that the previous introduction of alien DNA has either lessened or strengthened some of the DNA coding in Andromeda. If the other Trojans were given just the Andromeda serum, then none of them would be like Evie, and she would be unlike any of them."

17

Still tangled up between hope and dread, I watched Luc slowly approach the bed. "Well, I guess that was all good news. I mean, even if she isn't right about the whole rebooting thing." *God, I really hope she is.* "She confirmed that I'm healthy even after sleeping for four days."

"Yeah." Luc stopped beside the bed. "Viv is one of the smartest people I've ever met. Her theory could be on point."

That little kernel of hope grew. "If so, then I'm not a risk. I won't go all hive mind on everyone." I sought the same relief I felt in his expression but found nothing but a blank canvas. "You're not happy to know that there may be a chance I'm not going to flip out one day and run back to the Daedalus?"

"I didn't think you were going to in the first place." He frowned as he stared out the window near the bed.

"But you believed that only because you didn't want to accept anything else," I pointed out, studying him in the faint afternoon sunlight. Something was up. "What's wrong? And don't say 'nothing'. Obviously, something is wrong."

"I don't . . ." Exhaling heavily, he sat beside me. He slid his hand over my cheek, catching strands of hair in his fingers. He drew them away from my face, his hand lingering along the back of my head. "I just hate this—the not knowing." A rough laugh escaped him. "I've always known everything, Evie. Everything. You'd say that's me being arrogant."

I would.

"But it's the truth."

It was, unfortunately.

"Being able to read minds and see through all the BS has left very little hidden from me, but you . . . everything about you is unknown," he continued, carefully extricating his fingers from my hair. "Do you have any idea how much I hate this?"

Considering how much control Luc did have in any given situation, I had a good idea of what this must be doing to him, all of this, and I hated that I couldn't do anything to alleviate his fear. That I was the source of his fear.

"I bet you think you do," he said, his voice as rough as his next breath. "But you don't. I would give up all other knowledge just to know what is happening to you. I know that sounds intense."

It really did. "All knowledge?"

"I would do it in a heartbeat. If I knew what was happening, I could fix it. I could do something other than *this*." He smoothed his fingers over my cheek. "God, Evie, do you know that you're the only thing I've ever cared about?"

My heart squeezed painfully tight in my chest. "Luc . . ."

He shook his head. "I don't care how that makes me sound. You shouldn't be shocked by it. I wasn't lying when I told you what I feel for you is intense."

A burn filled my chest, crawling up my throat. I scooted toward him, my legs tangling in the blanket as I touched his jaw with my fingers. "I'm not shocked by it."

He didn't seem to hear me as those luminous violet eyes met mine. "When I heard Grayson shout my name and I went outside, seeing you lying there? My fucking heart stopped, Evie. Everything stopped. And when minutes turned into hours and hours turned into days, I couldn't think. I couldn't eat. I couldn't sleep. Hell, getting up to use the bathroom scared me shitless, because what if something happened to you while I was gone those couple of minutes? What if—" He cut himself off, squeezing his eyes shut. "I've waited for you forever, and the only thing that scares me—that terrifies me—is that something is going to take you from me, and I won't be able to do a damn thing about it."

Tears crowded my eyes, and when I went to swallow, a lump formed in my throat.

"You don't remember any of this, but you were close to death so many times when you were sick. You would lie there, so damn still. It was like you couldn't hear me or Paris when we talked to you—like you already had one foot in the beyond. I would just sit there and watch you, making sure you were breathing. I hated even blinking." His body trembled as his hands wrapped around my wrists. "And there was nothing I could do then. That's how I felt when you were sleeping. That there was nothing I could do but pray, and I don't even know if there's a God listening, but I prayed, Evie, because if I lost you again, I don't know what I would do."

Dampness clung to my lashes, seeped onto my cheeks. "I'm sorry—"

"Don't you dare apologize." His eyes flew open. "You've done nothing wrong. You didn't cause any of this." He paused. "I caused this."

"No, you didn't," I told him. "You didn't cause this."

His head tilted, and he stared at me for so long, before a small smile that didn't reach his eyes appeared. "All of this started because of me and my choices."

My fingers curled against his cheeks. "I don't know if it started because of you."

"Evie—"

"I dreamed something, but I don't think it was a dream," I rushed on. "It felt too real, like a memory, and if it was real, none of this started because of you."

His brows furrowed as his stare turned questioning. "What did you dream?" He slowly brought my hands to the bed. "Or remember?"

Lowering my gaze, I watched him slip his hands off my wrists as I told him what I'd dreamed, everything from the spot on the floor to my mom telling me that I wouldn't remember any of what happened, not even him. The only part I left out was the suspicion that I might've killed my father. At some point, he rocked back, and when I glanced up, he sat stiffly, his jaw a hard, unforgiving line.

"They would've sent someone else if for whatever reason you and I didn't . . . I don't know, become friends or whatever." I, too, sat back, leaning into the cushions. My gaze flicked to the ceiling fan. It was still. "I think I was sought out by Jason Dasher because of my uncanny resemblance to his daughter. At least that's the impression Mom gave me, and if my father and Jason had known each other, it's plausible Dasher would've seen me before."

Luc was quiet, but I could feel his eyes on me.

"Do you really think it's possible that they made me sick? I mean, considering what they are capable of, it doesn't seem impossible, but . . ."

"But if they did, it would be a whole new level they have sunk to," he said. "You didn't get sick right away. It was a couple of years. How they could've exposed you to something like that would be difficult to narrow down. Neither Paris nor I watched you 24–7. It could've been at the club or a store or when you were out taking pictures by yourself. They could've put something in the damn water in the house. Paris and I wouldn't have gotten sick."

It all felt almost too much to consider, but I had to. "I don't understand why they would've let it go on so long if all of this was a way to control you. They could've waved that serum in your face at any time and you would've done anything. I could've died before you brought me to them, and then what?"

"I can't answer that," Luc said after a few moments. "There has to be a reason they waited and took that risk."

It would've been a huge risk. All that time and effort they put into Luc and me cultivating a friendship that would lead Luc to defy all logic could've been lost if I'd died. "I don't know. Maybe what I dreamed was just a dream—"

"Your father's name was Alan."

A shiver swirled down my spine as my gaze shot to his. I didn't know what to say at first. "It was?"

Luc nodded. "And he was in the military, but I never discovered any relation to Jason Dasher. Those records could've been expunged. There wasn't a lot to be found about him other than his rather vast work history. The man couldn't keep a job longer than a few months."

"Alan?" I gave a little shake of my head as I returned to staring at my hands where they now rested in my lap. "That's his name. Should I feel something learning that? Like relief or dread? It's the name of my father, my real father, and I feel nothing."

"You don't remember him, Peaches. That's a name of a stranger," he said, angling his body toward mine. "You don't need to feel anything."

"And maybe it's better that way, like not remembering my time at the Daedalus." I closed my eyes as an uncomfortable heaviness settled over me, oily and thick. "If the memory was true, I think he was abusive . . ." My stomach twisted with nausea at the thought of continuing, but I needed to say it—say all of it. I couldn't let it sit unspoken inside me, where it would fester and become a different kind of monster. "I think I might've killed my father. The night I ran away was right after Jason Dasher arrived, and I think I stabbed him."

My eyes were open again, and I was staring at my hands. Had they been covered in blood? "She didn't—I mean, I don't think you knew, because I think I made sure to never really think about it. I don't think I could think about any of it. Probably not the healthiest coping skill, but maybe it was a way I could survive it all."

"I knew."

My head jerked toward him. I seemed to have skipped a breath.

Luc's lashes lowered. "I knew. I always knew, but you didn't want me to. I think you thought I would judge you for it, and I think you needed to believe that I didn't know, so I never let on that I did."

For some reason, my nose was stinging. So were my eyes.

"I didn't pick it up from your thoughts. Not at first. You gave us your real name, and Paris was able to check out who you were a few days after you showed up. He learned that your father was dead," he told me, his gaze never wavering from mine. "He suspected that you'd done it. He also suspected you had a good reason. When you first came to us, you were jumpy. If either of us reached for you or if we raised our voices, you'd flinch and often keep yourself at least an arm's distance from us. You had a lot of faded bruises that looked like someone had made a habit of grabbing your arms. Hard." His eyes were as hard as granite. "Neither of us ever judged you. If anything, the discovery meant you fit with us way better than we could've guessed, as disturbing as that was."

A choked laugh escaped my lips, and I looked away, blinking back tears.

"You had nightmares the first year. You'd wake up screaming about blood," he continued, his voice so very quiet. "One of those nights, I picked up bits and pieces. I just never let you know."

Lips trembling, I pressed them together until I was sure I could speak. "I think Sylvia and Jason realized he was abusive. She said if they'd known, they would've come for me sooner."

"And if that garbage human being had still been alive when Paris looked into you, he wouldn't have been afterward."

Even though I couldn't remember Paris, if he was anything like Luc, I didn't doubt that for one second. "I just . . . I don't know how I'm supposed to feel about that." My palms felt sweaty as I rubbed them against the blanket. "I don't really feel anything other than, cool, my actual father has a name. I should be angry that he was a monster who hit his child—and I am, but it's like I'm angry for someone else, if that makes sense? Maybe if I remembered, things would be different. I don't know."

The bed shifted, and then Luc said, "Look at me."

Drawing in a shallow breath, I did just that. The moment our gazes connected, they held.

"If you end up remembering more down the road, you go through what you need to go through. We'll go through it together, but there is nothing wrong with feeling nothing. Just like there's nothing wrong with how you feel about Sylvia. You feel what you need to feel, whether that's feeling nothing or everything."

The next breath I took scorched my lungs, and I nodded. Or at least I thought I did. "I love you," I whispered. "You know that right? I love you."

He leaned in, touching his forehead to mine. "I know, but if you feel the need to remind me often, I have no problem with that."

I smiled, and I realized the heavy, sticky feeling was easing off. I knew it could come back, possibly bringing with it ugly memories, but if or when it did, I would face them.

"I think I need to fess up to something," I said, drawing back until I could see Luc's face. "I heard you when I was sleeping, on and off."

"Did you?"

I nodded. "I heard you say even Grayson missed me. I know that was a lie."

His lashes swept down as one side of his lips tipped up. "I would never lie about such a thing."

"I also heard some really lame pickup lines."

"My pickup lines are never lame, Peaches."

In my chest, my heart started pounding. "I also heard you say that if I woke up and didn't remember who I was, that you had enough love in you for me that it would be enough. That you'd still love me."

Those lashes lifted, and the intensity in his gaze stole my next breath. "You have to have known that."

"I did," I whispered. "I do."

"But what you don't know is that wasn't the first time I said those words to you."

"It wasn't?"

"No." He placed the tips of his fingers to my cheek. "I told you that I love you, that I would always love you, no matter what, once before." His throat worked on a swallow, and when he spoke, his voice was thick. "I told you that the only time I ever said goodbye to you."

His face blurred. "And what did I say?"

"You said, 'I know.'"

18

Hours later, after the sun had gone down and after Luc and I talked over everything Dr. Hemenway had said, while we ate what felt like a week's worth of veggies and cheese, Zoe showed up. Like Luc, I saw a deep violet, transparent aura tinged with white all around her before she rushed forward, all but tackling me where I sat under the covers. There were hugs.

Lots of hugs.

And maybe a few tears.

"Don't ever do something like that again," she said, arms wrapped around my shoulders. "Do you understand me? I was scared to death."

"Sorry." I squeezed her back as I tried to get air into my lungs and not think about the fact that her face was almost planted in my unwashed hair.

"Don't apologize!" she cried. "It's not your fault. I'm just so happy you're okay and you're not—" She cut herself off.

My gaze lifted to where Luc lingered, arms crossed as he leaned against the doorframe. Grayson was there, too, standing silently behind Luc. When he'd walked in, I'd seen the rainbow effect around him, but when I looked at him now, all I saw was the bluish-purple bruise.

The Luxen had a black eye.

I had no idea how a Luxen could have a black eye, but I was full of questions.

"That I'm not trying to kill everyone?" I finished for Zoe.

"Yeah," she whispered. "Heidi would never forgive me if something happened to you before she got here."

I had hoped that they'd made their arrival while I slept, but they hadn't, and I was doing my best not to freak out about that. Nobody seemed concerned, so I was taking that as a good sign.

"I missed you," Zoe said, squeezing me until I squeaked.

"Your girl is starting to sound like one of those dog toys," Grayson commented.

"True." Pushing away from the door, Luc approached and gently pried Zoe away from me, and I don't know what he said to her, but after a few more moments, and then a few more rushing back to the bed for one last quick hug, Luc and I were alone again.

"It's getting late," he said, returning from showing them out. A few more candles sparked to life as he passed them. "And I figured you'd want to take a bath—a warm bath. I know you want to do it yourself, but I think we can make an exception tonight."

I really did want to do it myself, but I wanted a warm bath more.

"Bath. Please. And then you." I scooted to the edge of the bed, throwing the blanket off. "You have to tell me why and how Grayson has a black eye."

"Sort of a funny story." Luc carried one of the lanterns into the bathroom, placing it on the sink counter. "I punched him in the face."

My mouth dropped open. "What?"

"Yeah. He could've healed it by now—" The water came on, drowning out whatever he was saying as he sat on the ledge of the bath.

"What?" I rose, my steps a little wobbly as I made my way to the bathroom. "What did you say?"

"I said he's wearing it like a badge of honor." The lantern didn't do much to beat back the darkness of the bathroom, but it cast interesting shadows along the back of his shoulders.

"Why did you punch him?" I tugged on the hem of my borrowed shirt.

"He told me." Luc glanced over at his shoulder at me. "He told me what he said to you."

Oh.

Wow.

Was not expecting that.

"Why would he do that?" I asked.

"Because he needed to." Luc reached over, turning the water off. "Do you want to see how I'm going to do this?"

I wanted to know why Grayson felt the need to tell Luc how much of a dick he'd been and why he hadn't healed his own injury, but frankly, I was more curious about how Luc was going to heat the water. Shuffling forward, I stepped behind him.

"I think of boiling water," he said, placing his hand in what had to be frigid temps. A faint burst of white light powered down his arm, barely noticeable as he lazily trailed his hand through the water. "That's all."

Before I could speak, I heard the gentle rumble of water and squinted, seeing the bubbles spring forth from his fingers. "That's all," I murmured.

He withdrew his hand. "It's not easy to control, though, so you need to wait a few minutes for it to cool down."

With that, he rose fluidly, and with me standing so close to him, there was very little room between us. I had to crane back, way back, to look up at him. I suddenly felt incredibly nervous. Not the bad kind, but the kind that was an odd mixture of hope and anticipation. I wanted . . .

I didn't know what I wanted other than I knew I wanted him, and I could sense he was about to leave.

"I saw the aura thingy," I blurted out, and Luc's forehead creased. My cheeks heated as I shifted from one foot to the next. "I saw the same transparent aura around Zoe that I saw around you."

"And Grayson?"

"He looked like a rainbow." I toyed with the hem of the shirt again. "A bruised rainbow."

One side of his mouth curved up.

"You shouldn't grin about that," I told him.

"He shouldn't have said what he did to you." The smile faded. "Do you need help with anything?"

I arched a brow.

"Dirty mind," he murmured, that half grin of his making an

appearance once again. "I was talking about the bath. Do you need anything?"

Somewhat disappointed, I looked around the bathroom. "I can get the stuff."

"Or you can let me be all helpful," he offered, and because I didn't want him to leave, I nodded. "What do you want?"

Luc went about grabbing what I asked for. Body wash and a loofah. Cleanser for my face. A big fluffy towel placed on a small wooden stool.

"I want to wash my hair," I said. "I need to wash my hair."

"Got it." He grabbed two bottles out of the shower caddy. "Let me grab you a pitcher. That should help."

Stepping aside, I waited until he slipped out of the bathroom before turning to the bath. I sat down on the ledge, curling my toes into the fluffy mat. The water was hot to the touch, but I thought in a few more minutes it would be cool enough, especially if I used the cold water to rinse the shampoo and conditioner out.

I pulled my fingers from the water and stood, my gaze sliding to the half-open bathroom door. I don't know what I was thinking, or maybe I wasn't thinking at all as I reached down and wrapped my fingers around the hem of the borrowed shirt. Maybe it was being asleep for so long and waking up to hear Luc whispering his innermost fears. It could be the little piece of hope Dr. Hemenway's theory gave me. Perhaps it was the dream that was really a memory. Or maybe it was hearing Luc say he loved me.

I didn't know, and I wasn't sure it even mattered as I pulled the shirt off and then shimmied out of my undies, dropping both items in the hamper.

There was no turning back now.

Stepping into the tub, I sank down, sucking in a sharp breath at the shock of the hot water. It took a couple of seconds for my skin to adjust, and then . . . goodness. Leaning back until my shoulders were underwater, I almost moaned as the heat of the water invaded the stiff muscles along my back.

I sat up, tucking my knees to my chest as I eyed the soap. My pulse was pounding so fast as I waited, having no idea how Luc would respond. I doubted he'd scream, "My eyes!" and run from the room. I was sure he would be more than happy to see me like this, but this was bold.

I liked being bold.

Grinning, I planted my cheek against my knee and closed my eyes. It was only a minute more when my heart skipped a beat. I sensed Luc's return, and it had nothing to do with any alien DNA in me. Even with my eyes closed, I could feel the intensity of his stare, heavy and as hot as the water.

Opening my eyes, I saw him standing in the doorway, an old-fashioned white pitcher in one hand and a large plastic storage container in the other. He didn't move. I wasn't even sure if he breathed as he stared at me with pupils that shone like stars.

Heart still thrumming, I said, "I didn't want to wait."

"I see."

He spoke only those two words, but they were full of so much want and need that I shivered. I took a small breath. "I thought you could help me wash my hair."

All Luc did was place the pitcher on the vanity, the container on the floor near the tub, and then he backed up again, returning to the doorway.

"And I thought since you heated up the water, you should get to enjoy it while it's warm. The tub is big enough." And it was. The tub wasn't a Jacuzzi or anything like that, but it was definitely wider and longer than a normal tub. He still hadn't moved. I lifted my cheek but kept my knees to my chest. "If you want to."

His mouth opened and then closed. He took a moment. "I don't know if I can."

I had not expected that response.

At all.

A different kind of flush swept over my skin, having nothing to do with the heat of the water or the fact I was completely super-duper nude. Oh, man, I'd made a mistake. A big one. A big old naked mistake, and I was going to drown myself—

"You misunderstood. Or I misspoke," he cut into my thoughts. "I don't think I trust myself to just share that bath with you and wash your hair. There's going to be a physical reaction. From me. For you. It's going to be obvious, and that should probably embarrass me, but it doesn't. You could be wearing a hazmat suit and covered in cow dung and I'd still have a physical reaction to you."

My lips twitched. "Cow dung? Seriously?"

He met my eyes, and it was then when I realized Luc wore many masks. He'd let this one slip, and stark need swept across his features, sharpening them. Heat licked his eyes, intensifying the amethyst hue and turning his pupils a brilliant white. "Seriously."

A flush crept into my cheeks, and something far warmer and headier slipped through the rest of me. "Wow."

"Indeed," he growled, and the fire in his eyes lit up my veins. "So, as long as you know I'm not going to be a detached caregiver giving you a bath and you're okay with that, I'm more than willing to help you." One side of his lips curved up. "Like, you have no idea how willing I am."

"I don't want you to be a detached anything," I whispered. "I want you to be you."

"Thank God." Then, without further ado, he reached around to the nape of his neck, grabbed a fistful of his shirt, and pulled it over his head. He dropped it where he stood.

My gaze was greedy as they swept over his broad shoulders and defined chest, lingering on the lean length of his torso.

He made me want to do really irresponsible things—

I suddenly recalled Grayson's taunts. "Can you and I have, you know . . . ?"

"Have?" He propped his arms up on the threshold of the doorway, and when he leaned in, the movement did interesting, sinuous things to the muscles along his arms and shoulders. I was confident he was aware of that. "Have what?"

Keeping my arms around my bent legs and my gaze above the shoulders, I frowned. "Any other time you're reading my mind, but now you're not?"

Amusement curved his lips up farther. "You're not being loud."

I wasn't sure I believed that. "Can I get pregnant?"

"In general?"

My eyes narrowed. "From you, you asshole."

Dipping his chin, he bit down on his lower lip. "No, you can't. I was not designed for potency to bring anything other than a release. Husher believed that the ability for an Origin like me to father a child would only hinder growth of my physical or mental abilities."

Designed? I hated how that word was used as a way to remind him he was a thing created instead of a person. I absolutely hated how he used that word and others. And I hated how that choice had been taken from him at birth.

"And before you ask, like the Luxen, the Origins are not carriers, nor are we susceptible to diseases that can be transmitted," he explained. I had been wondering how to ask that question. "Are you surprised? About the baby thing?"

I gave a little shake of my head. "A little. It was just something Grayson said."

"I've got to ask why you're naked thinking about something Grayson said. Not that I'm judging. He's very attractive, and a lot of people find that standoffish 'I've been deeply wounded so I lash out at everyone' routine to be very alluring."

I rolled my eyes, not dignifying any of that with a denial. "He said I probably had enough alien DNA in me to make things compatible enough for you and me to make a currently really bad life choice."

"He may be right for other Origins, but he wouldn't know my current baby-making-abilities status. The most recent Origins were also sterile. After all, what could be more distracting than having a child?" He pushed off the door, lowering his arms as he took a step forward. He stopped by the vanity. "Does that bother you?"

I wasn't sure how to answer that, because kids were something that hadn't even begun to be something I'd thought about. So, I decided to be honest. "I don't know, because I don't even know if I want a kid many, many years from now." I thought of Kat's screams and shuddered. "I don't know if I'd ever want to do the whole birthing thing. Babies sort of scare me."

"What about ten years from now? Twenty? When we're not dealing with the Daedalus any longer and it's just us raising a herd of llamas?"

The fact that Luc was thinking that far in advance—thinking about *us* that far in advance—caused my heart to skip happily in my chest. Not only did he think there was a future for us, there was potentially a future for us that didn't involve the Daedalus or being stuck in the middle of a fight for world domination—

Wait.

"Raising a herd of llamas?" I repeated.

He shrugged. "Always thought it would be cool to have a herd of llamas."

I grinned. "I like llamas."

"I know."

Picturing us with a small house and a herd of llamas in our backyard made me laugh. It was the most ridiculous future.

The best future.

"We could always adopt one day," I said. "If that's what we wanted."

"We could." His head tilted. "Is the water still warm?"

I nodded.

"Do you still want me—"

"Always," I said, not needing to hear anything more.

That rare, full smile of his appeared, and I melted like snow on the first warm winter day. And then he was stripping off the rest of his clothing.

I should look away. Wasn't that the polite thing to do? But I couldn't. And I didn't think Luc wanted me to, either.

Even with just the light of the candles, I got an eyeful of everything. It felt like my skin had been heated with the Source, just like the water. This wasn't the first time I'd seen him, but it felt like it, because there was a certain awareness that throbbed between us, full of sharp anticipation and bone-deep yearning.

I started to scoot forward, but Luc's hand on my cheek stilled me. He tilted my head back as he knelt on the outside of the tub, kissing me.

"Let me wash your hair first," he said when he lifted his head.

"You don't have to." My blood trilled. "It was just a ploy."

"To get me naked?"

Grinning, I nodded. "It worked."

"It did." The pitcher ended up in his hand. "But I want to do this. It'll give me time."

"For what?" I watched him from my curled position, still keeping myself from being exposed. It seemed fairer now since the wall of the tub hid all of Luc's interesting bits.

"So I don't end up embarrassing myself."

It took me a moment to realize what he meant, and when I did, all I could whisper was a soft *Oh*. Despite all of Luc's experience and his playfulness, this could be his first time.

It could be our first time.

Luc was quiet as he set about washing my hair, taking his time. I'd never had anyone wash my hair. Or at least I hadn't remembered it, and I didn't think I'd like it, but instead of feeling coddled, I felt . . . loved. He was careful not to tangle his fingers in my hair, and he warmed each fresh pitcher of water, making sure none of the suds or the conditioner ran down my face but into the container he'd brought in so that we wouldn't be soaking in the water used to wash my hair. I honestly wouldn't have thought of that.

"Thank you," I said.

"You don't have to thank me."

"I just did, and I think I'm now spoiled and I'm going to forever demand that you wash my hair. You're really good at it."

"It's not my first time. I used to wash your hair when you were sick."

Why was I still surprised to hear that? I watched him refill the pitcher, placing it on the ledge of the tub. God, he would've had to have been fourteen or younger, and something like that seemed like a simple gesture, but it required a level of maturity and intuitiveness that I knew even most adults lacked. Luc was, surprisingly, a care—

He rose without warning, and my eyes widened. This time I did look away, because goodness, he was . . .

Every inch of him was beautiful.

Because I had no sense of propriety whatsoever, I peeked over at him. His back was to me as he dipped his head over the sink, wetting his hair. Then he added some shampoo. That was all. No conditioner. Within five seconds, he'd washed his hair out in the sink, no worry about tangles and knots the size of my fist.

Such a dude—a dude with a lovely backside.

He was turning back to me, and I averted my gaze. "You going to join me now?" I asked, hoping my request sounded mysterious and sexy, and not as high-pitched and squeaky as it did to my own ears.

"Nothing in this world could stop me," he replied. "Not even a marching band. They'd just get an eyeful of my goodies and have to deal with it."

"Goodies?" Laughing, I scooted forward. The water lapped at my back as he stepped into the tub behind me and sat. I was trying to play it cool, but I felt as if I were seconds away from a heart attack. "They'd probably enjoy their eyeful."

"You did."

Smiling, I dropped my forehead to my knee. "I can't deny that."

"I wouldn't want you to." His legs slid against my hips, the hair along his calves sending a riot of shivers through me.

Taking a deep breath, I lifted my head and leaned back just enough that my front was no longer plastered to my legs. He touched first the center of my back and then brushed my wet hair over one shoulder. A heartbeat passed, and I felt just the tips of his fingers on my waist. A moment later, his lips touched the nape of my neck. I bit down on my lip as I reached back, curling my fingers around his hands. I guided them forward as I uncurled my legs and straightened.

"Wait." His hands left my skin, his arms wrapping around me as he reached for the bar of soap. I watched him lather up his hands again before placing the soap back on the ledge. His hands returned to my upper arms, sweeping down, the backs of his fingers grazing the sides of my breasts, causing me to jolt.

"Just being helpful," he said in a gravelly voice.

"So helpful," I murmured.

His soapy, slick hands continued on, back up my arms and then down, over my lower stomach. His hands left only long enough to soap back up, and then his palms were skating up my ribs and higher, lingering until I was clutching his legs and doing everything in me not to squirm.

"Making sure you're squeaky clean," he said against my ear.

"Uh-huh."

He chuckled darkly as his hands slipped into the water, and then he was retracing his earlier steps, washing away the soap with a washcloth that had to have appeared out of thin air. The material did strange, interesting things to my skin, but then he had that soap in his hand again.

"Lean back." His request was a rough one I immediately obeyed.

The contact of my back to his chest and my hips against him was a wonderful, exquisitely pleasing feeling, but it was quickly overwhelmed when his hands were making their way over my hips and my legs. He lifted one, hooking it over the edge of the tub, and then his fingers were slipping over my skin, back into the water.

I kicked my back against his shoulder, my entire body pounding. "You're being very thorough."

"Of course I am." His voice was like smoke. "I'm a perfectionist."

My hips jerked, rising out of the water as a sharp, intense throb shot through me. I reached back with one hand, clasping the back of Luc's head.

"I don't want to miss a spot," he continued. "You should make sure I don't miss one."

I was.

My eyes were open, fixed on how the lantern light flickered over the water and our legs. I was fixated on the way the tendons along his hand flexed as I tugged on his head. He didn't resist, kissing my neck and then blazing a trail up along the line of my jaw as I turned my head toward him. His lips met mine, and his kiss was full of hunger.

There were no more pauses for soap as my other hand cupped his, feeling those tendons I'd watched move against my palm. The aching pulse intensified as we kissed and kissed, our bodies slipping against each other and the sides of the tub. We both were taking quick, shallow breaths that were nothing more than pants. I felt like a rope stretched too tight as I pulled away and lowered my leg back to the water.

Placing my hands on the sides of the tub, I turned, sliding my knees on either side of his legs. It wasn't at all graceful. Water sloshed everywhere, and my right knee banged into the tub. My palms were slippery, and they were trembling. His hands landed on my hips, steadying me.

"Thank you," I whispered, switching my hands to his shoulders.

Eyes heavy-hooded, he shook his head. "I should be the one thanking you."

"I haven't done anything."

"That's where you're so wrong." His hands flexed, but stayed at my hips. "You're giving me everything I've ever wanted or needed. You always have."

His words rattled me to my very core, and for a moment, I couldn't move. My heart was squeezing and expanding in the best possible ways, because I knew he wasn't talking about just this. He was talking about *me*.

If I'd had any reservations about what we were doing, they would've jumped out the tub at that point, but I didn't have one doubt, one hesitation. Every part of my being knew this was the right moment. This was the right time, and I thought I'd felt sure before, even with my ex, Brandon, but I'd been wrong, because I never felt like *this* before. Like this moment could freeze for eternity and it wouldn't be long enough. Like this second couldn't possibly pass fast enough and when it did it was still too slow. Like I couldn't understand how or why we'd waited until now and yet be so very glad that we did, because this moment felt *right*.

I slid my knees to his hips as I sank my fingers into his wet hair. His grip tightened as I settled in his lap, shivering at the ragged sound he made.

Our lips met, and this kiss was powerful and deep as all the ones that came before it, but it was different. There was an edge of urgency to it, one that caused muscles low in my stomach to curl. My body moved in response, out of instinct, and when his hands slipped beyond my hips, tugging me more fully against him, I could feel the same fierce intensity building inside him. He trembled against me, and I could almost imagine that his control was a thin veneer, only moments away from cracking.

But Luc had handed over the reins to me. He'd done so the moment he'd climbed into the tub, letting me guide where his hands, his lips went. He'd given up all control in this.

I broke the kiss, his chest rising and falling heavily against mine. "We can stop," I whispered as I let my forehead rest against his. "We can do anything you want."

One of Luc's hands swept up my back to curl around the nape of my neck. "I want exactly what you want."

I shivered as I slid a hand down his damp chest and then lower, under the water. His back arched, and the way he said my name as my hand touched him kissed my skin. I lifted up just enough, and then there was just him and me and the strangled sound he made against my lips.

Neither of us moved for several long, stuttered heartbeats. There was a pinch of pain that was more of a discomfort as I adjusted to the feeling. Luc was just as still, his body hardened with tension.

Drawing in a shallow breath, I tipped my body forward, kissing him. Both of his hands tightened, one tangling in my hair at the back of my neck, the other digging into my flesh.

"Evie. God," he breathed, shuddering when I moved tentatively. "I . . ."

My hands were back on his shoulders. "Is this okay?"

"It's more than okay." His lips touched mine. "It's perfect. It's just that I thought about how this would feel. Hell, I probably thought about it too much." He pulled me against him more tightly, wringing a gasp from me and a groan from himself. "But I never knew it could feel like *this*. I had no damn idea, Evie. None."

"Me, either," I said, and that was the truth.

Our mouths came together, and I began to move once more, slowly as I tried to soak in how he felt against me, in me, and how every inch of my skin became hypersensitive. My heart was thundering in my chest, completely lost and unprepared for the heady wave of sensations that seemed to sweep through me, through us.

Then, in the center of the keen madness, a bolt of fear pierced me. What if I did forget again? There was still a chance. There'd always be a chance. What if I had no memory of the beauty of these moments, the bliss of this? I could—

"I love you, Evie." One of his arms was curled around my waist, holding me so tightly to his chest as his hips chased the rhythm of mine. "You won't ever forget that. You won't ever forget this. Neither will I. It's *impossible*."

My fingers dug into his shoulders and then tugged at his hair. "Impossible," I repeated, opening my eyes to lock with the raw stare of his.

Eyes locked, there was no sense of rhythm at that point, no thought of the water swelling and falling, only to rise again, spilling over the rim. There was a rattling and then a creaking of the slowly swaying bathroom door. Soft white light flickered along his shoulders, and I looked down us, beyond his chest and mine, to where a constellation of dark dots appeared along my stomach, moving and twisting with my body—with our bodies.

"Beautiful," he murmured, his hand finding the spots and following them over the curve of my hip. "You're so beautiful."

I felt like that in the moment. How could I not? And there was no room for words. There was just us, and how we felt for each other, and that became a potent force, electrifying the space until I could hear the crackling of the air around us charging with the Source, lighting up the very air we breathed, as if the bathroom were suddenly full of a thousand fireflies, a stunning display of just how powerful our love for each other was.

19

It's weird," Luc was saying sometime later. We were lying in bed, neither of us speaking while he played with my hair and I used his chest as a pillow. I'd been lying there trying to determine if my vision was better than before I slept, because I couldn't remember being able to see the room so clearly, or if it were my imagination. "Sex is weird," he added. "I mean that in a good way, but it's like my brain is having a hard time processing it. Like it doesn't change anything, but it changes everything. I know that doesn't make sense."

"It does make sense." I smiled, because I'd been wondering if Luc had noticed how being in each other's arms felt more intimate now or if it just felt that way to me. "When I did it before, it was sort of . . . really awkward afterward. Like it was over and we both were like . . . okay. That's it? Or at least that was how it felt for me. It was done, and I think he said something nice, and then rolled over and started messing around on his phone."

"It doesn't feel that way for you now, does it?"

I lifted my head so I could see him. "It doesn't feel anything like that, Luc. I feel comfortable and completely at ease being like this." My gaze searched his in the dim light. "What does it feel like for you?"

"Better than I could've ever imagined. It feels like words would be inadequate even I tried to even describe it."

"Does it bother you that this wasn't my first time?"

"Honest? It doesn't bother me. Not in the way you meant. Was I jealous? Of course, but that's on me. And like I said before, it's not like I've kept my hands to myself over the years." He touched my cheek. "You were living. I was living. That's all any of that was."

My smile returned, and I stretched up, kissing him. His hand slipped back into my hair as I settled against him once more. Silence fell between us, and for some reason, my mind wandered its way to what Grayson had said before I had gotten dizzy.

"How long has Grayson been here?" I asked.

"Well, he arrived at the zone around the same time we did, perhaps a few seconds—"

"That's not what I meant. Was he born here, on Earth, or was he a recent arrival?"

He looked at me for a few moments, and then his lashes lifted. "That's another impressively random question. Let me guess. Something Grayson said?"

"Yes. He said Kent was the first human he met and that he was sixteen when that happened. Unless Grayson is aging incredibly gracefully, that couldn't have been more than a couple of years ago."

"He met Kent four years ago."

I sucked in a sharp inhale. "Grayson was . . ." I lowered my voice for some bizarre reason. Wasn't like anyone was hanging around in the closet listening to us. "Did he come with the invasion?"

Those lashes lifted. "I think you already know the answer to that."

Wow. I had so many questions. "Is that why he seems to hate humans?"

"Grayson is an equal opportunity species hater," he murmured.

That was believable. "How did you two meet? Did he want to kill humans?" Another thing occurred to me. "That means he rapidly assimilated a human's DNA to look like us! He took someone else's face! Did he want to put us in people zoos?"

"People zoos?" Luc chuckled under his breath. "I can tell you that he didn't kill innocent humans. Well, not many, at least."

My brows lifted. Not many? Uh . . .

"He's not a bad guy, despite what he has done and despite his less-than-stellar personality, and I know you're dying to know all about Grayson, but a lot of that—all of that—isn't my story to tell. It's Grayson's. I have to respect that."

Which was his way of asking me to respect it, too. It was killing me not to ask a million questions and demand answers. I'd never met one of the invading Luxen—well, at least I didn't think I had. Hell, I could've and never known.

But knowing that Grayson legitimately hadn't been around humans until four years ago explained why he seemed to stand out so much from humans, unlike the majority of Luxen who'd been here for decades or been around humans since birth. No wonder he felt so . . . inhuman.

Honest to God, I wasn't sure how to feel knowing that Grayson had been a part of the invading Luxen. But he hadn't killed innocent people—well, other than whoever's face and body he'd stolen, *Invasion of the Body Snatchers*–style . . . and however many "not many" actually was. Okay. That was semantics, but if Luc trusted him, there had to be a reason, one that went beyond pesky moral gray areas.

Luc twisted my hair around his finger. "I think you heard my thoughts earlier."

I lifted my head again, no longer thinking remotely of Grayson. "What?"

"I think you heard my thoughts," he repeated, looking incredibly cozy with his arm tucked behind his head.

"I can't hear your thoughts."

"But you did." He tilted his chin toward me. "When I left to get the doc, what did I say?"

My head was still a little all over the place, so it took me a moment to remember. "You said you didn't want to leave."

One side of his lip quirked. "But I didn't say that."

"Yes, you did." I rose onto an elbow, bracing myself on Luc's chest. "I heard you."

"I didn't say it out loud, Peaches. I thought it," he explained. "And when we were talking about everything after the doc left, you heard me again."

"When?"

"I thought, 'I caused this,' and you answered as if I'd spoken the words out loud, but I hadn't."

All I could do was stare at him. My first response was to deny that was possible. There was still a huge part of me that operated on the belief that I was an ordinary human. After all, I'd had years and years of being just that.

But if Luc said he hadn't spoken out loud, there was no reason he'd lie. I'd heard his thoughts.

I heard his thoughts.

Holy crap!

"How?" I exclaimed. "How did I hear your thoughts?"

"That's a good question. I can only theorize that it's one of those latent abilities waking up, and I was most likely being loud during those moments. It's possible Trojans can read thoughts like Archer and I can. It would make sense that the Daedalus would attempt to work that into the Andromeda serum. It would give the Trojans yet another leg up," he said. "Or it could be something else."

"Like what?"

His eyes closed. "I've healed you several times."

"Like after Micah?" I hadn't just gotten banged up in my fight with that Origin. I'd been near death.

"Yes. You were always getting yourself in trouble. Falling down and cutting open a knee or a hand. Once, you broke your arm," he said, his tone light. "Another time, it was your right foot."

The corners of my lips turned down. "It sounds like I was a klutz."

"You weren't a klutz. You were simply fearless." His eyes opened. "You would always jump before looking."

"Well, now it sounds like I was a badass."

"You're a badass now," he told me. "And when you first got sick, I attempted to heal you. I know hybrids can often telepathically communicate with the Luxen who mutated them. So, it could be that. Even though I didn't mutate you, you were given the other serums that helped mutate other hybrids."

"I want to try now." I popped upward, pushing off his chest. Luc grunted. "See if I can read your mind."

"Okay," he murmured, eyes going half-mast.

I drew in a deep breath and shook out my shoulders. I had no idea what I was supposed to do, but I figured it should require concentration.

Silence filled the room. Nothing but silence.

"I hear nothing."

"I'm not really thinking anything," he murmured. "Sort of really distracted at the moment."

"Why?" It was then when I remembered that I was naked. "Luc!"

"Sorry." He chuckled. "But it's probably a good thing you don't know what I'm thinking right now. Well, not thinking. More like picturing—"

"You need to focus." I started to scramble over him, but my gaze landed on the stack of shirts on the dresser that belonged to him. They were the ones that had already been here, brought over by Dee a few days ago.

I didn't have to get up.

I could be lazy like Luc and Zoe. My heart skipped a beat as I dipped my chin. Fully aware that Luc was still staring at me, I didn't allow myself to be distracted by that. I focused on the low-level hum inside my chest and then pictured the top shirt—

I squeaked as the shirt winged across the room, smacking me in the face. It fell to Luc's chest.

"Nice," he remarked.

"But I did it!" Happy and surprised, I picked up the shirt and tugged it on.

"Boo." Luc pouted.

I grinned. "I can't believe I actually got that shirt to, like, just come to me. Maybe I should try the bottled—"

"Nope." He curled his hand over mine. "Let's hold off on the liquids while we're in bed. Don't need a second bath."

He had a point.

"Plus, after the whole sleeping thing, you—"

"Do not say I should take it easy. I feel fine. Great, even."

"Well, that has everything to do with me and that tub."

I shot him a bland look. Luc smiled back at me.

My heart danced happily, because it was stupid. "We don't have

an endless amount of time to take it easy. In the morning, we practice some more. Moving things with my mind—"

"It's not really with your mind, it's with the Source."

"Semantics."

"Sure. You're right. Just semantics of an ability you have very
little control or understanding of."

I opened my mouth but snapped it shut again. Yet another good
point. Ugh. "Moving things with the *Source* is not helpful when
said item smacks me in the face."

"I'll have to agree with you on that. I also have to agree with
you on your shirt of choice."

Brows furrowing, I looked down and saw that it read COMMAS
SAVE LIVES. I shook my head. "Where do you get these shirts?"

"From Amazon."

I looked up. "Really?"

Luc grinned. "Yes. Guess what?"

"If you say *chicken butt,* I'm going to punch you."

"I didn't say, 'From Amazon,' out loud."

My lips parted on an inhale. "Really?"

He nodded.

Excitement thrummed through me. Rising onto my knees, I
squared my shoulders. "Think something. See if I can hear it."

He lifted his brows. "Hear anything?"

I listened with my ears . . . my mind . . . the Source. Whatever.
"No."

"Good. Because I was blocking my thoughts."

"What the hell?" I threw up my hands. "What good is that?"

"I just need to make sure you can't read my mind whenever you
feel like it." He winked. "I like my privacy."

I smacked his chest, and he rolled onto his side, taking half the
sheet with him as he laughed. "Oh, you like your privacy? Must be
nice! How do you think I feel?"

"Like you don't have any privacy?" He looked over his shoulder at me.

"Oh my God."

Still laughing, he shifted onto his back. "I can teach you how to shield your thoughts, if you'd like."

I took a deep, long breath and then another. "You know, I was about to ask why you're just now offering that, but I'd probably hit you again, so moving on."

"Yes. Moving on. One baby Trojan step at a time. If you can read my thoughts, it could come in handy for when—"

"We need to talk privately," I cut in.

"—I want to talk dirty to you in public," he finished.

I closed my eyes and then reopened them.

Luc looked utterly innocent.

"Luc." I sighed.

A half grin appeared. "Let's try again. I won't block you."

"You'd better not."

I promise.

A wave of goose bumps erupted over my skin. I'd been watching him, so I didn't see his lips move. "I heard you."

Look at you, reading my thoughts.

The shivery feeling across my skin intensified. "How? How can I read them but not everything else? Or are you shielding your thoughts nonstop?" If so, that sounded exhausting.

"I was projecting, for lack of a better word," he explained. "I concentrated on wanting you to hear me. It's just like speaking."

And that meant I could do it, too. Instead of him picking up random, often inconvenient thoughts, I could control—

Something occurred to me. "You weren't lying when you said you only hear me when I'm being loud."

"Mostly. There have been times when I went digging around, but you know that."

I did. "So, is it possible that the reason why I'm so loud is because I'm projecting without realizing it? Thinking about you at the same time?"

"You're right," he said, and I was a second away from clapping. "And you're wrong."

Good thing I didn't clap.

"Most of the time, it's because you're projecting without

realizing it." Shifting onto his side, he propped his cheek onto his fist. "Other times, it's because your emotions are heightened, and any natural shield that the mind possesses—and yes, some of the blocking is organic—collapses. Building shields to block mind-reading jerks like me isn't easy."

"Of course not," I muttered.

But you know what is?

The shiver that accompanied knowing I was hearing his words in my mind was intense. "What?"

Responding to me like this.

"But—"

Think of me and say what you want, but do so in your mind.

Responding like a normal human being was, well, what came naturally, so I had to stop myself from doing that. I concentrated on Luc, but I didn't look at him. That felt like cheating. *Can you hear me?*

Yes.

My head snapped toward Luc. He was watching me with those hooded eyes. "Really?"

He arched a brow as he tapped a finger off his temple.

Really?

Totes.

The corners of my lips tugged up. *This isn't some sort of wish-fulfillment hallucination?*

Luc smiled. *This would be a weird thing to wish for.*

Not when you wanted to feel like you were actually accomplishing something.

But I was totally talking to Luc telepathically, and that had to be the coolest thing ever.

Okay. Maybe moving a shirt with my mind—with the Source—was equally as cool.

Who was I kidding? All of this was cool, and I . . . holy crap on a cracker. I wasn't afraid of these abilities. My gaze dropped to my hand, and I saw very faint black dots, barely visible under my skin. I wasn't afraid.

I looked to Luc, and he was watching me. *You know what?*

What?

I feel like a badass.

His answering smile was swift and it was wide, and before I could track what he was doing, he moved. In a nanosecond, I was under him. *You have always been a badass. Do you know how that makes me feel?*

My body flushed hot. *I have a pretty good idea.*

Luc's lips touched mine, and there wasn't any talking from there, not vocally or in our minds.

Hours later, I very slowly, very carefully extricated myself from Luc's embrace.

It took a while.

Even sleeping, he held on to me like I might disappear on him again, and knowing that was a very real concern for him caused my heart to ache.

But the fact that Luc didn't wake up proved just how exhausted he was. He needed to sleep a day or two, but I couldn't sleep yet.

Restless, but nowhere near as much, I found a pair of leggings in the dark and pulled them on. In the back of my mind, I knew I would've had one hell of a time finding those black pants before, but I didn't obsess over that. Improved eyesight was definitely a cool benefit, but I'd talked to Luc *telepathically* tonight.

I'd also moved a shirt with the Source.

Luc and I had also had sex.

I wasn't sure which one of them felt more life-altering. All of them were for different reasons. So, there was a lot I could obsess over, rightfully so, but I didn't want to stress over any of it.

An idea had occurred to me while I'd lain there in bed, and I didn't know why I hadn't thought of it before. Heading to the kitchen, I quickly grabbed a few cans of food and a couple of bottles of water, placing them in one of the paper bags stacked on the floor of the pantry. If Nate had come by while I'd been sleeping, he could've been looking for food and gotten scared off by the presence of so many different people in and out of the house.

Even if he hadn't been, maybe if he found the bag, he would come back.

With the bag in hand, I slipped out into the cool night and looked around. Spotting the furniture by the firepit, I figured that would be a good place to leave the bag. I placed it on the cushion and then turned, looking up. The sky was blanketed with tiny dazzling stars, some brighter than others. Had the sky always looked like this, or were my eyes just registering it better now? I had to think the fact there were no light sources of any significance for miles and miles had to be why so many stars were visible.

Either way, it was absolutely beautiful.

The soft wail of a baby broke the silence, and I turned to Kat and Daemon's house. The cry came again. A soft, very frustrated wail that was most definitely coming from outside.

My feet were moving before I told them to. Curiosity had taken hold as I walked along the fence line, toward the front of the house and through an area that was only six feet wide and was more grass than stone. As I grew closer, the *owh*-sounding wail weakened, and I felt the creepy-crawling sensation along the back of my neck. My gaze tracked over the covered porch as I inched out into the front lawn.

Daemon was on the porch with the baby. I didn't see him, not through the heavy curtains, but I didn't feel that sensation when I was around Kat.

Low, masculine shushing sounds came from the porch, and they were answered by an even sleepier whimper.

Feeling like I was intruding, I turned away, but one of the curtains peeled back, and there Daemon was, glowing like a rainbow to my all-new, extra-special Arum eyes, and in his arms was this tiny thing that glowed white with a purplish tint.

A baby Origin.

The light show faded until it was barely visible. There was a whole lot of skin to see, as Daemon was shirtless, but it was the child who had my attention. He was wrapped up in a fuzzy white blanket—which was normal, I supposed—but this blanket had a teeny-tiny hood, and that hood had half of a face and ears—

"Is that a llama hood?" I blurted out, and the baby let out another cry. "Oh my God, I'm sorry. I probably shouldn't be talking if you're trying to calm him or something."

"Nah, it's cool. Talking doesn't stop him from sleeping. A bomb going off probably wouldn't stop him from sleeping." Daemon sighed as he looked down at the child. "And yes. It's a llama blanket, hood thing."

Relieved, I stared at the llama blanket. "Luc?"

"Who else?" He descended the steps, his feet also bare. "I hope Adam's extra-strength screams didn't wake you."

"No. I couldn't sleep." Surprised that Daemon was actually walking across the driveway to where I stood instead of rushing the baby away from me, I just stood there.

And like a doofus, I said the stupidest-sounding thing possible. "I've never seen a baby."

His steps slowed.

"I mean, I don't remember ever seeing a baby, but I've never been close to one in real life." I paused. "As opposed to seeing one on the TV or something. God, he's so small. Like, wow, that is small."

And like, wow, I needed to shut the hell up.

"Yeah, he's a little guy." Daemon grinned as Adam made a tired sound that vaguely resembled a yawn. "He does this crying thing, about an hour each night, at the same time. He's not hungry or anything. According to one of the books Kat read, it's just a thing babies do."

"How is Kat?" I asked, folding my arms over my waist.

"Good." He was still staring down at the infant, and I realized he was moving as he stood there, swaying and rocking gently. "Perfect, actually. She just fell back asleep not too long ago. Up feeding him. God, she's a freaking goddess." A brief, wider smile appeared as several thick locks of black hair toppled over his forehead. "I don't know how she did this." Awe filled his tone. "I honest to God don't. So, I'm keeping the little guy company at night so she can get some rest until he gets hungry again, which is a lot. This is a walk in the park."

I smiled at them. "She's incredibly strong. I'd probably be hiding in a bathroom, sobbing in panic if I were in her place."

Daemon chuckled as he looked at me. "Kat said the same thing more than once, just so you know." He turned, angling his body so I could see Adam's face. "Looks like me, doesn't he?"

Opening my mouth, I wasn't sure what to say. The little, scrunched red face didn't look like either Daemon or Kat. In fact, he looked like a little, tired old man. And then his eyes widened from the sleepy, thin slits. I couldn't see the color, but I knew they'd be a stunning shade of amethyst. I saw his pupils, though. Diamond white. He gave me a rather judgy look for a four-day-old infant.

"Um . . ." I shook my head. "He looks like you?"

"Right answer," he replied. "By the way, glad to see you up and moving around and not dead."

I blinked.

"Luc would've been . . . well, 'a real pain in the ass for the entire world to deal with' would be an understatement if he lost you again," he went on, and I couldn't help but think of our conversation back at Luc's club. "Hell, he was about out of his mind when I checked in with him."

"You stopped by?" Shock splashed through my system.

Daemon nodded as he swayed. "Got about halfway into the house each time before Luc made me leave. I think he was afraid I was going to make things worse. Can't exactly blame him for that, all things considered."

I was struck speechless.

"Anyway, Viv updated Kat and me earlier. Said you were awake and doing well. We were going to stop by, but she suggested we give you guys some time." That admittedly downright charming grin appeared again. "I told Kat that about three times since Viv left. Figured Luc wouldn't want any interruptions. I know I sure as hell wouldn't want any if Kat had been sleeping for four days."

"She wanted to come over? After giving birth? With the baby?"

He looked at me as if he were wondering where exactly the baby would be if not with them. "She's been worried about you."

"But she just gave birth," I whisper-yelled like he didn't know.

"Like I said, my girl is a warrior goddess."

"Yeah. Yeah, she is." I was half-afraid, but I had to ask. "Why are you not worried about me being so close to your baby now? You don't want me here, and I totally get it. I'm working on controlling the Source, and I knew who I was when I woke up, but I get it. I do."

Moonlight sliced over his face as he lifted his chin. "Not sure if you know this or not, but I wouldn't be standing here holding my child if not for Luc. Adam decided to come into the world his own way, feetfirst. There was a lot of bleeding and the umbilical cord was cramped and he was losing oxygen. He could've suffocated. Luc made sure that didn't happen. He saved my son's life, and there's no way I could ever repay him for that. No way at all." Voice rough, he dipped his head, kissing the top of the llama head. "The very least I could do is be a little less of a paranoid dick about his girl."

The back of my throat burned as a knot of emotion lodged itself right there.

"But that also doesn't mean I stopped worrying," he added in a tone that was surprisingly gentle. "I saw what you are capable of. I felt it. I hope for everyone's sake nothing comes from that worrying."

Easily recalling Kat's warning, I nodded. "I will do everything I can to make that the case."

"I know." There was a stretch of silence. "You probably should get back inside soon. If Luc wakes up and finds you gone, God only knows what he'll do, but it will likely be loud and make all my hard work here with Adam go to waste."

Grinning as the baby gurgled sleepily, I nodded. "You're probably right."

"Usually," he replied, and there was a hint of a teasing grin.

"Well, I hope the night is a quiet one and all of you get some rest."

"I hope so myself, but if it's not . . ." He looked down at the top of the baby's covered head. His features softened, impossibly so. "Wouldn't trade a damn second of this for anything."

Oh my goodness.

My heart imploded into goo.

"Good night," Daemon murmured, completely unaware that I was melting like chocolate on a hot summer day. He turned, his large hand still protectively folded around the back of his son's head as he began whispering to the sleeping child about someone called Princess Snowbird.

Watching him disappear back up the driveway and through the canopied carport, I thought that we'd actually had a decent conversation.

Maybe Daemon didn't hate me, because he was giving me a chance to prove that I wasn't a danger. And maybe babies were actually cute, because Adam was cute with the odd little sounds he made. Especially ones that didn't all but rip their way out of me when they made their appearance in the world.

Babies.

I shuddered.

I stared at the darkness of the looming city. Right now, babies made me want to scream and run in the opposite direction. I was smart enough to know that could change down the road, because there would be a down the road, but that was a bridge Luc and I would cross. Together. If we wanted children one day—I shuddered *again*—we could adopt. Being able to conceive a child didn't make a mother a mom or a father a dad. It didn't mean a child was loved any more or less, and it sure as hell didn't make one lesser than the other in any way.

I knew that better than most.

Mom loved Evie—the real Evie. I could see that when she told me about her and in the memory that had surfaced. And I think that she had loved me, despite all the lies. Or maybe that's what I needed to believe, because I did miss her. I missed her smile, the way she smelled, and her hugs. I missed that I could think of her without guilt and hatred.

And for the first time since I'd learned the truth about everything, I *almost* found myself wishing that I could forget her.

20

"D idn't we already discuss this?" Yanking my hair back, I twisted the mass into a bun and then shoved the first of a million bobby pins into it. "I told you I wanted to get back to training as soon as possible."

Luc stood in front of the television, and it looked like the painting of the archangel Michael was seconds away from smiting him. Luc was still shirtless, and I had a strong suspicion he was trying to distract me.

"We discussed this," he replied. "But it was sort of a one-sided discussion with you saying you wanted to get back to training."

"And you agreed."

"I do, but I also think there's no harm in taking it easy."

"I don't need to take it easy after sleeping for four days." I shoved another bobby pin in, nearly scalping myself in the process. Ouch.

"I just don't want you to overdo it, Evie, and then have you pass out again." Luc picked up a shirt.

"Dr. Hemenway didn't say something like that would happen."

"She also doesn't know what will happen." His brows knitted. "How many bobby pins do you need?"

"A lot. And I feel perfectly fine." One more bobby pin and I was somewhat confident my hair wouldn't topple over when the lightest breeze touched it.

"You do look perfectly fine." He tugged the shirt on. *Finally.* He arched a brow. "Didn't realize my man chest was so distracting."

"Man chest?"

"It's just skin and nipples, Peaches. Don't make it awkward."

I stared at him.

He grinned.

"Don't be cute."

I can't help it. I'm adorable.

A sharp whooshing motion tumbled my stomach. All morning, Luc had been shifting back and forth from talking out loud and through the Source, a different form of training from the kind we were arguing about.

I focused on him, imagining a cord connecting us. *You're annoying.*

He feigned a scowl. *I'm rubber, and you're glue. What you say bounces off me and sticks to you.*

"Oh my God." I laughed. "How old are you? Five?"

Luc nodded. "I'm a big boy now."

"Seriously. Stop being cute. I'm irritated."

"I can't help who I am." Luc didn't just walk toward me. He *swaggered*. "I know you're ready to get back to training, and I know I'm probably just being paranoid."

"You're definitely being paranoid."

"I am."

I concentrated on the cord between us. *But I do understand why you're paranoid. I would be, too, if it had been you who had passed out for four days.*

His gaze flickered over my face. "I'm glad you understand." He switched over to the more private way. *It's not that I'm trying to control what you do or that I don't think you're capable of getting back to training. I just worry. A lot.*

"I know."

He brushed back a wisp of hair that had escaped one of the many bobby pins already. *I know you didn't sleep much last night.*

Luc had been awake when I'd returned, probably mere seconds away from launching a search and possible rescue, but all he'd remarked on when I climbed back into bed was how cold my toes were. He'd gathered me close, tucking me against his chest, and promptly fallen back to sleep.

I slept enough, I told him and then switched to the form I was more comfortable with. "The only thing I do feel is a little restless, but nothing like before. Remember how Grayson said he could feel the Source, like an internal buzzing? That's how it feels. Maybe it's something I just need to get used to."

He tucked away another fine strand of hair. "Probably. I know it takes a while for hybrids. Just promise me that if you start to feel weird or dizzy or anything, you'll let me know immediately."

"I promise."

Running his fingers along my jaw, he tilted my head back. "I feel like I should apologize."

"For what?"

"I woke you up this morning."

I frowned. "You did?"

He nodded. "When I woke up, you were still sleeping and you were so still against me, I had this moment of panic, thinking you weren't going to wake up again. So, I just about shouted your name. I'm surprised you didn't wake up screaming."

"Luc." My heart squeezed. "You don't have to apologize. I would've done the same."

"Remember you said this after a year or so of me shouting your name in panic in the mornings."

"I'll remember."

Lowering his head, he kissed me, and each kiss since yesterday felt different—sweeter and heavier with promises. I stepped into him, gripping the front of his shirt. The sound rumbling from deep within him sent a shiver curling its way down my spine.

Evie. Luc smiled against my lips. "If we don't leave now, we're not going to be leaving for quite some time."

"That doesn't sound like a bad thing," I said, eyes still closed. "Does it?"

"No." He slid his hand over my hip. "It sounds like all the best dreams coming true."

My nose brushed his as I tilted my head. "But . . . ?"

"But we're going to be mature and responsible," he said with a sigh so disgusted, it drew a grin from me. "You want to get your abilities in tip-top shape. Prioritize, Peaches."

"You kissed me."

"Your lips were begging mine."

Laughing, I opened my eyes and pulled away. "Come on."

He caught my hand in his, and we walked out the front door into the bright, sunny November morning. The skies were such a clear blue, and the clouds fluffy and low. I yearned to capture it on camera. As we made our way down the driveway, I fantasized about replacing all the angel paintings with photographs of the sky, some in color and others in black and white. Alas, that wasn't going to happen anytime soon.

"Want to race?" I asked at the end of the driveway. We were going to the same place as before, the old packing warehouse.

"I thought we'd make a pit stop first. Unlike you, I haven't gotten the chance to really check out the newest addition to the world," Luc said. "It was probably a minute or so after he was born that I heard Grayson."

"That's fine with me." I'd told Luc about the surprise meet and greet, but I hadn't mentioned what Daemon had told me last night about what Luc had done. "You're amazing, you know that, right?"

"Obviously." He squeezed my hand. "But what made you decide to finally acknowledge it?"

"I'm pretty sure that wasn't the first time I've acknowledged that." We crossed the front lawns, heading for where the curtain was already parted. "But I know what you did for their baby."

"Oh." He was looking up, at the sky. "I didn't do much. Nothing to be impressed over."

"Nothing to be impressed over? You kept the baby stable. How were you able to do that?"

He stopped just below the porch steps. "I got lucky. We all got lucky that it was a compressed umbilical cord—something physical and not something biological. If so, there would have been nothing any of us could've done."

I looked up at him, keeping my voice low. "I think everyone got lucky that you were here."

His gaze lowered to me. "All I did was do what I could. I kept the baby's breathing steady. That's all."

And that kept the child alive, but to hear Luc speak, it was like he'd simply helped unload groceries or something.

Stretching up, I kissed his cheek, and when I rocked back onto my feet, he watched me. I tugged on his hand, and he followed me up the porch.

Daemon answered the door before we knocked. "Look who's blessing us with their presence."

Luc smiled. "I knew you were probably missing me."

The Luxen chuckled. "Like a hole in the head."

"That might actually be an improvement," Luc replied.

"He's here to see the baby," I jumped in before the two devolved into a "who could out-snark the other" contest.

"Is he jealous that you saw him first?" Daemon asked.

I nodded.

"I'm going to start calling you Benedict Peaches Arnold," Luc muttered.

That made me snort-laugh.

"You're in luck." Daemon closed the door behind us. "Adam is awake."

"It's because he's eager to meet me."

I rolled my eyes as we followed Daemon back to the bedroom. Once again, I was a little awed by the number of books in this house.

Can you hear any of Daemon's thoughts right now? Luc's voice made me jump, and I looked at him.

I hadn't heard anything the night before, but it wasn't like I'd been trying then. Focusing on Daemon's back, I concentrated and heard nothing.

I don't hear anything, I told Luc.

Interesting. He's thinking about how beautiful Kat looks and—yikes, I am not repeating what I hear now. Luc's brows lifted. *Maybe it's unique to us, because of my healing attempts and the other serums.*

If it was unique to us, then could that mean the other Trojans would be unable to communicate this way or hear others' thoughts? If so, Luc and I had a leg up on the other Trojans. Or it could mean that other Trojans could hear the thoughts of all others like Luc could, and I was somewhat defective because of the other serums.

You're not defective.

I shot a look at Luc. *Get out of my head.*

He grinned.

What we needed was another Trojan. That was the only way to test many of our theories or find any answers, but that was likely not going to happen.

"I think Adam knew you were coming," came Kat's voice from the end of the hall. "He's usually napping at this time of the day, but he's been awake."

Since Origins were all a little different, that could be possible.

"Then he must be as excited as I am," Luc responded as he stepped into the room. I lingered back.

Kat looked up from where she sat, rocking gently in the chair, hair swept up in a knot that looked as messy as mine felt and cheeks flushed a healthy pink. The baby was nestled against Kat's chest, looking and blinking at whatever babies looked at.

Without the little blanket hoodie, I saw that the baby boy had a lot of thick, dark hair. A head full of it!

Kat smiled as her husband crossed the room, dropping a kiss on her cheek and then the top of his son's head. She rose from the chair, the pale blue dress gliding around her feet as she walked forward, stopping in front of Luc, who stood as if spellbound.

"Kat—"

Rising onto the tips of her toes, Kat kissed his cheek, silencing him. "Thank you," she whispered, her eyes glimmering with tears as she stepped back. "Those two words aren't nearly enough, but *thank you.*"

I pressed my lips together as I inhaled sharply through my nose. Luc slowly shook his head, and I knew he was about to give her the same line he'd given me, but Kat was having none of that.

"Losing him would've killed us in the worst possible ways, and I don't know if we would've recovered from that, but the three of us are here because of you," she told him. "And I wish there were some way we could repay you—some way that you could truly understand the depths of our gratitude."

Luc was still speechless and back to being as still as a tomb, so I intervened. "He likes grilled cheese sandwiches."

Kat's gaze darted to me, eyebrows raising.

"A lot," I added. "Like, so much so, he's in a committed, long-term relationship with them. A lifetime supply of them would go a long way to proving your gratitude."

Kat smiled as she glanced over at Daemon while Luc's shoulders began to relax. "I think we can make that work. Right, babe?"

"I can cook up a mean grilled cheese," he said.

Thank you, came Luc's soft reply.

I blinked back the dampness in my eyes. *Now I don't have to worry about making you any.*

He sent me a grin over his shoulder and a look that said he knew better.

Kat turned slightly, and at that moment, little Adam stretched out a tiny, chubby arm toward Luc as his little head bobbed and weaved behind Kat's hand. He let out a soft baby noise. "I think he wants to say hello."

Before Luc could do or say anything, Kat was tucking the baby into Luc's arms. "Just make sure you support his head. Like this." Kat made it so that Luc's arm and then his hand formed a cradle. "There you go. You're a pro."

Luc looked like he'd been handed a bomb.

"Oh yeah, you look like a natural," Daemon remarked.

Kat sent a look at Daemon that made him chuckle. "He's doing just fine." She smiled up at Luc. "You're doing great."

"He's really small," was all Luc said.

"Sure didn't feel like that four days ago," she replied wryly, and I barely managed to hide my cringe.

Creeping closer, I could see that the baby was staring up at Luc with eyes identical to his. Adam was incredibly quiet as his sock-covered feet wiggled.

"I think he likes you," Daemon said. "Which is really going to tick off Archer. The moment he gets near, Adam scrunches up his face and starts wailing."

"That's my boy." Luc's grin was slow as he turned to me. "Want to hold him?"

"Nope!" I held up my hands. "No offense, but I do not trust myself not to do something wrong."

"I thought the same thing the first time I held him." Kat reached out, touching my arm. "I'm so glad to see that you're doing well. We were so worried."

"Thank you," I said. "And you look amazing, by the way."

"I feel like a ten-ton truck drove *through* me, and I'm exhausted." Her gaze drifted to Luc and her child. "But I'm absolutely loving it." She reached out, straightening the little sock on one of his feet. "Do either of you or Viv know why you slept for a few days?"

Actually relieved that she'd asked, because I was beginning to really wonder what kind of bizarre stuff these two had seen that they hadn't questioned it yet, I told them what we knew. Then Luc chimed in after Daemon retrieved his son, explaining Viv's theory.

"Damn," Daemon murmured. "All of it sounds insane, but it also makes sense."

Kat was toying with Adam's foot again. "I saw some of their labs while I was at one of their compounds. Dasher showed them to me, actually." She smiled at her baby. "There is nothing I don't think they're capable of, so coding a mutation to act like a dormant virus doesn't really surprise me."

Daemon's jaw hardened. "But if Viv's theory is right, and those additional serums changed the game, that would explain why you didn't attempt to head back to the Daedalus and why you didn't recognize us."

"You were rebooting," Kat said. "And something that Luc said or did either sped up the process or snapped you out of it."

Something had been said. I could almost hear it. Whatever it was, it bloomed on the fringes of my thoughts and then slipped through my fingers like smoke as I stared at Kat. My brain did cartwheels trying to recapture it, but I couldn't.

"You've used the Source since, right?" she asked.

"Yes," I told them, refocusing. "I used it to retrieve a shirt. I think it's going to make me lazy."

Kat sent me a grin. "Girl, when I first I got control of the Source, I used it for everything."

"Is it possible that the whole sleeping thing was possibly the final reboot? Or update running?" Daemon asked.

"It's not impossible," answered Luc. "We won't know until, well, we know."

Daemon handed Adam back over to Kat. "And working with the Source isn't the same as doing what you did in the woods."

"I know." I met his stare. "But we're starting out small, and I guess eventually, we'll go full throttle. Luc has a way to, um, ensure I don't get too out of control."

"He does?" Kat sounded surprised by that as she returned to the chair. Sitting, she placed the baby so he was resting cheek-down on her arm. He looked super-happy there. "How?"

When Luc didn't answer, I did. "He can basically shut me down by taking control. Knocking me out without, you know, actually knocking me out."

Kat's gaze shifted from me to Luc as she rubbed her hand up and down Adam's back. "That sounds extreme."

"What would happen if he doesn't will be way more extreme." I met Kat's eyes, willing her to remember the warning she'd given me before, and she must've, because she nodded.

"I want to be there when you go full throttle," Daemon announced.

My brows flew up. "Uh, I, um, don't know if that's a good idea."

"Same," Luc stated.

"I think I need to be clearer." Daemon then fixed those ultra-bright green eyes on Luc. "I want to be there to help make sure it doesn't get out of hand."

Quiet, Luc tilted his head, and then after a small eternity, he said, "Okay."

Okay?

He's being genuine, Peaches. His voice echoed in my thoughts without warning, jolting me. *He wants to make sure that nothing bad happens so something really bad doesn't go down.*

I thought that over. *You mean so I don't end up ticking off Cekiah and getting booted from the zone?*

You will never get booted from the zone. "I'll let you know when we're ready."

"Good." Daemon folded his arms, looking like the badass Luxen I knew.

"Good," Kat whispered and then louder, "Dee's going to be thrilled to hear you're awake and doing okay."

"Surprised she's not here." Luc picked up what appeared to be a stuffed banana and frowned. "I got him better toys than this."

Daemon ignored that. "She and Archer are out. She has several interviews."

My little old ears pricked right up. "With that stupid senator?"

"Among other stupid people." A brief grin appeared, but it quickly faded. "Remember that Sons of Liberty guy? Steven? He was talking about a flu?"

"The one weaponized with the mutation," I said. "He said it had been released in small batches."

Daemon nodded. "Well, it appears it's been released more widely. A lot of people are getting sick. Some are acting violent. Some are dying."

My stomach dropped, and immediately, I thought of James, of everyone I'd seen day in and day out at Centennial High. "How widely?"

"From what Dee has learned, the initial outbreaks in Kansas City and Boulder have spread. I don't know how many are sick, but it's enough that people aren't able to leave or enter the cities," Daemon said, and I pressed my hand to the center of my chest. "There's been another in Orlando, one in New Orleans, and . . ."

My breath caught as dread exploded inside me. "Where?"

There was a quick glance at Luc before Daemon answered. "Columbia, Maryland, and some of the surrounding cities."

"No," I whispered, my knees suddenly wobbly. I wanted to turn right around and find my way back to Columbia. It sounded crazy. What could I do? But I wanted to make sure that James and my friends were okay.

"How bad is it?" Luc demanded.

"Same as the other cities. They're locked down, trying to stop the potential spread." Kat's hand stilled on the center of the baby's back. Adam was asleep. "Or so they claim, but if the Daedalus is responsible for the flu, you know there's either a reason they're containing it right now or it's a lie."

"There are no estimates on how many are sickened?" Luc asked.

"The only thing Dee has heard is that in Boulder they're saying it's about three percent of the population, but it's higher there because of the large Luxen population." Daemon's jaw worked. "That's what the officials are saying, and that's probably a little over three thousand based on when we lived there."

"Dear God," I gasped. "If less than fifty percent get the flu vaccine and you use those statistics, that could mean at least fifteen hundred of them will die or mutate."

Daemon said something, but I wasn't tracking. A steady stream of faces flashed before me, some of them I knew, others nameless, and then that stream turned into a river of faceless people, all of them innocent. Nausea twisted up my insides.

"And let me guess, the Luxen are being blamed and the public is buying it hook, line, and sinker?"

"Yep," Daemon clipped out.

"We have to do something," I said, heart thumping.

"There's nothing we can do." Luc faced me.

"There has to be something." My thoughts raced for an answer, settling on the one thing Mom had always stressed. "Flu shots. Dee could get a message out there to make sure people are getting their flu shots. It would be some protection—"

"There's a nationwide shortage," Daemon cut in. "A very convenient one. If people haven't gotten their shot, they won't get one."

I lifted a hand, running it over my brow. "There's got to be something else. People are going to mutate or they're going to die."

"Something is being done," Luc said.

"You just said there's nothing—"

"*We* can do," he repeated. "As in you and me, and everyone in this room, including the adorable sleeping baby. We can't fight a flu virus, Peaches. Not with our fists or the Source, unless we use the latter to firebomb the hell out of cities, and I don't think anyone wants that."

"I know that."

"Dee is doing everything to get the word out there that the Luxen aren't making humans sick," Daemon explained. "That the flu is spreading like any other flu, through human-to-human contact. She's not blaming the Daedalus or the government. If she went at them like that, she'd be shut out. No one would hear her. We have to hope that people are listening to her and taking the right precautions instead of buying into catchy nicknames."

"We have to *believe* that," Kat corrected. "There are a lot of humans out there that aren't afraid of Luxen, who have to see through this BS."

"And then what?" I asked, looking between the two of them. "What if they do listen? What if they don't? Once the flu does its damage and kills or mutates millions, or even if there are no more outbreaks, what are we going to do?"

Neither Kat nor Daemon answered.

I sucked in a sharp breath. I knew what that meant—what it still meant even though Daemon was willing to give me another chance and even be there to help Luc stop me before things got out of hand. Neither of them trusted me, not with what they planned to do.

That still stung and it still angered me, but what crushed me was the knowledge that I had yet to give them any real reasons to trust me.

I could feel Luc's gaze on me when he asked, "What is this catchy nickname for the flu?"

"It's the most uninventive thing you could imagine." Disgust dripped from Daemon's tone. "They're calling it ET."

21

Three days after learning the flu with the stupidest nickname ever was spreading and the only thing any of us could do was hope that people would listen to Dee, I caught the stuffed banana that flew out of Zoe's hand, winging straight for my palm instead of my face.

"Aha!" I shouted, thrusting the toy Luc had stolen from Daemon and Kat's house into the air.

"You did it again!" Zoe clapped, a much more helpful and enthusiastic audience than Grayson.

"Congratulations," came the gruff voice that was surprisingly more irritating than Grayson's dry one. "You stopped a stuffed banana from physically assaulting your face." A pregnant pause. "After twenty-three attempts."

I counted to ten as my gaze slid past Luc's bemused expression to the old man sitting in the folded metal chair.

Unfortunately, Zoe hadn't come alone the last two days.

General Eaton sat there, rubbing the knee of his stiff leg. He had more comments than a sports broadcaster. When he'd showed up yesterday with Zoe, he'd claimed he'd wanted to see for himself that I was—how had he put it? "Awake and breathing and not trying to kill everyone in sight."

Lovely.

"It was not twenty-three times," I snapped, resisting the urge to turn the banana into a real projectile and launch it toward his head.

"It was more like fifteen," Luc interjected.

I narrowed my eyes at him. "You're so not helping."

Luc grinned, but there was something off about it. I couldn't put my finger on what it was or if there was anything truly off about it. *You're hot when you're mad.*

Don't try to sweet-talk me.

Chuckling, Luc lifted his hand, and the banana flew from mine straight to his. Over the last couple of days, Luc constantly shifted from speaking out loud to not, and while it was still a shock to hear his voice so clearly, sending what I wanted him to hear had gotten easier. And despite Eaton's less-than-supportive attitude, I was significantly better at using the Source. Yes, my aim was sometimes a wee bit off, but from day one, as Luc was referring to the first day after waking up, there been a marked improvement. No more misfires when I was attempting to move something. I didn't have to concentrate as hard, and I was feeling pretty darn kick-ass, to be honest.

"We're going to try to do something harder," Luc announced, tossing the banana into Eaton's lap. The general frowned down at it. "I want you to move animate objects—something that can fight back."

Zoe lifted her hand. "I volunteer as tribute."

I crossed my arms. "Not sure I'm comfortable with that."

"I am." Slipping the hair band off her wrist, she pulled the mass of tight curls back from her face. "Move me. I dare you."

Eaton arched his brow.

I looked to Luc. His shoulders were tense. Moving a stolen stuffed banana was one thing. Forcing my friend to do something was entirely another.

It's okay. You're not going to hurt her, Luc's voice came to me.

How can you be sure?

Because I'm not asking you to toss her through a window.

My lips thinned as I shifted my gaze to Zoe. "Are you sure about this?"

She nodded. "We used to do this all the time when we were training. It's how we learned to work with the Source."

Well, that didn't really make me feel that much better. "And you're okay with doing this again?"

"Get on with it, girl." Eaton scratched at his chin. "The day isn't getting any longer."

"If you're bored, you can always go find something else," I suggested nicely.

He tipped forward. "I got a piece of advice for you."

"You do?"

"That's why I'm here," he replied. "If you want to take what was done to you and do something good with it, you've got to get over yourself."

I blinked. "Excuse me?"

"Eaton," Luc sighed, turning to the older man.

"Naw, hear me out." He held up a hand. "You keep thinking like you're a human—like you're surrounded by fragile, little humans. You aren't human. Not anymore. And these two have never been human. You need to stop thinking and acting that way."

"He has a point," Zoe said after a moment. "You're not going to hurt me."

Luc said nothing as I shifted my weight from foot to foot. The thing was, I *could* hurt Zoe, but Luc was right. I wasn't going to try to throw her out a window or anything. And Eaton was also correct. I was still thinking like a human. Kind of hard not to.

"Okay." I unfolded my arms. "Let's do this."

"I want you to push Zoe back without touching her," Luc instructed.

Zoe skipped her way over to where I stood, stopping in front of me, smiling brightly. "Move me."

I stared at her.

"Do it. You know what to do. Make me move." She pushed my shoulder, and I rolled my eyes. "Make. Me. Move."

"You don't have to be this annoying."

"Oh, you know you haven't seen anything yet," she replied. "I can be way more annoying than this. Remember that time you and Heidi wanted to watch that creepy show about bugs inside people and I was not about that kind of life?"

I grinned as the memory surfaced. "You started dancing in front of the TV, doing a really bad interpretative dance routine."

"Oh yeah." She lifted her brows. "I can be a tree again. A tree being knocked down." Raising her arms above her head, she started to sway back and forth. "A sad tree, being knocked down."

"What in the hell," muttered Luc.

Trying not to laugh as Zoe started to dip to the right and then the left, I tapped into the hum of energy in my chest and pictured Zoe moving—"Oh, shit!"

Zoe's feet skidded along the floor as she *flew* backward, her shirt rippling around her. Throwing a hand out, she caught herself before she slammed into the wall.

Eaton chuckled. "Well, hot damn, things just got interesting."

"Oh my God, I'm sorry!" I started toward Zoe.

"That was freaking amazing!" Zoe exclaimed, and I drew up short. "Holy crap, it was like being hit by hurricane-force winds." Her wide-eyed gaze swung toward Luc. "Did you see that?"

"I saw it." A faint smile marked his lips. "Do it again, but this time, Zoe, fight back."

"I did." She straightened her shirt as she walked back to where I stood. "I fought back."

"Fight harder."

Her nose wrinkled. "Okay." Facing me, she was all business this time around. No interpretative dance routines. Chin dipped, arms at her sides, she nodded. "Move me."

I did what I did before, picturing her moving, but this time Zoe's pupils flared white and she didn't fly backward. She scooted back several inches.

"Push her back," Luc ordered, his jaw clenching.

I pushed, fingers curling inward. Zoe's lips pressed together, and white veins appeared underneath her skin even as she moved another foot.

"Dammit," she growled, her tank top plastering to her stomach and chest.

A second later, she lost the battle, sliding backward. Letting up, I looked to Luc.

He was frowning. "Are you really resisting, Zoe?"

"Yes!" She threw up her arms. "I thought I had it for a moment, but she's . . ." Zoe shifted her gaze to me. "Dude, you're strong." Her gaze flickered over me. "And your skin right now? It looks pretty damn cool."

A wealth of pride swelled in my chest, and Zoe and I squared off once more. Zoe was able to resist for a handful of seconds the next couple of times, but after that, I pushed harder, and there was no resisting.

Zoe had to tap out shortly after that, and Luc took her place. She had volunteered to help the doc carry out general wellness checks on all the humans. I had a feeling they were checking and double-checking for any signs of a flu, even though it was highly unlikely that anyone would've come into contact with it.

Luc stood in front of me, legs wide and braced. I pushed—pushed hard. His shirt blew back against his body as his hair whipped over his forehead. His pupils flared intensely, and for several seconds, he didn't move.

And then he did.

Luc slid about a foot before catching himself. White burst to life, lighting up a network of veins along his cheeks and throat. He didn't budge after that.

Sucking in air, I shook out my arms. "That's all I can do."

Luc straightened, the light receding from his veins. Brackets of tension formed around his mouth. "You are powerful. We already know that, but you know what else I know?"

"What?" I caught the water he tossed me and took a drink.

"I know you are way more powerful than that." He stalked toward me, taking the bottle I offered. "I have firsthand knowledge of that."

My stomach tumbled a little as I watched him take a drink. "What I'm doing right now isn't what I did in the woods."

"True, but you have that kind of strength in you. You should be able to send me flying across the room."

I smothered a yawn, wondering why Luc was so eager to be thrown across a room.

"Tired?" Luc stepped closer, his voice low.

Sleep hadn't come easily since I'd awakened from my short-term coma. Well, staying asleep was the problem. Falling asleep had been all too easy. I had no idea if it had to do with the whole mutating thing waking me up, worrying about Heidi and Emery, or learning about the flu, but either way, I'd spent a lot of quiet hours thinking everything over. Dee and Archer were slated to return today, and I hoped she carried with her some update about the flu and what was really happening.

But there was something that kept nagging at me, existing just out of my reach. I kept thinking it was something Kat had said when we'd visited her, but I couldn't put my finger on it.

"I'm fine," I told him, and then privately I added, *I promised you that I would tell you if I'm feeling weird or anything. I'm not.* "I don't want to toss you across a room."

Luc set the bottle aside. "And that is the problem."

I stiffened.

He curled his fingers around the hem of my shirt, straightening it. "Eaton could've said it better."

"I thought I said it just perfectly," the general muttered.

Luc ignored him. "But you are thinking like a human. You're treating us like we're humans. You held back on Zoe. I know you did," he said when I opened my mouth to disagree. "She shouldn't have been able to resist at all. And you didn't push as hard as I know you can with me. You need to stop worrying about hurting me or Zoe."

I placed my hands on my hips. "Easier said than done, Luc. I am capable of hurting you, and I don't know exactly what the limit is."

"Knowing your limit is easy." His eyes met mine. "You don't want to hurt me, then you don't hurt me."

My brows lifted. "That may sound like it makes sense to you, but it doesn't to me."

White light erupted from his palm, and he lifted his hand. Energy crackled softly as he cupped my cheek. His palm and the Source were warm as he touched me, sending soft jolts of energy skittering over my skin.

"Does that hurt?" he asked.

"No."

"But you've seen me use this to kill, haven't you? You've seen me place this very hand on someone and burn them from the inside out, right?"

Chest tightening, I nodded. "Not like I'm going to forget that."

"The Source is the Source, Peaches. The only difference is the will behind it—the who behind it. I don't want to hurt you, so I don't. You don't want to hurt me, so you don't."

He switched to a much more private form of conversation. *The night of the nightmare, you panicked and lost control. You had no will behind what was happening, and when the Source is left on its own, it often just becomes pure, raw destruction.*

"Try it," he said, lowering his hand. The Source flickered out. "Summon the Source and touch me."

The mere idea of doing that caused my heart to speed up.

"I have a feeling you two are doing that thing Kat and Daemon do all the time," Eaton grumbled. "Talking to each other the way you all do."

Luc held my gaze. "Someone sounds jealous." *Try it, Evie. I trust you.*

Pulse pounding, I knew I had to try. *You'll stop me if it hurts you? It won't.* A pause. *But I will if it does.*

Taking a deep and calming breath, I summoned the Source as I lifted a hand. A mass of churning light and darkness blossomed from my palm. Eaton muttered a sharp curse as the energy licked over and between my fingers. Under the Source, glittering dots appeared like shards of onyx embedded in my skin. *I don't want to hurt him. I don't want to hurt him.* I kept repeating that as I reached out, placing my hand on his arm. Luc jerked a little, and I started to lift my hand.

"I'm okay," he said. "Keep going."

Drawing in a shallow breath, I nodded. The energy pulsed around his arm, but it didn't do what it did before, climbing up his skin as if it were trying to swallow him whole. My gaze flew to his face.

Luc lifted his brows. "Feels like you're tickling me."

"Really?"

"Yeah. Kind of tingly." Those eyes of his deepened in hue as tiny sparks of the shadowy-white light danced over his skin and then disappeared, either fading out or seeping into him. "I kind of like it." He bit down on his lower lip as his eyes drifted shut. "A lot."

I flushed to the roots of my hair.

"Jesus, Mary, and Joseph," grunted Eaton. "I don't want to know what you're doing to him, but you aren't hurting him. Let's move this along."

Jerking my hand back, I willed the Source to fade out. Luc, on the other hand, slowly opened his eyes, his grin pure wickedness. The taut lines around his mouth had disappeared. "When we get done here, I'm going to make sure you know how to heat up water. I'm really looking forward to a bath later."

The flush spread, and muscles low in my stomach trembled. Luc and I hadn't done it since that night. It wasn't for lack of trying. We spent almost all day working on the Source, and then there was everyone else. Whenever we were alone, it didn't last. Whether it was Zoe or Grayson appearing or someone who needed Luc for something, which was, like, every evening, by the time Luc returned, I was passed out, and when I woke in the middle of the night, he looked too damn peaceful to wake up.

Though I doubted he'd mind.

"Promise?" I asked.

"Pinkie—" His head swung toward the closed double doors. "We're about to have company."

Case in point, I thought wryly, and we weren't even alone. I followed his gaze, sensing absolutely nothing—

Fists banged on the door. "Eaton! You in there? We got a problem—a big one," a voice I didn't recognize called out from the other side of the door. "Like, a really giant one."

I turned back to Luc. "How in the world do you do that?"

"I've got talents," Luc replied. I was willing to bet whoever was out there was human.

Sighing, the general ambled to his feet, letting the stuffed banana fall to the floor. "When is the problem ever small?" he grumbled.

Luc made it to the door before Eaton took a step, and when the door opened, my early suspicion was confirmed. A young human man with deep brown skin stood there, no transparent aura to be seen. Blood splattered his light gray shirt and olive-green cargo pants.

Relief saturated the man's face when he saw Luc. "Thank God you're here. We just got a package, and it's a mess."

A *package* usually meant a group of Luxen or others who needed safe entrance into Zone 3, and based on the blood, I had a feeling something had gone terribly wrong. I immediately thought of Heidi and Emery. They weren't expected, but . . .

"Where are they, Jeremy?" Luc's demand was as cool and calm as still water.

Jeremy's chest rose and fell with rapid breaths. "At the entry house. Doc Hemenway is heading over there now. I know Daemon is with Kat, and Eaton has medical knowledge, but you can heal, right? Zouhour is there, but—"

"She's not going to be able to do a damn thing." Eaton dug into the pocket of his jeans. Keys clanked together as he snatched them up. "Who's down?"

"Spencer." Jeremy's hands opened and closed at his sides. He glanced in my direction but seemed to not see me. "It's not good, man. Not at all. His chest—" He sucked in a sharp breath, his voice ragged when he spoke next. "It's bad."

I had no idea where the entry house was or who Spencer was, but when Luc sent a quick look over his shoulder at me, I said, "Go."

He nodded once, and then he was gone in the time it took me to blink.

"Come on." Eaton wheeled around, heading for the door. "I'll drive us over there. Faster than walking, and you can tell me what the hell happened."

Sending me another questioning glance, Jeremy unclenched his hands and rubbed his palms over the hips of his pants. "I'm not exactly sure. We were expecting Yesi and her group back this morning, transporting three unregistered, and friendlies, but only Spencer and the two friendlies arrived. He was hurt, and all I was able to get out of one of the unregistered was that they were ambushed at the state line."

"ART officers?" Eaton stopped at the door, looking back. "You coming? Or do you want to stay here and move this stuffed banana around some more?"

Unable to hide my surprise or my unwillingness to move a stuffed banana around, I snapped forward. "I'm coming." Catching up to them, I followed the two out of the door and the stale, dusty air.

"Assuming it was ART," Jeremy answered. "They've been picking up more and more patrols in Oklahoma and Louisiana. Got some of us thinking they may know something is going on here."

Eaton didn't respond to that, so I asked, "Are friendlies humans?"

"Yeah." Jeremy swallowed. "You know, like allies in war? A military thing, I guess. Or that's what I heard."

"Makes sense." I watched Eaton cut through the weeds that had broken through the asphalt, his limp evening out as he waded toward an old UTV like the one the doc had. I glanced over at the young man. "I'm Evie, by the way."

"Jeremy. But you probably already know that." A brief smile as he extended his hand and then jerked it back. "Sorry. Blood." He climbed into the back of the cart as Eaton jammed the key into the ignition.

I scrambled into the passenger seat, and not a second after my butt hit the thin, rain-rotted cushion, the cart jerked into motion. He gunned it, throwing me back against the seat. The next heartbeat, he hung a sharp left. Reaching above me, I grabbed the bars before I slid right out of the cart and ended up in what looked suspiciously like a continent's worth of poison ivy. The cart zoomed between the warehouse and a chain-link fence, the space barely wide enough to fit the cart. My wide-eyed gaze swung toward Eaton as the wheels bumped over rocky terrain and then hit the asphalt of the road in front of the warehouse. He picked up speed and the wind caught strands of my hair, blowing it back from my face.

He sped down the road, past the rusted-out cars. When he whipped the vehicle left, he narrowly avoided colliding with a truck that must've been a bright, cherry red at one time. White-knuckling the bar, I pictured myself flying out and face-planting in the road at any given second. Heart thumping, I almost missed the movement. Something darted out from behind the truck, running behind the work van with faded letters. The glimpse had been quick, but I saw bright auburn hair.

Nate.

The bag of food I'd left out had been there the following morning, but it was gone the next time the sun rose, and I'd been so very hopeful that it had been Nate who'd retrieved the food and not a strong squirrel who'd carried it off.

I almost shouted for Eaton to stop the vehicle, but if he did, there was a good chance we'd all go flying into the air. Not only that, I didn't want to delay getting to someone who sounded gravely injured.

Cranking my neck, I tried to see if Nate reappeared, but he seemed to have vanished. At least he was still alive. That was good.

"Evie?" Eaton snorted, shaking his head as he one-handed the steering wheel of the cart and sped down the steep hill.

I turned toward him. "What?"

"Makes me laugh when you introduce yourself and answer to that. One of these days . . . ," the general said. He spun the wheel, and the cart went up on two wheels. Under the rumble of the engine, I heard what I thought was the Lord's Prayer coming from Jeremy. "You're going to take back the power the name you were born with gave you."

22

It was strange how something I'd been trying to figure out could leap right out of General Eaton's mouth and smack me upside the head.

Take back the power the name you were born with gave you.

Kat had said there had to be something Luc had done that snapped me out of it in the woods. There was something he'd said. It was the same thing that had pulled me out of my sleep.

Nadia.

He'd used my real name, or as Eaton would say, the name I was born with. And that wouldn't be such a big deal except that the Daedalus hadn't trained and programmed me when I'd been Evie.

I'd learned everything when I'd been Nadia.

There had to be a connection there.

What, I had no idea, and right now wasn't the time to figure it out.

I was trying to stay alive.

General Eaton drove like we were in the safety of a steel tank, and Jeremy had definitely been reciting a prayer. Several times I almost flew right out of the vehicle, and I was only seconds away from joining in on that prayer when we bumped over a meadow where grass was as tall as the sides of the cart.

I half expected a damn velociraptor to pounce on us.

Except it wasn't a dinosaur from Jurassic Park that almost took us out as we cleared the tall grass but a slow-moving *cow* getting her late lunch on.

I almost died three times in the ten minutes it took us to get where we were going.

The entry house turned out to be a farmhouse, one that was still operating based on the cattle Eaton dodged with impressive ease.

When the cart slammed to a stop beside a similar one, I jumped out of that thing with speed that even impressed me.

"Doc Hemenway is here." Jeremy looked like he might vomit as he poured himself out of the back of the cart. He looked down at his stained clothing. "Good. That's good." He was trying to convince himself, and all I could think about was the blood covering him and what kind of wound would cause that.

My steps slowed as I neared the back door. The home looked normal, but at the same time, it seemed to pulse as if it had a heartbeat. Or as if the bones of the house were having a hard time containing whatever was inside. I hadn't felt anything like that before, not with a Luxen or an Arum. "Spencer is a . . . friendly?" I asked.

"Yeah." Jeremy's voice was hoarse. "Yeah, he is."

Eaton was stalking toward the open back door, the limp all but gone now. "Where are they?"

"In the dining room." Jeremy motioned me to follow.

Eaton had already disappeared into the recesses of the farmhouse as we entered through a cleared-out mudroom. Different types of awareness swept through me. There was definitely a Luxen here. I could also feel what I now recognized as an Origin, and the sensation that accompanied a hybrid, but my skin was prickling in a peculiar way. I felt something *else*. It lay on the tip of my tongue, tasting like summer in the streets. Heated asphalt.

Leaving the mudroom, I entered a narrow hallway, and I wasn't thinking about unexplained sensations or tastes.

Guns.

That was the first thing I noticed. Actually, pretty much the only thing I noticed. A llama could've belly-danced in front of me and I would've only seen the guns.

So. Many. Guns.

Rifles of every length and caliber leaned against the wall of the hallway, enough to arm a—wait. I did a double take. Was that a *rocket launcher*?

A scream of pain tore through the house, snapping my attention forward. Jeremy took off, his boots smacking off the worn hardwood floor.

I didn't see the kitchen I crossed through as my steps slowed, every part of me fixated on the tableau in the dining room. A room that had presumably once hosted family gatherings, holiday parties, and had once been a place of joy, but it would be hard to remember that seeing the tragedy playing out in the room now.

Out of everyone in the room, I saw Luc first. It was as if every cell in my body knew where to find him. He was at the side of a trestle table, his hands planted on a chest that looked oh so wrong. I couldn't see his fingers under the intense white glow of the Source, but I saw the blood smearing his forearms. Stark concentration marked his face as he stared down at the man, who bucked and withered.

"Stop fighting it. Come on, man, stop fighting it," Luc ordered, his jaw clenching.

An older man stood at the head of the table, snow-white hair sticking out from under a straw hat, with a grip on the fallen man's head that said he'd seen a lot in his day. Tendons popped along the sun-spotted forearms revealed by the rolled-up sleeves of his bloodstained denim shirt.

Blood. There was so much of it, running down Spencer's sides, pooling onto the table, and spilling onto the floor.

Doc Hemenway rushed forward from behind Luc, holding what reminded me of an air pump combined with a giant syringe. Except for Luc, everyone in this room was human, but there were Luxen here. There were others, and there was something *else* in this house. That feeling had not only lingered but intensified. I didn't want to bother him, but instinct told me he needed to know.

Luc, I called out to him. *I feel something strange.*

His eyes lifted to mine for a brief second. *What?*

There's something different here. My palms started to sweat.

"Who's in this house?" Luc asked.

"Two human girls," the old man answered. "That's all. Zouhour is with them. They're pretty freaked out."

There was definitely something other than a human girl in this house.

Whatever you're feeling, it's going to have to wait. I'm losing the battle with this guy, Luc responded directly to me, and he was right. Anything and everything else had to wait.

"I just need you to get the bleeding stopped," the doc said as she leaned around Luc, jabbing the end of the pump in the pool of blood forming in the sunken cavity of Spencer's stomach. "Then I can see what we have going on here." She pulled back the handle of the syringe, and the pump filled with deep, red blood.

"You don't have a whole lot going on here," Luc bit out. "He's got several arteries blown out—" A wave of white light rolled over Spencer, and his back bowed. "And every damn time he moves, he tears the goddamn one I just fixed."

"His aorta still has to be intact or he'd already be dead." The doc stepped back. "Keep him alive for ten minutes, Luc. I need ten minutes for the Fuse to filter this blood and get it into a bag." She glanced down at the tool she held. "Thank God for innovation."

The ghost fingers along the back of my neck intensified.

"Not sure all the innovation in the world can help him at this point," Grayson's droll voice stated from behind me less than a minute later. I looked over my shoulder at him. Was he the Luxen I sensed? I didn't think so unless he'd been in another part of the house. Grayson didn't take one peek in my direction as he propped a shoulder against the doorframe. He pulled a Blow Pop out of his pocket.

Jesus, he had to be the most unhelpful Luxen known to man.

Doc Hemenway shot Grayson a look that should've fried him on the spot. "If it weren't for three intelligent and compassionate human women who wanted to make sure developing countries could transfuse blood without electricity, Spencer would be dead and I would be shoving my foot so far down your throat, you wouldn't be able to think of a sucker again without shuddering."

My eyes grew as round as saucers.

One side of Grayson's lips curved up in a smirk right before a cherry Blow Pop went into his mouth, but then Spencer reared up again, and Luc's curses signaled another spurt of fresh blood.

"Jeremy, get over here and grab one of his legs!" Eaton shouted, going for the one that was curling. "Evie, grab his arm. Now!"

I did as ordered, grabbing the man's arm and pressing it to the table. Ignoring how cold and clammy and all-around wrong his skin felt, I got an up-close and personal look at the wound. "Dear God," I whispered, stomach churning. His skin was ripped open. Skin peeled in strips, revealing shattered cartilage and torn muscle.

"Don't look at it, Peaches." Luc's voice was soft as the Source flared. "Look at me. I'm pretty to look at."

The old man holding Spencer's head snorted.

I couldn't pull my eyes away from the mangled mess. "What did this? A grenade?"

"If it was a grenade, pretty sure he'd be dead," Grayson commented. "Well, he'd be deader."

"Thanks for the clarification, Captain Douchebag," I snapped, and the doc looked up across from me.

"I knew there was a reason I liked you." She smiled again. "We should become friends."

Spencer pushed against my hold as I said, "I'd like that, Doctor—"

"Call me Viv," she reminded me. "Everyone else does." She pinned Grayson with another blistering look. "Except you. You call me Dr. Hemenway."

"I wouldn't dare think of calling you anything else, *Dr. Hemenway*."

"Get ready," Luc said, his pupils flipping white before he closed his eyes. His veins lit up under his skin, starting at his cheeks and then fanning out across his face, down his throat, and then out from under the sleeves of his shirt. He was really pulling on the Source. An aura spilled into the air around him, outlining his body in white. Static charged the atmosphere, and I inhaled, tasting *life*.

My breath halted.

God, the kind of power Luc wielded was mind-numbing, but something different was happening inside me. It felt like the Source inside me had tightened into a tiny ball, and now it was unraveling, opening up, and it built, not in the back of my throat or in the pit of my stomach but in the center of my suddenly aching, empty, and cold chest. Pulse pounding, my grip started to loosen, but Spencer's entire body tensed as if he'd come into contact with a live wire. I snapped out of it, pressing his arm down as Viv did the same across from me. The scream pierced my ears and brought tears to my eyes and . . .

And then I felt a wall of ice press against my back.

Goose bumps pimpled my skin, and Luc's eyes flipped open. His all-white pupils expanded as his gaze met mine. Breathing halting in my throat, I looked over my shoulder. Grayson was stepping aside as a mass of rippling, stretching shadows pulsed in the kitchen, so dark and deep it could be a black hole. No, not shadows. A man. A man made of shadows and skin a shade of alabaster that somehow managed to appear devoid of blood without looking ghastly. His hair was so black that under the glow of the gas lamp, it tinted blue like a raven's wing. With strong jaw and straight nose, features hard, as if he were carved out of granite, he was handsome in the same way Grayson was, remote and cold. Perhaps even cruel.

He wasn't alone.

A short black-haired woman was behind him, a small hand curled around his biceps as she stared down at the table and her brown eyes flecked with green grew wide.

She was human, but he was an Arum.

His eyes, a blue so pale it was almost as if all color had been leached from them, flickered around the room, coasting over me, and then snapping back to where I stood.

This was the first time I'd been able to feel an Arum. There was no doubt in my mind that was why it felt like I'd been drenched in ice, but was he what I sensed that felt different? I wasn't sure, but I couldn't shake the crawling sensation of awareness that tasted like heated asphalt in the summer. His head tilted to the side in a movement as fluid as water and so snakelike it reminded me of the Arum I'd met outside of Foretoken. The one called Lore.

The one who'd asked what I was.

He'd sensed the Arum DNA in me, and it was obvious this one did, too. His nostrils flared, and then he took a step toward me, pulling free from the human woman's grip.

"Serena," he said, his voice so deep it spoke of dreams and

nightmares, and somehow manage to rise above Spencer's screams of pain. "I want you to get out of this house. Now."

"What?" Confusion filled the woman's voice.

The Arum never took his eyes off me, but I saw, along my periphery, Grayson remove the Blow Pop from his mouth. "Because you've already seen too much horror to last a lifetime, and I don't want you to watch as I kill this thing standing in front of me."

23

I should've felt fear—more like pure terror. This Arum looked like he could cash that check his mouth was writing. And I should've been thinking about grabbing that rocket launcher, because the edges of his body suddenly looked like they were shaded in charcoal. The blurred effect started to spread, causing his features to lose their clarity as deep shadows bloomed under thinning skin. The woman called Serena was backing up, reaching around to her back.

Spencer went quiet, all the stiffness seeping from his body. He was still, and I had no idea if he lived or breathed . . .

And something colder and *other* was waking from the cavern of my chest, and *it* slithered up, mingling with my thoughts, tracking not only his every breath and the slightest movement but also the human woman's, through *my* eyes.

This was not like the night of the nightmare, nor was it anything like what I'd felt when I'd been training. It reminded me of the woods, of the fight with April, when something *other* than me whispered through my veins, seizing control and erasing me in the process.

This was the Source—the kind of power that wasn't used to just move objects or to speak telepathically with Luc.

And *it* was not afraid.

It wasn't even slightly concerned that *it* somehow knew the woman was reaching for a gun.

The Source had simply sensed a threat, like it had done in the woods, like I suspected it had done with April. But this was also vastly different.

Because I still had control.

I would have to overanalyze all of this later, along with the whole Nadia thing. Right now, when an Arum wanted to straight up murder me, was not the time for any of that.

I met the Arum's gaze head-on, and his lips peeled back in a snarl as smoke and shadows stirred around him.

"Hunter." Luc's voice was calm in the way that sent a shiver of warning down my spine. "I like Serena, and I like you, so I'd hate to have to kill you in front of your wife."

Hunter.

What an accurate name, because I felt hunted, but I was not prey.

That was what the Source was feeding me as my chin tilted back a notch.

Grayson threw his Blow Pop in a small plastic trash bin. "I was told you were out meeting with Lore and Sin."

"I just got back," Hunter replied, and I swore the temperature dropped twenty degrees. I bet he and his wife had no problem in the hot, humid Texas summer.

Evie, I want you to move to stand on the other side of the table, but move slowly.

I heard Luc, but I didn't move. I didn't need to.

Half of Hunter's body became nearly transparent. "If you know what that thing is and you're thinking to protect it, we've got a problem, Luc."

"I know exactly who I'm protecting." Heat pressed against my back. "And I also know what will happen if you take one more step toward her. You will become nothing more than a pile of ashes. She is not responsible for what happened, and man, I'm sorry to know that went down. He was good. Better than you. He didn't deserve that."

I had absolutely no freaking clue what Luc was talking about, but I figured he was picking up the Arum's thoughts. I tried to hear something, but there was nothing coming from the Arum.

"Get out of my head, Luc," the Arum snarled.

"Someone's got to be in there," Luc said. "She is not what you think she is."

But I am exactly what he thinks I am, the Source whispered back to Luc.

Heat flared, pulsing against the corners of my vision. *Evie?*

I blinked. *I don't know where that came from.* A lie. *But I'm still here.*

You have control?

Yes? No. Maybe? I decided *yes.*

The shadows intensified around Hunter, and I didn't think he was going to listen to Luc.

My hands slipped off Spencer's arms as Eaton stepped back from the table, grabbing ahold of Jeremy and hauling him aside. The young man had gone as still as a statue.

"What in the hell is going on here?" the old man demanded, and there was no answer.

"Hunter." Serena stayed a foot behind him, to his side, where she had me in sight in case she decided to use that gun I knew she was now palming. The fact I even knew that almost disturbed me, but at this point, I figured it was another Source-fueled instinct. "We trust Luc. Maybe we should listen to him."

"We do not trust Luc."

"Now you're just hurting my feelings on purpose." Luc's tone was light, but I knew it would be a poor life choice if one judged his mood on his words.

Hunter's pale eyes flared. "One of those things killed my brother."

"Which one?" Grayson asked, his posture lax, but when he threw away his Blow Pop, something I wasn't sure I'd ever seen him do, he meant business.

"Lore." Hunter dropped the name like a bomb of pain and heartache. I jolted in recognition. He'd been alive on Halloween. How could he be gone?

But Kent had been alive that night. So had Clyde and Chas.

So had my mom.

"Damn," Grayson murmured.

"I am really sorry to hear that," Luc repeated. "Lore was one of the good ones. He really was, but she had nothing to do with your brother's death."

"She is not natural," seethed Hunter.

"Neither am I." All pretenses were gone from Luc's voice. "And I clearly recall you realizing not all that long ago that I could kick your ass into the next galaxy, and buddy, you were not wrong with that estimation. This conversation is getting old, and I'm starting to become bored. Do you want to know what happens when I become bored?"

Serena's arm moved—

"She has a gun," I warned, and I wasn't sure who I was warning. Everyone in the room or the woman herself. The hairs all over my body started to stand up.

"I know, Peaches, but she's not going to use it." Luc paused. "Are you, Serena?"

Hunter blinked at the nickname, and Serena said, "I don't want to."

"Then don't."

"I would strongly advise that you didn't," Grayson chimed in, finally adding something of value. "If you're alive later, I'll tell you what happened to the last group of men who pulled a gun on her. They were kind of all over the place by the time she was done with them."

I wanted to smile, which felt all kinds of wrong, so I managed not to.

"Things are getting a wee bit tense here," murmured Jeremy.

"I don't know what is going on here, and I don't care. You all need to take it elsewhere," Viv barked out, returning with an IV bag full of the blood in one hand and one of those manual bag valve masks. She tossed the latter to Jeremy. "I'm trying to save Spencer's life, in case anyone cares."

"I care," Jeremy confirmed.

"As do I. My wife is in this house, tending to the girls Spencer brought in," the old man said, and I distinctly heard a shotgun cocking. "And those girls are already scared as jackrabbits hunted by wolves. They don't need to get caught up in this."

Spencer murmured something under his breath, but all I could make out was "them," and the rest was too weak.

Viv was at his side, sliding the needle into his arm and then lifting the bag of blood. "It's okay, Spencer. Everything is okay. I'm going to look at your chest while these overly aggressive aliens take their beef outside. Isn't that right?" she asked, and I knew without seeing her that she was staring at Hunter and Luc. "Or at least take it to another room."

"What do you say, Hunter?" Luc's voice was closer, his energy tickling over my skin. "Kitchen? Outside?" Then he was in front of me, his entire body humming with power. "Or option C?"

"What is option C?" Hunter's lower half solidified.

White lightning crackled across Luc's knuckles. "Option C is me ending this before you even realize it's started."

Shadows and smoke pulsed around Hunter, snapping out against the threshold of the doorway. Where the inky substance touched, a scorched mark was left behind. What Hunter wielded was the darker and equally dangerous form of the Source.

Fully expecting Hunter to strike out, every muscle in my body tensed. I would *not* allow Luc to come to harm.

"Let's hope it doesn't come to that," Luc murmured, having picked up on my thoughts.

I was hoping it didn't, because I had no idea if I really tapped into the Source, I could control it, but in that moment, I realized I would risk it to protect Luc. I didn't care how crazy or wrong that was.

"My brother is dead, and something like her killed him." Raw pain turned Hunter's voice to chips of ice.

"I'm sorry," I said, and his gaze shot to mine. The hatred and grief was hard to see. "I met your brother briefly, outside Luc's club. He was . . . he wasn't mean to me." Couldn't exactly say he was nice, but he hadn't wanted to kill me, so there was that. "I really am sorry to hear that he's dead, but I'm not like whatever killed him."

"And I'm just supposed to believe that because you claim so?" Hunter demanded.

"Or because I've spent the last however many minutes of my life telling you just that," Luc replied.

Several tense moments passed. "What are you?"

"I'm not quite sure," I answered. It was a shock to realize how true that was. It finally struck me that I really wasn't like other Trojans.

"Luc," Viv called, urgent. "I need you. He's sprung another leak."

Luc didn't budge. "I need to know I can trust you, Hunter."

"I'm okay," I said. "Help them."

Hunter solidified, the wisps of shadows and black fire fading into nothingness. "Help the human. We'll be waiting outside."

Luc turned back to Spencer only when Hunter had stalked into the kitchen, arm wrapped around his wife. Grayson caught Luc's eye, and with a nod, he pivoted, following them out.

I stood there for several moments and then stated the obvious. "She's human."

"They love each other." The white glow appeared around Luc's hands as he placed them just above Spencer's chest. "Obviously, Serena doesn't have the greatest taste."

"Is that common?" I asked while Eaton took over holding the bag of blood and Viv rolled out a leather satchel. Medical instruments gleamed in the light.

"Not particularly."

"How can I help?" I looked around, seeing that Eaton had established another IV and Jeremy had his fingers on Spencer's wrist.

"Stay right where you are." Luc's brows furrowed in concentration. "It's not that I don't think you can handle yourself, but I'm going to worry nonetheless, and then I'll get distracted."

Every muscle in my body twitched. I wanted to go outside and talk to Hunter so I could find out as much as I could about this other Trojan and what had happened, but Luc being, well, Luc, he would worry. Right now, he needed to be 100 percent focused on Spencer.

"You can help me," Viv offered, glancing up from Spencer's chest as she worked alongside Luc to close the wounds. "I've got a bag over here by Georgie's feet," she said, and I was assuming the older man was Georgie. "In there, you're going to find a lot of stuff. I need you to find the clear pouch. It'll be full of needles."

Hurrying to the zippered tote, I knelt and quickly peeled it open. She wasn't lying about there being a lot of things in there. Stacked boxes and rolls of gauze among other medical-looking thingamabobs. Rooting around, I quickly found the zippered pouch, and boy, was that a trigger for anyone scared of needles.

"Got it," I said.

"Perfect. Open it and you're going to see that those needles are labeled. Grab me one labeled *morphine*," she instructed. "Don't worry. They're capped. Put it on the buffet table behind you."

Relieved to hear that, I pulled out the needle. The thing was massive. Turning, I went to set it down but got hung up in staring at the framed photos I hadn't noticed until then. Pictures of Georgie and a silver-haired woman I guessed was the wife cluttered the surface. From young, skin unlined, to laugh lines and more, the pictures chronicled the decades they'd been together.

"Don't mind the pictures, sweetheart. Doris will straighten up anything knocked over," Georgie said.

Still, I carefully placed the capped needle beside a picture of them when they were in their twenties, perched on the tailgate of a pickup truck. And as I turned back around, my skin was still crawling with the odd, thick awareness.

"Viv," Luc murmured, and my heart dropped. I knew that tone. It carried a different kind of softness, a heavy one.

"I know. I know," she clipped. "Not giving up. Evie, there's another needle in there, labeled *epinephrine*. Grab that and uncap it—carefully."

That was another massive needle. I uncapped it, waiting for further instruction.

"What's his pulse, Jeremy?" Viv asked.

"Viv," Luc repeated.

Sweat dotted Jeremy's brow. "It's fast. Like, I don't think I'm counting right."

"What did you count?"

"It's over three hundred," he whispered.

"Shit," muttered Eaton.

"Ventricular fibrillation," Viv spat. "Eaton, get the blood pressure cuff. Check it."

Eaton did just that, pumping up the manual cuff, cursing as he watched the little red needle. He said a number, one that sounded entirely too low.

The white glow receded from Luc's blood-soaked hands. "Viv."

"I know!" she shouted, shoving white gauze into one of the wounds. "Evie, hand the epinephrine to Eaton. He knows what to do with it."

Eaton took it and then asked for the cap. Handing it over, I watched him place it back on the needle. Georgie was shaking his head.

"What are you doing?" Viv demanded, a lock of hair falling across her face. "I need you to be ready to use it when his heart stops."

"You know we need to shock him, Viv. We don't have that here," Eaton replied. "No point in wasting this when we could surely use it later."

I folded my arms over my waist.

"That doesn't mean we don't try."

"That shot is just going to cause spontaneous circulation. You know that," Luc said quietly. "It's not going to do anything else."

"No. We can still try." Viv's eyes flew to his just as blood soaked through the bandages. "We need to try to save his life—"

"We have been, but Georgie is breathing for him. There is no way we can replace that amount of blood," Eaton argued. "His heart is about to stop, and even if we get 'hit the lottery' kind of luck and we manage to restart it, we can't keep doing that."

"Yes, we can," the doctor argued. "Luc can keep healing the—"

"I can't."

Those two words silenced everyone in the room. All eyes turned to him.

"I can keep stitching up the tears and eventually they'll stop ripping open, but there isn't anything in there," Luc explained, wiping his forearm along his brow. "There's massive damage in his brain. They look like lesions."

"Lesions?" Viv whispered, and when Luc nodded, she returned to packing the wounds with more bandages. "It could be a water-shed stroke. Spencer is young. He—"

"Let him go, sweetheart." Georgie had stopped squeezing the bag and placed his hand on Viv's shoulder. "You've done all that you can. We all know that. Spencer knows that. Time to let God do the rest."

Jeremy's eyes closed, and slowly, he lifted his fingers off the young man's wrist as Viv looked up to the older man. "He shouldn't die like this," she whispered.

"Ain't nobody out there that should die like this." Georgie squeezed her shoulder.

Evie? Come?

Quietly, I stepped back and then joined Luc. I followed him out of the room and to the kitchen, where he walked up to an old, scratched farmhouse sink. There was a pitcher of water there, and I grabbed the bottle of hand wash, pumping the lemony-scented foam into his hands. Soapy red splattered the basin, quickly circling the drain.

I took a heavy breath. "You did everything you could."

"I know." He continued to rub his hands together. "There are some injuries even I can't heal. He was dead before his body even hit that table in there."

"Did you . . ." Hairs all over my body began to rise. My gaze left Luc's profile and zeroed in on the doorway. "Did you know him? Spencer?"

"Just in passing." He turned off the water, and I felt his gaze on me. "You okay?"

The humming in my chest grew stronger. "Do you feel that?"

"Feel what?"

A scream rang out from the dining room. "He's dead? Oh my God! He's dead."

Luc was at the door faster than me, but I was right behind him. I saw several things at once. Viv was sitting on a wooden chair in the corner, her bloodied hands clasped together under her chin. Jeremy and Georgie were spreading a navy-blue sheet over Spencer while Eaton stood beside Viv. Three women stood in the doorway, two humans and a Luxen. One had gray hair flowing to her shoulders. I recognized her from the photos. Doris. She had her arm around the other human girl, the one who'd screamed. Hands covered her mouth as she trembled against the older woman. The woman with pale skin and eyes a golden hue was a Luxen. The rainbow aura gave that away.

Doris comforted the girl, making soft soothing noises as she started to move her back to the door where another girl stood. It took me a moment to recognize her. There were two main reasons for that. First being the weird, rippling overlay effect that briefly obscured her features, as if there were two of her standing in the same spot—one light, one dark.

And the second reason was because when that aura disappeared, she looked different. The last time I'd seen her, her blond hair had been limp, she'd had veins that looked like black snakes, and she'd been spewing a blackish-blue bile everywhere before she'd jumped out of the window of Luc's club.

I suddenly knew exactly what I'd been feeling in this house the whole time. It hadn't been Hunter who had caused my skin to prickle and crawl. It had been *her*.

Sarah, the sick human who'd mutated into a Trojan and then disappeared, stood before us.

24

"This day literally *cannot* get any more messed up," Luc growled, and then to me, *This is what you felt?*

Yes. I knew that without a doubt.

I didn't feel her. At all.

That wasn't good, but I wasn't surprised. After all, a Trojan would go undetected, wouldn't it?

"You're looking a lot better since the last time I saw you," Luc said.

Sarah didn't seem to hear Luc—didn't seem to even know he was there. She stared at me, her head cocked to the side like a dog catching a note only it could hear.

"What's going on here?" the pale-skinned Luxen asked, her dark brows furrowing as she moved to stand in front of what she believed were three humans.

"Just long-lost friends coming together for a chat." Luc moved a foot forward. "Why don't you take Doris and the very traumatized human girl out for some fresh air, Zouhour? Georgie will help you. And while you're at it, I think the doc could benefit from that. What do you think, Eaton?"

"I'm thinking we all could use some fresh air." Eaton stood like a rod as he made eye contact with Jeremy.

Confusion flickered over Zouhour's face, but she thankfully listened. She started to turn to Sarah, to include her—

"Nah, not her." Luc's tone was calm, even pleasing. Out of the corner of my eyes, I saw Eaton take Viv by the elbow, bringing her to her feet. "She's going to stay."

"A walk sounds really nice, the more I think about it." Eaton led Viv around to the other doorway. "I know a good place. The long way down by the river."

Whatever Eaton said meant something to more than half of the people in the room. Faces went impressively blank, one after the other, like a row of dominoes.

Zouhour's grip on the crying girl tightened. She'd taken one step, and I saw Sarah's gaze shift to her.

Instinct fired warnings left and right, and I felt the Source building in my chest, expanding and stretching. The *other* in me, the Source, retracted into the center of my chest, tightening and curling. My heart rate kicked up, sending my pulse into overdrive.

I've been looking for you. Her voice was a sudden intrusion, like talons in my mind. I jerked back a step. *Our massster is very displeassed.*

The Source pulsed and then began to unfurl, filling my veins. I tasted it in the back of my throat again. Heated metal and stone. It was happening so fast—the Source was taking control, seizing hold of muscles and nerves, responding to the presence of another Trojan.

A threat.

A challenge.

My fingers twitched as my vision seemed to sharpen, and deep inside me, where the Source radiated, a door was opening.

I didn't know what the end result was going to be, whether I would remain or if I was about to become something else. Panic didn't have the chance to even set in. There were only seconds for me to warn Luc.

It's happening, I told him. *Get everyone out of here. Now.*

An audible gasp came from the female Luxen, and the gravelly curse that followed was all Eaton.

Sarah blinked, and her irises were pools of onyx, the pupil a bright star.

And then the proverbial poo hit the fan.

Framed photographs floated into the air as inky shadows edged in white light spilled out from Sarah. Those in the room scattered, all except Luc. He . . .

Stupid, idiotic knight in shining armor grabbed my arm, thrusting me back behind him as Sarah stepped toward me. A crackling, spitting, intense white light erupted from Luc. He was powerful, unthinkably so, but Sarah was a Trojan.

And a Trojan's power was unfathomable.

No.

I would not allow him to be hurt.

Absolutely not.

The door in me flung all the way open, and raw, potent power flooded my system. My skin came alive as tiny, glittering spots appeared and my mind collapsed into the Source, into instinct.

I pushed—pushed *hard* with my mind, shoving Luc and everyone in the room out. There was nothing any of them could do. Not even . . . *him*. Purple Eyes. I shoved them all out not just from the room but out of the house, and there was just her and me.

The Source receded from her as she slid her hand into her pocket, pulling out something black, something like a key fob. The small device sparked memories of pain and loss. Different hands had held that. A small, feminine one. A larger, punishing one. The device hurt. It *stole*. A growling hiss crawled its way out of my throat.

Never again. Never again. Never again.

I moved like a cobra striking, catching her wrist and twisting. A bone cracked, and her scream of rage turned to pain. Her fingers spasmed, and I snatched the device out of her hand. As I closed my fist around it, the Source throbbed in an icy, burning pulse. I opened my hand.

Dust fell to the scarred floor.

She watched the particles fall for a moment and then her gaze lifted to mine. A heartbeat passed, and then she spun, taking off through the house.

Wiping off my palm, I followed after her, passing through a living room and then out the front door, onto a porch.

People were there, backing away. Humans. Luxen. Others.

Faces.

Names.

One kept them back. Amber Eyes. She kept them back as I went down the steps, wood creaking under my feet. I scanned the area, finding the Trojan caught between a blond Luxen and *him*. Purple Eyes. His head cranked in my direction.

The Trojan shifted toward *him,* the Source sparking to life along its hand.

I knelt, slamming my hand into the packed, dry earth.

"Shit," Purple Eyes grunted. "Get back, Grayson."

Too late.

The ground split, spilling the scent of fresh soil into the air as the tear raced across the space, splitting into two as it reached the three of them, branching off and digging down deep. I opened the ground up under their feet, sucking them deep and out of the Trojan's reach. Their shouts faded to background noise as the Trojan started toward the humans—toward the Amber Eyes who guarded them.

I wouldn't do that.

The Trojan's muscles tensed, toe turning to point in their direction as its head shot back to me. The Source sparked from my body, charging the atmosphere. Static poured into the air around me. Wind picked up, lifting my hair as the sky darkened above us, full of thick clouds.

"Jesus," someone whispered.

"Jesus ain't got nuttin' to do with this," another responded.

The Trojan's hand opened, and the sky erupted in intense white light. A bolt of lightning struck the space between her and them. Another came and then another. Someone screamed, but the sound was lost. Thunder exploded, rattling the windows and the house behind me. The blinding lightning strike receded. Grass smoked, and the Trojan was running toward a distant tree line, her blond hair a flag streaming behind her.

Primal instinct kicked in, the urge to chase, to *hunt* greater than the desire to end this. I took off after her, and she was fast, but I was faster.

Crashing into her from behind, I brought her down, my hand on the back of her head. She grunted as I slammed her face into the hard ground.

The Source pulsed out from her. I'd made a mistake. Got too

close. I knew better. The power expanded, thrusting into me like a speeding freight train. It threw me back, slamming me into a tree. Pain flared all along the back of my skull. I slid down, catching myself before I fell. Wetness tickled down my neck.

She scrambled forward on her hands and knees before springing to her feet. She took off again, and so did I.

A bolt of Source cut through the trees. Bark splintered beside me, tiny pieces slicing my cheek. As I slid to a stop, the tree behind me ripped from the ground, thick clumps of dirt hanging from roots as it winged toward me. I hit the ground as it flew over, scant inches above me. Lifting my head, I caught sight of the tree and stopped it. The tree hung suspended, needles showering the ground as I shifted my gaze to where the Trojan popped out into a beam of sunlight. I sent the tree spinning toward her.

She jumped to the side but wasn't fast enough. The roots smacked into her, the speed ripping into her skin and flesh. She stumbled backward into another tree, writhing. Her eyes widened, and I recognized the glaze. There was pain, but behind it was something far more potent.

Fear.

Smiling, I pushed up and rose to my feet. She slipped around the tree, and then she was running once more. I started after her, slow at first and then picking up my pace.

The trees were a blur as she cut between them, darting in and out of streams of lights breaking through the heavy branches, and then we exploded out from them, cutting through the tall reeds of an open field. Houses loomed up ahead, rows and rows of identical flat, one-story homes.

She cut to the left, heading straight for the first house. The front door swung open, ripping off its hinges as she raced up the cracked driveway. She entered the house, and I slowed, my gaze flickering over it. Boarded-up windows. Tears in the roof. My senses crept out from me as I stalked across the porch. The house was empty except for her, and the air was dusty, stale. I walked through a barren, dark room.

Shouts came from the outside, but they meant nothing to me as I tracked the Trojan through the house, to the kitchen stripped of appliances and counters.

I inhaled deeply, taking in the scent of dirt and blood. I wondered if she would run again. The corners of my lips curved up. I hoped so. My body thrummed with the possibility. It would be far too easy. She was wounded, but wounded prey was still fun.

I prowled forward.

Breathing heavily, the Trojan backed up as she wiped the blackish-blue blood from below her mouth. She didn't engage, though there was opportunity and weapons. Floorboards she could rip up. A ceiling she could bring down on me. Discarded tools that could cut and maybe even kill.

She used none of that, still moving away from me, her chest rising and falling.

I halted in the center, studying her. *Why?*

She seemed to understand what I was asking. "I don't know how."

My lip curled.

"They haven't trained me." She wiped at the blood again. "Taught me just the basics. I'm supposed to . . ."

Sssuppposssed to what?

"Find you." She lowered her hand. "See if the Cassio Wave works this time. If it did, I was to bring you back with me."

And if not?

Her breathing slowed. "Then I had failed. You know what that means."

I wasn't sure. My brain was a chasm of memories and thoughts, needs and desires. I slipped past them, past the glimpses of laughter and eyes the color of amethyst jewels, shoving aside grief-soaked images to the one where he stood behind me, his hands on my shoulders.

I knew that man.

Jason Dasher.

And I also knew I did not like when he stood behind me. Only a fool would take their eyes off him. He could move as fast as any of us, even *faster.*

"Failure," he said into my ear. "Failure is the option of those who court death. I do not, will not tolerate it. Look. Open your eyes and look to see what failure is."

I opened my eyes, and before me was what remained of another like me, clothing and skin soaked with blood, the white floor stained with a river of crimson that seeped to the center, to a rust-colored drain. The blood slowed there, forming a grotesque and shocking pool of wasted life and infinite, soulless ambition.

Hatred filled my chest, and with the Source, it found a home. I curled my hands into fists. My gaze met hers. She stared at me in silence, eyes black except for white pupils. She did nothing, said not a word from there.

The Source spilled out from me, rippling in shadows of dusk over my body. The taste of burned ozone coated the insides of my mouth. My skin crackled as the Source pulled and pulled. Wind roared through the room, whipping my hair across my cheeks as it lifted anything not bolted down. Hammers. Broken chairs. Dirt-covered tables. Empty bottles. Trash. All of it became weightless.

I became weightless as all that power saturated the air around me, turning the room to shades of dusk and dawn. Glass cracked and shattered. A great wrenching shook the house as the roof peeled back like a page turning in an ancient book, revealing dark storm clouds.

"Evie!" someone shouted, voice close by.

Sarah stepped forward, whitish-black light erupting from her palm—

The whirling cyclone of energy, a combustive mix of power and hatred, rose inside me, and it found a target. I let the Source build until it burned my skin and crowded my insides, leaving almost no room to breathe, for my heart to beat, and then, when I could no longer hold it in, I let it go.

The burst of power left me in a wave. Flung up and outward, the explosion of the Source was more than a bomb detonating. Once released, the Source was a concussive force, simply disintegrating whatever was in its path the moment the shadowy light reached it. Brick. Plaster. Wood. Cloth. Steel. All of it turned to glittering ash, surrounding me like a thousand fireflies, slowly drifting to the ground, where no worn carpet stained by years of living existed. No subfloor or crawl space. The sparkling ash blanketed the reddish-brown clay and loam that lay several feet from where I hovered.

I stared at the spot where she had stood. Nothing was there. Not even ash. A keen sense of satisfaction swept through me.

She failed.

I had not.

I smiled as I surveyed what remained. The absolute destruction seemed to be limited to the ground below where I floated; however, the blast had released a shock wave, shaking the nearby homes and shattering some of their windows. Curtains now drifted out of the gaping holes and into the silence of the built-upon hills and valleys overlooking a steel tomb of a city.

"You can fly?" a tiny voice asked.

Strands of my hair lifted off my shoulders, flowing out and around me as my gaze lowered.

A small child stood barefoot on the cracked sidewalk, a young girl of four or five. She wore overalls, the legs rolled up and one strap unbuckled and hanging loose, revealing the blue shirt covered with yellow-and-white daisies. Her hair reminded me of the darkest chocolate, too wild to be kept in the pigtails that were desperately trying to rein in the waves and curls. A fluffy stuffed llama was clutched to her chest as she stared up at me with wide, stunning eyes the color of violets.

Her eyes reminded me of something.

Of someone.

"Can you?" she asked, creeping closer to the edge of the sidewalk, to where the raw earth was exposed.

Could I? "I'm not sure."

She tilted her head to the side. "You should try to find out."

The little girl was right. I should try to find out. So I willed myself forward, toward her, and I drifted through the air.

"You can fly!" Her heart-shaped face broke out a wide, uninhibited smile as she shoved a little fist in the air and hugged the llama closer.

The corners of my lips tilted up. "I can."

"I wish I could fly. I can only make other people fly. I've tried to do it myself, but Mama got real sad when I tried, and Daddy yelled." Her nose scrunched. "It's the only time I've heard Daddy yell." She lifted her llama to her chin. "Did you do this?"

"I did."

"Is your daddy going to yell?"

"I . . ." I wasn't sure how to answer that. "I don't have a daddy."

"But you have two names." An impish grin appeared. "I want two names."

I did have two names, because I was two people, and I was something *other*.

"Ashley! Oh my God!" A woman raced up the sidewalk, a fuzzy pink blanket gripped in one hand as hair the same dark chocolate color streamed out from behind her.

The little girl named Ashley glanced at the woman. "Mama is gonna cry again." The devilish grin reappeared when she looked back at me. "I was supposed to be napping, but I felt you."

The woman only spared me a brief glance before she scooped up the little girl in her arms. She backed away, pressing the blanket to the girl's back. The woman looked at me then, her gaze never leaving me as she moved farther away.

Movement all along the street caught my attention. People coming out from behind the warped, cracked fence across the street. Bodies moving forward. One was Blue Eyes, his face smeared with dirt. He came to a stop on the stained pavement. "Oh, shit."

Behind him was a female Luxen, eyes amber. Both were powerful. That, too, I could sense, but neither could take me. Blue Eyes looked pale, appearing thunderstruck. The female looked . . . *ready*.

The back of my neck crawled as power pressed against me. I looked over my shoulder. Purple Eyes stood there, his hair blown back from his dirty face—a face full of tiny scratches. He'd been too close to the house. He wasn't alone. A man made more of shadows than flesh stood kitty-corner. On the other side was another Luxen, one who I knew I'd made bleed before. His green eyes held the memory of that.

Blue Eyes at my back. The Arum to my right and the Green Eyes to my left, and *him* to my front.

They were caging me in, and I didn't like that. And I didn't understand it, because I didn't wish to hurt them. I wasn't sure why, but I knew it wasn't my will. I rapidly calculated the most threatening.

Purple Eyes. He was powerful. His body shone with it. He could be a threat, that I knew, but I did not want to hurt him. Nor did I want to hurt the others.

My gaze shifted to the Arum. He was a different story. He wanted to hurt me. I remembered that. There was a reason, a sad one. I remembered feeling sad, but now . . .

He was a predator.

But I was *the* apex.

Rising upward, I pulled on the Source, and I felt it sputter before it sparked, weakened but there. I turned to the Arum.

"Dammit, Hunter," Purple Eyes growled. "Tone it down."

The darkness around him flickered and then faded, revealing a dark-haired man. He didn't look happy, but he was backing down. I watched him, not trusting the retreat.

"Look at me," came a soft command. I only obeyed because it was *him*. Purple Eyes took a step forward, hands lifted at his side. Soil caked his fingers, and I imagined he and Blue Eyes had had to dig their way out. I doubted they'd liked that, but they were alive, weren't they? "Evie?"

Evie. That was one of my names.

"You remember me? Right? You remember all of us."

I did. I know I did. I just needed a moment to make sense of what I remembered.

"It's okay," Purple Eyes continued, and his voice was soothing. I liked it. I loved it—the sound and how it made me feel. "You did good. Made sure she couldn't hurt anyone here. You did really good."

I didn't fail.

Relief flickered across Purple Eyes's striking, dirt-smudged features. He was solely focused on me, only me. "No, Peaches, you did not fail."

I lowered myself, and my feet had just touched the ground when there was a sharp, cracking sound, a popping noise. Pain exploded in my back, between my shoulders and then my chest, stealing my breath away from me.

25

Everything happened so fast.

Purple Eyes spun toward the green-eyed Luxen, who was also turning around. A man stood there, hands clutching a gun.

"What have you done?" the green-eyed Luxen gasped.

"She's the intruder, right?" The man kept the gun pointed. "She has to be, right? She just took out the building! I had to—"

Stunned, I looked down at my shirt. It was a light gray color, and a small dark stain had appeared in the center of my chest, an irregular circle that doubled in size within seconds—

The sound that tore through the air was a roar of pure, unfathomable rage, and it came from *him*. From Purple Eyes as a network of veins filled with the luminous glow of the Source, spreading across his cheeks and down his throat.

Green Eyes spun. "Luc—"

His arm cocked back as the bolt of energy exploded from his right hand. A streak of crackling energy shot like lightning across the space, finding its target. The man's scream ended just as it began, cut off as the Source consumed him, burning through clothing and skin, obliterating muscle and bone.

Seconds, only seconds had passed between the popping and the burned patch of ground.

I tried to take a breath, but red-hot pain swept through me. Managing only a thin, wheezy inhale, I lifted a hand to my chest. Blood stained my fingers, seeped through them. Wet warmth trickled down my back as I stumbled back a step and then my knees went out—

Someone caught me from behind. A Luxen. The one with blue eyes, the one who always had a lollipop. "She's down!" he shouted, and I tried to pull away, but I didn't seem to have control over my body. Blue Eyes was holding me as he went to the ground, on his knees. "Luc!"

Confusion clouded my thoughts as I stared at my hand, at the blood coursing down my arm, over the rapidly churning black dots.

I hadn't seen the shooter. I hadn't known the threat was there.

An arm slid under my neck, and the scent of pine and burning leaves surrounded me. Instinct fueled by the Source told me I would heal—that I just needed to find somewhere safe, and where I was now wasn't safe. I needed to get away, but whatever messages my brain was sending to my body weren't getting there. I tried to summon the Source, but the flutter in my chest was even weaker. The marks on my skin no longer appeared like glittering shards of onyx. I couldn't move, and I wasn't safe—

"You're safe, Evie. I got you," a deep voice intruded, a voice that belonged to hands gently brushing my hair back from my face. "I won't let anyone else hurt you. You're safe."

I was being laid down, and the rapidly scattering dark clouds were replaced by a face I knew, by eyes the color of wild violets, pupils a brilliant white. *Him*. I knew his name. It was on the tip of my tongue.

Moving his hand from my cheek, he placed it on my chest. Mine had fallen limp and useless to my side. As if it were some long-buried reflex, I kept trying to summon the Source, but the hum of energy was faint and growing weaker.

"I think it went in through her back," the blue-eyed Luxen said. "The chest is where it exited."

Purple Eyes tugged at my shirt, lifting it. With a curse, he started to turn me onto my side, toward him—

Burning pain shot across my shoulders, so sharp and sudden that I screamed. The Source throbbed in response to the pain, pulsing out from me.

Purple Eyes grunted, jerking back, but he held on tighter. "I'm sorry, Peaches. I'm so sorry." He continued to turn me until I was on my side, the agony an endless wave that tore another scream from me. "I know I'm hurting you. I'm sorry."

The Source didn't respond this time, not even when he shifted, pressing his hand to the throbbing pain. Heat flared from his hand, beating back the ragged stinging. The warmth flowed down my back.

"Open your eyes. I need you to do that for me. Please. Open those beautiful eyes."

Please.

They weren't open? My body seemed to obey that almost desperate plea as I forced my lids to lift.

His entire body glowed, not just his eyes, and the pulsing warmth was everywhere, ebbing and flowing. "There you are." He smiled, but I thought it didn't look right. "You're going to be all right. Do you hear me, Evie?"

"I . . . failed."

An emotion akin to pain tightened the lines of his features. "You did not fail, Evie. You did not. I failed."

I opened my mouth, but a wet cough came out instead of words—a cough that tasted of rich iron.

"It's okay." The beautiful man's face above me grew fuzzy around the edges. "It's okay. I promise you. Just stay with me."

He bent over me, and a shock of electricity flowed through me as he pressed his lips to the center of my forehead. Memories flashed of him doing just that time and time again. His lips against my temple, against my skin and my own lips. He'd kissed me many times before, because he was . . .

"I'm your everything," he whispered, curling his body around mine. "You're my everything."

I woke up remembering everything.

Sprawled atop Luc with my cheek plastered to his chest, we both were nude from the waist up. A sheet was draped over us, and I had a vague recollection of Viv and Zoe stripping away my blood-soaked shirt and bra to examine the healing wound.

I cringed. Things were spotty, but I clearly and unfortunately remembered clinging to Luc like a squirrel monkey when Viv and

Zoe tried to separate us. I was so bad that Luc had to carry me here.

God.

He was probably never going to let me live that one down.

My behavior probably had something to do with the fact that I couldn't remember who Viv and Zoe were at that moment, and in my weird Source-infested mind, I'd felt safe with Luc because he'd healed me.

I also remembered Viv being rather excited about my behavior, something to do with it giving further credence to her rebooting theory. At that time, I had no idea what she was talking about, but now I did. When I had let the Source take over, it had done so in a way that had been different from in the woods. I had been different but not randomly homicidal. So that was an improvement.

Getting shot, though? Not so much.

I couldn't believe I'd been shot or that I was alive and felt okay except that the space between my shoulder blades was sore. And I had Luc to thank for that.

I had a distinct impression I would've healed without his intervention, but the same instinct was telling me it would've been a longer, more painful process. Did I have regenerative abilities? Or was it like how Luc had removed those bullets from himself? He'd thought he could heal himself once he got them out, but those bullets had been different. They'd been modified with a weaker form of the EMP, designed to wound and not kill. Would I have known how to heal myself? I had no idea.

Luc's chest moved in the deep, steady rhythm of sleep under mine. The fine hair along his chest tickled my sensitive skin. I didn't remember falling asleep like this, but based on what I did remember, I probably climbed right on top of him. While I was a little embarrassed that others had witnessed me turning into a DEFCON 1 clinger, I wasn't ashamed that he'd evoked such a response from me while I hadn't entirely been myself. That was a sign that maybe I was less dangerous than before. At least to him.

But not to that girl.

Not wanting to think about any of that right now, I opened

my eyes. A gas lamp flickered softly from the nightstand, casting light across the bed, and another sat on the dresser, pushing at the deepest of shadows—

I zeroed in on the chair nestled in the corner, just outside the reach of the lamp's faint glow. The chair wasn't empty, and that wasn't a shadow shaped like a person.

Grayson.

The breath I took hitched as he rose from the chair and crossed the room, as silent as a ghost. He knelt a foot from the bed, his head turned to Luc, and then his gaze drifted to mine.

He didn't speak. Neither did I.

And then he did, his voice so low I doubted it would wake even Luc. "He's not unstoppable, you know. He can weaken."

My stomach hollowed at the thought. Luc always seemed incredibly larger than life itself, never weak, never tired, but I knew better than that. "I know," I whispered.

Grayson closed his eyes, and then a golden glow radiated from the center of his chest. The light washed over him as he slipped silently into his true form. A human-shaped being of light so bright it was almost like looking into the sun. His arm rose, and from within the light, I saw his hand, his fingers as he placed them on Luc's arm, the one closest to him. A ripple of light danced up Luc's arm, scattering across his skin in a glittering, golden wave. I felt the warmth and the low-level buzz of energy where my skin met Luc's.

Luc still slept, his breathing even deeper, and Grayson was giving Luc some of his own energy, replacing some if not all of what was surely lost from trying to save Spencer and then healing me.

Grayson withdrew his hand and then stood, gliding back from the bed, his true form fading until he was once more in his human form. He left without saying another word.

Not too long after Grayson left, Luc's arm around my lower back shifted, tightening and then relaxing. I lifted my head to watch his eyes flutter open. His gaze focused, meeting mine and holding.

"Hi," I whispered.

"Hey." His voice was rough with sleep as he lifted the arm Grayson had touched. He placed his hand against my cheek. "How are you feeling?"

"I feel okay. My back aches a little, but I don't feel like I've been . . . you know, shot in the back or anything."

"Good." His gaze remained locked with mine, and there was an intensity in his stare that I was only beginning to recognize and realize had been there every time he looked at me. It sent a shiver of *knowing* over my skin.

"You?" I whispered.

"Like brand-new."

I wondered how much of that had to do with Grayson, but I said nothing. I had a feeling Grayson didn't want Luc to know what he'd done for him.

"You sure you feel okay?" he asked. "That was one hell of a wound. Got one of your lungs. Nicked a couple of vital arteries."

My skin chilled at the knowledge unspoken in his words. If I'd been human, I most likely would've been like Spencer, bleeding out before anyone could do a single thing. "I feel fine," I told him. "Because of you."

He still hadn't looked away. "I killed that man."

"I know."

"He didn't know who you were. Eaton had managed to get an alert out that there was an intruder. He saw you and thought you were it. He was just doing what the community trusts him to do, and I killed him."

My gaze searched his as I rose a little onto my arms. There was a tender pull against the skin of my back, but nothing more. "Luc—"

But he hurt you. He made you bleed. His voice slipped through my thoughts. *I don't regret what I did.*

"I would've done the same," I admitted, and that was the truth, right or wrong. It was the truth.

"I know." He dragged his thumb along my jaw and then slid it to my throat, where the pad of his finger rested over my pulse. "I had no idea if you could die from a wound like that or if the SOL guy was right about what could kill you."

Massive brain trauma. That was what Steven had claimed could take out a Trojan, and apparently blowing them to smithereens could, too, but that wasn't something we knew for sure. Especially if I was different from the others, and it was really beginning to look like that was the case.

"You were bleeding everywhere. That blood still stains your skin right now. It stains mine. That's the second time in a very short period of time that I feared I'd lose you."

"I'm—"

"Don't apologize, Evie. Don't." He cupped the back of my head as he eased upward into a sitting position. The motion was fluid, causing little strain on the area between my shoulders. "There are a lot of things we need to talk about. Sarah. Hunter. What happened with her—with you—but right now, I need you. I need to feel you, be surrounded by you." His forehead pressed to mine. "I need to forget that we're both stained with your blood."

Closing my eyes on a shuddering breath, I cupped his cheeks. "You have me."

Luc kissed me, and there was nothing slow or tentative about the way his mouth moved or how his lips parted mine. The kiss deepened, and there was an edge of desperation to it, a hint of lingering fear.

The sheet tore away from us, landing somewhere near the foot of the bed on the floor. He broke the kiss, easing out from under me. Before I could question what he was doing, his lips pressed to the space that ached between my shoulders as I felt his fingers curling around the band of my pants.

Cool air washed over my now bare lower half, but the heat of Luc quickly chased it away. He moved behind me, skin against skin. A shiver rolled up my spine as an infinite spark transferred between us, something that could never be forced or fabricated.

The sight of his hand planting into the mattress beside my head and the feel of the hand at my hip flipped and twisted my insides into a heady mess that had me digging my fingers into the sheets.

Desire wasn't the only thing that charged the air around us. There was so much more as he pressed against me, into me. Love. Fear. Relief. Acceptance. I reached out, placing my hand over his, threading my fingers between his.

A long, antagonizing moment of stillness passed, his body coiled tight as a rope about to snap, and then he moved. The sound from the back of his throat seared my skin, and there was no sense of control or restraint. We fell in together, headfirst and without reservation, sinking deep into the flurry of sensation that went beyond the physical. I lost track of everything except Luc, the way he felt, the way he moved, and how there wasn't anything he wouldn't do for me. How there wasn't anything I wouldn't do for him.

And when we both toppled over the edge, we went spinning, falling together, and I don't know how long we stayed there, bodies fitted together, trembling and hearts racing.

Luc dropped his forehead to my shoulder, keeping his weight supported by his arm, the one I had, at some point, all but curled my upper body around. "I haven't hurt you, have I?"

"No." I kissed his hand, and I felt his shudder travel all the way down his arm. "Did you hurt yourself?"

Luc chuckled. "I might've pulled a muscle."

I laughed at his dumb joke. "Good."

"I probably should've controlled myself," he said, his breath warm against my neck. "This was wildly inappropriate of me."

"Yes, it was."

He shifted behind me, and I felt his lips touch the achy area between my shoulder blades once more. "But I'm thinking you like it when I'm wildly inappropriate."

I smiled. "Yes, I do."

Another kiss against the place a bullet had ripped through hours before. "Which one of us is the bad influence? I'm going to say it's you."

"What?" I laughed again. "How do you figure?"

"I was a good, conscientious boy for years, Evie. Years."

I snorted.

"You doubt me?"

"You were *not* entirely a good boy just because you hadn't had . . ."

"Because I hadn't had . . . what? You can say it. It's just three pearl-clutching letters pieced together."

I rolled my eyes. "Sex."

"Are you blushing?"

"Are you?" I shot back.

"Yes. Because I am still a pure—"

"Ass?"

"Is that an invitation?"

"Oh my God." I laughed even harder now. "Yeah, you sound like such a good boy."

"Like I said, I was." He moved again, this time stretching above so that his lips brushed my cheek when he spoke next. "But now? With you?" He moved his mouth to my ear. The words he whispered in my ear scorched my skin and sent a tingle down my spine. "That's who I am now."

Biting down on my lip, I closed my eyes as my toes curled into the messy blankets.

"What do you think?" he asked, his teeth catching the skin there.

I opened my eyes. *I love who you are.*

A dark rumble of approval skated over my skin. *Evie?*

Somehow I knew what he was asking. Maybe it was in the way he said my name. It could've just been the ever-present bond there, forged over years I couldn't remember and strengthened from the moment we came back into each other's lives.

I lifted my head, turning it toward him. His mouth found mine, and it was the kind of kiss that made me believe spontaneous combustion was possible. The kiss was a match striking, and I was on fire. We both were.

26

It was sometime later when Luc shifted onto his side, facing me with one foot tucked between my calves.

He toyed with the strands of my hair while I lay there, eyes closed and enjoying the gentle tug and release of his fingers. "It's time," he said with a sigh. "For us to be mature and responsible. We need to talk."

We did. "I wish we could stay like this, like right now, forever."

"You have no idea how much I agree with that statement," he said, and I was thinking I kind of did, but I opened my eyes. "How much do you remember?"

"Everything," I answered. "Well, everything up until you were healing me. Things got fuzzy then."

"How convenient," he murmured.

"I remember attaching myself to you—"

"Like we were made of Velcro?"

"Shut up."

"Focus," he teased. "Tell me what you remember."

"I remember everything from the moment the Source slid into the driver's seat." I told him about the Cassio Wave and what Sarah had claimed, what I'd felt during the whole time. "It was different. I didn't have control, but I wasn't psychotic."

"You think you didn't have control?" He arched a brow.

"I had no idea how I did what I did. The Source did it. Not me."

"You didn't hurt a single person. Not when you forced us out of the house—which, by the way, you ever do that again, I will straight up lose my mind."

I opened my mouth.

"I get why you did it. You recognized what she was, what she was capable of, and you wanted to protect us. That's admirable. Hell, more than that." He let go of my hair. "But I don't need you to protect me. I don't need you to worry about protecting me. That will distract you and could've made you vulnerable."

I stared at him as I rose onto my elbows. "Are you done with your rant yet?"

"Actually, no. Sarah could've kicked my ass from here to kingdom come and back. She might've even hurt me. Doubtful, but hey, stranger things have happened," he went on, and my eyes narrowed. "You may be a badass Trojan, but I'm yours. You're mine. That means when you go toe to toe with anyone or anything, you go to battle with me beside you, and if I go down fighting to back you up, there won't be a single part of me that regrets that. It's my choice, and you took that."

I couldn't believe what I was hearing. "Are you done now?"

He smiled. "Yes. I am."

"You would've done the same thing, right? And don't you dare lie. You would've dragged my butt out of that room if you could've. It wouldn't have mattered how many other people get hurt, as long as I'm okay?"

"Right."

"Wrong."

His smile faded.

"First off, I know you want to protect me, and yeah, it's one of the reasons why I love you," I said, and his little frown turned upside down. That didn't last long. "But I'm not about letting everyone crash and burn around us. I can protect you while I'm protecting others, so I know damn well you can do it. Secondly, the whole 'it's your choice, and I took it'? That's a two-way street, buddy. I cannot even count the number of times you whisked me away to safety while everyone else, including you, took huge risks. Remember your little rant next time the crap hits the fan and you stand in front of me instead of beside me."

Luc stared at me, and then he said, "Shit."

"Yep."

"You got me."

"I know." I smiled then, big and bright.

He didn't look quite so thrilled.

Whatever.

"Anyway, glad we got *that* out of the way so we can get back on topic," I said. "You think I had control just because I didn't hurt anyone?"

His eyes narrowed, and then he leaned over, kissing me. "It's a good thing I think you're adorable." He pulled back. "You blew a house and a Trojan to teeny-tiny little glittering bits and only shattered a couple of nearby windows. So, yeah, I think you had some level of control, whether you realized that or not."

"You think I had control on a subconscious level?"

"I think you weren't afraid of what you are. I think you trusted yourself," he said, and I didn't know if that was true or not. I'd been scared of the risk I was taking, but—"But you were more afraid of Sarah hurting someone and you were more afraid of her turning you into something else."

"Yeah." Disappointment rose. "I wish I hadn't destroyed that Cassio Wave. We could've studied that, even used it to see what it would do. She made it sound like the Daedalus wasn't sure."

"It would've been good to have that, but it's best that it wasn't used on you."

That wasn't the only thing I wished I had possibly handled differently, and maybe that was why I was reluctant to accept that on some level I did have control, because that meant . . .

That meant it was me who'd killed Sarah.

"Evie?" His voice was soft.

"Sarah hadn't been trained like I have. She admitted that when I cornered her in that house. She knew it was over. That she'd failed. I could've backed off, let her live. That would've been the smarter thing. We could've questioned her, could've compared her to me to see just how different I am—"

"But that's not what happened."

"No," I whispered. "She stopped fighting me, Luc. Closed her eyes and stopped, and I was disgusted by the fact she had failed, and if I had control, that was me. That wasn't the Source, not completely."

"It's not entirely unheard of for the Source to make hybrids more aggressive. The key is to recognize when it is having that kind of effect on you. It's not something you can't change." His finger touched my upper arm. "I have a question for you."

"Okay."

"If you were cornered by a Trojan who you believed could beat you, what would you do if it backed off once you stopped fighting?"

"I would—" I stopped myself before I answered in the way I would've a year ago. "Honest?"

He drew his finger down to my elbow. "Honest."

"I would attack," I admitted, feeling cruddy. "I mean, that's what would make sense."

"It would." He dragged his finger back up my arm, making little circles. "Showing mercy can be a weakness that can be exploited."

"You think that's what Sarah would've done?"

"Possibly."

I wanted so badly to latch onto that, so I could tell myself I'd done the right thing.

You did the only thing you were trained to do.

"That doesn't make it okay."

"Doesn't make it wrong, either." Luc curled his hand around my bent elbow. "Having Sarah here to question would've been great, but it would've been a hell of a risk. We have no idea what she would've done or if we could've even contained her. You did what I would've done, and I know that's not saying much. I am a bit more trigger-happy than you will ever be, but she was here to see if she could turn you into something like her. What if you let that heart of yours, that beautiful but soft heart, make that call and she hurt you? Hurt someone else? You would never forgive yourself for that."

He was making all kinds of sense, but what if Sarah wouldn't have attacked? She'd known she'd been defeated, that she had failed and it was over. She was ready to die—

"Do you think the Daedalus would've trained any of you to lie down and die? You don't remember your time there, but I do. So do Zoe and Kat. Dawson and Daemon and Beth. Ask Archer." His thumb smoothed over the skin above my elbow. "She may have only spent a short time there, but you can be damn sure that fighting to the death was drilled into her. Not a part of me believes for one second she wasn't playing possum. To the Daedalus, failure—"

"—is the option for those who court death," I finished.

His jaw flexed. "You had another memory? You didn't tell me that."

"It was just a brief one. It wasn't important."

"Anything you remember is important." He tugged on my arm and wiggled a few inches closer.

I told him what I remembered. "That was all. Nothing big."

"You saw someone dead, bleeding out on the floor, and that's not a big deal? Jesus." He scooted the rest of the distance, folding his arm around my shoulder. I snuggled in under his chin. His hand curled around my hair. "I'm right about Sarah."

"You're saying that because you think you're right about everything."

"I am."

My laugh was muffled against his chest.

"And I'm definitely right about this."

"Okay." I let it go. For now. "I can't believe I destroyed a house."

"It's fine."

"Fine?" I drew back enough that I could see his face. "How is blowing up a house fine?"

"It was unlivable and basically being scrapped for parts." He paused. "What you did was really badass."

A small smile tugged at my lips. "It was."

Dipping his chin, he brushed his lips along my forehead. "There's something else we need to talk about."

"What Sarah was doing with them in the first place?"

"Yeah, that, too, but something else."

"Oh, goodie."

His arm tightened. "When the Source took over, you went quiet. I couldn't pick up any of your thoughts. Not until the whole house thing. Then I could hear your thoughts again."

I tossed an arm over his waist. "What do you think it means that you couldn't hear me at first?"

"I don't know," he said as I rubbed my nose against his chest, and he sucked in a breath. "Why is your nose so cold?"

I giggled. "Sorry."

"No, you're not."

That was true. I thought about what he said. "Maybe Viv is completely right, and I was rebooting, and when I got close to coming online"—man, that sounded weirder than I'd ever thought possible—"you could hear me again. Doesn't explain why you couldn't hear me in the beginning."

"Could be because that was when you started to reboot, and I couldn't—"

"Oh my God!" I jerked, wincing as it pulled at my back.

Concern flashed across his face. "Are you okay?"

"Yes. Fine. I just remembered something I figured out before everything went down," I exclaimed. "It's Nadia!"

He jolted. "What?"

It wasn't often that I saw Luc so caught off guard, and it was sort of amazing. I wanted to revel in it, but now wasn't the time for that. "Kat said something the other day that has been driving me crazy. She said you might've done something in the woods that snapped me out of it. And you did. It was the same thing you said when I was doing the deep-sleep thing. I heard you, and that's what woke me up. You called me Nadia. Both times."

Luc swallowed hard, and then his expression smoothed out. "Yeah." He cleared his voice. "I did both times. I know you hate that—"

"I don't."

A brow raised.

"Okay. I did at first, because it was confusing, and it's still weird.

I mean, I don't know her—I mean, I don't know me." Groaning, I tried again. "It's just weird. All I know is that it doesn't upset me anymore because I am her, and that part of me responded to you. I was mutated and trained as Nadia, not Evie, so that has to mean something, right? There has to be a connection there."

He smoothed my hair back. "I think it means exactly what you said a few moments ago. That you are her, and I'm thinking that because you went through the mutation as her, there's a level of consciousness there that I can reach." He exhaled slowly. "That's good to know. It's another avenue if things escalate. Something I can try before shutting you down."

"Did you try to shut me down today?"

"No." He tucked the hair back behind my ear. "You went quiet so fast, but—"

"But you could've done it the moment I told you I was losing control."

"I could've, but I wanted to see what you'd do first."

"Oh my God, Luc." I stared at him. "What if I did go banana-pants crazy and you couldn't reach me?"

"I was willing to hedge my bets that you wouldn't." He dropped his hand back to my arm. "I told you this before, Peaches. I believe in you; I believe that you won't ever let yourself get to the point you did in the woods, and you haven't. Not since you had that nightmare, and the big difference there? You started to use the Source. You stopped being afraid of it. You started to trust yourself, and it's far past time you start believing in yourself."

My heart flipped over. God, he was right.

"I know."

I ignored that comment.

"Why is it so hard for you to do so?" he asked quietly.

Man, that was a hard question to answer, to explain. I shifted onto my back, relieved to discover it didn't hurt. There was a dip in my stomach when I thought again that I'd actually, literally been shot earlier. My brain couldn't process that as I slipped a hand under the sheet and found the small, ultrasmooth patch of healing skin. "Will it scar?"

"The one on your back? The entrance wound? It's already a faint mark. By tomorrow, it will probably be gone. The chest will probably scar, but it won't be too noticeable in a couple of days. It will look like a scar from a wound that occurred years ago."

"That's weird. Like, I can't even fathom that." I prodded at the skin, wincing. "It's tender."

"Yeah." He reached over, pulling my hand out from under the sheet. "So try not poking it."

"Good call."

He was quiet while I resisted the urge to poke around more. "Peaches?"

"Hmm?"

"Why won't you believe in yourself?"

"I don't know," I sighed, staring at the dark ceiling. But was that really true? I didn't think so. "I think Eaton was right. I keep allowing myself to think like I'm the Evie from before and that things are out of my control, because . . ."

Luc rose onto his elbow. "Why do you think that's easier?"

I closed my eyes, the truth hard to speak, to acknowledge. *Because that's how I've always felt. Like I've never had control in anything.*

"That's not entirely true."

Opening my eyes, I turned my head toward him. "How so?"

"Before, even when you faced things that were out of your control, like your father and getting sick? You did everything to gain back as much control as you could. You faced things head-on, no matter what cards you were being dealt," he said. "And that fierce strength is still inside you. That couldn't be stomped out by any serum, not completely."

Nadia was a badass, but she was me, and I wondered just how much of her still existed in me. If who I used to be was why, as Evie, I always felt so stifled and aimless, as if I'd been shoved into a skin that didn't fit.

"Your life as Nadia was mostly erased, but even the night you walked into the club, I saw so many of Nadia's qualities in you. It wasn't just the certain foods or drinks you liked or didn't. It was more than your love of photography. It was in the way you wouldn't let me intimidate you, how you pushed back even before you knew if you were safe with me or not. That was all Nadia. So is your inherent strength. Most people would've cracked under the pressure and everything you've been through. You haven't. Just like you didn't when you did what you needed to do to get away from your father. The same as you did when you were diagnosed with cancer. You kept going."

His gaze searched mine. "They may have taken your memories and put you in skin that didn't fit, but you have always been in there, and I have to think having that strength and that willpower leashed for so long made you feel like there was no control. Maybe it was even your subconscious trying to tell you something wasn't right."

I thought about what Eaton had said. "Time to take back the power of my real name—my real identity."

Luc didn't respond to that, but I knew that was right. It was far past that time, and realizing that wasn't a life-altering moment, not in any way that I could feel. It wasn't like all of a sudden I had no fear and believed that I was capable of everything and anything. Nor did it mean that I would suddenly start answering to Nadia, but it was a long-overdue step in the right direction and then some.

Because I knew in my bones, Nadia would trust that no matter what, she wouldn't hurt innocent people. She would believe in herself just as much as she believed in Luc. She sure as hell wouldn't take the path of least resistance. She would explode right through any and all obstacles. And she'd do it dancing.

The corners of my lips turned up.

"You hungry or anything?" Luc broke the silence. "Daemon brought some food over. Or at least that's what he said when he was here."

My smile halted. "Daemon was in here while I used you like an inflatable mattress?"

One side of his lips kicked up. "Yep."

"Oh man," I groaned.

"I didn't mind. I found it oddly soothing." He trailed his finger along my arm. "You were like one of those gravity blankets. We need to sleep like that more often."

He had been surprisingly comfortable, but our possible sleeping arrangements weren't the most important thing at the moment. "Was Daemon able to tell you anything about how Sarah ended up with these people?"

"Yeah." The half grin faded, and my stomach dipped. "The other human girl? Her name is AJ. She was able to fill in some of the blanks once she calmed down. She was with an unregistered Luxen, a friend she'd grown up with. They were concerned about what was going down and wanted a place to lie low. We have contacts in Luxen outreach centers who vet those who are looking to escape. AJ and her friend passed the vetting, and they were given the details on where to meet up with Spencer and Yesi. AJ claims that Sarah was already there with a Luxen, waiting to be moved here. She said that Sarah and this male Luxen kept to themselves, which is ordinary. They're instructed to not even share their names until they're here. The same goes for those moving the packages. They don't tell anyone who lives here or even where they are going. It's one way to protect the zone in case any of them are captured in the process. The ones retrieving the packages are the zone's most trusted. They will go down without speaking a word, no matter what."

Luc lifted his arm and I rolled over, into him. "According to AJ, things went south when they arrived at the area where we had to ditch the car. Yesi had started ahead with Sarah, the mystery Luxen, and another. We think that's when Sarah attacked them. Why, we don't know. Sarah would've entered at that point no matter what. Maybe Yesi saw or sensed something, but AJ said that they heard muffled sounds of fighting in the dark, and before Spencer could check it out, AJ said something came out of the woods and slammed into her. She was knocked out, and when she came to, everyone but her, Sarah, and Spencer were dead."

"Oh God." I shuddered.

"She said that she and Sarah helped get Spencer to the wall. She had no idea that it was Sarah who'd hurt them." Luc ran the tips of his fingers down my spine. "Dawson and Archer went out to where Sarah said she believed they were attacked. They found the bodies of four Luxen, which has to include the one Sarah was traveling with. So while there's not a threat that this Luxen may have gone back to the Daedalus, it doesn't tell us how she hooked up with him or why she turned on him."

"Do you think maybe the Daedalus made a Luxen go with her and she was ordered to kill him before he could possibly warn others here? Because if that's the case, it would be a huge risk once this Luxen got around others who could help him." I spread my hand out over his chest, above his heart. "But then that would mean the Daedalus would know about the zones."

"If the Daedalus were aware of who was here, they'd be storming those walls yesterday," he replied dryly. "But they most definitely have to know that unregistered Luxen are being moved and hidden somewhere. They have to figure that we've disappeared into one of these places. Pairing Sarah with a Luxen they are controlling one way or another ups their chances of Sarah being trusted and allowed into at least one of the places that the Luxen are being held. Either she got incredibly lucky with ending up at the right place or she gained some inside knowledge that the contacts she went to worked with our zone."

"Do the contacts know where the unregistered Luxen are being moved to?" I asked, thinking that would be one hell of a risk if so. I could easily imagine the Daedalus kidnapping family members of those who worked there to force the contacts to spill secrets.

"No. The zone is still secure." Luc rubbed his chin over my head. "Daemon also had a message for us. Cekiah wants to see us first thing in the morning."

27

Everyone is staring at me like I'm a freak.

Not everyone. Luc responded as he caught my hand, tugging me back and down where he sat, so I was perched on his knees. *Kat isn't staring at you.*

My gaze flicked over a few familiar faces and a whole lot of unfamiliar ones. Vibrant Luxen gazes mingled with ordinary human ones stared back at me in open distrust. Being stared at by a bunch of legit aliens like I was the weird one to be wary of was quite unsettling.

Kat was sitting at the long, conference-style table, her chair pushed back as she gently rocked baby Adam.

That's because she's focused on the baby.

Luc folded an arm loosely around my waist. *Daemon's not staring at you.*

That's because he's staring at his wife and son. Which was true. His dark head was bent as he touched the tiny, sock-covered feet.

Everyone is staring at you because you're beautiful.

My lips twisted as my stomach grumbled. Luc and I had eaten breakfast about thirty minutes before, but I felt like I hadn't touched food in a week, and that reminded me of how it had been right before I did the mini-coma thing. Which would be more concerning if I weren't currently in front of what felt like a firing squad. *Uh-huh.*

And because you blew up a house with your mind.

I sighed. *You're not helping.*

His answering chuckle tickled at my mind. Only Luc would be utterly unconcerned at the moment.

Cekiah cleared her throat, drawing my attention. Her braids

were swept back from her face, piled into a fascinating, intricate design that made the dyed blue braids really pop. She didn't sit at the head of the table. Actually, no one sat at the head. There weren't even chairs there, which I thought made an interesting statement.

No one here was at the head of anything.

Cekiah's eyes, a more honeyed color compared to Zouhour's, were fixed on mine. "I hope you've fully recovered."

I nodded. "I have. Thank you."

Her gaze slid to the space beyond my shoulder. "I wish the same could be said about Jonas."

"As do I," Luc replied smoothly while I tensed.

"Jonas was a good man, and he was doing his job," an older Luxen male said, his skin still mostly smooth with the exception of a few creases at the corner of his eyes.

"I'm sure he was an amazing person, Quinn, but he shot Evie." Luc's tone didn't change. "Who he was before that no longer matters."

Daemon looked up at that, and our gazes connected. What he had said to me one evening at Foretoken was all too easy to recall.

We aren't the bad guys, but we aren't the good guys, either.

Quinn's jaw hardened. "No one plays judge or jury here. No one has that kind of power."

"Are you sure that no one is playing judge or jury?" Luc asked as he surveyed the room. "Sort of seems like that's what occurring right now. The only difference is that I don't hide it when I do."

"Luc," Cekiah said in soft warning.

He shrugged. "I'm not sure what you want me to say about Jonas other than you should train your humans to be very sure who they are shooting before they pull the trigger."

Eaton lifted his brows from where he sat on the other side of Cekiah. "Duly noted."

I didn't even have to look to know Luc was smiling.

"Any of us would've done the same as Luc," Daemon spoke up, straightening.

"Right or wrong, that's just the way it is," Dawson chimed

in. He sat beside Dawson, and I wondered if they chose to sit side by side to mess with everyone. He looked down the table at Quinn. "Just like you would've done the same if Jonas had shot Alyssa."

Quinn sat back in his chair, not saying a word, and I had a feeling Alyssa was someone very important to him.

"His silence means he knows exactly what he'd do," Hunter added from where he sat reclined, a leg kicked up on the table. Serena was next to him. Luckily, today neither were trying to kill me. "But he's a *civilized* Luxen."

Daemon snorted. My eyebrows started to climb up my forehead.

"What happened to Jonas is a shame, one that should've been avoided," Bethany cut in from the other side of Dawson. "But I don't think we were called to this meeting to discuss that."

Beth sat so close to Dawson that their arms brushed, and my empty stomach dipped as I recalled the horror in her voice. She'd been so afraid for her daughter, of what I'd done.

Of what I might do.

"You're here to talk about me." I decided there was no reason to beat around the bush. "And whether or not I should be allowed to stay here. You did warn me that there'd be problems if I proved to be a risk."

Surprise flickered across some of the human's faces, but not Cekiah's. "I also warned Luc of this. I kept your secret until I could no longer do so."

"We weren't aware of the fact that you were anything but human until yesterday." The features of the female Luxen from the day before were taut. "Needless to say, none of us were all that pleased to discover that not only Cekiah had kept the secret from us but so did several trusted members of our community."

I really had no idea what to say to that, and none of those trusted community members looked all that bothered by being called out. Frankly, Daemon and Dawson looked bored.

"And here I thought we were going to talk about important

things like how close the Daedalus came to discovering the community." Luc planted his cheek on his fist as he propped his arm on the side of the chair. "And what will be done to ensure that never happens again."

"That is what we're discussing," Cekiah responded. "That thing was obviously here because of Evie."

That *thing*.

"And that means the community is at a risk," a human said. She was young, probably in her thirties. "Another could come looking for her the same way this thing did."

There it was again. *Thing*. My hands curled into fists. I wasn't like Sarah, but did they understand that? Was I a *thing* to them?

"Are we to stop transporting those in need of safety here?" A male hybrid joined in. "Because how else would we prevent something like that from happening again?"

My skin chilled. I thought about Heidi and Emery still out there, and all the other unregistered Luxen who needed shelter. If they closed up shop, would the other zones follow out of precaution?

"You can't do that," I blurted out. "There are still Luxen and others who need a safe place to go. If you or the other zones start turning people away, they'll be defenseless. Anyone taken into custody and processed has never been seen again. If these zones shutter their doors, you'd basically be signing their death certificates."

"I'm relieved to know you're thinking about those who need our help." Zouhour eyed me from where she sat, her nose pinched. "You understand the importance of what we do here."

"I do."

"Then you have to also understand why we'd be concerned about how you jeopardize what we do here."

And I did.

Lifting a hand, I rubbed it against the wound, the one that would've surely killed me if I were human and Luc hadn't been there. I needed to be here, where I was presumably safe with the exception of being shot, so I could learn more about what I could do and just how much control I truly had over the Source, but

I could not be the cause of others basically being left to fend for themselves.

I wouldn't.

Evie. There was a world of warning in how he said my name.

I closed my eyes. *It's not right.*

A faint charge of electricity danced along my back, coming from Luc. There was no doubt in my mind that the others felt it, too. "She understands fully, more than any of you probably would want to give her credit for. Except you, Kat; you have a heart as big as hers."

Kat didn't look up from her sleeping son's face as she said, "From what time I've spent with Evie, I know she wouldn't want to do anything that puts anyone or what we do here at risk." She smiled down at her son. "I'm sure she's mere minutes from volunteering to leave. That's what I would do."

Daemon sighed heavily as he nodded in agreement, sending Luc a rare look of sympathy.

"I don't care if one or a hundred more come looking for her. I brought her here because it was the safest place I could think of." Luc shifted behind me, his arm tightening around my waist as a brutal edge hardened his tone. "There is not a single thing that I will not do to ensure she remains as safe as possible."

"*Luc.*" I shot him a look over my shoulder.

He ignored me. "Not a single thing," he repeated.

"Trust me," Eaton grumbled as he dragged his thumb over his brow. "We all are completely aware of that."

"Then I don't know why we're having this conversation," Luc retorted.

"That's the thing, though." Kat looked up then. "It doesn't matter if Evie leaves this afternoon. The Daedalus won't know that unless she's spotted outside the zone. If more will be sent, they'll come even if she's not here. While that concern is a valid one, it's a pointless one, and we can't shut out others who need our help."

Lips slowly parting, I stared at Kat while the human female twisted toward her. "Then what do you suggest we do?"

"Make sure those coming here are being truly vetted and have every single one of our contacts looked over with the finest-tooth comb possible, because I don't for one second believe that this girl and the Luxen she was with could've been all that vetted. Not saying we have a spy in one of our contacts, but I think we have someone who screwed up," she said, and baby Adam softly cooed. "But that's just a suggestion, Jamie. A measured, less extreme response."

"Are you suggesting I'm fearmongering?" the woman demanded.

"I wouldn't dare think of suggesting that." Kat met the woman's stare. "But what do you think the Chicago zone will do if we stop allowing packages in? They'll follow what we do."

Looks were exchanged throughout the table, and it was Zouhour who spoke. "You're right."

Luc relaxed behind me. "Do you ever stop and think how incredibly lucky you are to have such a brilliant wife, Daemon?"

Daemon smiled. "Every. Single. Day."

"An additional risk does lie in our contacts. We need to find out how this thing was vetted and allowed in," Quinn said.

"She wasn't a thing," I snapped as the gnawing ache in my stomach moved upward. "Her name was Sarah, and whatever was done to her was done against her will. We saw her when she mutated. She had no idea what was happening to her. She may be as close to evil as one can get now, but a little bit of empathy never killed anyone."

The human woman opened her mouth.

I wasn't done. "And just so we all are on the same page, Sarah and I both were changed by the Daedalus. We're not alike, and I'm also not a *thing*."

Luc's hum of approval blended with my own thoughts as his arm briefly squeezed my waist.

"My apologies." Quinn bowed his head. "You're right."

"You say you aren't exactly like her, but you both were changed." Cekiah crossed one leg over the other. "I know what Luc and Zoe have told me. I know what you yourself have said, so what has changed that you suddenly know what you are?"

I could practically feel Luc gearing up for a biting response, but this was my battle. I rose, and Luc didn't stop me. "I know that whatever I am, it's not like her. I don't think I'm programmed like her and the other Trojans."

"You don't *think*?" she questioned.

"Yeah. I don't *think* I am. I didn't kill that one." I nodded in Hunter's direction. "Even though he really wanted to kill me."

"That is true," the Arum muttered.

Luc turned his head in Hunter's direction, and the Arum rolled his eyes as he pulled his legs down off the table.

"And I owe her an apology for that," Hunter grumbled. "I'm sorry."

My brows lifted. Before I could respond, his wife leaned around him. "And I was reaching for my gun. She didn't attack me." A small, sheepish smile appeared. "And I, too, am sorry about that."

"It's, uh, okay." I blinked, never thinking I'd be in the position of accepting an apology from two people who had wanted to murder me the day before.

"But what does that tell us, really?" Zouhour asked, and there was a genuine curiousness in her tone.

"From what we understand, the Trojans were trained to sense a threat, a challenge, and then eliminate it. They wouldn't have backed down from that," I explained.

"So you were able to show restraint this time?" Jamie said, arms crossed over her chest.

I met her stare. "I was able to show restraint, take out the Trojan who most likely would not have shown restraint after she attempted to turn me into exactly what she is. I stopped her from hurting anyone, and I did all of that without harming a single person. That's what I did this time."

"You blew up a whole, entire house," she returned.

"But did you die? Did anyone other than the bad guy die? No." Luc leaned forward, hands on his knees. "Does that answer your question, Jamie?"

She didn't dare look Luc in the eye as she said, "All that being said, it still doesn't mean she won't become a risk next time around."

"She's been working on controlling the Source," Eaton said, stretching out his left leg. "She and Luc. She's been using the Source."

Breathing a little easier, I nodded. "It's not that I don't believe they didn't try to make me just like the others, but I don't think it worked. Viv—Dr. Hemenway—thinks it's because I was given three different types of serums and having the other two in my system could've somehow interacted with the Andromeda serum."

"Those are theories," countered Cekiah.

"One of those Trojans killed my brother, and you all know—" Hunter sucked in a breath. "You all knew him. He was not weak. He put up one hell of a fight. So did Sin and I, but that Trojan showed no restraint. It came at us as soon as we left Lotho's place and came aboveground."

Lotho?

He's the leader of the Arum, answered Luc. *And he's a little eccentric.*

A little eccentric? Interest bloomed. *Speaking of Hunter, I want to talk to him. I want to know how he sensed either Sarah or me.*

Already on it. He's available later today.

I seriously hoped there was a later.

"It was like it was waiting for us. Between the three of us, we were able to injure it, but he was still alive when he escaped." A muscle worked along Hunter's jaw. "Never have I seen anything like that. I've never seen anything like her, either, but what we came across in Atlanta, it's different from her. I see that now."

My breath caught. Atlanta. *We were there, Luc.*

I know, came his quiet response.

I closed my eyes. Took no leap of logic that the Trojan had been there, looking for us—for me.

"The Trojan we faced down showed no restraint," Daemon chimed in. "We barely were able to get the upper hand, let alone kill it. The Trojan reminded me of . . ." He trailed off, shaking his head. "It's hard to explain. There was something entirely inhuman about it."

"The one I saw reminded me of that one liquid robot from the Terminator movies," Hunter said.

I frowned.

"The T-1000?" Beth asked, and when several pairs of eyes shifted to her, she shrank back a little. "What? I loved that movie."

"Yeah, that one." Hunter ran a hand through his hair. "That blank, robotic expression that lacked all emotion. There was no fear. None whatsoever."

Dawson was nodding. "Agreed. The one we came across could've been the perfect T-1000."

"I have no idea what a T-1000 is," Zouhour murmured.

The male hybrid next to her patted her arm. "I'll fill you in later."

Cekiah started to speak, but I felt a dancing of fingers along the back of my neck and shoulder blades the same moment she must have. "It appears we're about to have company."

The door creaked open a moment later, and Zoe slipped in, along with Grayson. They stopped just inside the door, letting it swing shut slowly behind them.

Zouhour frowned. "I didn't realize you two were invited to this meeting."

"We weren't." Grayson leaned against the wall and folded his arms over his chest. "But we're here."

That response got more than just a couple of narrowed looks.

"What Grayson *meant* to say is that we know we weren't invited," Zoe explained. "But we also know what this meeting is going to lead to, and we wanted to be here."

"And what do you think this meeting is going to lead to?" Cekiah asked.

"Evie being kicked out of here, or at least you all trying to do just that. We're here to stop you from making a very bad life choice," Zoe replied, standing there as if she were ready to go into battle. "And I get why you all don't want her here. None of you have seen anything like her. She's different. You think she's a risk, but I've known Evie for years. So has Grayson."

Wasn't quite sure watching over someone for years meant Grayson actually knew me, but I'd take any backup.

"She's a good person who's been through a lot, and she needs the protection of this community. She deserves it," Zoe stated, and God, I loved her. I couldn't ask for a better friend.

"I'm sure she's a wonderful person, but this isn't personal," Quinn responded, and there wasn't an ounce of dismissal in his tone. I believed what he said. "You're right, though. We've never seen anything like her before. None of us, including her, knows what's she capable of."

"And humans had never experienced anything like the Luxen before. They still have no idea what you're capable of, and their fear of the unknown is why this community exists. Don't each and every one of you expect to be given the chance to prove that you come in peace and all that crap?" Zoe challenged. "Or do humans and Luxen share that one common flaw?"

"Oh, burn," Luc murmured as the corners of my lips tipped up.

Those rocking alien DNA paled or drew back from the in-your-face hypocrisy. Jamie, the lone human female, looked less than pleased, but there was even a glint of doubt in her brown eyes.

"Actually," Grayson cut in with a long-suffering sigh. "Nearly everyone in here, including her, thinks she needs the protection of the community. That's not true. Not remotely. What is true is that you need her."

My head jerked around to him in surprise. Was Grayson actually actively defending me?

"She is more powerful than everyone in this room combined," he continued, unfolding his arms and reaching into his pocket. He pulled out a sour apple Blow Pop. "The Daedalus have more like her, and when they decide to break up this little militia you have going on here, even someone who isn't particularly intel-ligent would know what a good idea it would be to have her on their side."

The world just stopped spinning on its axis. Pigs were flying. Santa was real. Hell had even frozen over.

"But I'm thinking most of you are all too human." Grayson wasn't done as his gaze flicked dismissively across the Luxen in the room. "You force her out, you lose Zoe. You lose me. And you also lose Luc. And you'd have to be a unique kind of stupid to not take what that means into consideration."

Luc smirked as he leveled a stare on every single one of the unofficial but totally official council members. "He does have a way with words, doesn't he?"

"That he does." Cekiah tapped her fingers under her chin. "But we're not completely defenseless here. We've done just fine without any of you being here."

"How will you do without us?" Daemon asked, and another burst of shock rippled through me.

"Or us?" Dawson leaned back, draping his arm over the back of Beth's chair.

Hunter's smile was like smoke. "Or without me and every Arum here?"

I needed to sit down.

"And I'm sure Archer and Dee would be right behind us," Daemon added.

I really needed to sit down before I fell down. Backing up, I plopped into the empty chair that I didn't think had been beside Luc moments before.

Luc wore the kind of half grin I knew was beyond infuriating to anyone who was on the receiving end of them. "What were you saying again, Cekiah?"

Her lips had thinned. "I don't appreciate the not-so-veiled threat from any of you. Some of you I'd expect better from. Not you, Luc. I'd expect nothing less."

"And that's what you'll always get," he replied.

She coughed out a dry laugh as her gaze slid to Daemon and crew. "You would really leave here with a newborn? You'd risk that child's life by standing with them?"

"You want to hear something interesting?" Kat asked. Baby Adam had woken up, stretching a little hand up. She pressed a kiss to the tiny knuckles. "I told Evie what we would do if she proved a threat. That any of us would risk certain death at the hands of Luc to ensure the safety of Zone 3. And do you know how she responded? She didn't get mad at me, nor did she yell or break down. She said that she understood, and I believed her. Still do."

The room had fallen quiet as Kat said, "I don't want to go out there. Not until the Daedalus is truly destroyed and it's a world that I'd want to raise my son in. Isn't that what we're preparing for?"

Several severe looks settled into the faces of those at the table, but Kat would not be silenced. "We are training every person capable of fighting back to do just that." Her clear gray eyes lifted to me. "That's what we're doing in the Yard."

Someone, and I think it was Quinn, sounded like they were having a cardiac arrest.

"Kat—" Jamie started.

"Interrupt her and it won't be pretty," Daemon replied casually as if he were giving directions. "And it's not me I'm warning you about. Adam kept both of us up late last night. My girl is cranky."

Jamie snapped her mouth shut.

Kat's smile was downright bloodthirsty. "We knew even before we had proof the Daedalus was still operating that sooner than later, those in charge would come for us. They always do, but we will be ready. It will be the last thing anyone who attempts to destroy us will do. Then we will go out there and we will hunt down every single member of the Daedalus and everyone who has aided them and allowed them to put a president in office who won't just stop at genocide of the Luxen. And oh yeah, he's totally on our list. Not everyone in this room helped save the entire world when the Luxen invaded, but half of us did, and that's no exaggeration. We will not allow what we bled and sacrificed for to be turned into something far worse than what the invading Luxen could've ever hoped to achieve. The world beyond these walls belongs to all of us. We will make damn sure it does."

I might've stopped breathing at that point.

"Each Luxen and hybrid is being trained to fight with the Source, and every human who is able is being trained to fight hand to hand and then some." She kissed Adam's fist again. "Those who can't are learning how to fight back in different ways, from providing medical assistance to a multitude of other essentials that are necessary."

That's what the building blocks of this community were, why they were able to care for everyone, no matter their age or capabilities. Everyone pitched in, whether it was washing clothes or growing food, caring for the elderly or teaching the children, and they all did so with a common goal.

To take back their world.

Kat smiled at the soft sound Adam made. "I've heard that Dasher claims he has an army. Well, so do we, and it's bigger than you can possibly imagine and the Daedalus could ever dream of."

"Remember when you asked if people ever left here?" Zoe asked from behind me, and I nodded. "They do. Both here and Chicago. They go out and meet others, setting up enclaves all over the United States. They recruit family members and friends who were told that they were dead. Doesn't take much to open their eyes to the truth of what is going down."

No, I didn't imagine that it would.

"There are dozens of locations strategically placed throughout the States, each one commanded by either one of the zone leaders or a trusted, ex-military-minded human," Dawson said. "Eaton has helped coordinate and vet them."

"There are outposts in other countries, places that haven't aligned themselves with the administration's current policies." Serena smiled. "The Daedalus may have a lot of connections, but they may have forgotten how well connected some of the Luxen have become, especially in Europe."

"We are tens of thousands strong," Kat said. "And when we fight, we won't be fighting for someone else's greed or their thirst for power. We won't be doing it for a paycheck or for accolades. We'll be fighting to survive."

"I'll take those odds any day." Hunter tapped his hand off the *day.*

"So, we will not raise our child in the same damn type of society that we're going to overthrow, a community full of people who damn well should have known better, who have been given second and third and fifth chances and yet refuse to extend the same to another because they're different." Kat eyed every single one of the members at the table. "If we turn Evie out? That sets the kind of precedent that has ripped the world outside these walls apart for centuries. It will be the same precedent that will carry over into the world we will try to build."

"We are better than that." Beth's quiet voice drew all eyes. "At least that's what I've always believed, but listening to some of you today, I have grave concerns that I may have been misguided."

"Bethany," Quinn said gently. "How can you not be worried?"

"None of us are saying that we aren't worried about what she could do or become. God knows, I was scared half to death yesterday when I saw Ashley standing before her." She swallowed hard as Dawson brushed a strand of her hair back, his hand lingering on the nape of her neck. "But Ashley isn't afraid of her. All she did yesterday was talk about her new friend who could fly."

Oh.

Oh.

That was me, totally me.

"And our baby girl is often a better judge of character than nearly a hundred percent of the people we know," Dawson said. "If Ashley wants to be friends with her, then Evie has got my vote."

"I gave her good enough reason to attack me, and she didn't," Hunter added. "She has mine."

"Ditto." Serena raised her hand. "I was totally pulling a gun on her. She did nothing but warn me." She cringed. "Again, really sorry about that."

"She has mine," Kat said. "If that wasn't obvious already."

"Seeing what I saw yesterday?" Daemon met Luc's stare, and this was also about Daemon repaying Luc. But that wasn't the main reason. I wasn't going to lessen what they were doing by throwing their hats in with me. They trusted me. "I want her on my team when the day comes that we end this."

"She has mine," Zouhour announced, and a feather could've knocked me out of the chair. "Kat and Bethany are right. We are building a better world. We cannot do that if we let fear of what we don't know or understand guide us."

I clenched the arms of the chair to stop myself from doing something stupid, say, like climbing over the table and hugging all of them, and even baby Adam.

Cekiah looked around at the faces at the table, and one by one, they all nodded, even Jamie. There was a ghost of a smile on her face as her gaze returned to me. "Well, I guess someone should introduce you to the Yard."

28

The Yard was exactly that and then some.

Still a little dazed by what had gone down in the meeting and definitely still cringing from my gushing stream of words when I'd attempted to thank Kat and everyone afterward, I listened to Cekiah as she gave me a tour and Luc hung a few feet back, following at a rather sedate pace.

The Yard itself was behind a high school, encompassing the parking lot, football and soccer field, and a baseball field.

But that wasn't all. As we drew closer to the open double doors, I picked up the faint, repetitive popping. "What is that?"

"The auditorium had already been soundproofed, so it's made the perfect firing range," Cekiah explained. "We didn't want the children or those who are vulnerable to be frightened by the sound of guns. Of course, we could only stop so much sound transfer, and there is a level of distastefulness to use a room inside of the school for this purpose, but unless you were on this part of the property, you wouldn't hear it."

"That makes sense." From where we stood, I could see shapes of people moving about just inside the door. With the exception of the Trojans and the like, they'd be using guns. After all, it seemed like guns were mankind's weapon of choice. Fight fire with fire.

"We also use some of the classrooms for strategic planning for those who have been recommended for possibly leading an outpost," Cekiah explained. "The school has two gymnasiums, and we use them for grappling training."

"Sort of like wrestling," Luc expounded. "But a bit more intense since it often incorporates mixed martial arts. The Daedalus often uses it in their training."

"Considering how I took out April, I imagined I was trained in something like that, but I guess it's locked away."

"I find that fascinating." Cekiah turned to me, eyes widening. "Not that I find what was done to you fascinating but more so the fact that what you know exists on an unconscious level. How you're able to tap into that knowledge and use it, I find very interesting."

"You and me both," I mumbled.

"It would be interesting to see if you can access those training techniques under the right circumstances." Luc pulled his gaze from the sprawling brick building. "I imagine it would be a lot like with the Source. Once you use that training, it will become more natural to you."

"I don't know." I folded my arms. "Being able to use an alien source of power seems more believable than my suddenly knowing jiujitsu."

Luc grinned. "As easily imaginable as you being able to run faster than I can?"

I smiled at the memory of doing just that, basking a little in that moment of victory.

Shameless.

Don't rain on my parade, I told him. "Who is doing all the training?"

"A mixture, but for the most part, people who are skilled in whatever area they are training in. We got lucky with Eaton. He knew a lot of men and women who weren't happy with what was coming down the pipeline. Even a few who, like he was, were aware of the Daedalus and in the beginning had believed that there was good that they could accomplish."

"Do you believe that there was good in the beginning?" I asked, curious to know where she stood.

Turning away from the school, she gave a small shake of her head. "I think anything that involves humans isn't cut-and-dried. The same would go for Luxen, for any species that has the capability for emotions, desires, and wants." She glanced over at me. "History has shown that some of the greatest atrocities were aided along by well-intentioned people."

"Well, they do say the road to hell is paved with good intentions," Luc said, shoving his hands into his pockets.

Cekiah steered us away from the entrance, toward the chain-link fence. "The football field is one of the areas where we train the humans for hand-to-hand combat," she explained as we walked through the parking lot. "As you can see."

I could definitely see.

There were several stations set up across the field where the plain marking yards had long since faded, some of the stations led by a Luxen or hybrid, others by humans.

Several dozen humans were in the midst of either laying the smacketh downeth or being on the receiving end of one. One group near the rusted goalpost appeared to be straight up tackling one another on bright red mats.

Something about that tugged at the fringes of my subconscious. "Are they learning . . . ?" There was a word for it, and it wasn't *tackling*. Not how they were being instructed to use their legs or how to drag their opponent down by the arm. The word suddenly popped into my brain. "Takedowns! Are they learning takedowns?"

"Gold star for you," Luc murmured from behind us.

I shot him a look over my shoulder, and my stomach took that moment to grumble loudly.

He raised his brows.

Cekiah nodded. "In any fight, the odds are better if you get your opponent on the ground. They are also being taught how to take a fall in a way to avoid as much injury as possible, but to also be able to get to their feet quickly."

At other stations, they were learning punches and kicks and more complicated techniques that resembled something you'd see in mixed martial arts. There were faint popping sounds as we walked along, nearing the soccer field. The moment I got a clear eyeful of that, my mouth dropped open.

"Holy crapola," I whispered.

"Impressive, isn't it?" Cekiah smiled. "This was Eaton's baby in the beginning, and it took us nearly a year to put together."

"It looks like a marine-level obstacle course." I blinked, beyond impressed, because that's what it did look like, and it was in use at the moment.

"That's basically what it is," she confirmed.

Two women kicked off, jumping easily over the first hurdle, which appeared to have been constructed out of telephone poles, and then they vaulted over one that was several feet off the ground. They reached a high bar that was at least eight feet off the ground. Both women jumped, executing a pull-up where they got one arm and one leg over the bar, and then they dropped to the ground below. Cheers erupted from those on the sidelines as they vaulted over the next hurdle and then reached a log. Stepping onto that, they jumped up to grasp what looked to be a very large and long monkey bar. They swung their way across, dropping to a set of sawed tree trunks that they ran across.

They weren't done.

Hitting a six-foot wall, they climbed their way up and then went over the top. Once over the other side and on the ground, they raced over several different logs set at varying heights. They reached another high bar, but this time there were two of them. My jaw was on the ground as the jumped, their hands smacking down on the first bar. They swung their bodies, gaining enough momentum to then lift their legs and bodies over the bar about a foot higher while never letting go of the lower bar.

The women dropped to the ground and then met the final obstacle, the rope climb. Up they went, using their upper- and lower-body strength to make the climb. They reached the top and then came back down the same way they'd gone up, neck and neck.

Shouts and claps sounded as they hit the ground at the same time. Both women popped up, hugging each another.

"I'm exhausted watching this," I whispered, shaking my head. Like I needed to sit down after viewing that.

"This course builds endurance and stamina." Cekiah started walking again, just as a man and a woman kicked off at the beginning. "And according to Eaton, a sense of support and confidence among each other."

"I would never stop gloating if I completed that," I admitted.

"But you don't have to complete that," Cekiah said, and then nodded in the direction of the baseball field that resided at the bottom of a small slope. "And neither do they."

My breath caught as static charged the atmosphere. Down below, several Luxen were summoning the Source. The white light circled their palms. My heart rate kicked up as the Source hummed to life in my chest. The jolt of antsy energy coursed through my veins, but it was faint. The emptiness in my stomach seemed to spread to my chest as movement at the other end of the field caught my attention.

Three Luxen stood down there, holding balloons. Letting them go, they then used the Source to move the balloons in erratic bursts of activity.

On command, one by one, the Luxen and hybrids stepped forward. Tapping into the Source, they took out one balloon after another. The pure, deadly energy didn't pop the balloons. It swallowed them whole, disintegrating the balloons without a sound.

"Moving targets," I gasped. "They're practicing hitting moving targets with the Source."

"Their targets won't remain still, now will they?" Cekiah asked as the breeze caught the edges of her thin blouse, lifting the ruffled hem. "You are more than welcome to make use of the Yard, but I would ask that you do so under Luc's supervision." She paused. "Or one of those who spoke up for you during the meeting."

"That's doable," Luc agreed while I tried to imagine Hunter assisting me with any level of training.

I nodded when Cekiah glanced in my direction. I may not be kicked out of the zone, but that didn't mean Cekiah or the others were ready to allow me to have free rein. I couldn't blame them for that.

She drifted over to where a male hybrid was climbing the hill, his gaze darting back and forth between us and Cekiah. Watching the Luxen and hybrids down below, the cold knowledge that they were indeed preparing for war didn't just sink in. It dive-bombed me.

Kat's speech wasn't for dramatics. It was a reality, and it wasn't like I didn't know that when I heard it, but seeing it was a whole different ballpark.

Looking out over the field, I suddenly thought of Nate. This might explain why Nate was so afraid. Any of this would give one a healthy amount of fear, especially if he didn't know why this was occurring. Hell, I knew why this was happening, and it was still a little frightening to see.

"You okay?" Luc asked, voice low as he approached me.

"Yeah." I exhaled roughly. "No?" I looked over my shoulder just as another round of balloons evaporated. As far as I knew, only some Luxen could do that with the Source. Most would leave a wounded, smoking body behind. Either way, hitting a human with the Source would be nothing like taking out a balloon. "I don't remember much of the invasion. Before I learned the truth, I thought I must've buried the memories of what happened. Like it was so frightening and traumatizing that was the only way I could cope. Now I know why. I was Nadia when all that happened. Maybe if I remembered, all of this wouldn't be so unsettling.

"But it is," I admitted, facing Luc. "But I think if I wasn't disturbed then, there'd be a problem, you know? I mean, you're probably not disturbed by any of this because you've been around it your whole life."

"Sometimes, the reality of everything sneaks up on me." He took my hand, threading his fingers through mine. In the sunlight, his eyes were polished amethysts. "Usually when life feels like what I imagine normalcy is, the things I've seen catch me off guard." His head turned to the field below. "I may be able to take a life when necessary, and I may not even regret doing so, but I don't forget a single life."

Pressure clamped down on my chest as I squeezed his hand.

Luc squinted as he returned the gesture. "And before this is over, a lot of lives are going to be taken. On both sides." He looked over at me. "Are you ready for that, Evie? There are going to be more Sarahs. Enemies who became that way against their will. And there are going to be others who believe they're on the right side of history."

My stomach hollowed. "I have to be ready. I want to stop the Daedalus. I can't do that if I don't get my hands dirty."

"You're not going to get your hands dirty." He angled his body toward me, his eyes meeting mine. "You're going to get them bloody."

"I know." Another sharp dipping motion lit up my stomach, replacing the grumbling hunger.

His gaze searched mine as he lifted his other hand, placing the tips of his fingers to my cheek. "Soft heart," he murmured. "I don't want to see it hardened or destroyed."

"I don't, either." I curled my hand around his wrist. "But if I did nothing, that would do worse things to my heart, Luc, and we don't have any other choices here. We have to fight back."

"We have choices, Peaches. We always do." He stepped in closer. "We could disappear. I have other places, tucked away all over the world—places that would take the Daedalus decades to discover. We don't have to do anything."

It took me a moment to really hear what he was saying, because I sort of got stuck on the whole he-had-places-all-over-the-world part. "For real?"

"Real."

"Where?"

One side of his lips kicked up. "I have a small villa in Greece."

I blinked. "A small villa?"

He nodded. "Paris bought it a year or two before the invasion. You picked the location."

"I . . ." It wasn't exactly a surprise to hear that I would've picked Greece. As Evie, who I was now, I'd always wanted to visit there. "And you have other places?"

"I have a flat south of London and an apartment in Edinburgh," he told me, and all I could do was stare. "There's also the house in Puna'auia."

"I don't even know where that it is."

"I can show you exactly where it is. Just say the word and we can disappear." His head tilted. "We'd even take your friends if they wanted to go."

There was an allure to what he offered, a seductive, powerful one. There'd be no bloody hands to worry about, no Jason Dasher or Daedalus, at least for decades, and decades was an eternity. We could disappear with the people we cared about.

But the world wouldn't disappear with us. Neither would this virus or the Daedalus. They'd keep looking for us, and even if they didn't find us, they'd find others. The world would keep tiptoeing down a path that would change everything forever.

I lowered my gaze. "All of this . . . it's bigger than we are, Luc. If we disappeared and did nothing to stop this, I don't know if I could live with myself." Slowly, I looked up at him. "Is that what you want?"

"I'm incredibly selfish when it comes to you. You should know the answer to that."

"You're selfish, but you're not apathetic," I told him. "If you were, you'd forget those deaths you mentioned."

The hue of his eyes churned as his lashes lowered, and I spoke to him in the way only he could hear. *It would eat away at both of us.*

A long moment passed, and then his voice whispered in my thoughts. *It would.*

"You can show me all these places afterward," I said.

"I can do that."

"Promise?"

"Promise."

After gorging myself on cheese and some kind of cured meat that reminded me of jerky, I was still hungry as we left to meet up with Hunter.

"Maybe it's a tapeworm," Luc suggested as we walked the two blocks over to where Hunter and Serena had set up house.

Curling a lip, I looked over at him. "Really? That's the best you can come up with?"

He chuckled as he bumped his shoulder into mine. "I mean, if one has been in you long enough, you'd be eating constantly."

"I don't think that's how it works." I moved out of the way before he could bump my arm again.

"Well, there's this rare disease that—"

"You know, forget I even mentioned it." I hopped up on the sidewalk. "It's not as bad as it was before I took a mental vacay, so it's probably just my body trying to get used to the lack of sugar."

"How much sugar were you eating?"

"Not that much."

"How many grams?"

"How in the world would I know how many grams of sugar—"

Luc caught the bottom of my foot with his, causing me to stumble.

"Dammit!" Laughing, I swung on him, but Luc had moved wickedly fast, halfway down the block by the time I spun around. "That's cheating."

"More like that's you needing to work on your reflexes."

I flipped him off. Smirking, he came to stand by a yard shaded by large trees with burnt red leaves.

"You may be the most powerful Origin in the whole wide world—"

"Universe," he corrected.

I ignored that. "But sometimes you have the mentality of a twelve-year-old boy."

"A twelve-year-old boy who is also the most powerful Origin in the whole wide world."

Stopping several feet away, I stared at him.

He dipped his chin, grinning. "But you still love me."

A grin tugged at my lips. "I do." Then I sprang forward, willing myself to move fast, and I did. I knew I'd surprised him when I clasped his cheeks and he jerked back a fraction of an inch. Stretching up, I kissed him—really kissed him. Luc reached for me, but I darted away. He pouted as he let his arms drop at his sides. "Made you jump."

"You did." Eyes glittering, he watched me as I all but flounced past him. "Do you even know where you're going?"

"Nope." I kept walking. "I figured I'll know where I am when my extra-special alien senses tell me so."

Luc caught up with me as we walked down the block, the street lined with large trees. We'd crossed the street when I felt what reminded me of a breath of cold air along my back. Halting, I turned to my right. The yard was overgrown, but the sidewalk leading up to the curtained front porch was cleared.

"Give me one second." When Luc nodded, I walked a couple of houses down and came back when the feeling faded. I looked across the street and shook my head. "It's this house."

"Two gold stars for you in one day." He turned to walk up the sidewalk.

Trailing behind him, I waited as he stepped up on the porch. I kicked out, catching the bottom of his foot. He stumbled, catching himself as he spun around, brows raised.

"Three gold stars," I replied.

His smile started off slowly and then grew into the kind that caused my breath to hitch and my heart to melt. "Do you know what happens when you get three gold stars in one day?"

"What?" I went up the steps, stopping at the one below him.

Luc bent so that his mouth brushed mine as he spoke. "There's a reward involved."

My eyes fluttered shut. "Does it involve chocolate?"

"Something better." He dragged his lips over mine.

"Mmm." The fluttering in my chest moved lower. "Chocolate-covered popcorn?"

"Even better than that." Nipping at my lower lip, he caught my gasp with a kiss. We were so caught up in each other, neither of us were aware of exactly when the door opened behind us.

"I feel like there are better porches to do that on," came Hunter's voice. "Namely, any of them that aren't mine."

Eyes popping open, I saw Luc grin right before he gave me one more quick kiss and pivoted to face the Arum. "I'd apologize, but that would insinuate that I cared."

Hunter snorted as he glanced at me. "I don't know how you put up with him."

"If she knew you any better, she'd be asking Serena the same."

A semblance of a smile appeared as he showed us in. "True story."

Following Luc and Hunter inside, the first impression that I got of the small house was that it was very monochromatic. White, bare walls. Black couches and chairs sat beside black end tables and a black coffee table. Curtains and carpet white, there was literally no color in the house with the exception of the small, wooden figurines that were sprinkled through the living area. A wolf was perched on the end table beside a black lantern. A large bear stood on its hind legs between two white pillar candles that had burned halfway down. There was a horse mid-gallop on the other end table, and several small dogs lined up on what had once been a TV stand. Each of the figurines was detailed in a way I imagined took hours of making the smallest nicks and cuts in the wood.

Do you think he looked for the house that was already decorated in black and white? I asked, wondering how we ended up with angel-palooza.

Probably. He needed a place as deep and dark as his troubled thoughts. Arum are goth like that.

I snorted.

Hunter's eyes narrowed. "You two having a private conversation over there? Sort of rude to do that in someone else's house."

Suddenly finding the carved bear absolutely fascinating, I hoped he couldn't tell my cheeks were getting hot.

"We would never do such a thing. Where is Serena?" Luc swiftly changed the subject as he sat on the couch, patting the spot next to him. I took it as Hunter took the chair kitty-corner to it.

"She's visiting with Kat." He kicked a booted foot up on the coffee table. "Getting in some baby time."

"Why am I not surprised you're sitting that visit out?"

His shoulders shook with a silent laugh as he dropped his arm over his bent knee. "Few things in life scare me. Babies are one of them."

Huh. Hunter and I had something in common.

"So, you all wanted to talk?" The ultra-pale gaze flicked to me. "I'm really hoping you're not here for another apology."

I snorted. "No."

"And I also hope you're not here to thank me again. I don't think I can live through that again."

Pressing my lips together until I puffed up my cheeks as my eyes widened, I replied, "I may have been a bit enthusiastic in my response."

"I thought you were going to hug me."

"That you did not have to worry about. I don't make a habit of hugging people who wanted to kill me the day before."

A hint of white teeth flashed when he smiled. "Wise choice. So, why are you two here?"

Luc was silent as I scooted to the edge of the couch. "Before I ask you anything, I wanted to say I'm sorry about your brother."

"Why would you be?" His fingers started tapping along the arm of the chair. "Did you know him?"

"Actually, I did meet him. Briefly." I explained how I'd run into him outside the club. "He didn't attack me or anything. Sort of said goodbye and went inside."

A muscle flexed all his jaw. "Lore didn't make it a habit of attacking teenage girls."

"Good to know," I murmured.

"What are your questions?" he prodded, obviously not wanting to focus on his brother's loss.

More than anyone, I got that. Every time the image of Mom appeared, I immediately thought of anything else. I wondered if Luc did the same. "You sensed me, right? Or you sensed Sarah or both of us. How did you? Other Arums have—"

"Lore?"

I nodded.

His gaze flicked to Luc. "You can't sense her?"

"Nope. Neither can Luxen," he replied.

"Interesting," Hunter murmured. "I can do something you can't."

"That must be an amazing feeling," Luc replied. "I wouldn't know. You see, I've spent my entire life doing things you can't do."

Uh.

Hunter chuckled. "You're such an asshole."

"That's why you like me."

"True." He nodded. "I could sense the Arum in you, but it didn't feel right. It was too faint. I don't know if I was sensing just you or both of you. It felt like a heaviness in the air—"

"And on your skin?" I clasped my knees.

He was still for a moment, and then he nodded. "Exactly."

Looking back at Luc, I asked, "I wonder why Arums can feel me but not Luxen or Origins?"

"Hunter?" Luc asked.

The Arum gave a half grin. "I imagine it has to do with how we are able to perceive and see Luxen and anything with Luxen DNA. We are more sensitive."

"The auras I see now? You're talking about that?" I asked.

"Yes. Luxen like to think they are hunters. They're not. We are. Biologically, we are natural predators. Our senses are far more heightened than Luxen's—seeing, hearing, tasting, smelling. Apparently, the Daedalus has been able to replicate that. They have been trying for as long as I can remember."

"I felt Sarah as soon as I approached that house. I just didn't know what I was feeling." I took a deep breath. "I was able to communicate with her like I can with Luc, and I think I heard her in my head when she was mutating."

"Makes sense. We can communicate with one another that way." His fingers continued to move. "Can you hear other thoughts like Mr. Special beside you?"

I shook my head.

"Is that really a relief?" Luc asked.

Hunter's eyes narrowed. "Now you're just trying to prove a point, and you're going to annoy me."

"Can you communicate with me like that?" I asked before the whole meeting went down the drain.

"Already tried. You didn't hear me. And I can't hear you."

I frowned. "Maybe it's only other Trojans."

"That doesn't explain you two."

"He's healed me a couple of times or a dozen." I shrugged.

Hunter's pale gaze sharpened as he focused on Luc. Something was clicking together behind his eyes.

"How badly did you wound the Trojan?" Luc asked.

"Blew a hole through its chest. Like I could see through the bastard," Hunter answered. "That bad."

"Wow," I whispered.

"He didn't go at us like you did with the other Trojan. He could've blown up any of the buildings around us." Hunter's fingers stilled. "I'm guessing that's why a bullet took you down for the count. You expelled all your energy. Drained yourself dry, I imagine."

Luc shifted forward, all lazy arrogance gone. "Refresh my memory, Hunter. What happens when you go empty on the Source? When you don't feed?"

He arched a brow. "Like when we almost hit rock bottom? Not many choose to live that kind of life, but when they do, we grow weaker, become practically human. The first time is the worst. It's like detoxing. We get hungry."

I locked up. "What?"

"Hunger that no food can quench. Like the gnawing type of hunger that seizes up your stomach and chest," he explained, and it felt like the couch moved underneath me. "Many end up sleeping the worst of it off."

"Sleeping?" I squeaked. "Like for a couple of days?"

He eyed me. "Yes. Sometimes more."

"Oh, crap," I whispered.

"Jesus," Luc muttered as he looked at me. "I should've thought of that. You're part Arum. You started getting hungry after the woods, and then you slept for four days."

"Well, that should've been a dead giveaway," Hunter remarked.

Sitting there, I could only stare at the bear.

"Maybe to you, but she's not completely an Arum. I'm sure you've been filled in on her background."

"I have, but I didn't know she slept for four days," Hunter replied. "What happened when you woke up?"

Blinking, I eased my death grip on my knees. "I felt fine."

"You're part Luxen, so you probably took that time to replenish what you used. It was the first time you'd used the Source to such an extreme after activating, right? Doesn't poke holes in the doc's theory. Sort of proves it," he said, then laughed.

"What's so funny?" I demanded.

"Nothing," Hunter said, lips curling into a smile as he focused on Luc. "So how do you feel about becoming her own personal energy drink?"

29

Whatat?" I jumped to my feet. "You're saying I'm going to need to feed off Luc?"

Hunter arched a brow as he looked up at me. "Either him or a Luxen. Hybrids really won't be worth it. You feed off one of them and you're starving a few hours later. Humans, well, you'd feed off them for different reasons."

I started to ask why, and then, luckily, I thought of Serena and realized I really didn't need to ask that question.

My gaze bounced to Luc. His expression had gone thoughtful. My stomach dropped to my toes. "I'm not feeding off you."

He cocked his head to the side but said nothing.

"Then I'm sure you can find a willing Luxen to step in." Hunter dipped his chin. "You know, it doesn't have to be painful—"

"It's painful?" I whispered, clasping my hands against my chest.

"Only if you want it to be." Dropping his foot the floor, he tipped forward. "But you can make it so that the willing donor thoroughly enjoys themselves."

Warmth flared across my face. "I don't even know how to feed."

Hunter slid a knowing look in Luc's direction. "I know an Arum or two who would be more than happy to walk you through it."

Luc's gaze snapped in his direction. "That won't be necessary."

"You sure? Sin should be here soon." Hunter bit down on his lip. The Arum was clearly enjoying himself, the jerk. "And you know how helpful he is."

Luc's smile was all fire. "I also know how painful my fist in your face is about to be."

"It's just a suggestion."

"Oh yeah, you're being really helpful."

Chuckling, Hunter leaned back in the chair. "That's my middle name."

"And if I don't feed?" I sat back down. "I end up in a coma for days again?"

"Seems like that's the case. You sleep until your body can replenish what you've lost." Hunter put his foot back onto the coffee table. "In a way, you're lucky. If you were Arum, your only option would be to feed unless you wanted to lose the ability to harness the Source completely."

"Lucky?" I coughed out a dry laugh. "I guess."

"There is something else," Hunter said. "Opal."

"Opal?" I looked between them. "Like the gemstone?"

Luc nodded. "Remember how I told you beta quartz can hide the Luxen, neutralizing their wavelengths? That's not the only naturally occurring stone that has an impact. Some are good. Some are bad."

"Like onyx? I know that can hurt Luxen." It was everywhere outside these walls, installed like sprinkler systems in many of the public buildings, emitting a fine burst of onyx. The mixture had a bizarre effect on the alien DNA, causing Luxen to feel like their very cells were bouncing off one another. I'd forgotten about that. Would it affect me?

I shook my head. Focus on one WTF at a time.

Luc must've picked up on my thoughts, because he said, "Onyx and diamond mixtures have no effect on Origins. I imagine it will be the same for you."

"Diamonds?" I hadn't heard anything about diamonds before.

Luc nodded. "Diamonds have the highest index of light refraction. It won't hurt a Luxen or hybrid, but in large quantities, it can drain them of the Source."

"But opal is entirely different." Hunter let his head rest on the back of the chair. "It refracts and reflects specific wavelengths of light, changing the speed and direction. For anyone with Luxen DNA, it's a power booster. And for an Arum, if we have one, it gives us more power and limits how much we have to feed."

"Do you have a stray piece of opal lying around?" I asked Luc, hopeful.

He shook his head. "Ever since President McHugh took office, opal has been hard to come by. Most of it has been seized or destroyed."

"You don't have a stash of it?" Surprise filled Hunter's tone.

"I did," he replied dryly. "Two places, actually. One of them I had to leave rather unexpectedly from, and the other is quite the distance from here. Trust me, if I had one, Evie would be wearing it."

"Well, then, that's a shame." Hunter's gaze slid to me. "Feed or sleep. Those are your choices."

"There is no choice," argued Luc. "You need to feed."

Hands planted on my hips, I glared at where he was all but sprawled on the couch, one arm tossed along the back of the cushion, a bare foot resting on the edge of the coffee table. He looked mighty comfortable for someone who was five seconds away from getting smacked upside the head.

We'd been at it since we'd stopped by to see the doc, which was right after we'd left Hunter's place. I'd wanted to see if she thought there was anything I could do. Like, I don't know, a diet of all red meat or raw veggies. Maybe she had some vitamin B shots lying around. Luc humored me with the visit. There was nothing Viv could do or suggest. Apparently, she hadn't seen an Arum who didn't feed before. All the ones here, which weren't many, had willing Luxen donors.

Which had led to me asking Luc on the way back, "Who is Hunter feeding off?"

"You know, I don't want to even know," was his answer.

Like Luc, Viv had been annoyed that she hadn't picked up on the fact that since I had Arum DNA in me, I may need to feed. But who would've guessed that? Trojans were brand spanking new, and I was even uniquer.

I had learned on the walk home that the other stash of opal was at Luc's "small villa" in Greece, so no help there.

"I don't get why you're so worried about this." Luc kicked his other leg up, crossing them at the ankles. "Hunter explained how to do it."

And that had been as awkward as it sounded. The Arum had thoroughly amused himself, giving step-by-step instructions while repeatedly referencing "Luc or someone else who is willing."

To be honest, I was surprised Hunter was still alive.

When Hunter explained how to feed, he made the whole thing sound easier than I'd imagined it to be. Claiming that my body would know what to do, he admitted that he was shocked I hadn't already unintentionally fed on Luc. And then he explained how he'd accidentally done that with his wife, and frankly, that was just TMI for me at the moment.

"He also said it doesn't have to be painful," Luc continued. "And even if it were, I'd still be down for it."

I frowned at him.

"Look, I'll do anything to make sure you're okay—"

"I'm okay now."

One side of his lips twisted. "You just ate again and you're still hungry. How long before you start to feel dizzy and then pass the hell out?"

"I don't know." I threw my hands up. "I'll make sure I let you know when it's about to happen."

"It's not going to get to that point." Luc thrust a hand through his hair. "You slipping into what is equivalent to a coma is not an option. The fact that you even think it is actually boggles my mind."

"Boggles? Really?"

"Yes. Boggles. The. Mind. You were unreachable for almost four days. I had no idea if you'd ever wake up, and knowing that you will this time around doesn't make that any easier," he went on. "And what if something happens while you're sleeping?"

"That's a title of a movie, by the way."

His expression turned bland. "I know. It was one of your favorites," he said, and my heart skipped. I knew I had never told him that as Evie. "What if we're under attack here? Or what about when we're out there, fixing the world, and you have to replenish what you've used? You just going to take a time-out and sleep?"

My lips thinned.

"You think the Daedalus is going to give you that break? Call a truce while you recoup? Better yet, summon the Source now, Evie."

I pulled my hands from my hips.

He lifted his brows. "Or have you already tried and couldn't?"

I was seriously going to hit him.

"You already tried."

I had.

While I was in the bathroom, I'd tried to summon it, and only a weak, flickering ball of energy had appeared before quickly sputtering out.

I crossed my arms. "Why are you even asking that? You already know everything."

"So then you do realize you can't even work with the Source until you replenish it. Too bad there's no power here. We could marathon *Buzzfeed Unsolved*."

"You don't need to be such a smart-ass," I snapped. "Of course I've thought of that. I thought of all of that."

"And you still are fighting me on this? Seriously?"

"Besides the fact I'm not sure if I am going to hurt you or not, he also said I could lose control and drain you dry," I reminded him, which was something Hunter mentioned *while we were on our way out the freaking door*. "I don't like the idea of taking something like that from you. It's yours, and you need it. It feels wrong."

Luc stared at me, and then he leaned forward, dropping his feet to the floor. "What do you think I did when I took the Source from you the night you lost control? Did that feel wrong to you?"

I jerked.

"Because it's sort of the same thing, Evie."

"But you had to—"

"And now *you* have to." His voice softened. "I doubt you will lose control, but if you do, I'll stop it."

Taking short, quick breaths, I looked away. "I'm not trying to be difficult."

"I know."

"Do you? Do you get why this is . . ." I didn't even know how to describe it.

"Too much?" he suggested, and my head turned back to him. "Yeah, I get it. If our positions were changed, I'd be fighting you tooth and nail on this, and you know what? You'd be doing the same thing I am right now."

I pressed my lips together, hating when he was right, but it was even more than that. Just yesterday, Luc had used the Source to try to save Spencer and then to heal me. He'd been exhausted, and if Grayson hadn't done what he did, would there be dark shadows under his eyes, the taut line of tension around his mouth?

"I would've been fine without Grayson," he said quietly, startling me. "I didn't learn that by reading your thoughts. I knew. He doesn't know I do. It stays that way."

"You were exhausted, Luc. That was yesterday—"

"And today I'm a hundred and twenty percent charged. It's not like I won't make more of it," Luc said. "I just don't need to sleep for days to do that. I'll only need an hour or so tops to recover, and it's not like something you'd have to do all the time. If Hunter is right, it's only after you use extreme amounts of the Source." He scooted to the edge of the couch. "Do you know how many times when you were sick I wished there were more I could do? That I could somehow be your miracle cure? I couldn't then, but I can now. I'm not saying that to you as some form of emotional blackmail. It's just the truth. Let me give you want you need."

Unfolding my arms, I closed my eyes as I let out a ragged breath.

"I have no problems being your personal 5-hour Energy."

I shook my head as I opened my eyes. "This is not funny."

"There is humor in everything." His gaze caught mine. "If we forget that, we lose everything."

Something about the words rattled me. They were an echo in my mind and in my soul. Without a doubt, I knew I had heard him say them before, many times. I had no idea why that pushed me to make up my mind.

I was moving before I realized what I was doing, coming around the coffee table and sitting beside him. My heart was thundering as if I'd raced a mile to get there instead of walking a few feet.

His gaze never left mine, and he didn't speak as he angled his body toward me. I told myself I was going to do this, that I needed to. Because somewhere between his comment and when I sat beside him, I realized that if I didn't, I would be weak.

Therefore, Luc would be weak. Far weaker than he would be if I fed, because he'd spend days distracted and worried, and anything could happen in just an hour.

He waited until I was ready, and that took a small eternity, but when I made up my mind, it happened.

The hollowness in my chest pulsed, and the Source sparked. It was weak like before, but there, and it was as if it knew what I was about to do. I placed a trembling hand on Luc's arm.

"If I hurt you, you'll stop me."

Luc nodded, but a part of me knew that he was lying. He wouldn't stop me, and I didn't know if I wanted to yell at him or tell him that I loved him.

Drawing in a shallow breath, I placed my other hand on his chest like Hunter had instructed, right where I felt the Source inside myself. I closed my eyes, and a moment later, I felt Luc fold his hand over mine. Tears pricked my lids as emotion swelled so swiftly I sucked in a sharp breath. Instead of shoving the riot of feelings aside, I let them wash over me, and then I held all that love, all that acceptance close to my heart.

Hunter hadn't been lying.

Instinct took over. I leaned in, placing my lips a hairbreadth away from his, and *inhaled*.

Against his chest, I felt the Source flare, and then warmth flowed through my hand and down my throat like a cascading fall of sunlight. Deep in my chest, the Source pulsed again, this time stronger, brighter, like a morning glory opening to the first rays of sun.

Luc spasmed, sending a shock of fear through me. I started to pull back.

I'm okay. Seriously. His voice whispered among my thoughts. *It doesn't hurt. It's just . . . different. Continue.*

Listening to his voice for any hint of pain, I found none, which was good, because I needed more. I inhaled again, and this time, the warmth poured through me, into the pulsing center of my chest, and then Luc's energy was everywhere. My skin hummed with it, my blood sped up in response to it. The spark didn't flicker this time. It roared to life and—

Images suddenly and without warning pieced together. I saw myself, a younger me dressed in what looked like a white sheet with an opening cut out for my head and a silver-colored belt cinched around my waist. My hair was twisted into buns on either side of my head. I was spinning, the edges of the sheet lifting to reveal white leggings underneath as I swung a plastic lightsaber. Laughter. I heard laughter, and I *knew* it was Luc's as I shot toward the sound, jabbing the lightsaber as if it were a sword. The image was quickly replaced by another one of me, where I looked maybe a year or so older.

I was sitting on the floor beside a stunning man who looked as if he were made of gold and diamonds. His skin was such an astonishing shade of gold, hair like sunlight.

Paris.

Oh God, that was *the* Paris.

He was watching me as I shook my fist and then opened my hand. Dice fell out. All sixes.

"Yahtzee!" I shouted.

Paris grinned. "How many is that, Luc?"

A disgruntled sigh came. "Five. That's five Yahtzees, and you're totally helping her cheat."

I watched myself laugh in a way I had never laughed before, tumbling over onto my side.

That image evaporated, replaced by an older version, one where I wore a silvery, shimmering dress and my hair was long, a wild tangle. Cheeks flushed with anger and hands curled into fists,

I stood inside a doorway of an office. Wads of cash were stacked on a desk. Sitting on top of one of the stacks was some kind of hand-held game system.

"I hate when you do that," I said.

"Do what?" The nonchalant voice belonged to Luc. It was his, but nowhere near as deep as it was now.

"Don't pretend like you have no idea what I'm talking about! That couple and that guy that were just here. You didn't want them to see me. What was wrong with them? They looked—"

"It's not the couple I'm worried about," he replied. "It's the other one. He never needs to know about you."

My thoughts crowded with churning light and shadows, pushing back other images—

Enough. I had enough. I needed to stop.

But the taste of Luc was on my lips and inside me. I was surrounded in him, and I thought I could drown in him, and that would be okay. That would be more—

No.

If I drowned, Luc would surely go down with me. I had enough, more than enough.

I yanked my hand back as I lifted my head up. That was as far as I got. Somehow Luc was on his back and I was half on him, half on my side. His arms were tight around me, and underneath my chest, his heart was beating fast. His head was kicked back, eyes closed and mouth lax. My heart stopped with dread even as my entire body thrummed with power. "Luc? Are you—?"

"I'm fine." His throat worked on a swallow. "I'm not in pain."

"You look like you're in pain."

"I'm not in pain."

My brows drew down as I started to roll over him—

"Nope." His arm clamped my waist to his side. "Just stay right there."

I stared at him. "Okay. I can do that."

"Good. Great." Luc's jaw worked, and then his head tilted to the side, toward me. He opened his eyes, and the pupils were all white. "How do you feel? Did you get enough?"

"Did I . . . ?" I shook my head. "I just fed off you, and you're asking how I am?"

His brows knitted. "Why would I not?"

I stared at him, feeling tears crowd my eyes once more. "I love you," I whispered.

Expression smoothing, a small smile appeared. "I know."

My hand balled in the front of his shirt. "Thank you—"

"Don't thank me for that, not for doing what I needed to do."

His features blurred. "When am I supposed to thank you, Luc?"

"When I do something worth thanking me for." The light receded from his pupils while I wondered what in the world he thought was worth more than what he'd just given me. "You saw something, didn't you? When you fed?"

The question brought forth the image of me dressed in a sheet, swinging a lightsaber. I knew what I saw. It was me dressed as Princess Leia for Halloween. I knew that because Luc had told me about it.

"I saw your memories," I whispered.

"Yeah. Should've warned you that could happen. When an Arum feeds, they can see memories and sometimes capture emotions. I wasn't sure if you would, but I wanted to be prepared in case. I wanted you to see some of my good memories."

30

Luc had needed more than an hour to recover. He'd needed the rest of the evening, but by nightfall, he'd been back to feeling like himself. Mostly. He'd fallen asleep pretty early, and I tried not to be too worried about that. Luc said he just needed to rest for the evening, and he'd be back to normal. I had to believe that.

As I'd lain beside him, no longer feeling like my stomach was trying to eat itself, an idea came to me. I'd quietly slipped out of bed and moved silently through the house. I gathered up several cans of food I didn't think Luc or I would miss and placed them in a paper bag, along with a few bottles of water and another pack of fresh bread, but this time I added in something else. My eyesight had definitely improved, because I easily found an old notepad and pencil on the dark kitchen counter. I wrote a quick note to Nate, asking if he needed anything in particular. Dropping the pencil and a blank piece of paper in the bag, I started toward the door when I felt the presence of a Luxen. I didn't think I was feeling Daemon, unless he was trying to get Adam to sleep and had roamed into the backyard.

Placing the bag on the counter, I cracked open the door. The scent of rain followed the wisps of cool air as I scanned the stoop and the backyard. The tingle of awareness increased—

"You sensed me, didn't you?"

I didn't jump at Grayson's voice, for which I wanted to pat myself on the back. I stepped outside, closing the door behind me as Grayson appeared, having walked out from the narrow pathway that separated the house from Daemon and Kat's.

"I did," I admitted.

He tilted his head. "Well, that takes the fun out of sneaking around."

My newly improved eyes could make out most of his features. He wasn't looking at me but rather toward the bedroom. "I would say I'm sorry, but that would be a lie."

Grayson smirked.

"Are you patrolling or something?" I asked.

"In other words, why am I here?" he countered.

I couldn't see his eyes, but I could feel his gaze. "Pretty much."

"I ran into Hunter."

The muscles along my neck tensed. "He told you, didn't he?"

"Yes."

"Of course he did." I sighed, folding my arms. "I bet he took great pleasure in explaining what I had to do."

"He did." There was a hint of a smile on his face, but it was quick.

I now knew why Grayson was here. "Luc's okay. He's just sleeping right now. I didn't take too much or hurt him," I told him, cheeks heating as I focused on the firepit. I knew I shouldn't be embarrassed. Obviously, this was something Arum had to do, and I didn't have a choice. Not really. "And it's not like I wanted to do it. We argued for most of the afternoon about it, but I . . ."

"You had to do it," he finished, surprising me. "There is no way Luc would've allowed anything else. He probably would've sat on you until you fed."

I coughed out a short laugh. "Probably." Glancing over at him, I saw that he was staring toward the bedroom once more. "I won't hurt him," I blurted out. Slowly, Grayson faced me. "I know I did in the woods, but when I went after Sarah, I wanted to protect him. All of you. And the idea of doing anything that could hurt him, even if I don't have control of myself, scares the living crap out of me. I couldn't live with myself if I did."

Grayson said nothing, not for several moments. "I wouldn't let you do it again. I'd probably end up dead in the process, and if not, definitely dead afterward, but I won't let it come to that."

What he said wasn't a threat. At least I didn't take it that way, so I nodded. I don't know why, but I suddenly wondered if I'd misjudged the source of Grayson's loyalty. I thought about what Grayson had done for Luc after he'd healed me, and how shocked he'd been when he'd learned I was Nadia. There were other instances that now appeared in a different light to me, and I thought that maybe I now knew why he seemed to dislike me.

"Why are you staring at me?" he asked.

How he knew that I was doing just that since he was still looking at the bedroom was beyond me, and I told myself not to ask the question that was rolling to the tip of my tongue, but neither my brain nor mouth listened. "Do you love him?"

Grayson looked over at me then. "You think that's why I don't like you?"

Well, that was a blunt response, so I gave him an answer equally matter-of-fact. "Yes."

He dipped his chin, chuckling. My brows lifted as he slowly shook his head. "Would it bother you if I said yes?"

I mulled that over. "No. It wouldn't."

"Because he loves you?"

"Yes," I answered. "And he has to know that you love him. He knows almost everything. It doesn't bother him."

"I'm sure he does know." There was a pause. "But you're wrong about one thing. I don't hate you."

I opened my mouth to respond, but before I could even figure out what to say, Grayson had stepped back and disappeared around the side of the house. He didn't hate me? A strangled laugh escaped me as I turned back to the door. I saw no reason why Grayson would lie. Wasn't like he ever worried about my feelings before. I picked up the bag and then hurried over to the firepit, thinking that Grayson had to be the most complicated person I'd ever met.

And boy, wasn't that saying something.

The bag was gone by the following afternoon, no note left behind. I tried not to be disappointed about that and just relieved that Nate was still out there, surviving whatever way he could.

I didn't tell Luc about my conversation with Grayson, and if he'd picked up on it at any point, he didn't mention it.

And neither did Grayson over the next three days, while I'd become very good at using the Source to stop objects and even people. Grayson had been the test dummy for that round of training, much to his displeasure. Since he acted as if he and I never had that conversation, I decided I'd follow his lead. What he sort of admitted to didn't bother me. Luc was, well, he was lovable when he wanted to be, and I was just sort of relieved Grayson was capable of feeling any emotion instead of distaste or hate.

But even Luc had been impressed by how good I was getting with the Source. And it wasn't the empty, supportive kind of impressed, because I virtually froze Grayson and then later Zoe. Neither of them could break my hold on them.

It even had taken Luc quite a bit of time to snap free of my hold, and it had required me to use even more of the Source. By the time we were done, there was a tension to the set of his shoulders, and the lines around his mouth reminded me of the other time we'd worked on the Source. I'd worried it had to do with my feeding, but he assured me he was fine.

So, I was feeling pretty good about all of that, but when the classroom with wall-to-wall windows we'd commandeered that afternoon was pitched into sudden, complete darkness and the temperatures dropped to near freezing, I couldn't suppress the shiver that spun its way down my spine. I couldn't see anything, and based on Zoe's soft curse, she couldn't, either.

"Show-off," Luc muttered from somewhere inside the classroom. He'd been sitting on the desk. Now, he could literally be anywhere.

Somehow, Luc had wrangled Hunter into working on the non-Luxen variety of my abilities, which apparently included turning day to night. Part of me thought that Hunter might've been secretly relieved to be doing something. There was a haunting sadness that settled on his features every so often, and I knew he was thinking of his brother then.

I lifted my hand, unable to see it. "How did you do that?"

"*Ssskill,*" Hunter replied, and since he was in his true form, his voice sounded like shadows and smoke. It sounded just like the voice of Sarah, and mine when we had spoken telepathically to one another. "*I'm usssing the Sssource to obsssscure my presssence.*"

"Can I do that?" I asked.

"*I don't sssee why not.*"

"Would come in handy when you need to make a quick exit," Zoe said. "Like when you're at a party and there's someone annoying there."

"Or when I'm asked to help with training," Grayson commented.

"Or when Grayson walks into the room," I added.

"That's not nice," Grayson said from somewhere in the darkness.

I grinned.

The darkness suddenly stirred in front of me, thickening. I narrowed my eyes, sensing that Hunter had moved closer to me.

"You can beat that back," Luc advised. "That trick should only momentarily blind you. You let it go any longer than that, you've lost the upper hand."

Beat it back? Hmm. Summoning the Source, I felt it rippling through my veins. White and black light surrounded my palm, and I pictured it growing until the whole room was awash in light, but I didn't want to harm anyone. I just wanted to see.

The churning glow erupted, spitting half a dozen mini balls into space. Each one went off like a firecracker, showering the room in glittering bright light that fell onto the thick shadows, eating away at them like acid and then evaporating before they hit the floor. Within seconds, the darkness was gone and Hunter *had* moved closer.

"Cute," he said, having returned to his human form. "Now *that* is a party trick."

"I didn't want to hurt anyone in here." I paused. "Or you. I could've just taken you out and the shadows would've gone away."

Over Hunter's shoulder, I saw Luc's smug smile as Grayson leaned against the desk. "That's my girl," Luc said.

I beamed and then refocused on Hunter. "How did you make the shadows do that?"

"Most likely the same way you'd make it brighter." He walked over to the desk and picked up the apple he'd brought with him. "Minus the fireworks."

I glanced at Zoe, and she raised her brows. I started to ask for more detail, but from what I'd learned, using the Source came down to what you *willed* it to do, what you wanted from it. There was no reason to overthink it.

No reason at all, came Luc's voice.

Nodding, I lifted my hands and summoned the Source once more. This time, the balls of energy around my hands were more dark than light. I pictured them growing and expanding, and the energy pulsed, licking out from my palms and dripping into the air. Deep, intense shadows blossomed as the skin of my arms broke out with glittering black spots. The Source roared around me like a storm, rapidly seeping over the windows, blocking out the daylight. I smiled as all the light was sucked out of the room, but I could still see. Luc was sitting on the desk, staring up at the ceiling. Grayson was beside him, looking about as approachable as an angry warthog. To my left, Zoe had her hands clutched under her chin while her eyes were wide. Hunter stood in front of the desk, watching me.

All of them were in shades of gray.

"Can you see me?" I asked the Arum.

He shook his head. "No, but you can see us."

"I can," I answered, and Luc's chin snapped down. "Everything is kind of gray-washed, but I can see."

"All these shadows, as you call them, are a part of you, almost like an extension. They wouldn't hinder you," Hunter explained.

"Huh. That's pretty cool."

"It is." He crossed his arms. "Just remember that if you can do this, other Trojans will be able to do the same thing."

That took away a little of the coolness factor.

"How do I look gray?" Luc asked. "Still extraordinarily beautiful, I'm sure."

Rolling my eyes, I laughed. "You look okay."

"Lies," he said.

Zoe's wide-eyed gaze darted around. "I bet I look weird."

"No—"

Unfolding her arms, she wiggled them like limp noodles as she lifted her knees, hobbling from one foot to the next like a bizarre marionette.

"Yes," I corrected myself. "Yes, you definitely look weird right now. And creepy."

She grinned as she emitted a high-pitched giggle.

"Do I even want to know what she's doing?" Grayson asked.

"Nope." I watched Zoe puff up her cheeks.

"You want to be careful with this," Hunter interjected, drawing my attention back to him. "The shadows have a weight to them. You could seal up an entire room with it, and when you do that, you stop oxygen from getting in. You know that smell of burned ozone that often accompanies use of the Source?"

I nodded.

"It's the Source basically eating up the molecules that make up oxygen. In this case, you're not just blocking the light, you're virtually sucking the oxygen out of it faster than anyone can put it back into the air by breathing. You'd surely kill anything with a bit of human DNA in them, including yourself."

"Oh," I whispered, looking around in concern as I eased off, letting cracks of sunlight penetrate the darkness. "How long does it take to use up the oxygen in a room?"

"Three minutes if you're lucky," Grayson replied. "Maybe a little longer for those with Luxen DNA, but not very long." A ghost of a smile appeared, and I frowned. "Would be interesting to find out exactly how long."

My brow creased. God, he was scary sometimes.

The classroom door opened suddenly. Daylight poured in, along with Daemon, who drew up short as the rainbow aura around him faded to reveal that his brow was creased from how high he'd pushed his eyebrows up. "What in the world?"

I lost my concentration, and the mass of shadows lost their intensity, swiftly breaking apart and scattering.

Daemon looked around the room, his gaze landing on Zoe. She'd frozen mid-jig, or whatever she was doing now. "You know what? I don't even want to know."

Slowly, Zoe placed her foot back onto the floor and clasped her hands behind her back.

"I was learning how to block out light so no one can see me coming," I told him. "And apparently, Grayson would like to see how long it takes one of us to die from lack of oxygen."

Daemon lifted his brows. "Sounds about as I expected."

Grayson shrugged.

"What's up?" Luc asked.

"Sorry to interrupt," Daemon began.

Luc laughed. "Not really."

"True." A quick smile appeared. "Eaton said you all were in here. Need to ask a couple of you a favor."

"Sorry," Luc stated as I drifted over to him. Without saying a word, he snaked an arm around my waist and tugged me between his legs. "I can't babysit baby Adam. It's against my religion."

Daemon arched a brow. "You would be the last person I'd ask to babysit."

"I'm not the last person?" Grayson asked. "Shocked."

"Correction. You're the second-to-last person I'd ask to babysit Adam."

"Well, that's kind of offensive. I'm totally trustworthy," Luc argued. "And I give great gifts."

Daemon crossed his arms. "You once tried to gift Kat and me a llama because, according to you and literally no one else, they'd make a great family pet for a baby."

What?

Luc's smile turned thoughtful. "They will protect a herd—"

"A lone child is not a herd, Luc," Daemon sighed.

"One child is an equivalent to a herd of lambs." Luc folded his other arm around my waist, clasping his hands together.

"I won't argue that point—wait a minute." Daemon's eyes narrowed on the desk. "Is that Adam's stuffed banana? I've been looking everywhere for that."

Uh-oh.

"You might be having a stroke," Luc advised him. "There's no banana there."

The banana was totally there.

"We're really not even in this room," Luc continued.

"What is your favor?" I asked as I reached around Luc and picked up the banana. I tossed it to Daemon.

He caught it. "The favor is actually open to more than just Luc."

Don't, I warned Luc, able to tell he was about to say something incredibly sarcastic.

You're no fun. He rested his chin on my shoulder.

"There are a few med supplies we're running low on, and we're going to need to head out earlier than we'd expected," explained Daemon. "With Archer not expected back for another day or so, and with Jeremy and others going out to escort another package, we're down several people."

"You need me to go?" Luc surmised.

"We need a couple of people to go." Daemon shoved the stuffed banana into his back pocket. "It'll be an overnight trip. We'll leave tonight and plan to be back by tomorrow evening."

"We?" Luc lifted his chin. "You're heading out so soon?"

"Yeah, don't really want to, but it was Archer and I who scouted the place, and with him gone, only I know the ins and outs of it. That's why it's going to be as quick as possible. Dawson is going, too. We need at least two more."

"I know you just want to spend some time with me, so I'll humor you and go," Luc replied.

One side of Daemon's mouth tipped up. "Yeah, that's exactly why."

"I would if I could," Hunter said. "But Sin is on his way, and he could arrive at any point. Could be tomorrow. Could be next week. Either way, I need to be here with that happens."

Daemon nodded. "You need to be here when he arrives. God only knows what kind of trouble he'll get himself in."

"I can go." I pulled away from Luc in my excitement. I could actually be useful, working for all that food I'd consumed.

Which was a lot.

And what I'd been giving to Nate.

Which was also a lot.

"I don't know exactly what you need, but I've come a long way with the Source, and—"

"I'm going to stop you right there," Daemon cut in, and all that excitement sped into a brick wall going about 80 mph. "I don't want you to take this personally, and I'm not trying to sound like a dick, but things can get hairy out there. More than once, we've run into ART officers, and while you were able to control things with the Trojan, you're still working at that. We can't risk you blowing up another building."

He had a point, a big one, but my shoulders still slumped under the weight of disappointment.

"There's also the issue that you might be recognized." Sympathy filled Zoe's voice. "Your image was plastered all over the news in connection with Syl—with your mom's murder."

And another good point. Wasn't like I hadn't forgotten that I'd been conveniently blamed for her murder. I was just trying to not think about that messed-up factoid, but that reminder was a punch in the chest.

"Yeah, you guys are right." I leaned back against the table, and Luc's hands settled on my hips. He squeezed gently. "I know it's not personal."

Daemon's gaze met mine. "It's really not. I hope you know that."

"I do." And I did. Sometimes the truth was harder than something being personal.

And very few know when to step aside, Luc's voice whispered among my thoughts.

I took a deep, steadying breath. *I just want to be able to help out.*

I know. His hand slid to my lower back. *You will.*

"I can go," Zoe was saying. "I've done it before when I've been here."

"Perfect." Daemon looked toward Luc. "We'll meet tonight at the entry house."

I hoped that was a lot duller than the last time everyone was there. Wondering why Grayson hadn't volunteered, I waited until later that evening, while Luc was getting ready, to ask.

Sitting on the bed, I watched him root around in the stack of shirts. Damp hair toppled on his forehead as he bent, pulling out a plain, black shirt. The black cargo-type pants he wore were still unbuttoned. I was convinced either magic or the Source was holding his pants up, because those suckers were defying gravity at the moment.

"Why didn't Grayson volunteer to go?" I asked.

He shook the shirt out. "He knew he was needed here."

I started to ask why, but then it struck me. "He's staying behind to babysit me."

"I wouldn't call it *babysitting*." Straightening, he looked over at me. He seemed to freeze for a moment, eyes slightly wide as he stared at me. Shirt forgotten in his hand, he strode toward me. Stopping in front of me, he placed his hands down on either side of me and dipped his head, his lips finding mine.

His kiss was gentle and slow, the kind that threatened to shatter me into a million little pieces. When he kissed me like this, so softly, it told me what words could never capture.

Pressing his forehead to mine, he shuddered as he slid his hands up my sides. "I forgot what we were talking about."

I let out a little laugh, because I, too, had to think about that. "Grayson babysitting me."

"That." He shifted his head, kissing my temple. "He's just keeping an eye on things."

"Seems like that's his number-one job."

"It's his most important one."

I bit down on my lower lip as he pulled away, shirt in hand, the material now wrinkled. There was an ache in my chest. Luc had to know how Grayson felt, and making me Grayson's top priority just seemed wrong.

"I know."

I blinked. "What?"

His gaze met mine. "I *know*."

Grayson.

He was saying he knew how Grayson felt. "Then do you think making him stay back here is a good idea?"

"I know it's a good idea, because that's what he wants."

"That doesn't make sense," I admitted after a moment. "I mean, unless what he feels is this pure, unselfish type of love where he—"

"Protects you, because of what it would do to me if something happened to you?" he cut in.

I nodded. "I have to admit that I . . . yeah, I wouldn't be that good of a person."

"And neither is Grayson. I can't even believe you'd think he was. How many hours ago was he wondering how long it would take for people to suffocate? He's not selfless." Luc grinned. "You should see your face right now."

"I don't need to see my face to know it's the picture of confusion," I told him. "If he's not that good of a person, then why would he want to stay behind?"

"Because love can be complicated, Evie."

I lifted a brow. "Okay. That was unnecessarily vague."

"Look. Don't worry about Grayson. He's fine. If I thought he wasn't, he wouldn't be staying here." He pulled the shirt on over his head. "Unless him staying here makes you comfortable."

"It doesn't." I wrinkled my nose. "Well, I mean, half the time, I don't even know he's around."

"He's good like that."

"He's creepy like that," I muttered.

Thrusting his hair back from his face, he chuckled. "I've got to admit something." Luc zipped up his pants. "I almost pushed for you to come along."

"Really?"

He nodded. "For purely selfish reasons. I don't like the idea of leaving you here. Not because you can't protect yourself or that I think anything will happen." Buttoning his pants, he peered over at me through thick lashes. "I would rather have you by my side. I'm needy like that."

"I would rather be by your side, too."

"I know." Picking up a pair of black boots, he sat beside me. "But people out there are going to see us. It's inevitable. If you're recognized and the authorities are contacted, things are going to roll downhill from there."

I'd been thinking about that. "Do you think there's hair dye around here?"

Lacing up a boot, he looked over at me. "You thinking about dyeing your hair?"

I picked a strand. "And maybe cutting it. I'm going to have to leave here eventually, and it's probably a good idea that I change my appearance. Coloring and cutting my hair isn't going to make me unrecognizable, but at least it wouldn't be as easy."

His gaze roamed over me, and then he nodded. "It's a good idea. I don't know if they have any here. You can check with Zouhour. She keeps track of all the goods here, but I'll also keep an eye out for any while I'm out there. Any color in mind?"

"I don't know." I dropped my hair. "Probably brown? Something easy that will look natural. I always wanted red hair, but I have a feeling that will end badly with boxed color."

"Brown hair?" He laced up the other boot. "I think I'll dig it."

I grinned.

He lowered his booted foot to the floor. "You going to be okay tonight, all by your lonesome?"

"I'll be just fine."

"I don't think you'll be 'just fine.' You'll probably be up all night, hugging one of my shirts close to your bosom, sobbing."

"I'll probably get the best sleep of my life," I replied warily, but honestly, I wasn't looking forward to falling asleep without him there. Strange how I could get so used to that.

He pressed his hand to his chest, fixing a wounded expression across his face. "I will be clutching one of your shirts to my chest, sobbing all night."

Laughing under my breath, I shook my head. "Truthfully, I'll probably spend a good portion of the night worried about you guys. Every one of you are badass and all, but anything can happen," I admitted. "Promise me you'll be careful."

"I always am, but I promise." He touched my cheek, teasing gone from his voice. "Nothing will ever steal me away from you, Evie. Nothing."

31

It was only about a half an hour after Luc had left when I heard a soft knock on the kitchen door. I hadn't sensed anything, so I knew whoever was there was human. Hope sparked as I hurried to the door. I didn't know anyone who'd come to the back door other than Nate.

Telling myself I shouldn't get my hopes up, I cracked open the door and peered outside. At first, I saw no one standing on the stoop. The corners of my lips turned down, and then I caught a glimpse of orangey-copper hair peeking around the corner of the stoop. My heart about stopped. "Nate," I whispered.

A second later, his pale face appeared in the moonlight. He looked a little less dirt-covered than he had the last time I'd seen him. "Hi," he said, his nervous gaze darting behind me.

"No one else is here," I told him, stepping aside so he could come in.

"I know." He stepped out from around the corner, but didn't come in. "I mean, I saw the others leave. Him. The guy who lives here with you. I wasn't watching you—I mean, I kind of was so I could, you know, know when to come by."

"It's okay, but you can come by when he's here. You'd like him. He has dumb jokes," I repeated. Nate didn't look convinced. "Do you want to come in?"

He seemed to consider that and then took a deep breath before stepping in. He'd kept a wide berth around me as I quietly closed the door. "I, um, got the food you left out for me. Thanks for that."

"I'm glad to hear that. I was worried that a squirrel ran off with it or something." In the glow of the gas lantern, I thought he'd looked thinner than before, his cheeks hollower.

"That would be one big, scary squirrel."

"True."

A faint, uneven smile appeared and then faded. "I came by once before, but there were a lot of people at the house."

Not wanting to worry him, I nodded. "I wasn't feeling well, but I'm okay. I'm sorry I missed you," I added when he looked like he was about to push that. "Did you get the note I left you last time?"

He nodded. "I was going to write back, but I was afraid someone else would find it."

I wasn't exactly surprised to hear that. This kid didn't trust easily. Even right now, he kept looking around the kitchen like he expected someone to jump out of a cabinet. "I've been worried about you."

He blinked. "You have?"

The surprise in his voice was so genuine, it tugged at my heart. "Of course. I didn't know if you had enough food or water. Is that why you came back?"

"No. I was . . . I mean, I was hoping you had something that could help, like, disinfect the skin."

"Like rubbing alcohol or peroxide?" I knew we had both in the bathroom. When Nate nodded, concern replaced the relief. "Is someone hurt?"

"No." His nose scrunched. "I mean, not really. Not seriously. We have bandages and stuff, but nothing to, you know, clean the skin? And I don't know much, but I know that cuts and stuff need to be cleaned with something. That's what my mom used to do when I was hurt."

"What happened to your mom?" I asked, half expecting I wouldn't get an answer.

"She's dead. I didn't know my father." He shrugged. "He's probably dead, too."

"Did she die in the invasion?"

Rubbing a hand over his chest, he shook his head. "She died a few years before that. We—I mean I was in a group home when the invasion hit. Several of us were, and when people started dying or leaving, we were kind of just there."

Understanding crept over me. "You mean, you were left there by whoever was running the group home?"

"Yeah, but it really wasn't any different from someone being there." Nate gave another nonchalant shrug while anger rushed through me so fiercely, I felt the Source pulse in response. "We all pretty much took care of ourselves."

"That doesn't make it okay. No one should be left behind," I told him, wrangling in my emotions before he saw that I wasn't exactly human.

"Yeah, well, people were left behind before it all went to shit," he responded. "People who lived on the streets? They were already left behind."

He was right, and I told him that. "I know this is hard to believe, but no one in this community is left behind. Everyone is taken care of, and every one chips in one way or another."

Nate said nothing as he rubbed at his chest.

"Let me grab you some peroxide or something." I started toward the archway but stopped. "Don't go anywhere. Please. I'll be right back."

He nodded.

I stared at him a moment, almost wishing I could freeze him in place, but that wouldn't help gain his trust, so I hurried to the bathroom. It was somewhere between finding an old backpack and shoving the bottles of rubbing alcohol and peroxide in it, along with cotton balls and a bottle of pain reliever, when I decided I was going to make him take me to the rest of the kids. I knew it could be dangerous even though there didn't sound like there were any adults with them, and I also knew Luc would be furious when he found out, but based on how Nate looked now, he couldn't survive much longer like this. Maybe I wouldn't be able to convince him, but if there were others, I may have more luck with them. I also needed to know exactly how many kids were out there, fending for themselves, and just how hurt this other one was. I also reasoned it would be a good idea to see exactly how Nate was getting in and out of the city without being seen. I could defend myself, and helping Nate was far more useful than sitting here missing Luc and Zoe and everyone else.

Finding a tube of antibacterial cream, I tossed it in the bag. I had no idea if it was expired or not, but I figured it couldn't hurt.

Nate was waiting where I'd left him, his gaze glued to the archway. I thought I saw relief on his face when I walked back in.

"I got some stuff in here that I think will help." I placed the backpack on the island, leaving it open so he could peer inside. "But here's the deal." I waited until his gaze lifted to mine. "I know you're probably going to argue with me, but if you want this stuff to help your friend, then I'm coming with you."

His mouth opened.

"I trust you, Nate. Obviously, since I just let you into my house, and I hope you can try to trust me. I haven't told any of the community leaders here about you." That wasn't a lie. "And I am more than willing to help you, but I need to see who's hurt. You say it's not bad. I have no way of knowing that, and not knowing that is going to get to me. So, that's the deal. I'll even throw in some canned food and bread. Take it or leave it."

I felt incredibly adultlike in that moment, even though Nate couldn't have been more than four or so years younger than I was, but I sort of wanted to pat myself on the back.

Nate shifted his weight from one foot to the next, his little jaw flexing. Several long moments passed, and then he said, "Deal."

I was so surprised I might've needed to sit down.

He didn't look remotely happy when he'd agreed, but he'd agreed, and I wasn't giving him a chance to change his mind. I quickly grabbed some canned green beans, some kind of sausage, and bread.

"If you do anything to scare the others, they'll bolt," he said when I faced him. "They'll stop trusting me, and they can't survive out there."

"I won't do anything. I promise you that."

Nate blew out a ragged breath. "Aren't you worried that I'd

hurt you? That someone else will? You don't know me. You don't know who I'm leading you to."

The fact that he was asking that lessened any worry that I did have, but I met his stare as I zipped up the bag and reminded myself that I was, in fact, a badass Trojan. "I won't let you or anyone else hurt me, Nate. If anyone did try to, I can promise you that will not end well for them."

His eyes widened a little, but then he nodded. "Okay."

Slinging the straps of the backpack over my shoulders, I smiled. "Okay."

How Nate moved in and out of the community quickly became obvious the moment I realized he was leading me through a maze of cramped alleys in between abandoned homes, toward the same road Eaton lived on and all the way to end of it.

Hidden behind a car, we watched a Luxen patrol the chain-link fence that separated the community from a wooden area and the city.

The moment the Luxen had disappeared out of view, I looked over at Nate. "You know their schedule, don't you?"

He nodded. "It's like intervals, give or take a few minutes." He rose. "Follow me."

The fact that some kid without the aid of a watch could figure out exactly when the guards would be in a certain area was more than a little concerning. Filing that away to discuss with Luc when he returned, I followed Nate in the moonlight, across the cracked road and over a small patch of overgrown grass. Nate led me straight to a section of broken fence that was partially obscured.

Another thing that needed to be addressed.

We hurried through the trees, my eyes adjusting to the scarce moonlight. I had no idea how Nate was able to navigate, but I imagined it had a lot to do with repetition. He tripped a few times, though, over exposed roots and uneven ground.

The moment we cleared the woods and I could see the looming city, my stomach tumbled.

"This used to be a public park," Nate explained as he strode forward, the weeds reaching his hips. "There were trails and stuff, and a lot of people used to run them. They'd have concerts here sometimes."

Dead lampposts rose out of the grass, and every so often I'd see a shape of something underneath grass that might've been a bench. "Did you go to them?"

"Some of them."

We reached the end of the park, and I could feel the ground change under my feet, shifting from grass to cement. What I guessed might've been a parking lot had been converted into a temporary campsite. Tents sat every so many feet, some half-collapsed and others rippling in the wind. A chill swept down my spine as we walked past them and onto one that must've been a busy street at one time.

Cars sat untouched in the middle of the road, some with the doors wide open and windows blown out, while others looked virtually untouched with the exception of the wear and tear of the years of exposure. Papers and pieces of cloth drifted across the street, stopping only to be caught by the wind once more and carried toward darkened storefronts. I kept picturing a pack of wild dogs erupting out the shadows, but that didn't happen as Nate led me down a street.

Tall, dark shapes stretched into the night sky, silent and foreboding, but for a moment, I could almost imagine dozens of lights glowing from windows of the skyscrapers, the hum of traffic and people going about their lives.

And I thought of home.

My heart squeezed. I tried not to think of my old life, one in a bustling city full of sound and people and normalcy. Or at least the facsimile of normalcy, but seeing what had become of Houston made me wonder if there would be more cities like this, and it made me miss . . . *before*. Not that I wanted to go back to being blind to what was happening or to who I was or to be without Luc, but there was a simplicity that I missed, along with my friends and . . .

Mom.

A knot of emotion lodged in my throat. God, I missed her, and those feelings hadn't become any less confusing or easier to deal with. I hated her and I loved her. Just like I hated my fake life in Columbia but also loved it.

"Are you okay?" Nate's voice broke into my thoughts.

"Yeah." I cleared my throat. "Why?"

"You look like you're about to, I don't know, cry or something."

"Would that make you uncomfortable?" I teased.

"Uh, yeah."

I grinned. "Then I won't do it."

He tugged on the hem of his shirt as he glanced over at me. "But you're sad?"

"A little," I admitted. "I used to live in a city. Not as big as this, but it just made me think of home."

"Why aren't you there now?"

That would take all night to try to explain. "People were trying to hurt me and my friends. My mom was killed, and this was the only place we could go."

"Sorry about your mom." He looked away. "Why were they trying to hurt you and your friends?"

Unable to get too deep into why, I said, "Do people need a reason?"

"No." He sighed. "So, you're hiding."

"Yeah, I am." I paused. "Like you, I guess."

He nodded as he came to a stop, and I looked across the street at a square, one-story building that seemed out of place in between the taller, larger buildings. "Used to be a church. Like one of those small ones, but it had been converted into a place for people whose homes were destroyed in the invasion. Had a lot of beds," he explained. "It's one of the places we stay in."

"There are others?" I asked as we crossed the street.

"We have a couple of places." He walked ahead, stopping at the door. "They've probably already seen you out here." He nodded at one of the dark windows. "And they're probably hiding, so just don't say anything at first. Okay? Let me do the talking."

Heart rate picking up, I nodded and nearly held my breath when the door creaked open and Nate stepped in, motioning for me to follow. It was almost pitch-black inside the small reception room. Even with new extra-special Trojan eyes, I had a hard time making out what the shadows were stacked up against the wall, and it smelled like musk, people, and burned wood.

Nate walked down a narrow hall that opened up into a wide space that once had to be used for religious services. The altar at the back of the room was a dead giveaway, and so were the few remaining pews pushed along the sides of the room. Candles glowed from the altar and the makeshift tables scattered about the rumpled cots. Blankets and old newspapers covered the windows. There was a steel barrel in the center of the room with some kind of wire grille over the top of it. Beside it was a stack of pots and opened cans. I spotted what might've been creamed corn, and I caught the scent of burned wood. This was how they were heating their food.

I wasn't sure if burning wood in here was healthy, but they were probably too afraid to light a fire outside.

"It's okay," Nate spoke out loud, walking forward. "She's a friend who has been giving us some food and stuff. She brought some stuff with her now. Her name is Evie, and she's safe."

As he spoke, my gaze zeroed in on the pews against the wall. There was maybe a two- or three-foot gap between the seat and floor. The space was black, but . . .

"You all can come out. I promise you." Nate stopped, scratching his fingers through his hair. "She's not going to do anything."

There was a soft scratching from under the pews, but no movement.

Nate turned to me, sighing. "Show them what you've got."

Nodding, I slid the backpack off a shoulder and unzipped it. I started pulling stuff out—peroxide, cotton, food, water. I placed them on one of the tables.

"Jamal? Nia?" Nate called. "Come on. We don't have forever."

There was silence, and then from the darkness of one of the doorways behind the altar, a boy stepped out. He was a little taller than Nate, but as he drew closer, I pegged his age to be around

Nate's. There was either dirt or a bruise near his eye that darkened the rich brown skin. A second later, another one stepped out of the door, and this one was a girl, holding a hand to her thin pink shirt. Tiny wisps of hair had escaped her braid. Her light brown skin looked a little flushed as she inched forward, coming to stand behind the boy named Jamal. She, too, looked no older than Nate.

"What are you doing?" asked Jamal in a hushed voice. "You brought her here?"

"I know, but she wanted to help, and she's cool. She's not like them," Nate answered, and I kept my face blank. "She brought some stuff for your hand, Nia."

The little girl glanced at the table, but she didn't move.

I took a step back from the table but remained quiet. Three sets of eyes tracked my movement, and I believed many more had done the same.

"It's okay," Nate repeated. "She hasn't said a word to anyone." He drew in a bigger breath. "I told you guys about her. She's not like them."

Movement to my left drew my gaze. Out from under a pew, a tiny body unfolded itself. It was a girl, a small one who couldn't have been more than five or six. Her shirt was several sizes too big, nearly doubling for a dress over jeans. "Creamed corn."

I blinked.

Nate sighed again.

The little girl crept closer, and I saw she clutched something in her arm. It wasn't a doll or stuffed animal. It looked like a small blanket. "You gave us creamed corn."

"I did."

She lifted the blanket to her chin. "I like creamed corn."

"I brought some more. It's on the table."

The little girl glanced at Nate, and when he nodded, she rushed past the cots to the table. One grubby little hand snaked out, snatching up a can.

"That's green beans," I told her, slowly walking over. The little girl didn't run as I picked up the creamed corn. "Here you go."

She dropped the can straight onto the floor and took the other can, holding it to her chest. Then she turned and raced toward Nate. I bent down, picking up the can, and when I rose, my heart about stopped.

And it definitely broke a little.

Kids all but piled out from underneath the pews, most of them not much older that the little girl. Some were older, closer to Nate's age, their too-slim bodies having been bent into God knows what kind of contortions to fit under the benches. All of them were wary, their eyes bouncing around nervously like Nate's had at the house, and not a single one of them looked all that well. They were too thin, too pale or gray, and too dirty, and there was too many of them. My gaze darted over the faces. There had to be . . . good God, there had to be almost twenty? Maybe more? Because some moved into smaller groups, shielding the youngest among them, so it was hard to count.

I wanted to cry.

The knot that had been in my throat had lodged itself in my chest as I glanced over them, but I kept my emotions locked down as I exhaled roughly. I focused on Nia. "Are you the one who's hurt?"

She lifted a shoulder. "It's just a scratch."

"But scratches get infected," Jamal said.

"Does that happen a lot?" I asked.

Nate glanced down at the little girl. "Sometimes. We mostly get lucky, though."

Mostly. I swallowed. "I brought rubbing alcohol and peroxide. There's some cotton swabs here and some ointment. Nate said you had bandages?" *Clean ones,* I wanted to add.

"We do." Jamal answered as the others watched silently. "Is that aspirin or something?"

I nodded. "I think it's ibuprofen. I thought you guys could use it."

"Yeah." Jamal stared at the bottle as if it were a hundred bucks sitting there. "We can."

Nia started forward then, and I didn't dare move as she picked up a bottle. "This is gonna hurt, isn't it? I mean, it'll fizz and burn."

"Maybe a little, but I think that means it's working." Happy she was speaking to me, I decided to push my luck. "Can I see your hand?"

She glanced down at her hand and then slowly extended it toward me. She uncurled her fingers, revealing a thin, ragged slice across her palm.

"Is it bad?" asked Jamal.

The cut wasn't deep or wide, but the skin was an angry red around the wound. "I don't think it's bad, but I'm not a doctor or anything. My mom was, though, and I remember once her mentioning when there's an infection, you'll see lines sort of streaking out from the wound. I don't know if that's always the case or not." I looked up, wishing I had paid more attention when Mom had randomly talked about medical things.

"There's no pus or anything coming out of it," Jamal said. "I've been checking."

"And I've been keeping it cleaned," Nia said. "Trying to at least."

"That has probably helped."

Nate had walked over and unscrewed the lid off one of the bottles. "Let's get this over with."

Without further ado, he splashed some of the peroxide over the cut. Air hissed between Nia's teeth as the liquid immediately fizzed. We left it like that for a few moments, and then she let me dab up the liquid with a cotton ball. Nate moved on to the alcohol, which may have been overkill, but I had no idea. I tried to asked questions while one of the other kids appeared with a pack of unopened gauze. How long had they been here? How old were they? Was anyone sick? All I got were noncommittal answers or shrugs, but as the other kids got closer, I saw that others had bruises on them. Some on the arms. Others along the jaws. A few had split lips.

I looked to Nate as Jamal carefully wrapped Nia's hand. "What's up with all the bruises and stuff?"

Jamal's hand halted for a fraction of a second, and then Nate said, "Some of them fight. We're all like a family, though."

"A dysfunctional one," Nia muttered.

"Maybe you all should, I don't know, not fight so seriously?" I suggested.

Jamal cracked a grin. "Sounds like good idea."

"Were all of you in group homes?" I asked.

"About half of us. Some were homeless, I think. There were more, but . . ." answered Jamal, trailing off. He cleared his throat. "Some kids got sick, you know. Or there were accidents."

Pressure clamped down on my chest. "There were more kids who died?"

Nia nodded. "Yeah, and there were others—"

"Shit," Nate whispered at the same second a very deep, very male voice boomed.

"What in the hell are you doing here?"

32

The kids scattered.

They rushed back to the pews, all except Nate, who remained by my side as a man stepped out from the dark doorway Nia and Jamal had walked out of earlier.

And the moment my eyes locked with the man's, I didn't like him. It wasn't an irrational response. There were reasons, starting with the fact that he was a grown adult, somewhere in his thirties, maybe older, and he was by far cleaner than all the kids present. Not a speck of dirt on his pink cheeks or on the ball cap that was pulled on over his head, and his flannel shirt and undershirt looked as if they were in far better condition. He also didn't look nearly as thin as any of these kids, which caused warning bells to go off one after another for me. Most importantly, I had a feeling if I made a bet that this man didn't do the runs for food and supplies, I'd win.

And how in the world could an adult sit by and let children run around, retrieving food and supplies?

"What in the hell do you think you're doing being here?" he demanded again, kicking aside cots and blankets as he strode forward. The man was definitely human, that much I knew.

"She's the one who's been giving me food, and we needed something for Nia's hand. I thought—"

One look from the man silenced him. "I didn't ask you, boy."

Nate stepped in front of me, and I didn't think. I caught the back of his shirt and pulled him back so he was behind me. "Who are you?" I fired back, feeling the Source pulse to life in my chest.

The man threw out his arms, and I noticed several of the kids shrank back. A few even lifted their arms as if to shield themselves. Bruises and split lips appeared in my mind, and a shiver of knowing danced down my spine as his brows lifted, disappearing under the bill of his cap. "You in my house, asking who I am?"

"I am," I replied coolly, vaguely acknowledging that I should feel some level of fear, or at least, the old Evie would have, but I didn't. There was just cold, pounding anger.

"Name's Morton. These are my kids, and I know damn well where you're from. How did you get him to bring you here. Huh? Tell him you want to help? That those freaks up there in that community would welcome him? Welcome all these kids?"

Freaks?

"These kids may be a bit rough around the edges, but they aren't dumb. Well, not all of them," he said, and the Source pulsed once more. "They know better or should know better than to trust one of you. Bet you lied, didn't you? That's the only way they'd be standing here." He stopped a few feet from me. "Bet you told them you're human, didn't you?"

There was no stopping the surprise that widened my eyes, and I couldn't ignore how most of the kids backed even farther away.

Morton smirked. "You think I can't tell? Oh yeah, I know. You came down here with no visible weapon on you. There isn't a single human that stupid. One of them alien freaks? Different story."

"Should I have a weapon?" I asked.

"You'd be dumber than I think if not." He grabbed something propped against the other side of the table, lifting it—a bat.

Instinct took over, and I didn't stop it. The Source buzzed through my veins, and as I lifted my hand, it happened like I'd willed it. The bat tore free from Morton's hand and flew toward me, smacking against my palm. It stung, but I managed to hold on to it.

"You're wrong," I said. "I didn't come without a weapon."

Morton took a step back, and even if the kids hadn't have gasped, I wouldn't have felt like a badass. That took the wind right out of my awesome sails.

"What're you going to do?" Morton asked. "Beat me?"

Man, if my blossoming suspicious were true, I wanted to, but I didn't. Instead, I placed the bat on another table. "Why would I want to do that?"

Morton stared at me for several moments. "I told you all. Didn't I? I told each and every one of you." He scanned the groups of kids. "They can look like anyone. Even a harmless, little blond girl." He took another step back. "We don't need any help from your kind, and we don't want it."

"So, you've been going out and getting food and supplies, and not just one of these kids?" I asked.

The fingers of his right hand curled into his palm. "As I said, we don't need or want your help. We don't want or need to see you again, and if you think for one second of coming back here with any of your other freak friends, don't bother. We won't be here. I hope you remember the way out," he said. "Because you need to get going."

I didn't move, not until Nate, surprisingly, tugged on my arm. "It's okay. Come on."

I held Morton's gaze as Nate pulled on my arm again. I let the boy pull me away, turning just as I saw the man smirk once more. I didn't trust myself to even speak until we were outside the building.

"Who is that to you all?" I demanded the moment we reached the middle of the barren street.

"You lied to me," he shot back in return. "You said you weren't an alien."

"I'm not an alien." I stared down at him. "I'm just not completely human."

He threw up his hands. "And that makes a difference?"

"No, it doesn't. Not really, because there's nothing wrong with being an alien. Just because I'm not a hundred percent human doesn't make me evil or untrustworthy or a freak," I told him. "Who is that man to you all?"

Nate glared back at me for a moment, but then he shook his head as he stared back at the building. Jamal and Nia were standing there. "He's one of the adults that's still, you know, alive."

Aware of the other two's approach, I asked, "They were more adults?"

"My parents," Nia answered, coming to stop a few feet from

us, her fingers toying with the edge of the bandage Jamal had wrapped around her hand. "They got sick about two years ago, died one after the other."

"My grandma was with me," Jamal added, his throat working. "She got sick, too. Cut her hand or something, and yeah, it took her down."

No wonder he'd been so attentive to Nia's wound.

"There were a few others, some who I guess lived on the streets like Morton before," Nate said. "But yeah, they're all dead. Most didn't last the first year."

How convenient for Morton. "Does he ever go out and get the food? The supplies?"

None of them answered, and my suspicious were confirmed. This man was using them.

"Has he hurt any of you?" I looked at Jamal. "Did that to your eye?"

"No," Nate answered. "It's not like that."

I wasn't sure if I believed him or not. "What I'm about to say is probably going to come as a surprise, and it's also going to be painful to hear, but it needs to be said. The Luxen can heal humans—things that aren't caused by internal issues. Any single one of those Luxen who are *right there,* who aren't evil freaks or whatever, would've healed your grandma's cut on her hand, saving her life. Your parents? The others?" My gaze flicked to Nia and Nate. "They may still have gotten sick, but I can tell you that they would've had access to some care and would've been in a better place to recover. I hate saying that, because none of this is your fault, and I know all of you probably saw some horrible stuff during the invasion, but the Luxen and everyone who live there are not bad people. That man in there is feeding you all some bullshit."

Jamal shot a nervous glance at Nate, but Nia's lips twitched when I cursed.

"You all don't know me. Not really, but believe me when I tell you that if the Luxen in that community wanted to hurt you—if I wanted to hurt you—none of you would be standing here."

Nate's eyes shot back to me. "Is that a threat?"

"No, it's me pointing out that if I were going to hurt you, I would've already done it. If I wanted to hurt that man—and I use the word *man* generously—I would've already done it. And if I don't want to hurt you and want to help you, why in the world would you think the others wouldn't feel the same? I would get down on my knees and beg you all to believe me when I say not all Luxen are evil body snatchers. Just like not all humans are bad people." I took a deep breath. "We can help you."

"We're fine here," Nate replied.

"Really?" I arched a brow.

The other two looked away, but Nate nodded, and I swallowed a truckload of curses. I wanted to run back in there, grab all those kids, and run off with them. Their lives could be better, even if they didn't believe it at first, but I saw the truth in how they'd reacted when they realized I wasn't exactly human. I was shocked that these three were out here, still talking to me. If they were forced, it would take a lifetime to undo that damage. I had to give them the chance to see it themselves before I was a part of deciding what was better for them.

"I know you think things are bad, but you can't come back here, and you can't bring anyone with you. We don't need your help. Not like that," Nate said. "Don't even waste your time, because I'm sure we'll be gone tonight."

"And what if I did come back?" I challenged. "Would he hurt you guys?"

"I told you, it's not like that." The heat in his words was barely there. "You saw how the others acted. They'll run. And you saw how young most of them are. It will be all over for them."

I exhaled long and slow. "I won't come back, and I told you I wouldn't bring anyone here. I haven't lied, but I still want you to come to me if you need something, and if you ever decide that you want to give living in the community a chance or if you need my help to make that happen, you come to me. Okay?"

Nia dipped her chin, but she nodded.

"Yeah," answered Jamal.

I stared at Nate. "What do you think?"

"Okay," he muttered.

"Promise?" I persisted.

His gaze lifted to mine. "I promise."

Really hoping he meant that, I nodded.

"Do you know your way out?" When I said yes, he added, "You should get going. The ones who check this area will be back through soon," he said. "You can't get caught."

"I know. I won't." Not wanting to leave them with a man who treated them like his own hunting-and-gathering tribe of children, I lingered for another moment. "Be safe. All of you. Please."

After another round of promises, I started to turn. Jamal stopped me. "If you're not completely human and you're not one of them, then what are you?"

How did I answer that question? I had no idea, so I said, "I'm just Evie."

I left after that, darting between the two tall and dark skyscrapers and following the road out, doing my best to not think about how quiet and empty everything was. The moment I neared the exit ramp, I felt the presence of a Luxen.

"Shit," I muttered, dropping down behind some kind of bush. The feeling increased, and my muscles tensed to run. I could be fast—probably faster than a Luxen could see. I could—

The crunch of gravel under a boot too close snapped my head up.

Grayson stood above me, face impressively blank in the silvery moonlight.

"Shit," I repeated, slowly rising from my crouch. Part of me knew better than to be surprised that he was there. After all, he was on babysitting duty. "I didn't feel you until now."

"That's because I stayed far enough back that you wouldn't feel me until I wanted you to."

My lips thinned. "That's not fair."

"Fair or not, do you want to know what's stupid? You running off in the middle of the night with some random guy—"

"Random guy? You mean random *child*."

"Into a city you're unfamiliar with," he continued. "Without telling anyone, by yourself."

"Well, obviously, I wasn't by myself," I snapped. "When I was with a random child and you were following me like a Grade A stalker."

White flashed from his shadowy eyes.

"And I get it—you're going to want to yell and lecture me, but can we please not do this here? I—well, now *we*—need to get back before we're seen." I held up my hand when he started to argue. "I'll explain everything, and I will also sit still and be quiet and let you rant to your heart's content, but can we please get back to the community *now*?"

Grayson simply stepped aside, extending an arm.

Stalking past him, I shot him a look, and then I took off running and I dug in deep, picking up speed. Grayson stayed close as I raced across the clearing, straight for the tree line. I didn't slow down as we reached the broken section of chain-link fence, signaling that we were now back in the community. I didn't slow down until the row of houses came into view.

Still surprised by my own speed, I brushed several strands of hair out of my face as I stepped onto the asphalt of the road Eaton lived on.

Grayson caught the backpack, bringing me to a stop. "It's time for you to let me rant to my heart's content."

Pulling myself free, I faced him. "Before you do, let me explain what I was doing."

"I don't think that's the deal we made."

"That's because we didn't make a deal." Before he could say another word, I launched into the briefest, shortest version I possibly could about Nate and the kids. I even told him that Luc knew about Nate. "You can't say anything, not to anyone but Luc," I told him when I finished. "If we go in there, the kids could scatter, and that guy I saw—"

"Let me stop you right there." Grayson stepped forward, dipping his chin. "I don't remotely care about those kids, some guy, or their hunger and cuts and bruises."

My mouth dropped open.

"The only thing I care about is keeping you alive," he said, and my mouth then snapped shut. "Which is something that continues to be a full-time job, because only you would do something so incredibly—"

"If you say *stupid,* we're going to have a problem," I warned.

"Thoughtless," he growled. "You want to help all the lost children in the world. Awesome. But you don't ever just run off without telling someone."

There was a tiny part of me that got what he was saying, but a much bigger part of me dived straight into irritation. "I don't have to tell anyone what I'm doing. No one is my keeper, Grayson. Not even Luc, and certainly not you."

"Like I said, thoughtless."

"Thoughtless?" I gaped at him while I wanted to wing the backpack around and smack him with it. "I'm trying to help kids."

"Do you really have any idea what Luc would do if something happened to you? Again?" he demanded. "What it would do to him? And anyone in his path?"

"I know—"

"I don't think you really do," he cut me off as his pupils flashed diamond bright. "Because if you did, you would've stopped for one second and thought about the possibility of this being a trap. That you could've been led somewhere or to someone who had the Cassio Wave. That you could've been immobilized any hundred other different ways. You're not a hundred percent safe here. No one is, and yet, you just roamed right off without thinking twice." He was even closer, the heat of his anger radiating off him in waves. "Did you forget that I would be watching? Or was that why you felt safe enough to just leave?"

"I didn't forget." I stared up at him. "I just didn't think you were sitting around, watching me."

"Maybe you need to start thinking some more," he snapped.

"And maybe you could be less of a jerk?" I shot back, hands balling into fists. "And why didn't you intervene? If you're so worried that I could've been walking into a trap, why did you let me just roam off?"

"I wanted to see what you were doing."

"Oh. Yeah. That makes complete sense." I laughed. "Maybe you were hoping it was a trap."

The shock that rolled across his face was possibly the most emotion I'd seen from him. It was brief, but he'd been momentarily stunned before his jaw hardened and those luminous eyes narrowed. "You may hate me, *Nadia*. You may think I hate you. I wouldn't blame you for either of those two things, but do not *ever* insinuate that I would allow something like that to happen."

Heart pounding, I took a step back without realizing that I was doing it.

Grayson tipped his head back. "Do you really think for one second Luc didn't warn me about this kid?"

My mouth dropped open.

"That I didn't know the night I was outside that you were bringing out food for him?" he continued. "There isn't much Luc doesn't share with me, and he trusts me, even with you. I wouldn't fail him or—" He cut himself off, his chest rising in a deep, unsteady breath. "Go home, Evie. Just go home. Please."

There were a lot of times I would've flat out refused to do just that, but instinct told me to listen. More importantly, though, it was how unnerved I was by the fact Grayson had said *please*.

33

The following morning, I watched the angel figurines I'd collected from one of the spare bedrooms move up and down over the coffee table as if they were jumping hurdles.

I wasn't sitting around and entertaining myself. I was working on the Source instead of fretting over Luc and Zoe, Daemon and Dawson, or those kids and that guy.

Or thinking about what Grayson had said to me. I'd done enough of that when I'd lain awake half the night. I hated that he'd had a point. It wasn't like I didn't know there was a risk. It was just that I was willing to take that risk, and maybe that did make me thoughtless or, at the very least, reckless.

One of the figurines started to fall, and I cursed. I had no idea why, but using the Source to move lightweight objects was far harder to control than moving heavier things.

The figurine of a sea turtle with wings had just swooped over the winged rabbit when a knock on the door startled me. The figurines started to fall, but I managed to slow them down before they landed. Popping up from the couch, I hurried to the door. Since I hadn't felt anything, I knew whoever it was, was human. I also figured it wasn't Nate knocking on my front door in broad daylight.

Dr. Hemenway stood there, long brown hair pulled back in a ponytail. I hadn't seen her since everything had happened. Immediately, my stomach sank. "Is everything okay?"

"What?" Confusion swept across her face and then was quickly replaced by understanding. "Oh! Of course it is. Well, at least I think it is. I haven't heard anything."

I relaxed. A little.

"I stopped by to see if you would like to shadow me for the

day," Viv explained, much to my disbelief. "That probably entails us just sitting around and doing nothing for the majority of the day and maybe bandaging a minor cut or two, but you did really well with Spencer. You stayed calm and made a great assistant. Thought that maybe you'd be interested in helping out."

Another wave of surprise rolled through me and then gave way to eagerness. "Yeah. Yes! That would be really cool. I'd love to."

Viv grinned. "Great. We can head over now. I brought the UTV, so it's a quick ride."

"Awesome. I just need to grab my shoes."

"Take your time."

I did not take my time. Dashing into the bedroom, I toed on my sneakers and then ran back out. It was when we were walking to the vehicle that it struck me. I glanced at Viv as I rounded the front.

"Luc," I said.

"What about him?" She hopped into the driver's seat.

"This was his idea."

"It was," she admitted. "But when he brought it up, I was like, damn, what an excellent idea. He didn't have to talk me into it. If I didn't think this was a good idea, I would've put the kibosh on it."

I believed her.

"I hope you're not mad or anything," she said as I climbed into the passenger seat.

"No. I'm not." I sat back, smiling, and I didn't need to see myself to know it was a big, goofy smile. He knew I wanted to be useful here, to provide some sort of service, and he made it happen. "I'm glad he said something."

"So am I." Throwing the UTV into reverse, she eased out of the driveway and started down the street. "I've been training some people here, just in case I need an extra hand or something happens, so the more people who know more than just basic first aid, the better."

"Funny thing is, I actually considered becoming a nurse before . . . well, before everything." I watched the houses go by. "I used to think I didn't have the stomach for it."

"You do," she said confidently. "If you didn't, there would've been no way you could've been in the same room as Spencer." Squinting, she exhaled loudly. "Never in my life have I ever seen anything like that."

"That's probably a good thing," I told her as we neared the overgrown park. "You did everything possible to save his life. You didn't fail him."

"I wish it didn't feel that way." She squeezed the steering wheel. "But I know I did everything. We all did. It just sucks."

"Yes," I said quietly. "It does."

A faint smile appeared. "Tell you what, though—I'll never complain about being bored again, that's for sure."

I grinned and nodded as the market came into view. "Oh! Do you mind if we stop by the library really quickly?" I asked. "I need to see if there's hair dye here, and I have no idea where I'm supposed to find Zouhour."

"Sure?" She sent me a look full of questions.

"I need to change my appearance," I explained. "Eventually, I'm going to need to go back out there, and I need to make it harder for people to recognize me."

"Ah!" Viv laughed. "That makes sense. I was thinking this was a weird time for a makeover."

"No doubt," I agreed.

We swung by the old library, and after waiting a couple of minutes, Zouhour showed up with a thick binder that contained all the goods in storage. Turned out that there had been hair dye at one time, but the unused boxes had been tossed out since no one really wanted to put several-years-old dye on their heads. Understandable, because I sure didn't.

Hoping Luc was able to find one, I thanked Zouhour, and then Viv and I headed back to the medical office, driving behind the busy market. She parked the UTV right outside the office, and I followed her inside.

Enough sunlight poured in through the windows that the waiting area was brightly lit. Instead of rows of chairs, five examining tables had been moved out.

Viv saw me staring at them. "Weird location to treat patients,

I know, but there's too much natural light out here to let it go to waste." She tossed the keys onto a counter. "The back rooms are used when privacy is needed. All but one have windows to let some light in, and we'll fire up the lanterns if we need them." She motioned me to follow her. "Luckily, we haven't had to use them too often. With Daemon here, he can take care of most of the injuries, and now Luc. It will cut back on the stuff that makes me feel like my head is about to slip underwater."

"Are there no other Luxen here that can heal?" I asked.

"There are a few who can do minor injuries, but nothing like what happened to Spencer. If Luc couldn't keep him stable, Daemon wouldn't have been able to, either."

"I've been told that all Luxen can heal, but to varying degrees." I followed her along a narrow hall. Most of the doors we passed were closed.

"Yep. It seems like those who were most skilled at healing, well, they didn't make it here."

Anything could've happened to them, but I had a feeling that the Daedalus was more than just a little responsible. Those who could heal virtual strangers would've made excellent candidates for mutations.

"Here is the supply stash." Viv opened the door to what must've been a small laboratory before. Natural light shone in through the windows, casting a soft glow over the metal shelves lining the walls. My gaze roamed the room, and all I could think of was those kids and the grandma who died from a freaking cut on the hand. Right in front of me were several things that would've saved her life. There were boxes of bandages and latex gloves, cases of needles and bundled IV bags, row after row of pill bottles, numerous pieces of medical equipment, and stacked first-aid kits chock-full of everything needed to disinfect a cut.

"We were running low on a few things—namely, inhalers. Got a few people here with pretty bad asthma, and they're about to run out and—"

The bell above the door jiggled, signaling that someone was here.

"Coming!" Viv called out before raising her brows at me. "Let's see what's going on."

What turned out to be going on was a human man and Baby Wonder Woman—the little girl Ashley had made fly on the playground. The little girl was covered in an oozing, angry red rash that turned out to be poison ivy, much to the father's relief. Calamine lotion was given out, along with an oral antihistamine and a stern warning to not scratch, which the little girl promised not to do seconds before scratching at her arm as if she were trying to take it off. On the way out, the little girl had waved goodbye, and the father had nodded in my direction. That was the only time he really acknowledged my existence.

After that, there was the cutest elderly couple. The husband was worried about his wife. She'd been having chest pains, and after a brief examination that included taking the woman's pulse, blood pressure, and asking numerous questions, Viv was fairly certain it wasn't anything serious, but she recommended that the woman come in at any time if she experienced shortness of breath or nausea. Neither of them paid much mind to me, not even when Viv showed me how to use a blood pressure cuff.

When they left, Viv sat down on the rolling stool, shoulders lowered as she watched them shuffle toward the market. "She might be having heart failure," she said after several moments.

Pressure clamped around my chest. I didn't have to ask. The Luxen couldn't heal something like that. Not even Luc. "There's nothing that can be done."

Viv shook her head sadly. "No. Not here. We don't have the diagnostic capability to even test for it, and we can't blindly prescribe medication that could do more harm than good."

"That's got to be hard knowing that there may be something serious and not being able to do anything."

"There are a few things we can do." Viv toed herself around. "Last year, we suspected that one of the guys had cancer. He'd had it before, and all his symptoms pointed toward a cancer of the pancreas or liver, and that's something we can't treat here. We offered to escort him out to one of our outposts. We'd provide him with identification and some money. Without insurance, it would be a crapshoot, but it was still something."

"Did he take it?"

Viv gave me a tight-lipped smile. "No. I'll never forget this, but he'd said he knew all the treatment in the world wouldn't make a difference and that he would rather stay here. We can't force anyone, and something like the pancreas doesn't show recognizable symptoms until it's often too late. He was right. In less than a month, he was gone. Treatment might've extended his life, but it might not have been the best extra months given to him."

Heaviness settled over me, but I didn't have long to dwell on it. Another person came through the door, holding a blood-soaked handkerchief to his hand.

For a moment, I thought the dude might bleed to death right there, but come to find out, fingers just tended to bleed a lot. The guy only required five stitches. He didn't really say much to me beyond hello. The same went for the second man who needed his palm closed, having sliced it open helping repair a roof. A shot of lidocaine and a rather neat row of stitches later, he was out the door, replaced by what turned out to be a toothache, a case of indigestion, a bout of possible kidney stones, and what Viv believed to be an upset stomach.

"How do you know what to diagnose these people with?" Curiosity had gotten the best of me. "Not that I doubt what you're coming up with, but kidney stones? Indigestion?"

"I'm a mind reader," she teased. "Actually, you saw all those books back there? I've read every possible diagnostic manual I could get my hands on. I've been right for the most part." Her nose wrinkled. "Well, except for that one time."

"Do tell."

She laughed. "The woman was complaining of an upset stomach, vomiting, and fatigue. I asked all the standard questions. What have you eaten? When was your last period? Does it get better before or after food? Yada, yada. Nothing there to give me any indication of what could be happening other than just a stomach issue. A few weeks later, she came back with the same complaint, but she'd gained a little bit of weight. I asked her again about her period, but that time, she said she couldn't remember."

I started to grin.

"One pee-on-a-stick test later, we knew she was pregnant. So, that time wasn't my fault."

I laughed. "Well, I could see how it would be hard to keep track of months here."

"That woman was like five months pregnant. How do you forget not having your period for five months?"

My eyes widened. "Good point."

"Damn straight."

Looking out the window, I watched several men and women carry baskets into the backs of the stalls. "Can I ask you something?"

"Sure."

"Is it normal that the people here aren't exactly warm and friendly with new people?" I asked. "Or is it because I blew up a house?"

"Oh, everyone here is pretty wary of just about anyone." She lifted her brows. "And because you blew up a house, can you blame them?"

"No," I said and laughed.

"They'll warm up to you." Reaching over, she patted my arm. "Especially if you don't blow up any more houses."

"I'll try not to."

"Just don't try so hard that you end up not doing what needs to be done when it needs to be done." She rose. "I need a protein boost. And I have the perfect drink for you to try out."

Fifteen minutes later, I found myself staring at what Viv referred to as her Lunch of Champions, which was a concoction of raw veggies, some sort of powder she swore wasn't expired, and fresh milk. It looked like green slime. Green slime that had thrown up green slime.

I was *this* close to telling her about the children in the city when she took a huge gulp and then offered the glass. "Try it. It's not bad."

"Uh. I think I'll pass."

She pinned me with an arched look. "You are this alien hybrid who can blow up a house, but you're afraid of a protein shake full of vitamins."

I nodded.

Her lips thinned. "It's really not that bad. Kat loves it."

"Kat also just had a baby."

"Evie."

I sighed, taking the glass. "Fine."

"Great." She bit down on her lip, staring at me. "Try it. Come on. You can do it."

Lifting the glass, I didn't even attempt to smell it as I took a tiny sip—

"Drink like you mean it."

"I am!"

"That is not a real drink. You need to take a drink like it's your first spring break."

That made me snort, but I took a real drink, and the moment my tongue hit the thick, uneven mixture, my gag reflex woke up.

"It's good, right?" she asked.

Not wanting to hurt her feelings, I forced myself to swallow and then spent several precious seconds willing myself not to vomit. Only when I was sure I wasn't going to throw up on her, I said, "It's, um, different."

Her lip curled. "You don't know what's good for you." She snatched the glass back. "But I guess you really don't need vitamin and protein shakes, do you?"

I watched her down half the glass. "Thank God."

Still drinking, she slid me a sideways look.

"I bet you had a great spring break," I said.

She stopped long enough to say, "I don't remember most of them, so I'm going to go with a hell yeah."

I glanced out the front windows, feeling the shivery awareness along the back of my neck. I spotted Grayson and tensed. I hadn't felt him at all today, but I now knew he'd been around, staying far enough away that I didn't feel him. Which was mildly irritating.

I still had no idea what to make of what Luc had said before he'd left or my conversation with Grayson last night. I also wondered if Grayson ever slept.

"Oh Lord, here comes my most favorite person in the world," Viv grumbled, and I barely squelched my laugh as he walked in. "To whom or what do we owe the pleasure of your visit, Sir Grayson?"

Grayson arched a brow. "I doubt you find any pleasure from my visits."

"Nuh-uh," she replied about as convincing as a kid with their hand shoved into a cookie jar.

That ultrabright blue gaze slid from her to me. "I have news."

I sat up straight. "About?"

"I just heard that a group arrived. One of them is a human female with extremely bright red hair."

Jumping from the stool, I was sure my heart had stopped. "It's Heidi? Emery?"

"Unless you know of some other red-haired human girl that I would come tell you about, then I'm assuming yes."

"Oh my God." I spun toward Viv. "I'm sorry to do this, but can I—"

"It's totally cool. Go!" Viv shooed me, waving her hands. "Get out of here."

I whirled around to Grayson, nearly consumed with happiness and relief. "Where are they?"

"At the entry house."

"Thank you."

I didn't wait for his response—for anything else. I ran out the door, crossing the parking lot, and then I really picked up speed, knowing exactly where I was going. I ran as fast I had when I'd raced Luc. Wind tugged at my ponytail, tore at my clothing. I knew I was moving fast, but I could feel the presence of a Luxen close. Grayson was following.

I cut through the wooded area, not thinking about the last time I'd been there. In less than a minute, I was rushing past the two patches of disturbed earth that had been left behind when I'd sucked Grayson and Luc down into the ground.

Slowing down so I didn't burst through a wall, I bounded up the steps and in through the open door. I probably should've called out or something, because barging into anyone's house was rude, but my heart was thumping against my ribs as I heard voices—male voices and a softer, feminine one.

I stepped into the dining room and got a quick glimpse of the table, but I had to look away. It looked normal now. A white tablecloth covered it, and for one morbid second, I wondered if Spencer's blood had stained it.

Pushing the thought aside, I followed the voices into the kitchen. My extra-special senses were firing off. There was a dark-haired Luxen male standing just inside, the rainbow aura briefly blurring his features. A fainter buzz signaled a hybrid was also nearby, but it was the vibrant crimson hair I zeroed in on.

"Heidi!" I cried out.

She spun toward me, a smile breaking out across her face. "Evie! Oh my God! Evie!"

I crossed the distance in a nanosecond. Like, for real. Fast enough that I caught the wide-eyed look of surprise right before I crashed into Heidi, throwing my arms around her. "I've been so worried about you and Emery! Oh my God, you have no idea! I was so afraid something happened and I wouldn't know what to do. Wait. Where is Emery?"

"Right here," came the familiar voice, and my eyes flew open. Emery was standing just inside the mudroom, her raven-hued hair pulled back. The buzzed hair on one side of her head had started to grow out. She waved.

"Hi!" I yelled.

She grinned. "Hi, Evie."

"I missed you, too," Heidi whispered. "You and Zoe and Luc and everyone—" She pulled back, clasping my cheeks in her cool hands. "Girl, you moved fast. Like, superfast. I think I've missed a lot."

"Well, yes. There's a lot."

"Wait. What were those names again?" asked one of the guys behind us.

Heidi let go as she glanced over to Emery. "Oh, crap. After all this time, I slipped up and said names."

"I just shouted your name to the whole world," I told her, blinking back happy tears. In my excitement, I'd totally forgotten that those traveling were not allowed to share even the basic information such as names.

"It's okay now that we're here." Jeremy appeared behind Emery, pulling a black skullcap off. "Everyone can introduce themselves."

"What were those names?" the guy repeated, and I turned to him, still clutching Heidi like she'd possibly disappear.

The male Luxen wasn't who had spoken. He looked too terrified to do so as he stared at the man beside him. Light brown hair was swept back from the ruggedly handsome face of a hybrid. There was a network of faint white scars etched into his cheeks and on his nose, almost like a spiderweb of lines. Eyes a mixture of brown and muted green met mine. Recognition flared as he stumbled back in shock, his face paling.

"Oh God," he whispered.

My arms slipped away from Heidi as I became vaguely aware of Grayson entering the room. "You recognize me, don't you?"

"Jesus," he uttered.

Grayson struck like lightning striking past me. In a blink of an eye, he had grabbed the front of the man's shirt. Dishes rattled as Grayson shoved the hybrid against the cabinets. The new Luxen shouted, starting toward them as the glow of the Source surrounded him.

I didn't stop to think.

Summoning the Source, I *stopped* the Luxen. His body jerked as if his feet were glued to the floor. It wouldn't stop him from striking out with the Source, but I hoped it was a warning he'd heed. "Please don't attack Grayson," I said, and the Luxen's head swung in my direction. His lips parted on a sharp inhale. "I don't want to have to hurt you."

"Holy guacamole," Heidi whispered. "You're . . . Evie, you have black glitter all over you."

"I know." I kept my eyes trained on the Luxen. "That's one of the things you've missed."

"I don't want to hurt anyone, either," the Luxen responded. "Neither does he."

"You sure about that?" I asked. "You're starting to glow like a lightning bug."

"Sorry. It's a knee-jerk response," he said, and the glow faded until nothing surrounded him.

I nodded, but I didn't ease up on him, keeping him in place.

"Who are you?" Grayson demanded.

Beyond Grayson's shoulder, the hybrid's wide eyes were fixed on me. A cold chill knotted my muscles as he swallowed. "A dead man. I'm a dead man."

34

T hat's a strange-as-hell name," Grayson said, lifting the hybrid off his feet. "So you may want to think that answer over."

Georgie, the old farmer, walked in from the dining area, a woven basket tucked under his arm as he jerked to a stop. He took one look at the room and sighed. "Not again. Doris," he called out, setting the basket down. Straightening, he opened the old refrigerator door.

My eyes nearly popped out of my head. The insides had been hollowed out to hold yet another stash of rifles.

"What?" came Doris's voice.

Pulling out a rifle, he leveled it directly at the hybrid's head. "You may as well wait outside for a bit. We've got an issue in here."

Grayson lifted the hybrid even higher as the Source started to bleed into the air around him. "I'm starting to get impatient, and just so you know, I'm not known for my patience."

"I know their names." Jeremy had also grabbed one of the rifles from the mudroom. With one quick glance, I saw that Emery had Heidi behind her. The female Luxen's pupils were diamond bright. "They were vetted. The Luxen is Chris Strom," Jeremy answered. "The hybrid's name is Blake Saunders."

Neither name meant a thing to me, but they did to Grayson and Emery.

"Holy Christ," whispered Emery.

"That can't be right." The Source flared around Grayson. "I know that name. Blake Saunders is dead."

The hybrid said nothing, but the Luxen did. "It's true. His name is Blake, and I'm sure a lot of people believe him to be dead, but he didn't die. We're not lying. We not here to cause any problems. If we'd known that Luc was here, we wouldn't have come—"

"Why would it cause problems?" I demanded. "Who are you two?"

The hybrid's gaze shot to me.

"Don't look at her," Grayson warned. "Jeremy, I need you to get Hunter. Now. He'll be able to confirm exactly who these two are. And I need you to get him fast," Grayson instructed. "Don't talk to anyone else about this."

"On it," Jeremy said, and he then rushed from the room.

"Everyone should leave. Sorry, Georgie. I know this is your house, but I want you and Doris nowhere near here," Grayson instructed. "Take Emery and Heidi to Cekiah. She's at the old library. Tell her what is going down. Make sure it stays quiet. There are others here that don't need to learn of this."

"Others?" Chris asked, still frozen where I held him, his chest moving and falling rapidly. "Who else is here?"

His question was ignored as Grayson dropped the hybrid. He fell back against the counter, eyes flying open. His shirt was torn around his collar. He said nothing, keeping his gaze trained on Grayson.

"Evie," Grayson said as Emery took ahold of Heidi's arm and joined Georgie at the door. "Go with them."

"What?" I exclaimed. "I'm not going anywhere."

"I don't care where you go, but you're going somewhere that's not here."

"No, I'm not."

Keeping one hand planted on the center of the hybrid's chest, he spared me a brief glance. "I'm not asking."

"Good," I shot back. "Because even if you were, I'm still not listening. If you want me to leave, you're going to have to make me, and *that* is something I'd like to see."

The Source flared violently around him, and for a moment, I thought he was going to try, but then he gave me a tight-lipped smile. "It's your world, isn't it?" Then he turned back to the hybrid. "Sit. I want both of you to sit."

The room had emptied by that point, and there was a part of me that wanted to go after Heidi. There was so much I needed to tell her, and I wanted to hug her again, but instinct was going off left and right, telling me that I needed to stay here.

The hybrid slowly lowered himself to the floor, sitting with one leg drawn up, the other stretched out.

"That means you, too." Grayson looked at the Luxen.

"I can't," he replied. "I can't move."

"That's me." Pulling the Source back, I let the Luxen go.

Jerking as if he were attached to a string and it was pulled, the Luxen swung his head toward me as he sat a few feet from the hybrid. "How did you do that?"

I didn't answer, because I wasn't sure what I should admit in front of him.

"The Daedalus is how she did that," the hybrid answered. "The Andromeda serum, right?"

I shifted toward him. "I want to know how you know me."

"No," the hybrid said, his jaw hardening. "You don't."

Tiny knots filled my stomach as I started toward him.

"If you insist on staying, the least you can do is to stay away from them." Grayson's arm blocked me. "If they are who they claim to be, Luc wouldn't want you in the same zip code."

Those knots grew. Neither seemed very threatening at the moment. The Luxen appeared seconds from breaking down. Then again, all of this could be an act.

I didn't know them even though the hybrid seemed to know me. "Who are they?" I asked Grayson.

"Who are they claiming to be?" Grayson pulled a Blow Pop out of his pocket. "Two people who should definitely be dead."

"That tells me nothing."

"I never met you." The hybrid eyed Grayson from where he sat.

"No, you haven't." Grayson unwrapped the sucker. "But if you are who you say you are, I've heard the stories."

"From Luc?" he asked.

Grayson didn't answer.

One side of the hybrid's lips twitched upward as if he tried to smile. "If you didn't hear it from him, then I think I know who the others are who are here."

"Then you know your shocking return from the grave is going to be really short term."

"We didn't come here to cause trouble," the Luxen spoke up. "I swear we didn't. We were just looking for a safe place, and we heard that there were areas where we could go. We had no idea who was here. They told us nothing more. If we'd known, we wouldn't have come. I swear it. We would've risked it out there."

"It doesn't matter, Chris," the hybrid said as he tipped his head back against the worn, faded white cabinets. "They wouldn't believe us."

"Can you blame them?" the Luxen whispered.

Tilting his chin in the Luxen's direction, he shook his head. "No. I never blamed any of them."

The Luxen started to shift onto his knees, but halted when Grayson looked at him. He sat back, facing the hybrid. "You did what you had to do to survive. We all did."

"What did you do?" I asked.

Still staring at the Luxen, the hybrid pressed his lips together and then said, "Betrayed everyone. Everyone except Luc. He always knew. Can't keep much from him. But he never told the others the truth about me. Wasn't until later that I figured out why."

None of what he was saying made a bit of sense. "I want to know how you know me," I asked once more, ignoring the sharp look Grayson shot in my direction.

"Do you really?" The hybrid looked at me then with eyes haunted.

A world of unease settled over me like a thick, coarse blanket. "You knew me when I was Nadia."

His brows knitted, one of them split in half by a faint scar. "They took your memories. Wiped them completely."

Air halted in my lungs.

"That's right. That's what they'd said they would do. My memory is a bit spotty these days." A sardonic twist curled his lips. "I didn't know they did it. One day you were there. Then you were gone."

Oh my God, he knew me when I was with the Daedalus. Shaken, I didn't know what to say or do, because I felt split into two. Half of me wanted to launch into an interrogation, forcing him to tell me everything. The desire to learn about the missing time burned through me, making my skin itchy. But the other half? Based on the way Luc had paled when he'd realized I'd been Nadia at that time, how Kat and Zoe both said my lack of memory was a blessing, and from the brief memories I could grasp and hold on to, the other part of me wasn't sure I needed to know what was done to me. Or what I'd most likely done to others.

"I saw you with Luc even though he tried to keep you hidden," the hybrid said. "That was before the Daedalus." His gaze lifted to me. "Before I understood why he wouldn't tell the others who I was. It was because of you."

"That's enough." Grayson removed the Blow Pop. "It's quiet time."

I wasn't taking part in quiet time, not as I rapidly began to put what I did know together. Luc had used Daemon and Kat to get inside the Daedalus, to retrieve the serums he thought would heal me. Was this hybrid who claimed to be Blake involved, and were those he'd said he'd betrayed Daemon and Kat? If so, that meant . . .

Anger filled me. "You worked for the Daedalus?"

"Not by his choosing," Chris answered with a nervous glance at Grayson. "We grew up together. Close. Like brothers. There was an accident when we were younger. A bad one, and I healed him. He mutated, and the Daedalus found out, and ever since then—up until we finally got away—the Daedalus used me to control him. It was like that for more years than it wasn't."

"Really thought I said it was quiet time," Grayson said.

"They made him do terrible things—things he would've never done if they hadn't been able to use me. They controlled us. You have to understand that," Chris said—pleaded, really. "Everything he did, he did so that I lived, so that he survived. He did what anyone else would've done."

"Some would've done worse," the hybrid murmured, eyes meeting mine. "Have done worse."

A cold air pressed to my back, and while his words were unnerving, I knew the sensation meant Hunter was near. Seconds later, he entered through the mudroom and headed straight for the two men sitting on the floor.

Grayson stepped aside, and without saying a word, Hunter knelt in front of the Luxen. Static charged the air as the hybrid started to move, but Grayson was faster, catching him by the throat and slamming his head back.

"Don't even think it," Grayson said around the Blow Pop.

Hunter placed his hand on the center of the Luxen's chest and lowered his head. Then his hand went into his chest. Chris's body jerked and back bowed as his entire body lit up. He slipped into his true form, a being encased in rapidly flickering light as Hunter fed.

I was guessing that was how you made feeding painful.

Jeepers.

Hunter was taking the Luxen's memories, just like I had when I'd fed on Luc. It was as fascinating as it was horrifying to witness.

"Stop!" the hybrid shouted. "You're killing him! Stop."

My stomach dipped as Grayson laughed. "He's not killing." A pause. "Yet."

Hunter let go a few moments later, and the Luxen slumped back into the cabinet, his light still pulsing, but more slowly now.

"Chris?" the hybrid whispered.

Rising to his full height, Hunter looked over to the hybrid. "You *are* a dead man."

Cekiah and other Luxen arrived shortly after, and the two men had been carted off to a holding area until it could be determined what to do with them. I'd heard that both would be searched once more for any trackers.

It had been decided by Hunter that Kat and Bethany wouldn't be told about the newest arrivals, not until Daemon returned, and I knew then that whatever Blake had done, it had been one of those terrible things that Chris had referenced, and it did involve them. I couldn't imagine what it could be that they felt it was best to keep someone as strong as Kat in the dark, and that had been a ghost lingering in the back of my mind several hours later. Even now, as I sat at the house opened for Heidi and Emery, the empty one two homes down from the one I shared with Luc. Candles and lanterns lit the living room, fighting the coming night. I'd just finished filling Heidi and Emery in on everything that had happened since the night we'd all fled Columbia. Heidi had been sitting beside me on the couch, but she'd gotten up when I told them about Kent.

She sat on the arm of the chair, running her hand over Emery's head. "I don't know what to say." She bent down, kissing her temple. "I'm so sorry about Kent," she whispered. "God, I'm so sorry about Clyde and Chas. All of them."

Emery stared at nothing, her lips mashed together as she inhaled deeply through the nose. "They're dead?" she asked, blinking. "The men who killed Kent? They're dead?"

"Yes," I answered. "All of them."

Taking another long breath, she nodded. "Good."

I watched her turn to Heidi, and I looked away when she was folded into her embrace, giving them as much privacy as possible.

It was a while later before Emery said, "There's been a huge increase in ART officers, but the real issue was the National Guard."

Heidi nodded. "They were all over the place."

"Heavy patrol of the interstates and at the rest stops," Emery said. "Never have I seen anything like that, fully uniformed and armed. That's what took us so long. We had to keep backtracking, taking different back roads and lying low. The news kept saying their presence was to ensure that there was no traveling in and out of the quarantine cities, but they were in states nowhere near the places that have outbreaks."

"ET." Heidi rolled her eyes as she shook her head. "How stupid is that nickname?"

"Very," I said, leaning forward. "How bad are the outbreaks?"

She repeated basically what Daemon had shared. "But the thing is, no one is going in or out of those cities, and there's been some strange shit posted on social media from those areas."

"I created a fake account to try to check to see how James and some of the others that we knew were doing. I didn't want to log in to mine in case they were tracking that. When I was able to check last, he was okay, but schools have been shut down, businesses closed." Heidi tucked a piece of her hair back from her face. "He'd posted about a curfew and how the army had come in, pretty much taking over. There was this one post . . ." She trailed off, shaking her head.

"What?" I looked to Emery.

"I think she's talking about the posts about the dead."

"Oh God."

"Yeah." Heidi's shoulders rose. "He said that soldiers went around in his neighborhood, telling everyone that if someone got sick, they were to hang a white towel out the window or their front door. One of the houses next to him ended up putting one up. He posted that the next day he saw them carrying out three body bags."

I pressed my hands to my mouth.

"And then the last post was about the others." Heidi folded her arms around her. "The ones who got sick but didn't die."

"The ones who mutated?" I said behind my hands.

"I guess so," Heidi replied. "He wouldn't know that, but he'd posted something about him thinking they were the real reason the army was there. He said that people were acting weird. Attacking others and just, I don't know, raging out. He posted that nighttime was the worst. All you could hear were these screams. Said it sounded like something from a horror movie."

Having seen with my own eyes what Sarah and Coop had done, I couldn't even begin to imagine what it was like if dozens or hundreds more were going through the same thing. "What is the army doing? Straight up shooting them?"

"I don't know," Heidi said. "His last post was right before we reached Arkansas."

Fear was a bolt to the system. "Oh God."

"I don't know if anything happened to him. It seems like the social media was just turned off in Columbia and the other cities, but the news keeps telling everyone that things are under control. That fewer and fewer people are getting sick. If that's true, why would they shut those cities off completely?"

I let that sink in. "They don't want the world to know what's happening. That want everyone as unprepared as possible."

"And for the most part, people are going about their lives like nothing has happened and as if it can't touch them." Emery leaned back. "We met up with those two in Arkansas. I had no idea that was who they were. Why would I? I've heard the stories and was told they were dead."

"Who are they?" I asked, hoping for once I'd get an answer.

"From what I know, Blake was a hybrid the Daedalus often used to spy on recently mutated hybrids. See if they were viable— able to control their abilities and be of use to the Daedalus. Several years ago, he'd been sent to Petersburg, West Virginia, and enrolled in the school Kat and Daemon attended. The Daedalus knew that Kat had been mutated, and they wanted firsthand accounts. They had no idea who Blake really was until it was too late. He killed one of their friends—a Luxen who Dee had been seeing. Adam Thomson."

Adam. I sucked in a sharp breath, knowing instinctively that their baby was named after him.

"There's a lot more to it. The guy was or is a master manipulator and liar. He ended up getting Kat captured by the Daedalus, and while she was with them, Jason Dasher had her fight other hybrids—namely, Blake. She killed him," Emery said. "Or at least, that's what she and everyone believed."

"Dear God." I scrubbed my fingers down my face. No wonder they didn't want Kat to know until Daemon returned. "How is he related to Luc?"

Emery lifted a shoulder. "I don't know how Luc knows him. All I know is that he met him a couple of times, but I wasn't around then."

I had no idea if Emery was telling the truth or not. It was something I was going to have to get out of Luc.

"He knew me," I said, dropping my hands to my thighs. "I think he was there when I was at the Daedalus, being trained."

"And turned into the badass Trojan that can have disappearing tattoos?" Heidi rose from the arm of the chair and plopped down next to me. "Because that's what it kind of reminded me of. Or embedded stones . . . tattoos or stones that moved." She smiled when my gaze met hers. "It was really cool looking."

I cracked a grin.

"I'm going to be honest." She bit down on her lip. "But I am having such a hard time picturing you running fast anywhere. I mean, I remember you in gym class. You ran like you were on slo-mo."

A laugh burst out of me as I leaned into her, resting my head on her shoulder. "God, I've missed you."

"Same," she whispered.

Knowing it was getting close to the time that Luc and crew should return, we left for the entry house. Grayson joined us, having appeared out of freaking nowhere. The walk to the farmhouse was quiet.

It looked entirely different at night, the driveway and porch lit with torches and solar lights. It was so bright that I knew the Arum I felt as we neared the porch was Hunter. I could see him sitting on one of the rocking chairs, his wife beside him.

Doris stepped out of the house, a tray of glasses. "Figured we'd have more company than normal tonight. Made some sweet tea."

"Thank you." I took a glass and then sat on the top step. Taking a drink, I almost moaned in pleasure. It was truly *sweet* tea, heavy on the sweet part.

Heidi and Emery spoke with Hunter and Serena while Grayson lurked somewhere to my left. I nursed my sweet tea, having no idea how Daemon and Kat were going to handle the news.

"Hey."

I turned to my left, and just as I'd suspected, Grayson was there, just out of the reach of the lights. He stood in what must've been a flower bed at one time. For some reason, I thought about what he'd said last night. *You may think I hate you.* He sure didn't act like he liked me, and if he cared for Luc like he did, I really couldn't blame him for disliking me.

"I have a feeling this is going to go in one ear and out the other. I also have a feeling Luc is going to say the same to you," he said, voice so low that I doubted anyone else could hear him. "I know you want to talk to Blake, but you need to realize that whatever he tells you, you've got to take it with a grain of salt. He's not to be trusted."

I nodded.

Grayson was right. I did want to talk to Blake, but if given the chance, could I believe anything he said? That question was going to have to wait.

"By the way, I haven't said anything about where you were last night," he added.

"I figured if you had, someone would've yelled at me by now," I said. "But thanks for not saying anything."

He was silent for a moment. "But I will tell Luc as soon as this little drama plays out."

"I'm going to tell him," I whispered. "I wouldn't hide that from him."

"I'd hope not." He then turned away.

What was happening with Nate and those kids was important, but this Blake thing was going to take precedence.

Only a few moments later, I felt them before I saw them. I rose from where I sat, placing the glass of tea out of the way so it wouldn't be knocked over. I walked down the steps. Moments later, the small group appeared out of the darkness. Four had left. Four had returned. Each wore backpacks and carried duffel bags that appeared close to bursting.

I wanted to race down the driveway, meet him there, just like Heidi was doing, rushing toward Zoe, but I remained where I was, sensing that something big was going to happen the moment Daemon learned the truth. I watched Luc as he stepped farther into the lit area, his striking features breaking into a beautiful smile. It faltered the moment he picked up on my thoughts. I replayed everything that had happened, and I knew he read all of it.

His face went impressively blank as his gaze shifted to where Hunter sat in the rocking chair. Then he walked past me, stopping briefly to kiss me before he unloaded what he'd brought back on the porch. He waited until Daemon did the same, and by then Hunter had gotten his butt out of the chair and stood.

"Daemon," Hunter said.

The quietness of the Arum's voice must've sent some sort of warning to Daemon, because he went incredibly still. "What?"

"Blake Saunders is alive," Hunter told him. "And he's here."

35

Daemon took a step back, arms going to his sides. "That's not possible."

"It's true," Hunter said. "I fed on the Luxen. I didn't see how they're alive, but I know they're telling the truth about who they are."

"That son of a bitch is alive, and he's here?" Daemon started to turn, his pupils a stark white. "Where is he?"

"They're being held under the library," Hunter answered.

"Hold up," Luc said when Daemon started down the steps. "We need to talk about this."

"Talk about what? He's supposed to be dead. He needs to be dead, and there is no way in hell he's not going to be." A white glow emanated from Daemon as he stalked down the steps. "There's nothing to discuss."

Luc stepped in front of the clearly enraged Luxen. "You need to calm down."

"You need to get out of my way."

"I'm going to ignore that, because I get it. You're mad. You have every right to be mad, but we need to know how he's alive."

"Right now, I don't care. Whatever he tells us cannot be trusted." Daemon was losing hold of his human form. "You know that, Luc. None of us can trust him."

"I'm not suggesting anyone does."

Daemon looked to the side, the light flaring around him. He started to turn from Luc, but spun back. "Do you have any idea what he's done to Kat? Do you?"

"I know enough," Luc said quietly. "But we need to talk to him. We need to know how he ended up here and what he's up to.

He recognized Evie. He was with her while she was at the Daedalus. We need to learn what he knows."

"What part of *I don't care* do you not understand?" Daemon growled.

"I'm not asking you to care, but before you kill him, I need to talk to him," Luc reasoned, and a shudder rolled through me. "He can't lie to me."

That was the wrong thing to say.

Daemon's head swung back to Luc as the Source pulsed around him. Fine hairs raised all over my body as he said, "And he's never been able to, has he?"

Blake's words came back to me, and my knotted stomach sank even further as Daemon continued, "You always knew what he was—what he was going to do." He stepped into Luc, and I saw Grayson peel away from the shadows of the porch. "You knew Blake was going to betray us, but you needed access to those serums. We were just your delivery system. He killed Adam, Luc. He's killed others, but you don't care. Because only *she* mattered, right?"

"As if you wouldn't have done the same if you were trying to save Kat's life." Luc didn't even deny it.

"You know damn well I would've," Daemon admitted. "But that's not what happened."

"The Daedalus would've gotten their hands on you with or without me." Luc's pupils started to glow. "But with me, I had you both protected as much as I could on the inside, or are you conveniently forgetting that?"

"Your protection only went so far, Luc. They tortured Kat!" Daemon shouted, and lightning streaked across the sky. "They used her to force me to mutate others. They cut her open, Luc. The things she saw still wake her up in the middle of the night."

"And for that, I will never forgive myself," Luc said, and it was then that I realized all the humans, including Heidi, had been shuffled inside. Only those with some sort of alien DNA remained outside.

"But you wouldn't change a damn thing, would you?"

"No," he admitted, and I closed my eyes.

"Those serums didn't even heal her." Daemon sounded astonished.

"Those serums gave her at least a few more months!" Luc yelled, and I saw a crack of lightning behind my closed eyes. "They gave her enough time to be healed. If you all hadn't gotten them, she would be dead."

A bitter taste filled the back of my mouth as I opened my eyes. I'd known that Luc had put Daemon and Kat in jeopardy in his attempts to save my life. Daemon had told me as much. Back then, I hadn't known how to really process that, and right now, all I could feel was horror. I hadn't known what they'd done to them. I had ideas, terrible ones, but I never really knew.

Zoe appeared to my side, curling her hand around my arm. She tugged on it, but I couldn't move. It really hit me like a hundred-ton truck that I was the reason they'd been captured by the Daedalus. It didn't matter if the Daedalus would've gotten to them eventually. It happened then because of me.

Because of Luc.

And now, it was me again that was going to cause Daemon and Kat more pain.

"And if she had died, she wouldn't have ended up in the hands of Jason Dasher, going through God knows what while being turned into something designed to kill us all," Daemon shot back. "You did that, Luc. Congrats."

I sucked in a sharp breath, and Luc simply moved too fast. His fist slammed into Daemon's jaw. The Luxen's head snapped back, but he didn't fall. Dawson shouted, but it was too late.

"Stop it!" I yelled.

They crashed into each other like freight trains. Each of them landed a blow before both went down, Daemon on top for half of a second before Luc flipped him, fisting Daemon's shirt.

"Do you think I don't know that?" He lifted Daemon's upper body as he leaned down. "Do you think I don't know exactly what I caused?"

"But was it worth it?" Daemon asked.

"How can you even ask that?" White light poured into Luc's veins as he cocked an arm back.

I'd seen enough.

Later, I would probably be a little amazed by how I hadn't hesitated and hadn't for one second feared injuring anyone, but in the moment, all I cared about was stopping this. Raising my hand, I summoned the Source and lifted Luc straight off Daemon. He landed standing, several feet away, his chest rising and falling with harsh breaths.

With the weight gone, Daemon popped to his feet. He spat a mouthful of blood and then he charged toward Luc—

"Enough!" I froze the Luxen, holding him in place. Daemon's head swung toward mine, his lips pulling back in a snarl. "Are you two done yet?"

"Nah, we aren't." Luc smiled. "I need to blacken his other eye."

"I'll tell you what I don't need." Daemon turned his head back to Luc. "I don't need my girlfriend fighting my battles."

"Oh, how about you go fu—"

"Shut up," I snapped. "Both of you, just shut up."

"I wished you hadn't stopped them." Hunter was leaning against the porch railing. "This was just getting good."

"You shut up, too," I said, to which the Arum laughed. "You both are acting like freaking little boys."

"Sounds about right," Luc said. "Because he hits like a little boy."

"I'm about to hit you like a little boy," I warned, and Luc looked at me, brows raised. "Honest to God, I don't care if you two beat each other half to death, but I don't want to listen to either of you bitch and moan about it later. You two are friends. I don't even know how, and frankly, I don't care enough at the moment to figure that out, but you both are acting pretty shitty."

"How am I acting shitty?" Daemon demanded. "And seriously, you need to un-freeze me or whatever you're doing."

"Are you going to try to hit Luc again?"

Daemon seemed to mull that over. "Probably."

Luc snorted.

"Then you can stay frozen, buddy," I told him. "Basically suggesting that I'd be better off dead is pretty shitty."

A muscle flexed along his jaw as his gaze met mine. A moment passed. "I didn't mean that."

"You didn't?"

"Sure sounded like that," Luc tossed out there.

"I know it did, but I didn't mean that," Daemon insisted. "Sometimes I say asshole-ish things. Just ask Kat. She can confirm that."

"I can confirm that," muttered Dawson.

I nodded, accepting his apology only because it wasn't the priority at the moment. "You should be more concerned about going to your wife and figuring out how to tell her the guy she thought she killed is still alive and is actually here, instead of fighting Luc and running off to kill some dude. Because do you really think she's not going to find out? Or she's not going to be super-pissed when she learns you knew and instead of going to her, you went to Blake?"

Daemon snapped his mouth shut.

"She has a point," Luc remarked.

"And you." My head whipped in his direction.

"*Moi?*" Luc placed his hand against his chest.

"Yes, you. I don't know everything this Blake did, but I know enough. You cannot expect Daemon to go along with anything that doesn't involve a bloody murder," I said. "And I don't even know how I feel about straight up killing someone who isn't attacking you at the moment."

"He deserves it," Daemon grumbled.

"He does," his brother agreed. "Like, more than you will ever know."

"And what? I'm supposed to wait until he stabs that knife in my back one last time?" Daemon asked. "For shits and giggles?"

"Why couldn't you have frozen his mouth?" Luc muttered.

I ignored that. "I'm not suggesting that. I'm just being honest that I'm not like, 'Yay, murder is cool!' But I am saying that whatever Blake knows about me and about the Daedalus is not worth causing Daemon or Kat or anyone else more pain."

"He could tell us what was done to you while you were at the Daedalus," Luc argued. "He could tell us about the other Trojans."

"We don't know exactly what he knows—"

"That's the point. Blake could be a gold mine."

"But will that be worth causing your friends even more pain?" I asked, hands shaking at my side. "Because I can tell you that for me, it won't be worth knowing that I'm that root cause."

"You're not the cause." Shock splashed across Luc's expression. He all but blinked out of existence, appearing directly in front of me. "You did not cause anyone pain."

I know. I met his stare. *But you did, because of me. You're not a monster who doesn't care for others. I know that, because I couldn't have fallen in love with you twice if you were.* His face paled, and it killed me to see that. "I will not be the reason again."

Luc looked away, jaw clenched, and then his gaze swung back to mine. "I didn't want them to get hurt. I never wanted any of them to be hurt, but I had to." Stepping back, he turned to Daemon, and when he spoke, his voice was hoarse. "She is the only thing in my entire life I ever needed—the only person I've ever loved, and she was slipping through my fingers. I was watching her die day after day, and there was nothing I could do. I couldn't heal her. No one could. And I was going to lose her. I *was* losing her. Can you even begin to imagine what that feels like?"

Daemon closed his eyes. "No," he said roughly. "I can't. I don't want to."

"I hope you never have to. I know I did that to her." His voice cracked. "But I would not let her die. I couldn't."

"You didn't cause what the Daedalus did to me." I stepped toward him, but Luc moved out of my reach. I swallowed hard. "You had no idea. You cannot blame yourself for that, and you can't blame him for that, either," I said to Daemon.

"That was low," Dawson murmured, arms folded. "Lower than I've seen you go."

"I know." Daemon let his head fall back. Sensing that Daemon might not hit Luc again, I freed him from my hold. He didn't seem to notice. "I shouldn't have said that."

Luc said nothing.

"So," Hunter asked. "Are we going to kill this guy or not?"

"No one is killing anyone," Cekiah announced, startling me. I'd been so caught up in everything, I hadn't even felt her or Zouhour's presence, but both were standing in the driveway. "Despite what Luc did to the man who shot Evie, that's not what we do here, no matter what."

Daemon turned to them. "He cannot be left alive."

"He does not die," Zouhour said. "At least not tonight."

The argument about Blake's future had moved inside, and thankfully no one was throwing punches at this point. Although it looked like Kat was ready to start breaking things. Dawson had retrieved her, and baby Adam had been placed with Beth.

Hunter looked half-asleep on the couch, and Grayson lurked in a corner, not really adding anything other than his presence to what was happening—which was pretty much the only value I was currently adding. The only reason why I was still here was because Luc was. Emery and Heidi had left with Zoe, and Georgie and his wife had already bid everyone good night, wanting nothing to do with this conversation.

Kat paced the living room, her husband's eyes tracking her every move. "I cannot believe this is a conversation that needs to even take place."

"You think discussing killing someone isn't necessary?" Zouhour challenged from where she stood behind Cekiah.

"Not when it has to do with Blake." She made another pass along the frayed throw rug. "You guys have no idea who you have locked up right now."

"He was forced to work for the Daedalus," Cekiah answered. "They held Chris as leverage. Yes, he told us."

"And did he tell you what he did when he worked for them?" Kat demanded.

"He told us that he gained your trust and then betrayed you, subsequently causing the death of a friend and then your capture."

Cekiah stared up at Kat. "He told us that you were made to fight him, and you were led to believe you'd killed him."

She stopped, hands curling into fists. "I know I killed him. I saw his body—" Her voice caught, and Daemon reached out, snagging her hand. He pulled her into his lap. A moment passed, and when she spoke, her voice was steady. "I saw what I did to him. No one bleeds that much and lives."

"Apparently, he did," Cekiah said gently. "Chris healed him, and he was moved to another location to recover. He says it took months."

Kat rubbed her lips together as she shook her head. "I can't believe this."

"He cannot be trusted. The fact that he's even here is already a huge risk to everyone." Daemon smoothed his hand up and down her back. "He didn't just accidentally end up here."

"We searched both of them. Neither of them have any trackers on them," Zouhour said. "The Luxen DNA would interfere with any of the bio trackers they've used in the past."

"Not only that, they've been vetted," Cekiah added.

"And look how that turned out last time," Hunter said.

That was a good point.

"Be that as it may, we still do not kill people," Zouhour retorted.

"All except Luc," commented Daemon.

I glanced over at him. He was surprisingly quiet, shockingly so.

"That was a onetime incident none of us plan on repeating." Cekiah tipped toward Kat and Daemon. "You just spoke about how you wanted what we were doing here to be different— building a world you wanted to raise your son in. I agreed with everything you said. How is killing him going to be a world any different from the one outside of here?"

"Because Blake should not be a part of that world or this world," Kat said.

The argument continued around us, running in a vicious circle until Zouhour said, "It sounds like he has done enough in his past to warrant a death sentence, but we're not just talking about him.

Chris has been held hostage more than half his life. He has done nothing to any of you. We kill Blake, we kill him. Do any of you want that on your conscience?"

"It's a weight I'm willing to carry," Daemon said.

Neither Zouhour nor Cekiah seemed to have expected that answer. I wouldn't have, either, if I hadn't seen Daemon's anger. I still had no idea how to feel about this. They were talking about capital punishment, but without a trial, and I'd always been conflicted by the idea of a life for a life. Part of me thought that some people had committed crimes so atrocious that they forfeited their right to life, but the other part? How did taking a life make things right? But then I thought of Jason Dasher. He didn't deserve to live.

This was all too real, though. Beforehand, I would never have to seriously consider the idea of being a part of the decision to end someone's life. Now, I was witness to it. I guessed that was a part of the normalcy of my old life that I missed.

Glancing over at Luc, I saw he was watching everyone, but I could tell he was barely following the conversation. I knew he had no problem with the whole eye-for-an-eye thing, but he also wanted Blake alive, at least for a time. It looked like he'd get what he wanted. Except right now, as I studied his profile, I couldn't tell what he wanted. His expression was so unreadable.

Luc?

His lashes lowered and lifted. *Yes?*

Are you okay?

There was a beat of silence, and I heard his response. *Yeah.*

Heaviness settled in my stomach as I stared at him. I didn't need to hear his voice or see his expression to know that he was lying. What Daemon had said—what I had said—was still tearing at him. I didn't need to read minds to know that.

You want to get out of here? I asked.

Actually, I do need some fresh air.

I started to rise, but his voice stopped me.

Alone. I'll meet you back at the house. Don't wait up.

And with that, he left the room without a single look back.

36

I did wait up.

How could I not?

Having left shortly after Luc, I waited for hours, but Luc didn't show. It had to be several hours past midnight before I finally caved to the exhausting worrying that had me pacing the length of the dark house.

At some point, I'd felt the bed shift and the warm weight of his arm settling over my waist. I'd started to turn to him.

"Go back to sleep," he'd whispered, his arm tightening around me. "We'll talk in the morning."

Half-asleep and surrounded by Luc's familiar scent, the smell of pine and fresh air, I'd done just as he'd requested. I wished I hadn't. Luc was gone by the time I woke, and it was now past lunch. I hadn't seen him since, but a box of hair color was on the dresser, the shade labeled *rich mocha*. I'd left it there, thinking now wasn't the time for a makeover.

Concern wasn't just a shadow in the back of my mind. It was a full-blown, tangible entity that made it difficult to pay attention to the conversation around me. I knew exactly what was keeping Luc away from me. It was what Daemon had said the day before.

It was what I had said to him.

Will that be worth causing your friends even more pain?

That was what I'd said to him, and I couldn't take those words back. I wouldn't. Those words were the truth. Luc's attempts to keep me alive had put others in harm's way. They had hurt people. They had led to death, and that was something he had to live with—we both had to live with—but I didn't hold it against him. I couldn't regret how far he had gone to keep me alive. Even without reading my mind, Luc had to know that. He had to know that if it had been him, I would've done the same. It didn't matter who I used to be or who I was now, I knew I would've done anything to save his life.

"Do you really think they're going to kill them?" Heidi asked from where she sat next to Emery. We were outside by the firepit. They had taken up the love seat, and Zoe was curled up in one of the other chairs.

Looking around, it was almost easy to pretend we were in any pretty garden and things were normal. Or at least the new normal. We were all together finally. Only we were missing James, and they were discussing whether or not Blake would be executed.

So, like I said, *almost* easy.

"I don't know how they could let him live," Emery answered as she toyed with a strand of Heidi's hair. "Even if he's turned over a new leaf, he can't be trusted, and because of that, it's not like he can just be exiled or whatever."

"Because what if he's still working for the Daedalus?" Zoe asked, her arms looped around her knees. "He now knows too much."

Emery nodded. "Like what this zone is and *who* is here. The moment they learn this is where Daemon and Archer are? Kat? Dee? They're going to take this place out."

"Hell, Daemon and Archer? They hear that Luc and their missing Trojan are chilling here, we're going to be knee deep in Daedalus officers," Zoe said. "They'd already know if Evie hadn't stopped Sarah, and I can't help but think the entire zone is on borrowed time right now."

My gaze shot to her. There was something about the way she said that that made me think she was talking about more than just Blake. "What do you mean?"

Zoe nibbled on her lower lip as she shook her head.

"What?" I persisted.

"I don't know. It's just that I can't be the only person who's been thinking that Sarah had inside help. Even if the contacts out there, the ones at the resource centers, don't know where the packages are being moved to, it feels mighty convenient that Sarah found her way here."

I sank into the chair. "No. I don't think you're the only one."

"But if they knew what was going on in the zone, you don't think they'd be all over this place?" Emery asked.

"That's what I can't figure out. If they do know, why haven't they invaded?" Zoe shrugged. "Which means I'm probably just being super-paranoid."

"I don't think you can be too paranoid," I said, pushing back a chunk of hair blown into my face by the wind.

"But back to Blake?" Emery glanced at her girlfriend. "Things aren't looking good for him."

"I don't know about that," Zoe said, unfurling her legs. "Cekiah and Zouhour are not about straight up killing people, especially when it leads to the death of innocent Luxen."

"Presumably innocent Luxen," corrected Emery. "We really don't know the truth. Just bits and pieces of the story they want told."

And man, that was a truth that couldn't be argued against.

"I just don't know how I feel about that," Heidi admitted. "I mean, I get that this Blake guy did terrible things and he can't be trusted, but what if he's been, I don't know, reformed? Or what if he really was doing everything to keep his friend alive?" She looked around our small, incomplete circle. "We all would do anything to keep our loved ones safe. I'm here because of that. Not that I don't want to be with Emery, but I left my family so they'd be safe. They're now stuck in a city that's closed off to the entire world. I have no idea how they're doing or if they're even—" Her breath caught, and my chest squeezed. "I don't know if they're even okay. I want to reach out to them, but I know it wouldn't just jeopardize us; it would put them at risk if the Daedalus thought they could use them to get to us."

Emery dropped the piece of hair she'd been playing with and picked up Heidi's hand, her somber gaze latched to her face.

"The point I'm trying to make is that any of us, including probably half of everyone here, would do some terrible shit to save the ones they love." Heidi's eyes glittered with unshed tears. "We're going to punish others for doing what they needed to do to keep someone else alive?"

"What would you do if he did something that ended with Emery being tortured?" Zoe asked.

"I'd want him dead," Heidi said, causing Zoe to throw her hands up. "But I hope I'd have enough empathy left in me to try to understand why he did what he did if something like that happened."

"I wouldn't have that in me," Emery admitted, squeezing Heidi's hand. "I can't even lie. I'm not as good as you."

"I don't think it has anything to do with being good or not, because you are good," Heidi said, pulling their joined hands into her lap. "I'm just sensitive."

Zoe snorted.

Heidi ignored that. "Look, I'm against the death penalty. Can any of you be surprised by my confliction?"

"What about you?" Zoe looked over at me. "What do you think?"

I opened my mouth and then closed it. What did I think? There wasn't an easy answer. "I don't know, to be honest."

"Cop out," Zoe muttered.

"No. I'm serious." I leaned forward in my chair. "Part of me thinks he should be, I don't know, humanely put down. I have a feeling we only know half of what he's done, and what we do know is terrible enough. No one here is going to trust him, so it's not like he can be let out to roam, and we can't release him back into the wild."

"But?" Heidi said.

I sighed. "But if Blake dies, then so does Chris, and if Blake did do these things to keep Chris alive, then he was only doing what he needed to. The same thing any of us would do."

Zoe eyed me. "I feel like there's another *but* coming."

"There is." Feeling the prickly sensation of incoming Luxen, I glanced around as I lowered my voice, not knowing if Daemon was in the backyard next door. "But if he'd caused what happened to Kat to Luc or any of you, I'd want him dead. I just don't know how to feel about this."

Heidi nodded as she sat back, her gaze dropping to where she held Emery's hand. "Things used to be so much easier."

Understatement of the year right there.

Movement snagged my attention, and I glanced back at the house. Grayson stood in the narrow pathway that led to the front yard. My heart skipped a beat.

"Excuse me," I murmured, jumping to my feet. I hurried over to him. "Do you know where Luc is?"

His cool gaze flicked across my face before settling an inch above my head. "He's in the library. I thought you'd like to know that he's getting ready to talk to Blake."

I couldn't believe Luc was going to try to talk to Blake without me. I also couldn't believe that Grayson was telling me this.

Stomach twisting, I started to take off in a dead run but managed to stop myself. I turned back to the girls. "I have to go."

Curiosity marked their expressions, but I faced Grayson. "Thank you."

Grayson lowered his gaze, and I don't know why I did what I did next, but I touched him. I reached out and took ahold of his hand. His skin was warm, which was at such odds with everything else about him. I squeezed it. That was all I did, but his entire body seemed to jolt as if I'd shocked him. His eyes widened as his entire body stiffened.

"Sit with them. Talk to them," I said, letting go of his hand before he passed out. "I know they'd like that."

Icy-blue eyes met mine. "You sure about that?"

Well . . .

"I'm sure Emery would love to talk to you," I said, and then I grinned.

Only the corners of his lips curved up, but it was *something*. "You'd better hurry."

I found Luc less than two minutes later, having run as fast as I could to the old library. He'd been on the first floor, speaking to Cekiah as I all but burst through the front doors.

"Yes, I promise I'm only going to talk to him," Luc was saying as I skidded to a halt, a sheet of hair falling across half of my face.

He glanced over at me, an eyebrow arched as I shoved the hair back from my face.

Our gazes connected, and for one heart-stopping moment, I thought he was going to ignore me. That he'd pretend that I wasn't there, and I didn't know what I'd do. Actually, I did. I would be pissed. I'd probably make a scene, and then I'd go hide and cry like a mature person.

"Correction." He turned back to Cekiah. "*We* will not hurt a single hair on Blake's head. We just want to talk to him."

A rough breath punched out of my lungs.

Cekiah glanced at me, lips pursed. What felt like a whole minute passed before she said, "You guys have half an hour. That's it. You know where to find him."

I watched Cekiah walk back through open double doors that led to the main part of the library. From where I stood, I could see rows of books. Slowly, I shifted my gaze to Luc. He looked the same as he had when I'd seen him walk up the driveway, the same as he'd been before he'd left. The intriguing and stunning lines and planes of his face were all familiar, as was the breadth of his shoulders and the lean tautness of his body. Those eyes were still shockingly beautiful, a shade so bright that it looked like jewels has been placed there.

Something was different, though, as he stared back at me.

"I'm guessing someone alerted you to what I was doing."

"I'll never tell," I tried to tease, but it fell as flat as a board in the space between us. I wanted to talk to him about what I knew was bothering him, but now was not the time. "We didn't talk this morning like you'd said we would."

Luc said nothing.

I took a shallow breath. "You're going to talk to Blake."

He nodded.

"Did you think that maybe I would want to be here?" I asked, fully realizing that my voice was nowhere near as level as I wanted it to sound.

"I did."

My brows lifted. "And?"

"And I figured since God only knows what Blake is going to say, I decided it probably wasn't a good idea for you to be there."

Irritation rose. "Well, good thing you don't get to make decisions for me."

An emotion flickered across his features, gone too fast for me to track what it was. His expression smoothed out. "Come on."

Ignoring the tickle of unease and the ravaging flood of uncertainty, I followed him down the hall and toward the windowless door situated at the end, tucked beside an alcove that featured a glass case I imagined once showcased books. The hallway was dark and cramped, and even my new special alien eyes couldn't make out a step from the darkness, but that didn't last long. The glow of the Source spilled out around Luc's hand, lighting the way. He started down the steps.

Telling myself yet again that now wasn't the time to talk to him, I opened my mouth and blurted out, "Are you okay?"

"Yes," came his answer, and I knew it was lie.

"You sure?" I asked as we rounded the corner. "I'm worried."

He was quiet for several moments, stopping when he reached the next landing. He faced me, the glow softening his features. "If you're going to come in here and talk to Blake, you can't be worried about me. I'll know when he's lying, but you won't, and I might not be able to say anything before the damage is done. And then there is the truth," he said. "You have to be present in what we're doing. You understand?"

My heart turned over, but I nodded. "I do."

His gaze searched mine, and then I sent him the message again. *I do.*

"Okay." Luc turned, and the door creaked open.

Lanterns lined the walls of the basement, casting enough light that we didn't need to use Luc's hand like a flashlight. We walked past packed goods, boxed and labeled. I wasn't paying attention to any of it as the door at the end of the room opened into a space lit the same. I wasn't thinking of anything, because there was a cell. There were several of them, and all of them glimmered in the low light like they'd been doused with glitter.

"Onyx," Luc explained. "The bars are coated with onyx and diamonds to prevent Luxen from escaping."

"How did they make them?"

"I believe the bars already existed. They were moved here by humans," he said, and I couldn't help but think of who those bars had held at one time. But I needed to be focused on who the bars held now.

Blake was in the center cell, alone. He was sitting on a bed, one leg curled up, the other stretched out and resting on the floor. I looked around, seeing that the other cells were empty.

Chris is being held in the other room, Luc's voice filtered through my thoughts. *They didn't want them together.*

That made sense.

Blake lifted his head as we approached. A half-eaten sandwich sat on a plate beside the bed, next to a bottle of water. He didn't smile or show any emotion. "I've been waiting for you two."

37

Sorry to keep you waiting." Luc stopped about a foot from the bars. He didn't sound sorry at all.

Blake sensed that, because he smirked. "I see you haven't changed at all."

"I think if you have five seconds outside the cell, you'll find that even more people haven't changed," Luc replied.

The smirk faded. "I guess Daemon knows I'm here."

"He does."

He focused on the ceiling. That, too, shimmered with chips of onyx. "And Kat?"

"If I were you, I wouldn't even think her name, let alone say it."

"Yeah." He exhaled heavily. "They want me dead."

"Of course they do," Luc answered.

"But that's not why you're here." He lowered his gaze.

"Nope," Luc said as I stepped forward. "The story is that you're alive because Chris healed you."

"I did die. More than once. Kat kicked my ass, and I've got the scars to prove it." He gestured to his face. "They don't stop there. My whole body is covered in them."

"Am I supposed to feel sorry for you? If so, spoiler alert, I don't."

"I don't expect you to feel sorry," he answered. "Chris healed me. Brought me back, and then I was moved to another location, and if you want to know why they let her think I was dead, I have no idea."

"How did Chris heal you if you died?" I asked. "Wouldn't that have meant he would've died?"

Blake's gaze slid to me. "Good catch, but Luxen don't always die immediately when the hybrid they mutated dies. Some linger for a couple of minutes. Luckily—or unluckily—Chris lingered, but it's not like he didn't have help. The Daedalus kept restarting my heart and pumping more blood into me."

I glanced at Luc.

"He's telling the truth," Luc said.

"Why would they keep you alive?" I asked. "From what I can remember about the Daedalus, they don't tolerate failure, and if Kat beat you, you failed."

"They thought I was still useful," he said.

"And were you?" Luc asked.

"It took weeks for me to fully heal, and I spent most of the war being held, along with Chris, at Raven Rock."

"Raven Rock?" I frowned.

"A military base in Pennsylvania outfitted with all the things necessary to survive a nuclear war," Luc explained. "I razed that base to the ground." He said it as if he were talking about mowing the grass.

"That's what I heard, but we were moved out by then."

Luc's shoulders suddenly tensed. "You were moved to Fort Detrick."

My lips parted on a shaky inhale, and I knew. I didn't even have to ask, but I did. "That's where you saw me."

"I saw you before," Blake reminded me. "At the club. You were dancing."

"I should've killed you then," Luc snarled, and the vicious truthfulness in his words sent a shiver down my spine.

"You should've, but you needed me." Blake folded his arms over his chest. "I saw you again at the fort."

My heart started thumping. "I was trained at Fort Detrick? The whole time?"

Blake nodded. "In the part that's far underground, beyond their level-four biohazard. You didn't know about that place, did you, Luc?"

Luc didn't have to answer. He hadn't known that I had been there.

"What can you tell me about what I did there?" I asked.

"You did what they wanted you to do." He shifted, straightening out his bent leg. "Eventually."

"Cut the dramatics out, Blake. You know I have very little patience," warned Luc. "That also hasn't changed over the years."

His jaw worked. "You weren't down with the program when I first saw you."

"I fought back?" I asked.

"You did."

Hearing that made me want to smile. I knew that sounded insane, but the satisfaction learning I hadn't just gone along with what the Daedalus wanted was enormous.

"That didn't last forever," Blake added.

Oh. A little of the satisfaction deflated.

"Are you sure you want to know?" he asked.

Luc looked to me, and I could read what he'd prefer in his eyes. If he had his way, I wouldn't be down here. I wouldn't hear any of this. But I could handle whatever Blake told me.

"I want to know."

Blake shook his head as he let out a heavy sigh. "You pushed back as much as you could, refusing to learn how to fight, and when they forced you, you would refuse to use what they taught you against others." His eyes closed. "But they always found a way to get what they wanted. I didn't see you all the time, but when I did see you, you looked like you'd lost a fight with a heavyweight boxer."

Luc stretched his neck to the left side and then slowly to the right.

"They beat me until I caved?" I asked, oddly unaffected by the knowledge. Maybe it was because I wasn't all that surprised.

"Food and sleep deprivation. I know they used that, because they used that whenever they weren't getting their way. I also know they did that because the one time I saw you, you looked like you hadn't slept in about a week. That was in the beginning. I imagine they used other methods." He sounded weary and weighed down. "They could get creative."

I swallowed, not even daring a look in Luc's direction. "And then what?"

Blake looked at Luc before he said, "They broke you."

A charge of energy caused the air to thicken. The gas lamps flickered, and Blake unfolded his arms.

"Luc." I reached over, placing my hand on his lower back. *It's okay. I'm still here. They didn't break me.*

It's not okay. It will never be okay. Another ripple of energy rolled through, and then his chest rose with a deep breath.

Once I was sure Luc wasn't going to lose his mind, I asked, "So, I became a mindless minion?"

A grimace appeared. "I don't think you ever completely became a minion. You were different from the others."

Breath catching, I lowered my hand. "What do you mean?"

He scooted to the edge of the bed. "I wasn't around you all the time. It was sporadic, but you had a sense of awareness that the others never had. You tracked things differently, as if you were really seeing them. You thought before you acted, even when you did what they wanted."

"They? Do you mean Jason Dasher?"

"Jason and the others that worked with you all. He had me in the pen once with one of you." Blake sent Luc a quick glance. "I never fought her. I swear."

Luc gave him a chin lift I guessed signaled that he believed him.

"What do you mean by *pen*?"

"It was a room where they'd pit you guys against one another—"

"White walls with a drain in the center?"

He nodded. "Made cleanup easier for them to just hose the room down afterward."

Nausea rose as the image of blood circling the drain formed. I pushed past it. "I killed others like me?" When he didn't speak, I stepped forward. "I want to know."

"If I could forget one-tenth of what I've done, I'd gladly give it up. Why would you want to know?"

"I'm not you."

"No, I guess not." His chin rose a notch. "Yes. You killed others like you. You killed others not like you."

Shock splashed through me. "Others not like me?"

"Luxen. Hybrid. An Origin or two," he said, and the bile was in my throat. "Humans—"

"Okay," Luc cut in. "They made sure she could use her abilities to fight and to kill. Got it."

I pressed my hand to my stomach.

"I saw you afterward once. You were with him. You didn't look proud of yourself. Not like the others when they pleased their maker."

That was a relief. I guessed.

"You were with Dasher a lot," Blake said. "He treated you differently from the others. Brought you food in from the outside. Let you watch television. Had you sit with him while he worked."

That reminded me of Luc's relationship with Nancy. I think Luc was thinking the same, because his jaw was so hard it was no small wonder that he hadn't broken a molar.

"I'd seen them do that with hybrids or Origins throughout my time with them. Used to piss the others off." Blake lifted his brows. "Didn't seem to even faze the Trojans, though. Like jealousy was completely programmed out of them, which is strange as hell since they were competitive."

"Did you and I talk?" I asked, and when he nodded, I wanted to know what I would've said, how I would've acted.

"It was brief. Dasher was talking to my new handler, and he had you in his office. They weren't really paying attention to us. You looked at me and told me that you remembered me."

"And what did you say?" Luc asked.

"I asked about you." Blake looked at him. "I couldn't figure out how they got her. I didn't know she'd been sick. I heard that through the grapevine later. I knew they didn't have you. None of them would've been talking about anything else for days if that were the case."

Some of the old Luc snuck through then, because he smirked, and God, I had never been so relieved to see that.

"You told me that Luc was free," Blake said, and a fine shudder rolled through Luc. "And then you told me . . ." A grin cracked his lips, and he laughed lightly. "That I was on your list."

"My list?"

"Of people you planned to kill."

Luc chuckled, but all I could do was stare. "And how did you respond to that?"

The small smile faded. "I think I said you'd have to get in line."

"It is a pretty long line," I muttered, and I thought I felt a wave of amusement shimmer through my thoughts. "Did Dasher know I was different?"

"I don't see how he couldn't have. It was obvious to me."

"And that didn't upset him?"

"Didn't seem like it did." Blake rose slowly. "I kept thinking, even after you seemed to have disappeared from the fort, why in the hell did they have you? Why would they save you and then train you? It had to have something to do with you." He focused on Luc. "But that didn't make sense, either. You may have been big shit to them, but man, if you've seen the Trojans in action—and I mean in *real* action—you'd know they'd have no need for you. So why?"

"They just can't quit me," Luc replied, sounding bored.

Another faint smile appeared on Blake's face, but it was brittle, as if he hadn't smiled a lot.

"That's a good question," I said. "And I'm guessing you don't know."

He stopped in front of the bars. "All I know is that it can't be something good." His eyes met mine. "And that they have to have some sort of plan that involves both of you."

Eaton had suggested as much, but it still opened up a festering wound of unease.

"Do you know if Dasher was mutated?" asked Luc.

The question seemed to surprise Blake. "No. Why?"

"Sylvia shot him in the chest. Saw it with my own eyes. She would've had to heal him," Luc answered.

"I don't think he was. At least not in a way I could tell," he answered.

"Sylvia? Did you ever see her? See her with me?"

"A few times. When you were with Dasher in his office. She would come down."

I folded my arms under my chest, fighting not to feel anything in regard to that. "When was the last time you saw me?"

"I don't know exactly when, but I never saw you again after we spoke," he said. "I'd only learned bits and pieces about the Poseidon Project, but I figured you'd become whatever they wanted you to be. I guess that turned out to be Jason Dasher's daughter. They didn't tell me anything about you. They never asked if I knew who you were, and even after you left, I knew better than to ask questions."

"Are they still using the facilities under the fort?" Luc asked.

"I was able to escape about a year later, and they were then. I imagine they still are."

I opened my mouth and then closed it as I squeezed my eyes shut for a heartbeat before reopening them. If that was true, then my mom had to be still working for the Daedalus when she died. How could she not have if those facilities were still active under her feet? I thought about how she'd warned me the night she'd died and I'd run. How else would she know they were coming if she still didn't have something to do with them?

"Good to know," Luc murmured. "How did you escape?"

"We were being moved to a new location. I don't know where. They didn't tell us, but Chris and I were being moved together. It was our only chance. I don't think either of us thought we would succeed, but we were ready for the consequences if we failed."

"Death?" I said.

"Certain death," he confirmed. "But we were on the interstate, somewhere in Ohio, when they stopped to get gas, and then we ran. We've been running ever since. It was by some fluke that Chris met a Luxen who introduced him to one of the resource centers. If not, we'd still be running."

"And you'd be in a less precarious position," Luc finished for him. "Anything else of interest you want to share?"

"If I knew more, I'd tell you."

"Then I guess this conversation is over."

"Wait," Blake called out before Luc or I could turn. "I need your help."

"I'm sure you need a lot of things, Blake."

"I need to get out of here. If I don't, Chris is going to die, and I'm telling you, he's been innocent in all of this. You can read my mind and see that is true."

"I can, but I don't see how you think I can help."

"You know exactly how you can help." Blake gripped the bars, wincing as the onyx-and-diamond mixture began to work at the alien DNA in him. "If you don't help me escape, they'll kill me. That will kill Chris. He doesn't deserve it. The blood is on my hands."

"That blood can't be washed off, Blake. Ever."

"You of all people know I realize that." Blake still held on to the bars, the scars lining his face beginning to stand out more. "If I could somehow break this bond that ties Chris's life to mine, I would. God, I would've done it years ago, but I can't, and he doesn't deserve to die, Luc. He doesn't."

Heart twisting with unwanted sympathy, I looked to Luc.

"Please," Blake begged. "You're not helping me. You're helping Chris. Please. Daemon is going to kill me. You know he will."

"Can you blame him?" Luc asked.

"Hell no. I don't blame him at all. If it were just me, I'd welcome it. God, I would. You have no idea what kind of nightmares I have. You escaped, Luc. I didn't. But if you hadn't, I'm what you would've become."

I stiffened.

"I would've never become you."

"You sure about that?" Blake nodded at me.

Luc stepped forward, pressing his hands to the bars above Blake's. The hybrid jerked his hands off.

Blake backed away. His gaze darted to mine. "Please—"

"Don't." Luc moved, blocking me from Blake's view. "Don't ask that of her. You do, and your life ends here, right now. You know I'll do it."

There was silence and then, "You would."

Luc said nothing.

"I'll do anything. Anything," Blake whispered. "Think of all the favors I could owe you—"

"I can't help you," Luc said.

"Can't or won't?"

"Won't," Luc answered, and I felt like crying.

I didn't want Luc to help Blake. I didn't want Kat and Daemon to wonder where Blake was, nor did I want the community to live in fear that Blake would betray them—because I knew in my heart, he would if he were ever captured—but this was sad. It was a fucking tragedy, and I hated the Daedalus even more for what they had turned this man into—for putting all the nails in his coffin years ago. If Blake were killed and Chris did die, it may be by Daemon's hand, but it was the Daedalus that caused it.

I wanted to close my eyes, but I didn't. Blake came back into view, only because he was backing up. He sat down on the bed and tipped his head back against the exposed brick. His eyes closed, and he returned to waiting for what was surely coming his way.

Death.

And then, without saying a word, Luc took my hand and we walked out.

Luc let go of my hand the moment we reached the main level. That stung, because it felt odd and wrong, as did the fact neither of us had said a word.

"We need to talk," I said the moment we were out on the sidewalk, far enough away to prevent anyone from overhearing us. "Not about Blake—"

"I know." Hands in the pockets of his jeans, he turned to me. "We do need to talk."

The nauseous feeling from before returned. I expected him to say something stupid or silly. I didn't expect him to agree, and instinct screamed out warnings that caused a hundred knots to crowd my insides. "What Daemon said about—"

"How much pain I've caused people who deserved so much better than that?" he cut in, and it felt like a knife sliced open my chest. "What he said was true. What you said was true. You're right. They don't need to be caused any more pain, but at the end of the day, what you think or what Daemon wanted, didn't matter. Blake's alive, anyway. We got to talk to him. I got what I wanted."

And we didn't learn much beyond new nightmare fodder. "You did what you needed to do to keep me alive. People got hurt. People died." I took a step toward him, and he visibly tensed. "I wish they hadn't. I know you wished they hadn't, either, but I was dying, and you kept me alive. I can't hold that against you."

Some of the coolness seeped out of his crystalized gaze, and a spark of relief eased the knots. "I know, Evie. I didn't think for one second that you held any of that against me."

My gaze searched his. "I would do the same if it was you."

"Would you, though?"

I jerked back, stunned. "How can you even ask that?"

He looked away. "You wouldn't have done the things I've done. You wouldn't have hurt people. You're good, Evie."

Anger crashed into the agony his words were reaping. I wanted to hug him. I wanted to take him in my arms and show him just how grateful I was that he felt the kind of love that ensured my survival. And I also wanted to strangle him—strangle with love, of course, because he didn't know me as well as he thought he did.

"We need to go somewhere private."

One eyebrow raised as he turned his head back to me. "Peaches, I don't think what you have in mind is appropriate at the moment."

My eyes narrowed. "You wish that's what I had in mind, but you're not going to get that lucky."

"Well, now I'm really curious."

"We need to go somewhere quiet, because I'm about to yell at you, and we don't need half this community witnessing your embarrassment."

Luc's eyes widened as he stared at me in silence for several moments. "You sounded so much like her right then. Like Nadia."

"That's because I am her!" I shouted, sending a lone bird above me into the sky.

He continued to stare at me.

"Jesus," I snapped, storming forward. I grabbed his hand and started walking.

"Evie—"

"Nope," I cut him off. "Not until we're home or somewhere private."

"I was just—"

"Going to actually shut up?" I suggested. "Wow. Thank you."

Luc's answering chuckle set off every one of my nerves, because I didn't think I'd ever heard him so amused.

"What's funny?" I demanded, and when he didn't respond, I looked over at him as we crossed the intersection. "What?"

He blinked. "Am I allowed to speak now?"

I exhaled out of my nose. "You know what? I don't care about what you find so funny. No, you can't talk."

Luc's lips twitched as if he were fighting a smile or another laugh, but he wisely managed to fight it and to stay quiet the whole entire way back to the house. The moment the door closed behind us, I let go of his hand and swung around to face him.

"Are you going to yell at me now?" he asked. "Not too loudly, though. Daemon and Kat might hear us."

"If you say one more dumb thing, the entire world is going to hear us," I warned, and as much as it annoyed me, I also loved that glimmer I saw in his eyes. "I thought you knew me. I thought you knew me better than I knew myself. It sure seems like that most days, but I was wrong."

His brows bunched together. "I do know you."

"You know what I used to be like. Actually, I don't think you even knew me as well as you think you did then," I said. "There's no way you can if you really think that I wouldn't have done exactly what you did if our positions were switched."

"Evie," he began. "You wouldn't—"

"I would put people in harm's way. I would do it, and I'd hate it, but it wouldn't stop me if that meant making sure you were okay," I said. "And I have a feeling even before my memories were taken from me, I would've done it then. Does that make what you did right? What I would do if your life were in jeopardy? No. What you did and what I would do will never be right, but it is what it is. It's not like you don't care, Luc."

"See, that's where you don't know me as well as you think you do," he shot back. "I didn't care enough about others to not set things in motion that led to Kat being tortured and Paris being killed. I didn't care enough to give you back your phone and let you be. The moment I decided I couldn't—that I wouldn't—walk away from you again, everything that has happened since then has happened because of that."

I gaped at him. "You have no idea what would've happened if you hadn't made that decision."

"I know Kent would still be alive. Or in the very least, his friends wouldn't have had to watch him die like that. I know that Clyde would've lived to see another day, because my head would've been in the game and I would've gotten him and Chas out before we were raided," he argued. "There are more examples, but most importantly, you would never know the amount of blood that drips from my hands from what I've done to ensure that you're standing here, right in front of me."

My breath stuttered. "You do realize all of what you just said also puts all that death, all that blood, on me?"

"No. It doesn't. It never has touched you, because you never made those choices. I did."

"That's not true!" I took a deep breath. "You didn't set out to hurt them, or did you?"

"That doesn't change that it happened. It doesn't change that there has to be something wrong with me," he spat out, stunning me. "Do you know what I did all last night? All this morning? I walked and walked, trying to understand what they did to me to make me this way. To make me not care about anyone else—to make it okay for me to do the things I've done. Things that have hurt people. Things that have gotten people killed," he said, his hands opening. "Because there are more moments than not where I don't even feel remotely human. That if not for what I feel for you, I would be a monster. But I am one." He drew back a step, his eyes glittering. "I have to be one, because I sleep damn good at night, Evie. Those wounds I've inflicted and the deaths I've caused weigh on me, but they haven't changed me. I'd do it all over again. I would."

Oh my God.

Cracks spread across my heart; the tears crowding my eyes not for me but for him. How could he think any of this about himself?

The worst part was this wasn't something that just sprang up overnight. What Daemon had said had only pulled the trigger on the loaded gun that had always been there.

Shame burned my skin as I eased my fingers open. He was self-ish? Maybe he was, but so was I, and my selfishness was rooted in self-preservation while his stemmed from my preservation. My own immaturity was a shock to my system, and I was well aware of how immature I could be at any given moment, but this was beyond that. It was as if I'd dipped my head under scalding water.

This was the cause of those quiet moments when he looked as if he were caught in some kind of personal nightmare he couldn't wake from. This was what he couldn't hide in his eyes even if his features became an unreadable mask. I'd been so wrapped up in my own problems, my own baggage, I didn't take the time to really check out his, because if I had, I would've seen this.

Suddenly, I thought I really understood what Grayson had meant when he'd said Luc couldn't always be unstoppable. I'd thought he'd meant physically, but he was talking about something far more important. I just hadn't seen it. Grayson had, though.

Hindsight had such perfect vision, didn't it?

"I'm sorry," I whispered.

"You're sorry?" He shook his head in disbelief. "What do you have to apologize for?"

"Everything?"

He jerked as if someone had landed a blow, and my body was moving without me even realizing it. I went to him, and when he reared back, moved to put space between us, I wouldn't allow it. I placed my hands on his cheeks, stopping him. I didn't use the Source. I didn't need to. Luc always stopped for me.

I stared up into his eyes as I flattened my palms against his cheeks. "There is nothing wrong with you."

His pupils shone like bright stars. "Evie——"

"You have done monstrous things, but so has Daemon. So has his brother and half the people we know. So have I." Dampness clung to my lashes. I stepped into him, until the heat of his body beat against mine. "You do care. I've seen the weight you carry, but I should've *really* seen it."

Luc trembled as his hands folded around my wrists. He could do anything with his strength. Push me away. Hold me back. But the way he held my wrists felt as if he were holding me there. "I want to believe you. You have no idea." His voice was thick with raw emotion. "But sometimes I think I was more of a success than Nancy Husher ever realized."

"No." I leaned into him, feeling him shudder. "If that were true, you couldn't love me like you do. And that's why you did what you needed to do. Not because of the Daedalus or because something is wrong with you but because I was the only thing you ever needed in your whole life."

Another shudder rocked him as he lowered his head to mine. The tips of my fingers were wet from the tears, but not mine.

They were his.

"You're a gift. You've always been the most precious gift life has ever handed me. Can I ever be worthy of that?" he whispered. "Of you?"

Tears had hit my cheeks now, and they were mine. "You already are, Luc. You've always been. We just all have a little bit of a monster inside of us. How could we not when we love someone like we do?"

"I love you, Evie. I fell in love with you within the first week I met you. I loved you before I even knew what that meant, and I loved you even when you were gone, and I loved you when you became someone else," he said—pleaded, really. "And I fell even more in love with you when you walked through the doors of Foretoken. I've never stopped loving you. I never will."

"I love you." I closed my eyes, losing a breath and then two. "And every part of my heart and my soul belongs to you, Luc. You are a gift."

I don't know who made the first move, who kissed who, but our lips met, and everything—*everything*—was a heated, blinding rush that carried that edge of desperation that was always there. I'd tasted it in his kisses before, felt it in how he held me close at night. I tasted and felt them now as my back hit the door. It fed the greedy way our hands pushed and tore at clothing, the way his hands gripped my hips and lifted me. It was behind the near frenzied way his mouth moved against mine. I'd thought that it was from how close he'd come to losing me before, and I was sure that was a part of it, but I knew now it was also those scars hidden so deep within him.

It wasn't the only thing that drove us to the floor and to what felt like the brink of death. It was the raw power of what we felt for each other. It was love, the kind that could level entire civilizations, the kind that could rebuild them. Love was the thunder in our hearts, the lightning in our veins, and it was what kept us together where we landed, even after our skin had begun to cool and our breaths had slowed.

We lay there, his head tucked under mine as I stared at the ceiling, smoothing my hand over and through his hair. I made myself a vow, and I hoped he heard it. I hoped he knew how deep it ran.

What I told him hadn't healed the wounds that were in his soul. What we'd just done wasn't a magic fix, either, but I now saw the wounds that were there, and I would do everything to heal them.

I'd do anything.

38

It was sometime later that I'd told Luc about Nate and what I'd seen when I'd followed him into the city. I wasn't at all surprised when he'd sat up and leaned over me, his brows raised as he demanded to know if he'd heard me correctly. I had to repeat that yes, I'd gone with Nate into the city. As I'd expected, he wasn't thrilled, and I didn't think hearing that Grayson had followed me had helped. I had a feeling Grayson was going to have to explain why he hadn't stopped me, and I hoped for his sake he had a better answer than what he'd given me.

When Luc finally was done lecturing me on being safe, he asked, "You think that guy—what was his name?"

"Morton."

"You think he's abusing those kids or something? Because if so, how do we sit and wait for them to ask for help?"

Right there.

Right there proved Luc cared more than he realized. "Nate said he doesn't, so it's just my suspicion, but either way, he's most likely using those kids to scavenge food and supplies, and God only knows how dangerous that is."

Luc settled beside me. "We're going to have to do something."

I looked over at him. "I know. I just hope they come to us. If we force them, I think it will confirm their fears. Not only that, if we go there, they'll run."

"I have a feeling those kids know where to hide."

I nodded. "Do you think the others will be okay with taking them in?"

"Cekiah and the others would gladly take them in," Luc said. "I don't doubt that for a moment."

That was a relief to hear, and I hoped it was the case. We stayed there for a little while longer, but the warmth and silence didn't last long. Dee and Archer returned later that afternoon, having already known about Blake. Somehow Daemon had gotten a message to them. Had he used a carrier pigeon or something?

Almost everyone was at the old library, piled into the main room. Surrounded by stacks of books, the council who refused to call themselves a council took up one of the long conference-style tables. Luc and I sat side by side on one of the smaller tables, our legs dangling as we listened as one hour turned into two hours of them arguing about what to do with Blake and Chris.

Not entirely surprisingly, Dee wanted him dead. No ifs, ands, or buts about it. And also not entirely surprisingly, more than half of the unofficial but totally official council was stuck on the moral wrongness of it all.

I had a headache.

Okay, I didn't have a real headache, but I had an imaginary one that felt as painful as any I'd ever had.

"We should have a trial," someone suggested.

"Are you guys serious?" Dee exclaimed, throwing up her hands. Archer had stepped outside at some point, and I had no idea where or why, but I was so envious of him.

So envious.

"A trial?" Daemon scoffed. "And who is the judge?"

"Who would be the jury of his peers?" Zouhour asked. "Do we need to find a handful of people who've been in his situation before? A trial seems pointless."

"We have a jury of his peers." Cekiah gestured at those sitting at the table. "There are people right here who have been under the control of the Daedalus before. Who could possibly—"

"If you think for one second any of us can sympathize with him, you're out of your mind," Kat said. "And if you think we're going to stay here while he's here? Not going to happen."

"We don't want anyone to feel unsafe," Quinn, the older Luxen male, said. "And we understand your history."

Vibrant, enraged green eyes flicked to the Luxen. "I don't think you do."

Quinn leaned forward. "We have to take Chris into consideration. I've spoken to him. He's been nothing more than a hostage."

Slowly, I looked over at Luc. A moment later, two purple eyes met mine. I sighed. One side of his lips kicked up.

I can't take much more of this, I told him.

They just keep talking in circles, he agreed, glancing back to where Daemon looked like he was seconds away from flipping a table. At least that would be something different. *Why don't you head out of here? No reason for you to be in here.*

If I go, you go.

The other side of his lips curved up as he leaned over, kissing my lips. *I would love nothing more. Maybe we could have a repeat of this afternoon.* A pause as he leaned back. *Not the deep, dark part. But what came after. I think I got rug burns on my back.*

My face flamed with heat. "Nuh-uh," I gasped.

Cekiah looked over at us with a slight pinch to her face.

Running his hand over his mouth, he muffled his laugh.

I hate you.

That was not what you were saying earlier.

I looked at him.

He managed to wipe the grin from his face. *But I need to stay. I have a feeling Daemon is going to go Full Daemon, and I need to be here to stop him.* He placed his hand on my knee and squeezed. *Not that I really want to see Blake live, but that might actually get him kicked out of here, and even though they both were willing to leave if you weren't accepted, they need this place.*

Glancing over to Daemon and Kat, I thought of baby Adam. He was at home, being watched by Heidi and Emery, who apparently were all about watching babies. They did need this place.

I can stay.

Go. He squeezed my knee again. *Let me live vicariously through you.*

That made me grin. *I wanted to check in with Viv. I haven't seen her since you returned. I totally bailed on her.*

I'll look for you there.

I started to slide off the table, but stopped. Leaning over, I gave him a quick kiss as I thought to him, *You do care.*

Luc didn't respond, and that was okay. I knew he heard me. I knew he knew I believed in what I said, and if he didn't believe in those words yet, I would until he could.

No one else noticed my escape as I crept out of the room. They'd fallen back into a heated argument. Out in the hall, I looked down the end, to the lone door that led to Blake. What were they going to do with them?

Having no idea, I walked out into fading sunlight. Archer had left the meeting, but he hadn't gone far. He was pacing right where Luc and I had stood earlier. He stopped, looking over as I went down the steps. "They still at it in there?"

I nodded as I slowly approached the older Origin. "I couldn't sit and listen any longer. I'm going to go check in with Viv."

"Don't blame you." He folded his arms over his chest, his gaze falling to the closed door behind me. "I couldn't stay in there, not in the same building as Blake, knowing how he hurt Dee. He almost killed her, too."

"How is Dee handling it?"

"She's shocked. Angry. Things were a little rough when she first learned, but my lady is strong."

"She is!" I said, maybe a little too enthusiastically. "I mean, to do what she does, she has to be. I could never keep my cool like she does."

His grin kicked up a notch. "You should see her after she does the on-air interviews. Pretty sure she wants to blow things up." The grin was as gone as quickly as it had appeared. "I don't know how Daemon can stand to be in the same zip code as that guy."

"I don't think he can. That's why Luc is staying behind—just in case Daemon makes a go for him," I said, running a hand over my arm. There was a chill in the air that hadn't been there earlier. "What do you think they're going to do?"

"I don't know," he said, eyes nearly identical to Luc's sliding back to me. "I don't think it'll matter what they decide in the end."

I didn't think it would, either.

His head tilted. "How does that make you feel? Knowing that two people will die, one of them most likely innocent?"

"I don't know," I said, and then I took a long breath. "Actually, I do. I don't like the idea of Chris dying. I don't like the idea of anyone dying, but if he'd done those things to Luc, I'd be demanding his execution."

Archer watched me. "Death is never easy, not even when it's well deserved. Except the dead have a habit of not staying dead."

"Seems that way." I started toying with the hem of my shirt. "And I guess the same could be said about me."

"Luc never said you were dead. We just assumed you were."

I wasn't sure how to feel about a whole bunch of someones assuming I was dead. "How are things on the outside?"

"Where we film, things are normal, but the news isn't good. They are really pushing the Luxen narrative, even networks that don't usually fall in line with the administration's agenda. Only overseas news sources are questioning what is being reported as the cause of the flu." Lifting a hand, he scratched his fingers through his neatly trimmed hair. "The masses aren't really paying attention. If this flu spreads wider than the infected cities and the only thing humans do is avoid Luxen instead of one another, things are going to go south fast. Like, Spanish influenza fast."

I shivered as I tried to imagine a widespread outbreak. If Hollywood taught me anything, one person on a plane would bring the whole world crashing to a halt. To be honest, I was surprised it had only traveled to five cities and not more.

"Is there any news coming out of the quarantined cities?" I asked, hoping he had a different story to tell from Heidi and Emery's.

Pressing his lips together, he shook his head, and my heart sank. "Officials claim that aid is being rendered and that as soon as a vaccine can be developed, those uninfected in the cities will be the first to receive them, but we already know that's a lie."

We did.

Only the normal flu vaccine could prevent the mutation in the virus, and I doubted the officials were going to do anything to fix the nationwide flu vaccine outage—an outage I was sure they'd engineered.

"Sometimes I just don't get it. Like, how can the Daedalus have such a reach that the CDC isn't all over this? That there isn't a single person within the organization that's not holding up their hand and saying, 'Wait a minute.'"

"I'm sure there have been," Archer said. "And I'm sure many of them, if not all of them, have been silenced through conveniently timed accidents."

Jesus, I hadn't even considered that. "Just when you think the Daedalus couldn't get any eviler or more powerful, you're proven wrong."

"I learned a long time ago to never underestimate them."

My mind went straight to Luc, to what he'd shared. A twisting motion lit up my chest. Luc had escaped them so very long ago and he'd never become like Blake, but the Daedalus had made those first cuts.

"You doing okay?" Archer asked.

I blinked, managing a smile. "Yeah."

He arched a brow. "You do realize I can read minds, right?"

"You do realize it's rude to do that without someone's permission?"

Archer grinned. "I do, but you're—"

"Loud." I sighed. "I know."

He nodded and then cast his gaze in the library doors. "I've known Luc a long time."

Every part of me tensed. I really didn't want him to be picking up on what Luc had shared with me. No one needed to.

"No one will," Archer said, and those violet eyes met mine. "There are days when I think I don't know much, but I was with the Daedalus for a long time, virtually undercover. None of us walked out of there without scars. We all feared that we'd become exactly what they wanted, one way or another. A monster."

My mouth dropped open. How deep did he go into my mind to pull that out?

"It's Dee that keeps me human," he went on. "It's always been you that has done that for Luc, and I have a feeling, even if you don't realize it, he does the same for you."

The next breath I took scorched my throat. I was at a loss as to what to say.

Archer smiled. "I'd better head back in there."

I nodded, stepping aside as he walked past me. I watched him until the door swung shut behind him. More than a little freaked out, I slowly turned around and started walking, thinking over what Archer had said. Part of me didn't want to know how he'd picked all of that out of my brain, but he was right. Luc was there for the nightmares and all the scars I carried. If he weren't, I would probably be just as inhuman as I imagined the other Trojans were.

Walking along the empty lot that was behind the shopping center, I took in the stools that sat in front of the basins turned over to dry out. The clotheslines were bare, and as I walked under them, I couldn't help but think of how creepy it was—

A soft whistle drew my attention the right. My heart kicked against my ribs as I spun around, searching for the face I hadn't seen in days. There. Behind the dumpster, I saw familiar red hair.

"Nate." Relief seized me as I crossed the distance and then gave way to concern, because I seriously wasn't expecting to see him so soon. "Is everything okay?"

He'd slinked farther back into the shadows as I rounded the corner, frowning when he continued to move away. Nate was skittish, but this was different. "Are you all right?"

"Yeah. It's just . . ."

I saw his face, and rage poured into me like a violent summer storm. He'd been hit—hit *hard*. Around his swollen left eye, his skin was a deep purple and an angry shade of red. The Source pulsed in the center of my chest, flashing through my body. "Who did that to you?"

Nate drew back, planting himself against the back of the building. "Your skin." The one eye of his widened. "It's *moving*."

I didn't have to look at my arms to know the Source was making its presence known and he was scared. Who could blame him? Besides all the nonsense he'd been fed about the Luxen, I was sure I looked like something straight out of a low-budget science fiction movie.

"It's okay." I lifted my hands, and Nate flinched. Stupid move. I willed myself to calm. The Source pulsed and then returned to a steady hum. "I'm not going to hurt you. You have to know that. Right?"

Nate was still for several long heartbeats, and then he nodded. "You really aren't like them—like the ones who'd invaded."

"I'm not. Neither are the ones here." I managed a calming breath. "Who did this to you?"

His silence was an answer.

"Was it Morton?"

He folded scrawny arms over his frail chest and gave me one more nod.

The fact I didn't lose my shit right there showed just how much control I truly had, because now it was me who wanted to blow something up.

Namely, Morton.

Funny how I had just walked away from people arguing about whether it was right or wrong to kill someone, and here I was, fully ready to commit murder. Nate was just a child. All of them were just children. How in the hell could a grown man hit one of them? And I knew this wasn't the first time.

"Your eyes," Nate whispered.

"Sorry. I'm just upset for you. No one has the right to hit you, Nate. That's not okay." Surprised by how level my voice was, I slowly lowered my hands. "Please tell me you're here because you want our help. Please."

His head bowed. "After you left, Jamal and Nia . . . I think they wanted to go with you. So, I talked to the others. They're ready," he said. "They want out."

I almost hit the ground. Only a few hours ago, Luc and I were talking about this. Never did I dare to hope that Nate would come to us so quickly. "Okay. That's good. That's great. We can go now—"

"Not right now." Nate's chin jerked up. "It has to be later.

Tonight. When it's dark. We'll flash our lights when we're at the Galleria. It's the mall."

I had no idea where that was, but he peeled away from the wall. "Do you have to go back?" I asked, not wanting him to. "You can stay here. You'll be safe, and we'll go get the rest of them. You don't have to go back there."

"But I do." Nate straightened as he took a step, and that's when I saw him limp.

He wasn't limping before.

"Did he do that, too?" I jerked my chin at his leg.

"He kicked me when I went down."

I was so going to kill Morton. "Stay," I urged. "I can take you to the doc. She can give you something—"

"I have to go back. The younger ones. They get scared easy at night. Jamal and Nia can't handle them all by themselves."

"But—"

"Please. Just come tonight. Okay? When it's dark. I'll signal you from inside the Galleria. We'll be near the entrance."

Realizing there was nothing I could do to stop him that wouldn't scare him, I took a step back. "We'll be there."

"We?"

I nodded. I might have done a lot of stupid things, but there was no way I was going back into that city by myself again and trying to wrangle up a bunch of frightened children.

Plus, someone needed to lead them out while Morton was dealt with.

"Your boyfriend?" he asked.

"He'll be there. You'll like him. He wears really stupid shirts."

A tentative smile appeared, but it didn't last. He'd seen too much, been through too much. "Tonight."

"Tonight," I promised.

Watching him leave was one of the hardest things I'd ever had to do. A hundred different things could happen between now and when it was dark enough that the kids could make their presence known. Morton could go at Nate again, could go at any of the other kids.

My hands curled into fists.

But I knew if Nate didn't go back there, the kids wouldn't come to the mall. They'd scatter in a city they knew like the backs of their hands. We'd never find them.

Now I just had to convince Cekiah and everyone else that taking on more than a dozen children was the right thing to do. I could only hope that Luc had been right about Cekiah and Zouhour being more than willing to take the children in.

Spinning around, I raced back to the library and skidded into the main room. Everyone was still there. No tables had been flipped, but I hadn't been gone all that long. Viv was there, sitting in one of the empty chairs. I must've just missed passing her. I knew this was a terrible moment for me to tell them about Nate and the kids, but I really didn't have a choice.

"This is becoming—" Kat stopped mid-sentence as Daemon looked over his shoulder at me.

It's Nate. He's back. They're ready.

Luc's gaze shot to me, and with one quick nod, he stood. "The situation with Blake is important, and I'm sure all of you wish to continue arguing the same points over and over again, but Evie has something that's also important to share."

Figuring my thoughts were super-loud at the moment, I wasn't at all surprised when Archer's eyes narrowed and he leaned over to whisper in Dee's ear.

"Please tell me it's not yet another person whose right to live or die we'll need to discuss?" Quinn said wearily.

Well . . .

I was going to skip over that part at the moment.

"Remember when I said I saw lights in the city? I wasn't seeing the sunlight reflecting weird or anything like that," I said, noticing that Eaton no longer looked half-asleep as Daemon tilted his head. "There are people in the city. Kids."

That got everyone's attention. Human and alien eyes fixed on me.

"What?" Cekiah had twisted around in her seat.

"Shortly after I saw the lights, I came home to find a kid in the house. I knew he wasn't a part of this community, because he wasn't at the school. He was scavenging for food. His name is Nate, and I saw him again a few times, and talked to him once more. Then he came because one of the other kids was hurt. I went with him into the city—"

"You did what?" Daemon demanded.

"Trust me, she's already received the lecture I know you're about to deliver," Luc remarked.

I gave him a wince of a smile. "I know it wasn't the brightest idea, but I did it. I needed to see how many kids there were and try to get him to trust me. You see, he didn't want me to tell anyone, and he was worried that if I did, the kids would scatter into the city. There are over a dozen children in that city. All human. Nate might be the oldest, and he can't be older than thirteen."

Someone sucked in sharp breath, and there were gasps. I was hoping that was a good sign.

"How is that even possible? Where are their parents?" Jamie, who hadn't been exactly keen on me hanging around, had a hand pressed to her chest.

"Some were homeless or in group homes or something similar before the invasion, and just forgotten in the chaos," I said. "But one of the kids told me there used to be more children—there used to be parents, families, but many of them didn't survive the first year."

"Oh my God," whispered Jamie. "That is . . . I don't even have words."

"I have so many questions right now," Zouhour said. "How did you two even get past our patrols? We have guards constantly patrolling the outer edges of the city."

"The kids know this whole area. They know exactly where the guards are going to be at any given time—their schedule."

"Well, add changing up the guard routine to my mental to-do list," muttered Eaton. "I can't believe we haven't seen any of them when we've done our sweeps. We've scoured every inch of that city in the last four years."

"Like I said, they know how to hide and not be found," I told him.

"What do you mean they've been living there?" Jamie asked. "There's nothing in the city. No food. No real useful supplies other than just what they can take here and there."

"That's where some of the food has been disappearing." Viv cleared her throat with a slight grimace.

I scanned the group for expressions of censure, but all I saw was shock and dismay. "I wanted to say something as soon as I discovered them, but I knew if anyone came looking for them, no one would see them again."

"How do they look?" Viv asked.

"Underfed. I get the impression that there have been infections, mostly from cuts and bruises. Things that I imagine if they were living under better conditions they wouldn't have to deal with." I looked at Viv closer. Her cheeks were flushed. "Are you feeling okay?"

"Yeah. Allergies." She sniffed. "Too bad the EMPs didn't knock them out. Why haven't they come here for treatment? We would've helped them."

"They're scared," Luc stepped in. "I haven't seen any of the kids myself, but that's what they've told Evie. They're scared of us—of all the Luxen here."

"Good God," Quinn murmured, running his thumb along his chin. "Have they seen the Yard? Is that why?"

"I don't know what they've seen, but there's a man who's sort of fashioned himself as their guardian," Luc continued. "He's got them scared out of their minds when it comes to the Luxen, and I imagine he's got them thinking only he can protect them, and since he's human, he felt familiar to them."

"But he's not protecting them. His name is Morton. He's using them. I'm willing to bet most of the food and supplies go to him, and he's been abusing at least one of them. I'm sure it's more," I said. "I just saw Nate, and he had a black eye and had been limping. I asked if it was Morton, and Nate said yes."

Kat's hand fisted where it rested on the table. "That is unacceptable."

"It is," I agreed. "And none of them have confirmed this, but I think . . . I don't know, but it's awfully convenient and strange that all these kids survived, but only one adult did? Morton could have something to do with the other adults not making it. I'm just saying, I met him once, and he just gives those kind of vibes."

"What I'm hearing is making me stabby," Dee said.

I nodded. "I've told them we can help them. I mean, we would, right? They're just children, but they've been too scared to accept help." I drew in a shallow breath. "Until tonight. Nate said they're ready. They want help. I told them we would. I know I'm not on your unofficial but totally official council, and I don't speak for any of you, but I have to believe that the kind of world you all are building wouldn't let kids starve or turn a blind eye to them being hurt."

Gazes left mine and were exchanged all along the table until, one by one, they nodded. My breath halted as I shot Luc a nervous, hopeful look.

Luc winked.

"How many children are there again?" Cekiah asked.

"At least twenty. There could be more. They are all very skittish and move around a lot. Hard to keep track of," I answered. "If we do help them, and I am hoping that we do, a large group can't go in there. There can only be a few of us. Otherwise, I'm afraid some will bolt even if Nate has rounded them up."

"Finding lodging for all of them will be difficult." Zouhour was looking at Cekiah. "But we could set up temporary housing here until we figure out what to do with them." She glanced over at me. "How old is the youngest you've seen?"

"Five or six," I said, and Dee visibly paled.

"There are families I know who will be more than happy to take the young ones in. Even the older ones. I can name several off the top of my head right now," Viv said, sniffling. "And if there are any that are sick, I can house them at the med building."

Jamie was nodding. "We have to do something. They are just kids."

"Agreed," Quinn said.

Cekiah sat back. "We will help. We will do everything we can to help them."

39

Only a short time later, we were standing in the living room. I'd changed into leggings and a long-sleeved black shirt that belonged to Luc, thinking less restrictive and lightweight clothing would be a better choice.

There was going to be a lot of running in our near future.

"Is everyone about ready?" Eaton asked. He was going to wait for us at the warehouse, the closest point to the city. Cekiah, along with Zouhour and Viv, were getting the library and med building ready. Jamie and Quinn were handling notifying the community, both confident that by the time we returned, they'd already have homes for most of if not all the kids.

God, I hoped so.

But I mostly hoped that whoever stepped forward to take them in was patient. These kids had been through a lot, many even before the invasion. This wasn't going to be a Disney movie come to life.

"Yep." Daemon finished lacing up his boots. I hadn't expected him to volunteer, but he'd insisted on it. So had Kat.

Luc nodded. "Been ready. Just had to wait for Daemon to figure out how to tie his shoes."

Smirking, Daemon straightened and then turned to where Kat stood, holding a rather alert baby Adam. He took the small child from her, cuddling him close as he kissed the baby's cheek. "Can you say, 'Uncle Luc is a dick'? Huh? Say—"

"Daemon," Kat admonished, eyes widening.

"First off, I'm not his uncle. I am his godfather, thank you very much." Luc arched a brow, and I felt like I'd missed that announcement. "Secondly, I'll teach him better insults than that."

Kat whipped around. "No, you won't."

The kind of smile that crept across Luc's face said he was so going to do exactly what he said.

I honestly couldn't even begin to figure out Daemon and Luc's friendship. They went from throwing punches to joking around like nothing had happened. It had to be a boy thing.

Or an alien thing.

"That kid has no chance," Archer said from where he sat with Dee. They'd be joining Eaton at the warehouse.

I cracked a grin even though my stomach was in knots. So many what-ifs were circling around in my head. What if Nate changed his mind? What if he couldn't convince all the kids? What if Morton—

"It'll be okay." Luc draped an arm around me, tugging me into his side. "We're going to get them out. All of them."

Kat took the baby back from Daemon, and Adam promptly dropped his chubby cheek to her chest. "It's time to talk about what we are going to do with this guy. If he is using those kids and hurting them? If he's possibly killed others? He can't come here."

There was a reason why everyone waited until Cekiah and everyone else was busy to bring this up.

"I know," said Luc. "He's not coming back here."

"Zoe and Emery are going to lead the kids back here. We're hoping they'll go with them," I said.

Plastering a giant smile across her face, Zoe clasped her hands together. "They will. I have a very trusting face."

Heidi looked up at her from where she sat on the arm of the couch. "Please do not smile like that when you see them. You're going to scare them."

Zoe's eyes narrowed.

"If not, I'll have to go with them," I added, thinking that would be a high likelihood if Zoe did her flailing-arm thing.

"And then what?" Dee asked, her long, dark hair swept back from her face.

"And then we handle Morton," Luc said. "One way or another, he will not be a problem."

Kat looked around the room as she folded her hand behind her son's head. She nodded, and just like that, everyone here, including Eaton, accepted the inevitable.

Blake may not die tonight.

But someone would.

I stopped my mind several times over from really thinking about it. Morton may deserve it. Just like Blake. But killing some-one was still ending a life, and a twisted part of me really hoped Morton gave us a reason to do it. Killing someone in self-defense was a whole lot easier to swallow.

"Still not a fan of any of this," came a mutter from the corner of the room. I didn't have to look. It was Grayson, the final member of our six-person crew.

Frankly, Grayson was the last person I'd take if I didn't want to scare anyone.

Luc snorted.

I looked up at him, and he grinned as he said, "I don't think you're a fan of much, Gray."

"We don't know these kids." He peeled away from the wall and stepped forward. "Where they've been or where they're from."

Kat lifted her brows. "You make it sound like they have cooties."

"Well, there's a good chance they may have lice," Luc said, and my stare turned into a glare. "Hey, it's possible. No judgment here."

"He's right," Dee said, dropping her elbows to her knees. "There's a lot we don't know, but you know they're human, and if this is somehow some sort of trap, those kids are still being used and they still need our help."

"What kind of trap could it even be?" Kat asked, gently bounc-ing the baby. "If it was the Daedalus, do you really think we'd be standing here having this conversation?"

Daemon shook his head. "It's one thing to have kids hidden in the city and entirely another thing for people to get into that city without us knowing."

"Nothing is impossible," Grayson replied.

"Didn't say that it was, but we would've seen them," Daemon replied.

"I'm not suggesting it's the Daedalus. I'd hope you all would be able to see that," Grayson replied. "Doesn't mean that these kids aren't going to be a problem."

"Have you even been around kids?" Eaton asked as he laid a map out on the coffee table. "I'm thinking not, because they are always a problem."

Grayson's eyes narrowed. "I've seen kids. There's one right there." He gestured at Adam.

"That's an infant," Luc explained. "Vast difference between that and an actual kid, my friend."

"I know that." Grayson folded his arms. "Whatever. Let's go play Big Brothers, Big Sisters of the Alien World."

"Uh-huh. You see this?" Eaton tapped a line highlighted in blue. "This is the metro system. Runs aboveground mostly, but there are underground access points that lead to the walking tunnels about twenty feet below the downtown area. Those tunnels connect about ninety-five city blocks. Now, the wall cuts through one of the tunnels built below the metro," he explained, and I remembered him mentioning the tunnels the first day we'd talked to him. "One of the first things we did is close that tunnel off from the inside. We blew that section of the tunnel. It would take years for anyone to remove all the debris to make it remotely passable, and we would've seen activity coming from outside.

"We may have made some mistakes, but we've done our best to cover our bases. Now." Eaton moved his finger to the left, tapping a line labeled *Westheimer Road*. "This is where the Galleria is. It's in uptown, and the quickest access point from there is the warehouse. You're going to get on the 610. Daemon knows the quickest way to get there. The Galleria is right off an exit. In a car, with a clear road, it would take a good thirty minutes, but we've gotten most of the highway cleared enough that travel on foot or in a vehicle shouldn't be an issue."

"It will take us minutes," Daemon said, fixing the sock on Adam's foot. "The hard part is to get the kids back here."

"Jamie and Viv are going to meet me at the warehouse. They're rounding up every available vehicle that still runs," Eaton explained.

"We'll keep them moving," Emery assured. "And when we're ready for you guys, we'll send a signal."

"We're going to light up like—" Zoe stopped herself as I raised my brows. "We are going to light up in a manner that will not scare the kids."

"Then we come in and get the kids," Eaton finished. "Do you know what side they will be on once they're at the Galleria? That place is the largest mall in all of Texas. Three levels and a skating rink below."

"He said they'd be near the main entrance," I said.

"That's close to the tower—the big building you can see from here. Well, one of them," Daemon said when Eaton looked to him. "I know which side that's on. We can get right onto that one street. What's it called?"

"I think it was Hidalgo," Archer answered.

"That's it." When he saw my expression, he added, "We were in and out of the mall for a while. Got a lot of really nice supplies from in there."

"Ah, yeah." A dreamy look swept over Dee's face. "That's where all the Chanel came from."

Kat grinned at her. "I think—"

Without any warning, the map lifted up in the air and spun.

"What in the world?" Eaton leaned back and looked at me.

"It's not me!" I threw my hands up.

"Luc?" Archer asked.

He shot the older Origin a bland look.

"Sorry. It's Adam." Kat patted his back as Daemon snatched the still-spinning map out of the air and handed it over to Eaton. "He's been doing a lot of that lately."

"That must keep you on your toes," I said, thinking that I had, in fact, more control than a baby Origin.

"It does." Kat kissed Adam's cheek. "Especially when they're sharp items."

"Oh my," I murmured.

Luc slid his hand over my back as he looked out the window. "It's dark," he said. "It's time."

The six of us walked past where Eaton waited outside the warehouse, along with Dee and Archer. Soon others would join them, and hopefully, the group that would wait wouldn't be in vain.

"The terrain through here isn't bad, but it's uneven," Daemon said. "When we hit the highway, you want to stay in the center. All the unsalvageable cars have been moved to the side. It really should only take us two minutes tops."

"Sounds good to me," Emery said, the breeze lifting the strands of hair on one side of her head.

I stared out over the field. It was a clear night, and the moonlight cast enough light that between it and the new-and-improved eyeballs, I wasn't worried about running into a tree. My gaze tracked to one of the darker, thicker shadows that seemed to loom over the rest of the skyscrapers. The tower.

"Any questions?" Daemon asked.

Luc raised his hand.

I reached for it, because I had a feeling it would be utterly irrelevant, but I wasn't fast enough.

"Yes, Luc."

"Are you sure you're against me getting Adam a llama?" Luc asked. "Like, really sure?"

Daemon sighed. "Yes. I'm sure."

"Life ruiner," he muttered, lowering his hand.

I couldn't help it. A giggle snuck free.

"Don't laugh," Daemon said. "It just encourages him."

Biting down on my lip, I managed to stop the next one from slipping free.

"Any actual important questions?" Daemon asked.

Grayson started to raise his hand.

"Yes, Grayson, *all* kids are dirty, and they *all* smell funny," Daemon said before Grayson got the question out there.

Emery snorted-laughed from where she stood.

"Thanks for the heads-up, but that wasn't my question," Grayson drawled. "I was going to ask what is the plan in case Morton shows up and pushes back while the kids are still there? I'm thinking we don't want to fry him in front of a bunch of impressionable youngsters who are already terrified of us."

Impressionable youngsters?

Grayson had a good point, though. "We don't want to do anything to him while they're around," I said as I tightened my ponytail. "I could freeze him until we get the kids out."

"Yeah, you've gotten really good at that." Daemon stared pointedly at me.

I gave an awkward smile.

"Sounds like a plan," Luc said, reaching over and tugging my hair. "No matter what, we all stay together. The same goes for you two." That was directed at Emery and Zoe. "Don't separate when you're taking the kids out."

Everyone nodded, and it was time. Daemon slipped under the opening he'd created. Zoe and Emery followed, and as I stepped forward to do the same, Luc caught my hand, stopping me. I turned back.

Before I had a chance to speak, Luc kissed me, and it was sweet and slow, like we had all the time in the world. And I wished we did, because when he deepened the kiss, I wanted more. But we didn't have time, and there would be a later where we would.

Luc pulled back, his hand sliding from mine, and when he nodded, I took a breath and then slipped through the fence, the touch of his lips against mine lingering. Grayson was the last through, and then Daemon, Emery, and Grayson slipped into their true forms.

It didn't matter how many times I saw it, my breath still caught. Light spilled from them onto the ground. Daemon's burned more brightly, and it was hard to look at him without my eyes watering. My gaze shifted to Emery and then Grayson. It still wasn't pleasant to look directly at them, but if I looked close enough, I could see them behind the light, their skin soft and almost translucent. They looked like ethereal beings, raw and beautiful.

Then they were running, moving so fast they looked like lightning arcing across the ground. I glanced over at Zoe and Luc, and then I was racing across the field, keeping track of where Daemon was going.

Who needed a flashlight when they were around?

Wind picked up with my speed, tugging at my shirt and hair. Under my feet, the ground was uneven and rocky and the reeds reached my thighs, but the faster I went, the less my feet seemed to touch the ground.

Catching up with the Luxen within seconds with Luc right behind me and Grayson keeping pace, we moved farther down the highway, toward the quiet, looming city. The abandoned cars sat all along the shoulders, and the asphalt of the road had already begun to see the wear of lack of upkeep. Cracks had formed, and potholes riddled the whole way. Up ahead, the building that seemed as tall as a mountain grew closer and closer. Only a few minutes later, Luc held up a hand, and we slowed.

"The exit is there," he said, and I saw the sign for the road Daemon and Archer had mentioned earlier. It was cockeyed and rusted, probably days away from falling over. "All you Lite-Brites should dim down. A small herd of Luxen racing toward the meeting place isn't going to set anyone at ease."

One by one, the Luxen dimmed, and as the light receded, they had returned to their human forms.

Luc fell into step beside me as we made our way down the road. There were more cars here, and I doubted anything larger than a sedan could squeeze through.

"This is creepy," Zoe murmured, looking up.

She was right, and even though I'd already seen the city at night, it was no less unsettling. The tall buildings blocked a lot of the moonlight, and Daemon and Luc turned their hands into Source-powered lanterns. This area of town had fared far worse than what I'd seen. Windows in nearby buildings were busted out. Several storefronts and offices carried scorch marks. A few of the cars had been turned upside down. Bullet holes were scattered along a few windows that remained.

Following Daemon, we hung a right and the intersection—

"Wow," Emery murmured, stopping. "Look."

Ahead of us, movement stirred around an area that must've been a park or some sort of green space. A deer stepped out, its antlers enormous. Hoofs clanged off the asphalt as it moseyed across the road. It wasn't alone. An entire flock of them followed. Or were they called a *herd*?

Herd, answered Luc.

I smiled as I watched fawns amble after the adults, their legs not nearly as sturdy. *Why am I not surprised you know that?*

None of us spoke or moved until the last one had passed, disappearing from our sight.

"I bet Luc wishes they were llamas," I said.

Daemon groaned.

"You have no idea, Peaches. I would've befriended one and led it back to Daemon's house—"

"Dear God," groaned Daemon.

Luc looked at me. "And then the others would miss it and they would come, too."

I started to smile.

"Before Daemon knew it, he'd have a herd of llamas," he went on, and Daemon started walking. "Kat would be thrilled."

Laughing, I took his hand. "You're so bizarre."

"If wanting a herd of llamas makes me bizarre, then I lace up those shoes and rock it," he replied.

"You say that now." Grayson passed us. "Until the first one spits in your face."

"I think llamas will see me as one of their own and wouldn't dare think of doing that," Luc reasoned.

I shook my head as we walked under the shadow of the tower. Talk of llamas ceased as we took a left. My heart started thumping as a parking lot came into view. Rusted-out cars were scattered throughout, windshields shattered. I imagined that the cars and their owners must've been here when the EMP was dropped, and there was something sad about seeing the cars, some of them so weathered I could no longer tell their colors, and how it showed what people were doing when their lives were irrevocably shattered.

We waited under the line of trees, hidden in the shadows. Luc and Daemon spoke to one another in low, hushed voices, and whatever they were talking—or arguing—about had Emery and Zoe grinning. Grayson stood a few feet from me, his gaze fixed ahead, like mine. I don't know how long we stared at the letters *GALL*. At some point, the letters *ERIA* must've moved on to better things.

Like the ground.

I saw it first, the flash of yellow light. "There."

"See it," Luc confirmed, having been keeping an eye on the building. The light flashed two more times.

"That's Nate. Can we somehow send a signal back?" I asked.

Luc stepped forward, lifting his hand. The Source ballooned out from his hand and then flickered out before coming back again. He did this once more.

I held my breath, hands balled tightly until the light flashed from within the mall once more.

"Okay." I exhaled roughly. "He's here. They're here."

"Remember," Luc warned. "Stick together."

Nodding, I pivoted and stepped off the curb, onto the pavement. Joined by the others, we rushed across the parking lot, reaching doors that had long since been torn away.

"Lovely," Grayson murmured as we walked inside.

Zoe's nose wrinkled. There was an odor that reminded me of the dankest, darkest basements. To the right was an entrance to one of the office towers, and at the left was a hotel. Glass crunched under our feet as we walked on. There was a lot of light coming from the center. I looked up and up to where moonlight streamed in through the enormous skylight. Entire sections of glass the size of a compact car were missing, exposing everything inside to whatever elements the last four years had dealt, which explained the thick, cloying musty scent.

Storefronts were unrecognizable. Signs broken on the floor. Silvery moonlight bounced off shards of glass still in the windows of some of the stores and shone a light on a thin layer of what appeared to be mold. It crept along the walls between stores and up to the second floor.

"Are the kids staying in here?" Emery asked, voice low. "Because if so, this is like the opposite of healthy, clean air."

"I don't think so," I said, but then again, I had no idea.

"God, I hope you're right." Zoe looked down at the floor as she lifted a foot. "I think there is something growing on the floor."

I shuddered, scanning the entire length that was lit by moonlight. Gaping darkness existed at each end and straight ahead.

"The light came from the center." Daemon squinted. "They have to be around here."

Instinct told me they were. They were hiding, probably in the absolute emptiness in front of us, waiting to see what we'd do. Desperately trying not to think of all the horror movies, I stepped forward.

Evie, Luc's voice was a harsh whisper.

"It's okay. I'm not going far." I stared into the nothingness. "Just . . . everyone stay back for a moment."

I could feel Luc's unwillingness. It beat at my mind like crashing waves, but no one moved one inch.

"Nate? Jamal?" I called out. "Nia? We're here to help, like I said we would be." I paused, sensing that Luc had moved closer. "The guy *right* behind me is my boyfriend."

"Aww," Luc drawled. "That's the first time you called me that. Today, whatever today's date is, will forever be our boyfriend-girlfriend anniversary."

I shot him a look over my shoulder. Moonlight sliced over his cheek as he grinned. "He's a little different." I turned back to the darkness. "The rest are my friends. They're here to help, too."

Silence.

"Maybe they left," offered Grayson, and honestly, he sounded a little too relieved by the prospect.

Then I heard it, the soft shuffling of feet. Hope swelled. "Nate?"

Another too-long stretch of silence and then *whispers*. I could nearly sense Grayson was about to speak, but I held up my hand, silencing him.

Do you hear them? I asked Luc.

I hear something.

I think it's them whispering.

Have you've developed supersonic hearing? If so, that's sexy.

My lips tipped up even though I didn't think my hearing had approved all that much. *That's a weird thing to find sexy.*

I find everything about you sexy.

Now I was really smiling, and maybe that helped, because after a small eternity, the silence was broken by Nate's voice.

"We're here. We're coming out."

Glancing back at the others, I met Luc's gaze, and I let him see the broader, borderline creepy smile.

Peaches, came his voice. *Stop being so adorable.*

I love you, I told him, and then I turned back. The darkness had shifted, becoming solid as the children inched their way out. I moved backward with each of their steps, not wanting to crowd them. I ended up standing side by side with Luc. His fingers brushed mine, and then he took my hand in his.

I squeezed. Luc did the same.

I saw Nate first, and anger rippled through me all over again at the sight of his face. The bruise looked even worse in the moonlight, as if the entire area around his eye was black. He held the hand of the smallest child, one I hadn't seen before. Jamal had ahold of two kids, as did Nia. The other older kids stayed behind them, their wary gazes darting frantically. They looked *tired.*

"God," whispered Zoe in a thick voice.

Nia's gaze shot to her as she stopped, pulling the two children closer.

"It's okay," I told her. "That's my friend."

Zoe nodded eagerly. "My name is Zoe," she said, clearing her throat. "And you see this girl here with the really weird hair?"

Nia's gaze moved to Emery while one of the smaller children cracked a grin. Nia nodded.

"My hair is not that weird right now," replied Emery.

"It's weird." Zoe widened her eyes at the children as she nodded. "But she's going to help me take you guys to get some food."

"You're not taking us?" Jamal asked me and then turned to Nate.

"I will be right behind you guys. I promise."

"There's nineteen," Daemon said in a low voice. "Is that all of them?"

I scanned the group again, but it was hard to tell. So many of them had grime on their faces. "Is this everyone?" I asked.

"We couldn't find Tabby," Nia said, shivering in her thin shirt.

"I know where she is," Nate said as he led the little boy toward Zoe. The child stared up at her with big eyes. "He likes his hand held. Is that okay?"

"Of course," whispered Zoe, extending her hand without hesitation.

The little boy stared at her hand as if it were a coiled viper.

"Go ahead, Bit. Take her hand," Nate coaxed.

"Bit?" Emery asked.

"He, um, he doesn't know his name." Nate shrugged like that were commonplace. "We just named him Bit."

"He likes it," added Nia.

My throat closed up as Emery smiled and said, "I like the name, too."

Bit hesitantly reached out with his other hand, placing it in Zoe's. It seemed so small as he continued to stare up at her. "Are you an alien?"

"No." Zoe smiled, but I knew her smiles. She was struggling to keep it together. "I'm something far cooler than that."

Daemon scoffed under his breath. "I'm an alien. She's not as cool as I am."

That earned him distrustful stares, but goodness, Daemon could lay the charm on. That easy grin of his, the one that flashed just the hint of dimples, seemed to be working on even the kids. Half of them lost the wary stare and instead looked curious.

Man, I said to Luc. *He's good.*

Yeah, he is.

"Go with them," Nate urged, sending me a nervous glance. "I've got to get Tabby."

It took a little bit for Nate to convince them, especially the older kids, and all the while, unease blossomed in the pit of my stomach. Nate was like their unofficial leader. I didn't expect him to let any of these kids out of his sight.

Something's up, I sent to Luc, telling him what I knew. *He wants these kids out of here. Can you pick up anything from him?*

I've been listening the whole time, Luc replied. *He's scared. He just keeps repeating over and over "I can do this," and he's thinking about Tabby.*

The unease grew. *Nothing else?*

He's too afraid. It's clouding his thoughts. Luc was silent for a moment. *I can go deeper. Don't know if you know that, but I could push beyond the fear, but he'll feel that. I'll do it, but if he freaks out—*

I hadn't known he could do that, and I wondered if it was something he didn't do often, because I'd never felt him tinkering around in my head.

Picking up on surface thoughts isn't hard, he told me, proving he'd done just that. *But if someone is afraid, feeling heightened emotions, or using shields, then you have to get through that.*

Don't risk it. If he feels it and freaks out, it will scare the kids. I scanned the darkness ahead once more. *We just need to prepare for anything.*

We are, came his response.

Eventually, Zoe and Emery had control of the kids, with the help of Jamal and Nia. Nate had to reassure them again that he was coming, and then I had to, because I was the only face they barely recognized. Then Zoe and Emery were leading them back out the way we'd come in.

"They'll be okay with them?" Nate asked the moment they were out of earshot.

I faced him. "What's going on, Nate?"

"What?" he said.

As Daemon and Luc exchanged a look, I stepped forward, keeping my voice low. "You've given me the impression that you wouldn't let those kids out of your sight and you just handed them over like it was nothing?"

Nate's one good eye darted from me to Luc and then to the others. "I just need to get Tabby. She's—"

"Shit," Luc muttered, and I felt the charge hit the air the second before the veins under his eyes filled with white light.

Stumbling back a step, Nate almost toppled over. "You said he wasn't a Luxen."

"He's not," I said.

"I'm something very, very different." Luc took a step toward the boy. "So, you're going to want to think before you do what you're about to do next."

"What's going on?" Daemon asked.

"He's about to lead us right into a trap," Luc said, and my heart skipped a beat. "Isn't that right?"

"Nate," I whispered, my chest seizing in the painful grip of disappointment.

"I . . ." Nate's face crumbled. "I'm sorry. Evie, I'm sorry. I didn't have a choice. He has Tabby. He has my little sister."

40

Y our sister?" I exclaimed. I hadn't known he had a sister. "You never told me you had a sister." I stepped toward him—

Nate flinched as if I'd raised my hand. "I'm sorry. I'm so sorry. You've been so nice, but Tabby—she's the only family I've got left. You met her. She was the one who loves—"

"Creamed corn," I interrupted, recalling the first time he'd been at the house. "That little girl who grabbed the can is your sister."

"Yes. I didn't even think he knew she was my sister. She must've slipped up and said something. I'm sorry, but he's got my sister, and he'll hurt her." Nate dropped to his knees, clasping his hands together. "I'm sorry. I should've told you everything when I saw you, but I'm scared. I didn't want to do this, but he'll hurt her. I know he will."

Luc moved, and Nate swung his head toward him. He knelt so they were eye level. "I can read your mind, so it's best to continue being honest. I'll know when you're lying."

Nate gaped at Luc, and it was obvious that he'd never known that was possible. Anger flashed through me, directed at both Nate and Morton, but I wrapped my hand around Nate's arm, tugging him to his feet. "Tell us everything."

His lower lip trembled. "You're going to hate me."

"I think you need to worry more about us growing impatient," warned Daemon.

"You need to talk and do so fast," Luc agreed as Grayson casually moved so he was behind Nate.

"It's okay," I told Nate even though it really wasn't. "Just tell us everything and tell us the truth."

The boy seemed to pull himself together. "He had us all afraid of the Luxen—the people that live here. It wasn't hard. Many of us remember what it was like when they came. We all saw some scary stuff. I knew something was up when he asked that I—"

I heard it the same time Luc did, which was only a heartbeat later. Grayson spun around, and Daemon stiffened. Footsteps echoing from within the darkness. Multiple ones.

Grabbing ahold of Nate, I shoved him behind me as the darkness seemed to expand.

"They're soldiers," Nate said. "I saw them earlier. The others didn't, but Morton made me see them."

"Jesus," Daemon muttered. "How did they get in?"

"The tunnels," whispered Nate, fingers clinging to the back of my shirt. "He had us dig out the tunnel from the inside. We spent three years doing it."

If this was something they'd been working on for years, then I knew only one thing could be behind this.

The Daedalus? I said to Luc.

Unfortunately.

But it didn't make sense. If the Daedalus had been working to get into the city unseen for three years, then they had to know what was going on here.

"The other kids? Are they in on this?" Daemon demanded.

"No. I swear. They dug the tunnels, but they didn't know why. I didn't until a few days ago."

"He's telling the truth," Luc confirmed, and that part made me feel a little better knowing we weren't sending a bunch of foxes to the hen house.

"I'm sorry, Evie," Nate continued to whisper. "I'm so sorry. I didn't—"

"You can apologize later," I cut him off as the footsteps came to a sudden halt. I stared deep into the darkness. "I need you to be quiet now."

Tiny pinpricks of light appeared in the darkness.

"Brace yourself," Luc warned. "They're here."

Daemon and Grayson slipped into their true forms, twin intense lights.

And then they were here.

Dozens and dozens of ART officers spilled out of the darkness. Rows of them dressed in white, their shields hiding their faces. All of them carried rifles, the kind I knew were modified to carry a dangerous, often deadly electrical current.

They were all aimed at us.

I'll take care of the guns, Luc said. *You take care of them.*

Done, I said, letting instinct take over. All the practice had helped erase fear of losing control, but this would be different. I wasn't moving objects or people, but I couldn't let panic take grip. I tapped into the Source. The power in the center of my chest stretched as if it were waking up, and then it flooded my system.

"On the floor and in human forms. Now," one of the officers commanded. "Or we shoot."

Luc sighed as my skin tingled. "Boring." And then he lifted his hands. "I'd expect better."

Fingers twitched over triggers, but they weren't fast enough. The rifles were ripped from their grasps and flew toward the ceiling. Metal groaned and caved as the barrels were melted and bent. Electrical pulses lit up the chambers of the rifles, bursting out the back in mini, harmless explosions. I wished I could see the officers' faces.

I threw out my arms as I summoned the Source. Whitish light with swirling black shadows powered down my arms as I pictured them going in the same direction as the rifles.

Shouts erupted as the first row of officers lifted off the floor. I didn't let myself think about whether this would hurt them or if it would do worse. I couldn't. Not when I knew where they were from, most likely who sent them.

They flew up and up, all the way to the skylight. Some went through the holes already there. Others shattered the glass, their shouts of surprise ending in screams.

"Holy crap," Nate gasped behind me.

A dozen or so more officers remained.

A bolt of the Source streaked out from Daemon, taking one of the officers and sending him spinning into the wall. Another blast shot out from Grayson. He hit an officer, and he hadn't been holding back. The officer fell facefirst, body smoking when it hit the ground.

Luc sent three flying into the wall, their bodies hitting with a fleshy smack that gave way to the stomach-churning sound of bones crunching.

At that point, the remaining officers, just under a dozen, knew what was up. They started to turn, to run, and I couldn't let that happen. My gaze flipped up to the second-floor railing made out of heavy cement and glass directly above the officers. Daemon and Grayson took out another two. Luc threw another through the storefront.

Trusting that I wasn't going to do anything that would cause me to have to reboot or whatever, I dug deeper, and a burst of heavier, thicker power rippled through me as I stared at the ledge above. The cement cracked straight through the middle, sending a plume of fine dust into the silvery moonlight. Pushing out with my hands, I controlled the fall of the large swath of cement and glass. It swung down, catching the remaining officers as they turned to flee. They didn't make it far.

Lowering my hands, I looked to Nate as my heart pounded. "Are there more?"

Trembling, he nodded.

"I guess this is a bad time to say I told you so?" Grayson said.

Yeah.

Yeah, it was.

Luc lifted his hand. Sparks flew from his fingertips. The very air lit up, like I'd seen him do once in his apartment above the club. Glittering golden dots of light rolled out from Luc in all directions, spreading down the dark halls on either sides, eating away at the void.

The halls were empty.

"Where are they?" Daemon demanded, having returned his human form. "Where is this Morton? And be detailed, kid. I know there are over three hundred stores in this building."

Nate kept his arms close to his chest. "He wanted me to bring you to him." He stared at me. "He said he'd be in the park."

"The park?" I repeated.

He nodded. "The one beside the big tower."

"We just came from that direction. No one was out there," Daemon said.

"I don't know. I swear. That's where he said he'd be," Nate repeated. "He's there. He has to be. You've got to help me get Tabby back."

"We will," I told him.

Grayson shot me a look that said I shouldn't have said that.

"How many more officers did you see?" Luc asked, the pupils of his eyes diamond white.

Nate shook his head. "Maybe the same number as the ones that were here," he said.

"And what is he going to do once you lead Evie to him?" Grayson asked, returning to the dimmed, human version of himself. "He just going to hand Tabby over?"

"That's what he promised."

Grayson huffed out a laugh, shaking his head.

"What? What are you saying?" the kid shrieked. When Grayson looked away, Nate shuddered. "He promised. I did everything he asked. For years, we stayed away from you guys, but then he told me I needed to get supplies from you all. That's when I went into the community. He said that I couldn't be seen until I saw you."

My stomach sank even though we already knew. The Daedalus was here. They'd *been* here, and God only knew what was going to happen from here—what could already be happening in the community. And they were here because of me.

After everything I'd done, I still put the community at risk.

"He told me what you looked like, and he told me I needed to get you to follow me, but not right away. It would be too suspicious."

"Why did he want her to follow you?" Daemon asked.

"He had to confirm who she was." Nate started to pace in a tight, narrow line.

"That's why he was there that night." My fingers stretched as the Source sent an angry push of energy through me. "He needed to see who I was with his own eyes."

Nate shoved a hand through his hair, tugging at it. "He never told me why. He still hasn't. This whole time, he had us believing that we were opening the tunnel as a way to get out. He lied."

"And so you believed that he'd just give you back your sister after you helped him?" Grayson demanded.

Horror crept into the young boy's face. "What else could I believe?"

God, I understood the position he was in. He had to believe, because if he didn't, then there was only one harsh reality.

"It wasn't until we cleared the tunnel a few days ago. He told me it was time to get you to follow me." He tugged at his hair again. "I didn't know why, and I didn't understand why he acted the way he did when he saw you. He wanted to see you, but he made you leave."

Because he'd gotten what he'd needed to be sure of.

"Then earlier, he took me down to the tunnel and I saw them—the men in white. The soldiers. He told me that I needed to get you to come back with me," he said. "But I refused. I like you. You gave us food and stuff, and you were nice, and I'd already talked to Jamal and Nia. We were planning to come to you. I swear."

"But?" Luc whispered, and I stepped closer to him, knowing that soft tone meant he was seconds from doing something bad.

"But he hit me. He kicked me. I didn't care. Wasn't the first time. But then he told me he had Tabby." Tears streaked both cheeks, even the one under the swollen, bruised eye. "I didn't have a choice."

Did he?

He's telling the truth, Luc's repeated, his voice entering my thoughts. *He has a sister. This man has her or at least got him believing that he does.*

Part of me understood Nate's actions. Just like I understood why Daemon and Kat and Dee and just about everyone else wanted to kill Blake while recognizing, unwillingly, that Blake had been put in a god-awful situation.

But we all had choices.

We just never knew which side we'd fall on until we had to make that choice.

"I wish you'd told me the truth earlier. We would've still helped," I told him. "You have no idea what you're dealing with."

Nate closed his eye.

"Daemon," Luc said. "Go back to the community. Warn the others that the Daedalus is here. Get them ready."

Daemon took a step, and then he hesitated. He actually hesitated, and that said a lot, because his wife was back there, his baby. And it also said a lot that Luc was asking him to go and not Grayson. Luc had to know that Daemon wanted to be back there just in case this was something that had already turned uglier than we were aware of.

"Do you guys have this handled?" Daemon asked.

"Yes." Luc's gaze moved from Grayson to me. "We've got this."

I nodded. "We do."

Daemon met Luc's stare, and then he was gone, racing off to the community, to his wife and son, and I prayed things were as we'd left them.

"Let's go get your sister," Luc said. "I want to meet this Morton. Super-excited about it."

"If we go through that hall, it's the quickest." Nate pointed at the hall straight ahead.

"It is," Luc confirmed. "Daemon was thinking that just before he left."

Grayson snapped his fingers at Nate. "You. I want you right beside me. Within arm's length the whole way."

Frozen, Nate looked at me.

"Go to him," I said. "He won't hurt you."

Grayson lifted a brow.

Nate didn't move.

"You're not within arm's length," Grayson murmured. "I do not like to wait."

The kid gathered whatever courage he had in him and made his way to Grayson.

Luc stepped into me, his hand on my arm. "This isn't your fault, Evie."

I met his gaze as knots formed in my stomach. "They're here because of me, and if something happens to the people—"

"If it does, still not your fault," he said. "And I'll spend the next however long reminding you of that, but right now, I need you out of here."

"What?"

"They're here for you. The last thing we want to do is lead you right to them." He lifted his hand to my cheek. "You have to know that would be a bad idea."

"What's a bad idea is you not having me there. You all are bad-ass, but we really have no idea what's going to happen. What if they have a Trojan there?" I said, heart thudding as I lowered my voice. "What about Nate's sister?"

"We'll get her and we'll deal with whatever is there, Trojan or not."

I stepped back. "You're not going to fight my battles without me."

"Evie—"

"No," I repeated. "I don't need you to protect me. I don't need you to stand in front of me. I need you to stand beside me."

His eyes flared wide and several moments passed before he reclaimed the distance, cupping my cheeks with both hands this time. "If something happened to you—"

"You'd feel the same way I would if something happened to you," I finished for him. "You'd be destroyed. I'd be destroyed. Together, we'll make sure that doesn't happen."

"Together," he repeated, closing his eyes. "I hate this. Every fiber of my being hates the idea of you getting anywhere close to these people. That you've already been close and anything could've happened. I hate this, Evie."

"I know." I gripped his wrists. "So do I."

"No hesitation, Peaches. You're going to kill more tonight, and if things get out of control, if there is a Trojan, take them down," he said. "Use everything you have, and I'll take care of the rest— I'll take care of you after."

"I know," I repeated.

Luc leaned down, kissing me. It was far too quick, but it was just as powerful as any of the other kisses. Then he stepped back. So did I, and together we joined Grayson as he stood with Nate. One look at Grayson's expression told me he agreed with Luc. He didn't want me here, and I got that. I really did. They were here for me.

And it was me they'd get.

We walked down the corridor, past the broken men who lay scattered about.

"Cleanup is going to be a bitch," Grayson muttered. "I am not going to be on that team."

I shot him a look but said nothing as we reached a dark department store. Luc cut the light show, not wanting Morton and whoever else to see our approach. I walked into the darkness without hesitation. It wasn't like I wasn't afraid. I was scared. My heart was pounding, my fear feeding the Source and making my senses acutely aware. It would be foolish, deadly so, to not be afraid. I'd taken down one Trojan before, but Sarah hadn't been trained like I had been, like the others. I could fail. A lot of things could happen. I just couldn't think of them as we navigated the turned-over racks and fallen mannequins. This was my fight, and if I couldn't hold my own here, I wouldn't be able to out there.

We reached the doors and then, after warning Nate to remain quiet, we stepped out into the fresh air that did nothing to remove the lingering scent of mold. Luc led us to the right and we walked down the street, keeping close to the tower and out of the moonlight. I made out the cluster of trees we'd passed before and the space hidden within. There was an opening—

My skin erupted in goose bumps. My vision seemed to constrict and expand as instinct roared to life, taking over.

I moved fast—faster than Luc could've anticipated, shooting out in front of them. It was almost like when I'd seen Sarah. The Source seized control, but I was still there, and this time I was in the driver's seat; it's just that the Source was guiding my movements. My ears prickled, picking up a repetitive clicking.

Throwing out my hand, the word *stop* formed in my mind. It poured into the Source and then into the air.

They came to a stop inches from us. Over a dozen tiny cylindrical objects containing a bluish electrical charge in the center remained there, frozen all around us.

Nate gasped.

Stepping forward, Luc plucked one out of the space. His lip curled. "They're the same kind of bullets April's handler shot me with."

Which meant they weren't looking to kill any of us. They wanted us wounded, and that was actually worse.

"True story." Luc picked up on my thoughts, signaling to me that this time was different from before. He hadn't been able to hear my thoughts when I'd gone after Sarah. His fingers closed over the bullet as the Source swelled around his hand. He swept his arm through the air, and one by one, the modified bullets exploded. A second later, he lit up the air, sending the Source in every direction, and I saw the remaining officers. There were just as many, if not more, than the ones who'd come into the mall.

I was moving before I knew it, racing through the opening. Luc and Grayson were right behind me as I skidded to a stop, my eyes clocking the lowered weapons, sensing their willingness to fire once more.

"When will you guys ever learn?" Luc said, curling his fingers as if he were summoning them. The rifles went up and into the air, crashing into the tower behind us and into the trees.

These officers didn't run like the others. They came right at us, pulling something small and black from their thigh holsters.

"Tasers," Luc warned.

"Fun times." Grayson shoved Nate back as he slipped into his true form.

"Get back," I ordered, hoping everyone listened.

Dipping down, I slammed my hands onto the ground. The earth rattled and woke up with a deep, trembling breath. Geysers of dirt flew into the air, and then the ground expanded under my hands, rippling out in all directions, forming tunnels of churning dirt and grass.

There was a shout as the closest man jerked backward, his arm flying up. Electricity charged up the prongs of the Tasers as he hit the button in his panic. He went down, down deep, along with several others. I buried them under the thick, sandy dirt.

I didn't think they were getting out.

Ever.

Rising, I caught sight of Luc catching one of the officers by the arm. A bone cracked, and the Taser dropped to the ground. Luc slammed his hand into the officer's chest. The Source washed over the man. His screaming ended abruptly, just as the Source streaked across the area, smacking into another officer. Her pain-filled shout was drowned out as Grayson took down another.

I continued forward, the wind picking up around me as my eyes moved to the trees. Perfect, useful weapons. The Source guiding me, I spread my arms and hooked my fingers inward. Branches cracked like thunder, tearing from the trees.

Grayson and Luc knew what was up. They hit the ground like pros, Grayson taking Nate down with him. Not all the officers were fast enough.

The branches—now jagged, multiheaded arrows—hurtled across the clearing. They slammed into the men and then went through them, piercing shields, helmets, and armor.

The air smelled like metal as I lowered my hands.

Six more down.

Half a dozen left.

I scanned the grounds, looking for Morton and the child. An officer came straight at me, and I pushed with the Source. He flew backward as if the very hand of God had grasped him and he met an unhappy ending with some sort of cement wall that stood in the center of the park.

Where was—?

I spun, coming face-to-face with an officer who held a Taser mere inches from me. I had no idea what, if anything, it would do to me. I didn't want to find out. The officer jabbed the Taser at me. Electricity fired to life—

I moved.

Or I thought I did, because the officer stumbled forward, the Taser firing harmlessly against nothing, against—

Smoke and shadows.

Holy crap.

I'd done the Arum thing—the thing April had done. I was there, but not. The officer whirled, and I threw my hand out. It was there—the dark, fuzzy outline of it was, at least—and it went straight through the man's chest. Blood sprayed my face as I drew my arm back. The man's shout ended as he collapsed, folded like a paper sack. I watched my arm solidify, watched my legs become more than just the shape.

I lifted my head to where Luc stood feet from me. His wide eyes met mine. "Did you see that?" I asked.

He nodded. "You went all Arum there for a moment."

"I didn't know I could—"

Luc grabbed my arm, thrusting me to the side as he shoved his hand out. A bolt of the Source erupted from his palm and hit the chest of the man who had come up directly behind me.

"Thank you," I said, turning around and finding Grayson taking out another officer. I was going to have to take what I'd just done and set it aside to get excited over later.

Luc and Grayson made quick work of the remaining officers. Within minutes, the field was scattered with bodies, and the scent of burned flesh and blood was heavy in the air. I felt the sudden awareness of an incoming Luxen. My gaze darted to the sudden bright light that rushed through the trees. The Luxen solidified, becoming human.

"Daemon." Surprise gave way to fear. "Is everything—"

"Everything is fine, and they've been warned. I came back to help." He strode forward. "Doesn't look like you guys needed it."

"Told you we had it handled," Luc responded, reaching down and lifting the helmet off one of the officers. "Jesus. This guy can't be any older than we are."

I didn't want to feel the pinch of sadness over a life lost long before he entered this field, or what could have led anyone to sign up to work for an organization like the Daedalus.

They believe they're on the right side of history, Luc told me as he rose. *They always do.*

"Please tell me Morton is among them," Daemon said.

"Sorry," Grayson said. "He hasn't made an appearance yet."

"Are the others okay?" Nate asked from where he sat on his knees, arms tight to his chest.

Daemon spared him a brief glance. "They're fine. Being welcomed right now with blankets and warm soup, I believe."

Nate closed his eyes, shoulders caving in. I was relieved to hear that the children made it and that so far nothing had happened at the community, but—

Branches snapped under the fall of booted feet, and we spun back to the cement wall. Out from behind it stepped Morton. One hand was on the tiny shoulder of the small girl. She had her blanket. It trembled like a limp flag, and she looked too terrified to cry, to make a sound.

A nasty, bloodthirsty smile pulled at my lips as I walked forward. He would not hurt that little girl. He would not hurt Luc or Grayson or Nate. He would not hurt me.

"I wouldn't take another step forward," Morton advised, lifting his other hand. He held something small. "If you do, I'll push in on this button my thumb is already resting on. You're fast, but I'll hit this button in time. You may hurt me. You may kill me. But you *will* activate this time."

41

He held the Cassio Wave between his fingers.

The Source didn't care about that. The desire to lash out, to destroy him, caused tiny muscles all along my body to twitch as I forced myself still. My entire body trembled as I eyed his hand. I could take him. I could get to him before he pressed—

Careful, Luc's voice intruded. *You're fast, but his finger is on the button.*

Drawing in a deep, steady breath, I lifted my chin.

"That's right." Morton smiled. "You may be powerful. All of you are, but what I hold in my hand is real power."

My lip curled, and a sound came from me that I didn't even know I was capable of making. It was a low trill that I'd only ever heard Sarah make the day she mutated.

"Yeah, you don't like hearing that," Morton replied.

"Let the girl go," Luc said. "Whatever you think is going to happen here doesn't involve her."

"Please," Nate pleaded from where he was on his knees, within arm's reach of Grayson. "You promised if I brought—"

"You didn't do exactly what I asked, Nate. Not remotely surprised. Following basic instructions has never been your strong suit." Morton never took his eyes off me. "But she's right, what I know is going to happen here doesn't involve her."

Morton lifted his fingers from her shoulder. The little girl didn't move, her terrified gaze full of exhaustion and fear. I could tell she probably wondered if this was some sort of trick.

"Tabby," Nate called, voice shaking.

She burst forward, her thin legs and arms pumping as she raced toward her brother, not once looking down at the bodies. He caught her in his arms, rising with her in his embrace. Nate didn't wait around. He spun and took off, and all I could hope was that after, we could find him or he could find us.

My eyes narrowed on Morton.

If there was an after.

There will be, assured Luc, and then he said, "I'm surprised you let them go so easily."

"I don't need them."

"You sure about that?" Luc queried. "Less than a minute ago, you had a hostage. Now there's just you and us."

"And this." He lifted the hand that held the Cassio Wave, and I tensed. "We've been waiting for you, Evie."

"Is that so?" I asked, wondering how quickly I could reach him. I wasn't exactly skilled like the others at sending bolts of the Source.

Morton smiled. "We knew that eventually you'd come here."

Grayson shifted from one foot to the next. "So you've just been hanging around? Using little kids to go get your food?"

"More like making sure the children would stay away from the others until I needed them to be seen. Tell me, do the people in the community really think the Daedalus has no idea who's all here?"

"If you've all really known we've been here this whole time, why wait?" Daemon snarled. "Why not come after us?"

"Why would we waste precious manpower and time?" Morton asked. "What you're doing is no concern to us. You are no threat."

My brows lifted in shock.

"No threat?" laughed Daemon. "Okay."

Morton smirked. "We've known this whole time that some of the Luxen Outreach facilities have been fronts for moving unregistered Luxen and supporters to Houston and Chicago."

Holy crap. They really did know.

"We'll deal with all of you soon enough, don't worry," Morton said.

"Oh, we're not worried," growled Daemon.

"Are we all just going to stand around and talk some more?"

Luc asked. "Or are you just wasting time until more officers show up? If that's the case, I hope they're better at their jobs than the last two batches."

"More aren't coming."

I wasn't sure I believed him.

"I don't need any more. I've seen all that I needed to see," he continued. "I knew the moment you ripped that bat out of my hand, you were ready."

I sucked in a sharp breath. He'd goaded me with that bat to see what I'd do, and I'd exposed at least some of my abilities right then and there. That was so stupid.

You didn't know, Luc's voice entered my thoughts.

I didn't think that mattered.

Morton eyed me. "The Trojan who made it to Zone 3 was a test. I'm assuming that one failed. Shame, but Sergeant Dasher will be pleased to hear how adept Nadia's become at using the Source."

Air lodged in my throat as my skin hummed with barely leashed power.

"Do not speak that name," warned Luc, the air around him crackling. "Ever."

"What name should I use? Evie? That's not her real name. Why she still answers to that is strange . . . and interesting."

"How about you don't use either name," Luc suggested.

Morton laughed under his breath.

"Are you going to tell Sergeant Dasher yourself?" I asked. "You think we're just going to let you walk out of here?"

"You're going to show him, you see. The very second I press this button, you will activate."

Panic and fury seized at my chest. "I didn't activate last time, but if you've been here for three years, I guess you wouldn't know that."

"I've been updated by one of the men. I think he's one of those you buried in the ground," remarked Morton. "This is a new, improved device. You'll activate, and because I represent Sergeant Dasher, you will listen to me. Do you want to know what the very first thing is that I'll have you do? I'll make sure you kill them."

Whatever air I was getting into my lungs wasn't enough.

"These two Luxen will try to stop you, but they'll fail. They can't defeat you. Then your boyfriend over here will try to do the same, but he, too, will fail," Morton continued as ice hit my veins. "And then remember the dealing with Zone 3 later? Well, that's sooner rather than later. I'll send you there next, and you will take out every single person there."

My knees started to feel weak.

"Man, woman . . ." He paused. "And child."

No.

No.

My gaze swung to Luc. He was staring at Morton, his entire body seeming to vibrate with rage. I couldn't let this happen. There was no way.

"Why are you waiting, then?" Grayson demanded. "What's holding you back? If I were you, I would've already hit the damn button. You've seen what she's capable of. The fact that you haven't tells me you're not all that confident that the Cassio Wave is going to work."

A tiny bit of hope sparked, but . . .

But what if it did work? It was too much of risk, because if it did, there was no going back. And if the Daedalus knew what everyone was doing here, then they had to be confident that this device would work. Because if not, they'd just exposed their knowledge of them. They'd lost the advantage of a surprise attack, and there would be no way Morton would make it out alive.

I scrambled for a way out of this. There had to be something.

Too bad no one ever got those elephant tranquilizers Zoe had joked about. If I were knocked out, then at least I wouldn't be a danger—

I knew.

I knew what could work. "Just let me say goodbye to Luc."

"Evie," Luc started. "You don't—"

"Please," I cut him off as I sent him the message. *You need to take the Source from me.* "Just let me say goodbye."

There was no response from Luc as Morton laughed. "I'm supposed to trust you?"

"What can I do? I attack you, you hit the button. Any of them attack you, you hit the button," I reasoned. *If he hits the button, I will be completely drained. I might still activate, but I won't be able to hurt any of you.* "Please," I pleaded of both Morton and Luc. "I just want to say goodbye."

Out of the corner of my eyes, I saw Grayson and Daemon exchange looks.

"Please," I whispered. *You'll be able to take him out, and you'll be able to handle me. Keep me contained until you figure out what to do with me or—*

There will be no other option, came his swift response. *I will bring you back.*

But if you can't, you have to take care of me. You won't have long. I'll probably sleep eventually, but when I wake up, I'll be at full strength.

"You can say goodbye," Morton said, and I nearly sagged with relief. "But one wrong move, and that's it."

"Thank you," the words tumbled from me as I turned to Daemon and Grayson. "Don't do anything. Please. Just let me say goodbye."

Daemon stared at me like I was out of my mind, but Grayson nodded, and I knew he sensed Luc and I were up to something. He was going along with it.

"Go," Morton urged. "Make it quick."

My steps were jerky as I walked the short distance to Luc, my heart thundering as my gaze met his. Fury swirled in his eyes as static crackled harmlessly off my skin.

Promise me. I stopped in front of him as I placed my hands on his chest. *If I don't come back from this, please do not let me become a real monster.*

He cupped my cheek, his voice rough. "Evie."

"Nadia," I whispered, soaking in his features and committing them to a memory I hoped I didn't lose. "That's who I am."

Luc shuddered, eyes squeezing closed and then reopening. His pupils so white and large, it nearly swallowed his entire iris. "*Nadia.*"

I nodded. "I love you."

He dropped his forehead to mine as he folded his arm around my waist. *Promise me,* I told him. *Promise me you won't let me turn into something I'd hate.*

Luc hauled me to his chest, fitting my body to his. I inhaled deeply, letting his scent wrap around me, and when his lips touched mine, a sob shook me. He slid his hand from my cheek, down my throat. I leaned back just enough for him to fit his hand between us. His palm flattened against my chest. I kissed him back, tears streaming down my face as I clutched at his shoulders. My pulse felt like a trapped butterfly.

I love you, he said, and I felt the power of what he felt in his kiss. *I love you with every breath I take, Nadia. I will bring you back.*

I shuddered as his palm warmed against my chest. I felt the first soft tugging motion, and then it was stronger, harder. My body started to jerk, but Luc held me closer, stilling me and silencing the sharp cry building in my throat as the Source roared to the surface and then contracted rapidly, rippling back through my veins. Bright light flashed around Luc. There was a shout, and my heart seized.

Promise me, Luc. I started to fill dizzy. *Promise you'll end this.*

He kissed harder, deeper. Tongues and teeth clashed, and I didn't care. I wanted to remember this, remember him and then—

Never, he promised. *I will never give up on you.*

My eyes flew open as I realized what he'd promised, and that was not to do what needed to be done if I couldn't come back as me from this.

If he didn't, then this would be all for nothing. Once I regained my power, he wouldn't be able to contain me. He wouldn't stop me, and I would become what he feared he already was.

But it was too late.

Luc's head kicked back as he jerked his hand away. Strings of white light that pulsed with intense black shadows attached to his fingers. The Source throbbed in tune with my heart. I could feel it pouring out of me and into him in fast, crashing waves, and I saw it seep into his skin, sink through his bone and muscle, to his very core. His eyes went wide as streaks of white shattered the purple.

The mass of twisting, throbbing power swallowed him whole. His arm flexed around me, and then it was gone.

I hit the ground hard, weakened and unprepared for the sudden lack of support. Stunned that Luc had let go, had let me fall, I lifted my head and looked up as what was left of the Source throbbed weakly.

I couldn't even see him.

The light around him was so intense, stronger than the other night he'd done this. He had taken more this time, almost all of it. The swirling black-and-white light spun around him until it smoothed out and he was nothing more than the outline of a man colored in the shade of brilliant moonlight.

He blazed brighter than any Luxen, than any star. The entire area, as far as I could see, was lit up. He turned the darkest night to the brightest part of the day.

I stared at him, eyes watering, as he seemed to continue to grow in power, becoming even brighter, and for some reason I thought of what Eaton had said.

You had to know, Luc, that they would find some way to reel you back in.

It was the one thing neither of us could figure out, the one thing that even Blake had wondered. Why would they need to reel Luc back in when they had me, when they had the other Trojans?

You're the burning shadow and he's the darkest star, and together, you will bring about the brightest night.

The Brightest Night.

"Hell," Grayson murmured, having slipped out of his true form, just like Daemon had. He held his arm up to shield his eyes. "I'm hoping that's normal."

Slowly, I looked over to Morton. He should be panicking, and I should already be activating. Obviously, he had to have known by now that Luc and I hadn't simply said goodbye, but I felt the same, and Morton . . .

He stood there, a hand up to block some of the intensity. He wasn't freaking out. He wasn't hitting the button repeatedly. He just stood there like he'd expected this.

The Brightest Night.

Understanding began to dawn, one so horrifying and so final, I didn't want to accept it. I didn't want to believe. I just couldn't. Pulse pounding, I swung my head back to Luc. I tried to reach out to him, sending my thoughts directly at him.

Nothing.

Nothing and then—

A rush of ice and fire and power, so much pure, potent power— the kind that could level cities, wipe out civilizations, and erase entire histories. My mind immediately retreated, and the Source flared, deep in my core. It struggled, a mere spark compared to Luc's inferno, but it pulsed, triggered by a very real, very bad threat.

Suddenly, I thought of the dream I'd had when I'd slept all those days. Luc and I facing each another, a city utterly destroyed in the background. Slowly, I staggered to my feet as my gaze swept back to where Morton stood.

Lowering his hand, he stared back at me, and he nodded.

I almost fell again.

Nothing felt real as I was forced to accept that none of us, not a single one of us, had given the Daedalus enough credit. In every way possible, we'd underestimated their plans, their foresight.

This had been their plan from the very beginning.

I stared at Luc.

This had been Nancy Husher's legacy.

Pressing the back of my hand against my mouth, I turned to Morton.

Opening his hand, he dropped the device to the floor.

"That's just . . . ," Daemon said. "That's just an old key fob."

"I lied." Morton lowered his hand, his gaze fixed on me. "Sergeant Dasher will be so proud of you, Nadia. You didn't let him down. He knew you wouldn't fail him. Thank you."

I shuddered.

"What in the hell is this soon-to-be-dead man talking about?" Daemon growled.

"You may have been the strongest Luxen, but you were never the smartest," Morton replied.

Daemon took a step toward the man, snarling as the white haze of the Source surrounded him.

"Don't," I warned, and then I roped Daemon in place with my mind before he made his child an orphan.

He tried to lift his foot, struggled to move. His wide-eyed gaze swung to me. "You'd better not be doing what I think you are."

I was, and he was just going to have deal with it. So was Grayson as I leashed him to where he stood. I didn't know how long I was going to be able to hold them. I had no idea what would happen if any of them charged Morton, and I didn't need to be worrying about them. My focus returned to Luc. There was still a chance. He'd just taken the power. He was absorbing it, and once that happened, he'd be different, but he'd be okay. He was last time. There was still a—

"Tell me, Nadia, is this the first time he's fed from you?" Morton asked, sounding as curious as a child. "Did it only take this one time? We believed it would take no more than twice."

"Fed from you?" Grayson spat with disgust.

I refused to answer, attempting to reach out to Luc again, finding nothing but the barren space filling with unending, unchecked power, and I remembered what Luc had said after he'd done it before.

It would change me.

"Please tell me," Morton said.

I would become far worse.

"I must know."

I would be something to truly fear.

"You see," he persisted. "We have this bet going at the office—"

"You son of a bitch," I snapped. The Source sparked inside me, fueled only by the rage pounding there me. "You don't matter. At all."

Morton laughed softly. "Oh, I matter," he admonished. "You know who else does? Luc. That's all we've needed. That's why you were special. He wouldn't do what he just did for anyone but you. After all, he would do anything for you."

Luc slowly lowered his flaming arms.

"No one, not even that traitor general or the outdated Sons of Liberty, truly understood what the Poseidon Project was designed to do, why it was in conjunction with the Origins. Eaton should've known the sergeant wouldn't have showed him all his cards."

But Eaton had suspected there was more. So had Blake. We just hadn't listened.

"For those a little slow on the uptake. Daemon, I'm talking about you." He glanced at the furious, immobile Luxen. "The Andromeda serum didn't create Trojans. All it did was create an updated, state-of-the-art hybrid. One with the abilities of the Luxen and Arum, coded to answer to the Daedalus, and minus that pesky sense of self Origins and earlier hybrids have. They are just fine-tuned and perfected versions of an earlier, no-longer-necessary model." He paused, eyeing me coolly. "All except you. We'd hoped that when April used the Cassio Wave, you'd activate and then Luc would eventually feed from you in an attempt to weaken and control you, but you are somewhat defective, as it appears. The sergeant is very interested in discovering why you still have such a sense of self."

Ignoring what he'd meant as an insult but was actually a compliment, I tried again to reach Luc.

"You see, the Daedalus only had two choices when it came to Luc. With his power, we either had to kill him or find a way to control him, to use him. Nancy Husher had always insisted that killing him would've been too much of a waste, that we just needed a way to control him. It's a shame she's no longer alive to see how right she was."

"Shit," muttered Grayson, the next to truly get what was going down. Trusting that he wasn't going to do anything stupid, I gave him back his ability to move. Grayson showed no acknowledgment of it happening.

"The new hybrids are powerful, and they will become one of the most advanced armies man has ever seen, but he is . . ." Morton looked at Luc then with an expression that was part awe. "But he is *the* weapon of mass destruction. One simple show of his strength and he will end wars before they can even begin. There will be no resistance. There will be no opposition. Not when the world sees what he can do with just a snap of his fingers. He *is* the Trojan."

"If that's the case, then why do you even need the new hybrids?" Daemon demanded, and I eased off him. He, too, proved that he was just as smart and showed no sign that he could now move. "Why create the flu and mutate half the damn population if Luc is the ultimate weapon?"

Luc tilted his head at those words. My heart skipped. He was listening. He was aware, but was it him in there? That cold, apathetic Luc who wouldn't make silly jokes and talk about raising a farm of llamas? Or was it something else entirely different?

Something even he feared?

"Mutate the population?" Morton laughed again, catching my attention. "Who told you that? None of the humans who are infected with this flu will survive without our intervention, and we have already chosen who we will save."

As if they were gods.

"The rest will all eventually self-destruct, most likely taking out a few people with them. That's an unfortunate consequence, but it will create further chaos—"

"And hatred for the Luxen, because you convinced everyone else that we were making them sick," Daemon filled in the rest.

"Exactly," Morton confirmed.

Dear God, all those people who were bound to become sick? They wouldn't even mutate, and I wasn't sure which was worse, but they were all innocent. Billions of innocent people were going to die.

"If there's no need for your army of Hybrids 2.0, then why do you have them?" Grayson demanded.

"Because a weapon as fine as he is shouldn't be wasted on things that aren't even human."

Daemon blanched, actually paled when Morton's words sank in, and I thought I might vomit.

The hybrids would be used to exterminate the Luxen and any humans with alien DNA.

And it *could* work.

Most of the Luxen would fall fighting the new hybrids while the world shattered apart around them, ravaged by sickness—a sickness that would fuel further violence against one another and against the one thing that could save them.

The Luxen.

But that was only a possibility, because Luc hadn't made a move against any of us even though when I tried to reach him again, there was no answer.

"Luc," I said out loud this time. "You're still there. I know you are. You have to be. You're still—"

"He's no longer the Luc you knew," Morton said quietly, walking toward Luc. He stopped beside him. "Keep her alive. Your maker will want to know why she's defective. Kill the others."

Your maker.

I tensed as Luc lifted his head. The Source pulsed intently around him, and I knew if he struck out, no one stood a chance. He'd kill any of us with a half-formed thought.

Tendrils of the Source reached out from Luc, filling the area in a wave of static before rapidly receding, finally, *finally* revealing the features I loved so fiercely.

A face I barely recognized.

It was Luc—his broad, angular cheekbones and carved jaw, his full lips and his golden skin—but those eyes, amethyst fractured with white, ever-swirling streaks of light, were not his.

Those eyes tracked everyone present. Morton. Daemon. Grayson. Me.

And when he looked at me, he did so like he looked at everyone else. Assessing. There was no softness or warmth. No love or want. Just endless hardness and ice, devoid of all emotions.

This wasn't Luc whose gaze moved past me, back to the Luxen.

This wasn't even the Luc after he'd fed for the first time.

This was what he had warned me about.

My heart broke so utterly and so heavily in my chest I could almost hear it. There was a scream in my mind, and it was my own as my knees trembled. A sob choked me, and tears crowded my eyes even as I let the Source rush to the surface.

The Luc I knew, the Luc I loved, wasn't there. And that meant I knew something the Daedalus didn't, something that only in their supreme arrogance they wouldn't have taken into consideration.

"Morton?" I called out as Luc slowly turned his head in my direction. A shiver crept over my skin as those fractured eyes met mine. "I said you didn't matter. I wasn't wrong. You don't. Worse yet, you're dispensable. That's why you're here and not Dasher. Just in case . . ." I drew in a ragged breath. "You know, the Daedalus accidentally created something far worse than they could even imagine."

Morton frowned as he looked from me to Luc. "Do what your maker commanded, Luc. Kill the Luxen. Subdue her. We need her alive."

"Maker?" Luc finally spoke, and I flinched at the ice that coated the one word, the power that was so heavy I thought it might crush all of us.

Out of the corners of my eyes, I saw Daemon and Grayson react, taking a visible step back.

"Maker?" Luc repeated. "I am not *made*. I am a god."

Morton didn't even have a second to react. Luc turned those eyes on him, and that was it. The man *caved* into himself. Skin incinerating, taking with it blood and muscles. Bones shattered like glass, and within a heartbeat or two, Morton was nothing more than a pile of half-burned clothing and ash.

"Holy," whispered Daemon.

"Shit," Grayson finished.

Luc's gaze inched back to us, and the lack of humanity, the absence of *him,* in those cold, scattered eyes sent a bolt of pure fear down my spine.

How could the Daedalus create something like *this* and hope to control it?

Nothing could.

He zeroed in on me with those frightening, churning eyes, sensing out the uttermost threat. His head tilted once more. I saw the Source pulse around both Daemon and Grayson, and I knew they would try to contain Luc once they realized he wasn't right. They would die.

"Run," I told the others as the strands of hair lifted off my shoulders. Luc's eyes shifted toward Daemon, and I knew neither he nor Grayson could move nearly quickly enough.

Unleashing what was left of the Source, I let it wash over me, and I let it *out*. The blast of power roared faster than either Daemon or Grayson could respond to, sweeping them off their feet and carrying them away as far as I could get them before the Source sputtered to nothing. Their landings would be hard. It would hurt, but they would be alive.

At least for the time being.

Luc still stood. He hadn't even moved a centimeter. Only a single lock of wavy hair had moved, and it slowly drifted back to lay against his forehead. His lips—lips that had kissed mine, lips that had spoken words of love—twisted in a facsimile of a smile, perfect and empty.

Silvery light appeared around his open hands, and I knew I wouldn't survive this. I wouldn't live. I was empty, virtually human. There was no escape. All I could hope was that Daemon and Grayson recovered quickly enough to warn the others, to get as many people as possible out of Luc's path. That they had a chance to hide, because the biggest threat was no longer the Daedalus or their flu or even their hybrids.

It was what stood in front of me.

The Source grew around his hands as the icy burn of power ramped up all around me. The wind roared through the trees. Tears blinded me as I thought what would happen to Luc if he did come back from this and he remembered what he was about to do, and what was left of my heart withered.

He continued to stare at me, brows lowered and those eyes . . .

He *glided* forward, and I wasn't even sure if his feet touched the ground. Then he was right in front of me. My skin erupted in tiny goose bumps as he stared down at me.

"Luc?" I whispered, eyes widening as I watched him lift a hand to my cheek. The silvery Source danced around his fingertips. I didn't move. I couldn't. He held me there in place with just his stare. Not a single muscle could twitch. The fingers hovered near my cheek, and I had no idea what it would do when it touched me, because I no longer knew what the will behind the Source would be.

And as he stared down at me, I knew that whatever I was about to say would most likely be the last thing I ever said.

"I love you," I whispered, body shaking as the wind caught my clothing. "I will always love you. I love you, Luc. I love—"

His fingertips grazed my cheek, and icy heat drenched my body as the Source whipped out from him.

Outside of me, the world groaned and screamed. It shook and then fell to pieces. Cement broke apart and crumbled. Buildings as tall as mountains fell in a shower of fine dust. Roofs peeled off and shattered. Trees shuddered into themselves, and metal crunched and gave way as abandoned cars crumbled. Flames erupted from old reserves of gas or propane, the fire spitting into the sky like geysers. The air turned thick with debris as the shock wave rolled and rolled and rolled out from all around us for what felt like an eternity.

Inside of me, a different storm raged. It started in the recesses of my mind, where it was dark and cloudy, a rumbling and rattling of a locked door. The silvery light ripping through steel and cement then pierced straight through me, obliterating all the shadows in a blinding rush of pain that was a shock to the system as it raced down my spine, firing along nerves. It was so consuming, so powerful that I couldn't scream around it, couldn't even breathe as images flashed where the dark clouds had me. Faces and events and words and emotions that all held significance, and they kept coming, years' and years' worth of thoughts, desires, fears, and memories.

And then the storm quieted. The images stopped. The pain stopped. The world stopped.

I wasn't standing.

My arms dangled at my sides, and my legs were limp. Luc held me, an arm around my waist and his palm flat against my cheek. I couldn't speak as I stared into eyes streaked with lightning. Something was wrong with me. I couldn't move or close my eyes, speak or stop him as he lowered me toward the smoking, ruined ground.

Over his shoulder, I saw that the tower was gone, so was the Galleria. My eyes shifted just a fraction to my right, and oh God, there was nothing there. No buildings. No trees—

The hand at my cheek slid to the back of my head as I felt my legs and then my hips touched the ground. My head was guided down, and he was still above me, his lips inches from mine.

"*Never,*" he said, and the ground trembled under me. Brackets of tension formed around his mouth as his jaw hardened. His eyes squeezed shut and then reopened. The bolts of churning white light slowed. "Never come for me." He slowly slid his hand out from under my head as his lips brushed the corner of mine. "*Never* look for me. If you do, I will take everything from you."

Luc slowly pulled away, and for the briefest second, our gazes met. I thought I heard him whisper my name, but then he was gone, and there was nothing but heated stone and ash, glittering like a million fireflies. Nothing more than tiny specks of what was left of the city drifted back to the ground, where it fell upon me and everything around me like slivers of snow kissed by the sun.

I couldn't speak, but even if I could, Luc was now gone, so I couldn't tell him he was wrong. He'd given me everything, because I remembered.

I remembered *everything*.

Read on for an exclusive bonus scene featuring

DAEMON

Never in my whole damn life had I ever been so scared.

I thought it had been the moment I realized Kat had gone out there by herself, baiting that Arum to protect my sister and I.

I'd been wrong.

When I realized Blake had been working for the Daedalus, I'd been scared out of my mind for her, and when Will, the man who had used her mother to get to her—to us—had her in that cage, I'd been terrified for the nightmares I knew those hours would leave behind.

I'd been wrong.

Even when the Daedalus had her and everything messed up thing they did and all that came out after that, I'd thought I could never be more scared that she would be ripped away from me.

I'd been so damn wrong.

Now I knew.

Because the hours of pain and too many close calls as Kat struggled to bring our child into this world had truly been the most frightening moments of my life. And each time I felt her heart slowed to a sluggish beat, I thought that was it. She was an incredibly strong hybrid, and I was one of the most powerful Luxen in the world, but when her gray eyes had started to lose their focus, I was terrified that it wouldn't be enough.

And as much as it killed me to admit, it wouldn't have been.

The tiny body against my chest squirmed, drawing my gaze. My son. Our son. Wrapped in a white blanket, he was so tiny. I didn't realize infants were this damn small. I bet he fit in both of my palms. Not that I would try. God knows I was too afraid of dropping him.

Or breathing too heavily.

Or thinking too loudly.

He was asleep, and even now, his little legs and arms pumped under the blanket, as if he was ready to get out there and take on the world.

Just like his momma.

My gaze lifted from the wrinkling little face. Soft candlelight flickered throughout the room, dancing over Kat's cheek. Color had already begun to work its way back into her skin. There had been moments where she'd be too pale, when there had been too much blood. She was already healing.

Thanks to Luc.

I looked down at my son and it was like someone had punched a hole through my chest.

If Luc hadn't been here, Kat wouldn't have pulled through. She would've died. I would've gone with her, and if our son had survived, he would've done so without the people who loved him more than all the stars in the sky could.

Quietly, I turned to the wall that faced the house Luc and Nadia were in. *Evie*, I corrected myself for the umteenth time. Her name was Evie now. One of these days I would stop referring to her as Nadia.

Probably a long time from now.

But I needed to try.

I owed Luc . . . I owed him everything. He was why we were still here, healthy and whole.

Worry crept into my thoughts. I had no idea what happened to her, and all I knew was that she hadn't woken up, no matter what Luc did. If something happened to her. . .

Well, the Daedalus would be the least of the world's problems.

Right now I couldn't go there.

That would be a bridge I hoped to never have to cross. I hoped it all worked out. Luc infuriated the hell out of me, but he deserved happiness just as much as Kat and I do. He deserved to have his girl by his side.

Kat stirred under the blanket. One pale foot stuck out. I grinned as her toes curled. Any other time I would've grabbed that foot of hers. She would wake up swinging, thinking a demon or some crap got her. Courtesy of all those books she read, she had one hell of a vivid imagination. I would've made up for it, starting with that foot and following the length of one curvy leg.

Come to think of it, something similar was why I now held our son in my arms.

My smile grew.

Damn if I didn't get a little lost staring at her. Always did. Awe filled me once more. How she handled everything amazed me. Even when I knew she hurt, when I could feel her heart failing, she had held on to my hand with such strength.

Time and time again she proved that I wasn't worthy of her, and I was so damn lucky to have her. To have this.

Bow-shaped lips puckered and his little brow furrowed. Was he dreaming? Did infants even dream? I had no idea, but if he dreamed, I wanted them to be good ones. Rocking him gently until his forehead smoothed out, I had a feeling Kat and I were going to have our hands full with Adam.

There was never a name more fitting for our son. He would be just as fierce as his namesake and as brave and strong as his mother. And he would have me standing behind him. Always.

Everyone knew I'd burn down the entire world for Kat; watch it all go up in flames if I had to. I always knew I would. No doubt, but as I stared down at the tiny, scrunched up face, I truly realized the depths of destruction I would wreak to keep them both safe and happy.

"Nothing, and I mean nothing, will ever touch you," I said and kissed the downy softness on the top of his head. "That is a promise."

And that was one I would never break.

Cradling him close to my chest, I carried him back to where Kat slept. Careful not to wake either of them, I settled in beside her. I bent, brushing my lips over Kat's brow and then leaned against the headboard.

It was going to be a long night.

That was fine by me.

There was nothing else I rather be doing than watching over the two most important beings in my life.

ACKNOWLEDGMENTS

Thank you to my agent, Kevan Lyon, and subrights agent, Taryn Fagerness. Thanks also to Stephanie Brown, Melissa Frain, and the amazing team at Tor: Ali, Kristin, Saraciea, Anthony, Eileen, Lucille, Isa, Devi, and everyone else who had a hand in bringing this book to publication.

Luc and Evie's story would never have been a thing if it wasn't for you, the reader. I cannot thank you enough. Special shout-out to JLAnders. You guys always amaze me.

The Brightest Night was the first book I wrote without my writing pal, Loki. I want to thank her for nineteen years of friendship and cuddles. Snuggle Diesel for me.